D0438317

SECRET SINS

Recent Titles by Jeannie Johnson

FORGOTTEN FACES
JUST BEFORE DAWN
LIKE AN EVENING GONE
A PENNY FOR TOMORROW
THE REST OF OUR LIVES

LOVING ENEMIES *
SECRET SINS *
WHERE THE WILD THYME BLOWS *

* *available from Severn House*

SECRET SINS

Jeannie Johnson

This first world edition published in Great Britain 2007 by
SEVERN HOUSE PUBLISHERS LTD of
9–15 High Street, Sutton, Surrey SM1 1DF.
This first world edition published in the USA 2008 by
SEVERN HOUSE PUBLISHERS INC of
595 Madison Avenue, New York, N.Y. 10022.
This first trade paperback edition published 2008 by
SEVERN HOUSE PUBLISHERS, London and New York.

British Library Cataloguing in Publication Data

Johnson, Jeannie
Secret sins
1. World War, 1939-1945 - Social aspects - England - Bristol - Fiction 2. Pawnbrokers - Fiction 3. Bristol (England) - Fiction
I. Title
823.9'2[F]

ISBN-13: 978-0-7278-6554-0 (cased)
ISBN-13: 978-1-84751-028-0 (trade paper)

Except where actual historical events and characters are being described for the storyline of this novel, all situations in this publication are fictitious and any resemblance to living persons is purely coincidental.

All Severn House titles are printed on acid-free paper.

Typeset by Palimpsest Book Production Ltd.,
Grangemouth, Stirlingshire, Scotland.
Printed and bound in Great Britain by
MPG Books Ltd., Bodmin, Cornwall.

For Michele Roberts who suggested the idea

One

Curious eyes turned in the direction of the man in the gabardine trench coat. If anyone had been brave enough to look into his eyes, they would have seen they were the same colour as his coat, a sludgy hazel, not bright, not happy. If they'd had the guts to stop him and make conversation, they would have seen the hard line of his jaw and perhaps heard him grind his teeth.

No one did stop him. No one dared.

He walked straight and tall, his steps measured and his eyes missing nothing as he scanned the humble brick facades of houses built some time in the nineteenth century. The workers who'd lived in them had worked at the cotton factory in Barton Hill, a working class area in the centre of the old seaport of Bristol. They were small and cramped. Damp too.

Some doors were open. The smell of cabbage and meagre rations filtered out into the street. He wrinkled his nose. Even though he hadn't eaten for hours, the smells did nothing for his appetite.

The street was moderately busy. Women stood in gossipy groups on the pavements, small boys pedalled on makeshift bicycles and girls with dirty faces pushed doll's prams made from orange boxes.

He felt their eyes on him. If he'd needed to he would have asked questions, but he didn't. He knew the house number he wanted.

'Looking for someone?'

Although surprised and indignant that someone was brave enough to speak to him, his footsteps did not falter. He glanced only briefly over his shoulder at the brave soul who'd dared.

The woman wore too much make-up and carried too much weight. And that despite rationing? Incredible. He was loath to reply, so didn't. He'd reached the house he was looking for anyway.

Number seventeen had dirty windows. Lace curtains divided over an elegant statuette of a lithe woman and two equally elegant dogs; Borzois, he thought. Russian deerhounds. They were made of plaster and common. It was no more than he'd expected. No doubt the blackout curtains were folded behind the lace and prettiness, slumped against the wall.

The front door was brown. He eyed its dull surface. Couldn't whoever lived here make the effort to paint it?

His thoughts were trivial and easily brushed aside. He was here on serious business. In years past it hadn't seemed so serious, but recent events had changed all that. The world had changed and so had his take on it.

The sound of the door knocker echoed around the street. He sensed those that watched had fallen to silence, their interest transferred from local gossip to the stranger daring to walk down their street. And what was he doing at number seventeen? He resisted the urge to smile to himself. All would be revealed, but not to them. All secrets were for whoever lived here. The past was coming back to haunt them.

The door was old and swollen in its frame and creaked like old bones as it was tugged open.

Henry Randall looked him up and down. 'What can I do for you?'

He hid his disappointment. He'd expected a woman. *That* woman.

'George Ford, Attorney at Law.'

He preferred this description to solicitor or lawyer. It had more gravitas, struck more fear into guilty hearts.

He congratulated himself, pleased that his voice was level and self assured. He sensed the man who had opened the door had been about to tell him to clear off until he'd told him who he was. Amazing what the legal profession could do to people.

Henry Randall's appearance was not so much a disappointment as a goad to the man's seething anger. Although not exactly a tidy man, neither was Henry dirty, merely shabby. His shirt sleeves sprouted through the holes in the elbows of his woolly cardigan. There was a slight greasiness to the edge of his collar. A five o'clock shadow sullied his chin. Judging by what he knew of her background, he wondered how such a woman could have married such a man. It wasn't fair. It wasn't right.

Antagonism had flitted in Henry Randall's eyes when he'd first opened the door. Now there was only puzzlement, perhaps even confusion. The man calling himself George Ford pretended not to notice but broke instantly into his well-rehearsed patter.

'I'm looking for a Mrs Mary Anne Randall, formerly Sweet, daughter of Joseph and Lydia Sweet of Eastville. I am calling with regard to the matter of her Aunt Maude's will. Certain provisions of the estate deemed that I conduct a face-to-face analysis of the legality and identity of said beneficiary. Have I been rightly informed that she lives here?'

He beamed broadly. He was good at gaining people's trust. He had the knack of adopting a certain look, a certain tone that people always fell for – even surly sods like Henry Randall.

Henry's lax cheeks lengthened with his chin as he thought this through. His visitor waited until sure that his convoluted language was sinking in. Henry frowned. Gone were his days of foul language and stinking breath. He'd turned almost teetotal thanks to Mary Anne. All he wanted now was for her to notice him again, but not with the fear she'd once held for him. He wanted her to love him, but she wasn't having any of it. Since she'd left he'd tried all sorts of ways to get her back, but so far without success. Any excuse and he was round there. This lawyer was an excuse in a trench coat.

Henry glanced at the others who'd moved into this street since being bombed out in Bedminster. There were a few – about three families. Biddy Young was one of them. He glowered at her. Nosey old bat!

He didn't so much smile at the man, but merely let his face loosen a little – the closest he ever got to a smile. 'Well, you'd better come on in unless you want the whole street to know yer business.'

George Ford followed Henry up the stairs. 'I'm up here,' Henry explained. 'Biddy Young, my neighbour, lives downstairs. We both got bombed out at the same time in the old street.'

George Ford made no comment. He wrinkled his nose at the smell and state of the downstairs hall. Nobody had polished the stair's handrail in ages. Henry Randall's living accommodation wasn't quite as bad. The man made an effort, though everything was shabby and second hand, doubtless donations from the Red Cross and suchlike.

'Speak your piece,' said Henry without offering his visitor a chair.

George Ford wasn't fooled. He saw the curiosity in the other man's eyes.

'Money. I'm talking money.'

'So you say. I didn't know my wife had an Aunt Maude.'

George smiled with his lips, but purposely adopted a questioning look in his eyes. 'Do you know everything about your wife? Has she never kept secrets from you? People do, especially women. Not that I am attempting in any way to blacken your good wife's name. Besides being easily tempted, women love secrets. Look at Eve and that snake. How well did they know each other before she told Adam of his beguiling ways?'

All manner of expressions flickered across Henry Randall's face and eyes. George knew he'd unnerved him, knew he could manipulate him as easily as a wooden marionette if he chose to. And he did choose, and in time he would use him.

Henry Randall seethed with a jealousy George Ford could not possibly comprehend. He was finding it difficult to take in the glib words, so naturally fell back on his basic emotions. This was yet another young man in Mary Anne's life. She already had one. He wouldn't stand for another.

George sensed suddenly that he'd been wrong and that Henry would take a little more time to control. He smoothed the way for the future. 'So you don't know her address?'

'I already told you, no. And besides, I don't recall her ever having an Aunt Maude.'

Once the front door had closed, Biddy Young hurried over to where two of her neighbours were muttering together. Like Biddy they had seen the smartly dressed man go into number seventeen. Like her they were curious.

'So what do you think that's all about?'

One of the women was wearing metal curlers. They clinked together like stair rods as she shook her head.

'Don't know. P'raps he bin up to no good and that bloke's a copper.'

'Fancy a cup of tea?' asked the woman with the spiky curlers.

'Only if you bring it out 'ere,' said Biddy. 'I wouldn't want to miss anything.'

'Goes without saying,' the woman replied.

The three of them stood there, slurping tea from saucers and passing a single Woodbine between them. Bits of tobacco stuck to their lips. Their eyes stuck on number seventeen.

It was ten minutes before the man reappeared. He shook hands with Henry before marching off up the street.

'Right,' said Biddy. 'Let's go and find out what's going on.'

The other women watched as she made her way to number seventeen. Henry didn't take too long in answering.

His face dropped when he saw it was her, as though he were hoping to see someone else. *Too late for that*, thought Biddy, but she plastered on a painted smile.

'I'm out of sugar. A few teaspoonfuls will do if you got some?' She kept beaming.

'You'll be lucky!'

'Oh. Never mind. I expect you made a cuppa for your visitor. Not from round here, is he?'

She waited for Henry to tell her to shove off. Perhaps he wouldn't. If so there could be only one reason. It was something to do with Mary Anne.

Just at that moment, Stanley Randall pushed his way past his father, wheeling his sister's old bike. 'I heard it all,' he said, gleefully addressing Biddy, who he'd known since he was small. 'It's something to do with money left by her Aunt Maude.'

'You little—' Henry aimed a blow at his youngest son's head. It missed. In the past he would have gone after him and laid down the law. But not now. Henry Randall wanted the world to believe he was a changed man.

Young Stanley grinned cheekily. He mostly visited his father every Friday, sometimes staying the night. Today was Sunday and an exception, and he wouldn't be staying. Today he was off home.

Biddy frowned as she watched Stanley wobble away on his sister's bicycle, given to him when Lizzie had joined the Royal Army Service Corps. Stanley didn't care that the bike was designed for a girl. Having transport meant he could live with his mother at the pawn shop in Bedminster and visit his father on Fridays when fish and chips were on offer.

Biddy Young was a bit disturbed and not a little put out. She regarded herself as Mary Anne Randall's best friend. They'd shared secrets, disappointments and joys over the years – but perhaps they had not shared everything.

'I never knew she 'ad any auntie. Never mentioned one,' Biddy muttered, not to anyone in particular.

Henry looked over her head to the end of the street, his eyes following his visitor until George Ford had disappeared around the corner. Even then he kept his eyes focused on that self-same spot.

'She didn't,' he said. 'That's why I didn't give him 'er address.' He turned back to Biddy. 'Will you tell 'er when you see 'er?'

'Course I will, though I won't go round there today. I ain't 'ad a wash today. I'll pop round tomorrow and tell 'er.'

'Water ain't that scarce,' he said, and went back indoors.

Undeterred by his comment, Biddy hurried back across the road. Of course she'd tell Mary Anne. She'd tell her that her old man had refused to pass on her address because he wanted to hurt her, and what could be more hurtful than standing in the way of a family inheritance? If Mary Anne had a bit of money coming to her, she might be generous and pass a bit on to her good friends – especially those who'd helped her claim it.

Glancing back over her shoulder she saw that Henry had closed the door. Old skinflint. Leopards don't change their spots, and in her opinion, Henry Randall was still the brute he'd always been despite having given up the beer. He'd never forgiven Mary Anne for leaving him for another, younger man. Biddy didn't blame her. Michael was lovely and she was sure they'd be happy together once the war was over and he was back from all that secret stuff he was doing. In the meantime she decided to take it upon herself to protect Mary Anne's interests and so, first things first, puffing and panting she ran to the end of the street. She almost collided with a boy riding a makeshift bicycle made from pram wheels and a rusty frame.

'Oi! You!' She grabbed his shoulder. 'Go and fetch that bloke you just passed. Him wearing the khaki mac.'

'Give me a penny,' he said, stretching out his hand.

'I'll give you a clip round the ear!'

'I ain't doing it for peanuts, Missus!'

He was resolute. Biddy growled at him. How come kids were so sharp these days?

'Here you are,' she said, her hand diving into her generous bra cup. 'A farthing.'

He grimaced, thought about it, then took it, spitting on it before shoving it into his ragged pocket.

A few minutes later, George Ford reappeared, skirting a table of buckets, bowls and sweeping brushes outside the corner shop.

Biddy struck a provocative pose and flashed him a lascivious smile. 'You wanted Mrs Randall's address? Well I'm the one that can give it to you.'

Once the deed was done and he'd thanked her and walked away, Biddy turned back into the street smiling to herself. Even though she hadn't managed to get George Ford back to her place for a cup of tea and whatever else might take his fancy, she'd done her best friend a good turn and was pleased with herself. Now to take the news back to her neighbours.

'Guess what,' she said to the first neighbours she came across. 'That dirty old sod made a pass at me. I told him to sod off, told 'im I was a married woman.'

There were mutters of 'cheeky monkey' and 'who does he think he is?'. Biddy basked in their attention. She felt like Jean Harlow, blonde, curvaceous and irresistible.

Henry Randall watched her through the front window. He saw the women glance over and guessed they were curious. He scowled. Bloody women. They were all the same, fit for only one thing. He turned away, opened a bottle of beer and poured it down his throat.

Two

The air-raid siren was wailing its warning, the baby was crying and Daw was yelling but Mary Anne Randall carried on pouring the cups of tea they'd been about to drink into the thermos flask.

'I can't believe Adolf Hitler is sending over a raid on a Sunday,' she muttered. 'It must be another false alarm.'

Stanley was hovering, hands in pockets, shirt cuffs flapping around his wrists.

'Ma, who's Aunt Maude?'

Mary Anne continued to concentrate on the thermos flasks and sandwiches she'd prepared for going into the shelter.

'I don't know,' she said vaguely. 'Who is she?'

'A man called round at Dad's and said she'd left you some money.'

His mother stopped what she was doing and frowned down at him. 'I don't have an Aunt Maude.'

'So you won't be getting any money?' Stanley's tone was as disappointed as his expression. Pedalling back from his dad's he'd dreamed of a shiny new bike – a boy's version, not this silly girl's bike that Lizzie had left behind.

Mary Anne chuckled to herself. 'Chance would be a fine thing.'

Disappointed, Stanley shrugged and packed up his toy soldiers to take to the shelter. Grown-ups had strange ways that he didn't always understand. He thought of his eldest brother Harry and what he would advise if he told him how he felt about grown-ups. *Grin and bear it*, that's what he'd say.

'The shelter,' Daw was shouting. 'We've got to get to the shelter. Ma, will you leave that! Can't you hear the sirens?'

Mary Anne's voice was as calm as her exterior. 'Daw, you've always been a bit on the hysterical side. How many false alarms have we had? We're too far west for the Germans to bother us. Our Lizzie told me that.'

Daw's eyes were wide with fear. 'Ma, it's a raid! There's bombs dropping!'

Mary Anne tutted loudly as she screwed in the top. 'And on a Sunday too. Have they no respect?'

'There's loads of them,' shouted Stanley, her youngest, a lad of ten who was as much of an armchair general as his father. 'Watch out! Yer squashing me,' he added as Daw squeezed through the doorway, the baby still squalling in her arms.

Mary Anne was about to follow her, then stopped. 'The presents! Stanley, give me a hand here!'

Stanley poked out his tongue at his sister before racing back to help his mother.

There were glass-fronted cupboards on either side of the fireplace. Mary Anne plunged into the lower cupboards. Unlike the upper ones they were wooden fronted. She pulled out two brown carrier bags bulging with Christmas presents. Most were home made – scarves, handkerchiefs and things made from hand-me-downs. Stanley took one, carrying it tucked behind him so that it bumped against his legs. His mother followed.

'Hitler can bomb all he likes, but he isn't going to destroy these and ruin our Christmas.'

Daw was getting frantic. 'Come on!' The baby squalled even louder.

Mary Anne pushed the second carrier bag at her daughter. 'Take this.'

'Where are you going?'

Christmas wasn't just about giving presents. There was food in the larder, precious bits and pieces, some on ration and some acquired through friends of friends. Mary Anne headed for the small lean-to kitchen.

'You go on. I'll be right behind you. I'm not leaving the tea and flour and the Christmas cake.'

Daw didn't wait. Bundling baby Mathilda into her pushchair, the carrier bag bouncing between her knees and the pram, she broke into a run. It was her mother's opinion that the back yard was too small for an air-raid shelter. She preferred the public ones in Dean Lane.

'At least there you can have a jolly time before a bomb hits,' she'd quipped, referring to the sing songs, sometimes accompanied by an accordion.

'Mum, don't say that!' Being brave didn't come easily to Daw, whereas young Stanley took everything in his stride.

Mary Anne pulled everything she could from the cupboard: flour, tea, sugar, sultanas and precious tins of pink Canadian salmon. Plus the Christmas cake, of course.

'Take this,' she said, thrusting a bundle into Stanley's arms. 'Now go on after our Daw. I'll be right behind you.'

A sudden thought made Mary Anne stop in her tracks. She looked up, thinking that perhaps the scream of the siren had changed in some way. It hadn't, and yet some instinct telling her the sirens were different today had made her hesitate. And why had she gathered all her precious Christmas things together? She'd never done that before. Why today?

She shook the thoughts from her head. No matter what, she would follow her instincts. In the past she'd lived purely for her family, burying her true self beneath whatever they had wanted her to be. A mother. A wife. Now, since knowing Michael, she had become a woman, a mature version of the carefree girl she'd once been.

Jolting herself back to reality, she wove in and out of the furniture and out of the back door, locking it behind her. The front of the shop was securely bolted against the looters that bombing raids inevitably brought. A pawn shop was a magnet to such people. She'd kept things going in Michael's absence and wasn't about to lose it to thieves now.

She dashed off into the alley and down to Dean Lane. She was just in time to see Stanley disappearing down the steps of the shelter entrance. The sound of the sirens set her teeth on edge. She was glad to reach the shelter entrance, as being underground muffled the sound of the siren.

The shelter was bursting at the seams, but still she managed to push her way across to where Daw was sitting with Mathilda in her lap. The pram had been left outside. There was only room for people in here. The man on the accordion was squeezing away and singing 'I'll be with you in apple blossom time'.

The air was hot and rank with the smell of people. Normally it might have been bearable, but these people had little to eat, little water to wash with and hardly enough time to keep body and soul together. Everyone was beginning to look a bit grey around the gills.

Stanley found a few of his pals. As if by magic they all pulled conkers from their pockets and immediately started a game.

Daw was crying, big tears streaking her dust-covered face, the dust stirred up from the floor by tightly packed people. Her selfish temper suddenly took hold. She glared at her mother.

'I wish I hadn't come. It's all your fault!'

There had been many times when Mary Anne had hidden the hurt caused by Daw's comments. This was just another one, so she put on a brave face and tried to sound calm and collected.

'I had to get the Christmas presents, Daw,' she said as she squeezed on to the rough bench beside her daughter. She sighed. 'I was looking forward to a proper Christmas, Daw. That cake'll go down a treat. So will that salmon.'

'I don't care,' Daw blubbered.

Daw had always had a bit of a self-centred way about her. Even now, she pouted as though she were still nine years old. 'That isn't what I meant. It's coming to the pawn shop. If you still lived at home with Dad . . .'

Mary Anne clamped her teeth tightly together. Harry, Lizzie and even young Stanley accepted that Henry's violence and drinking had been too much for their mother to live with. They'd also accepted that she loved Michael, who had been left the pawn broking business by his uncle. They'd met at the beginning of the war when she'd been running her own little business from her washroom at the back of the house. He was younger than her, though she was still a looker for a woman of forty plus. At first they'd been in competition, but that had soon melted away. They'd both been escapees – her from Henry and he from Germany.

Mary Anne turned her face away until she had gained more control of her emotions. Her heart ached to see Michael again. Sometimes she screwed her eyes tightly shut and imagined his features, afraid that she might never see him again, afraid that she'd forget what he looked like. His letters were few and guarded and sometimes, when she was at her lowest ebb, she wondered if he would ever return; if he would ever *want* to return. To help keep the doubts at bay, she tried to fill her time with the pawn shop and helping out in the Red Cross shop around the corner in East Street. She'd donated some of the pre-war pledges that had never been claimed. Some of it was sheer tat, stuff that went straight into the bin. The clothes, crockery and cooking utensils went to the shop.

It took a while to control her feelings and by the time she could, the walls of the shelter were shaking. Someone shouted that a nearby shelter had been hit. The panic was palpable, rolling through the people like a tidal wave. Shouting and screaming, a host of humanity clawed their way to the entrance, terror in their eyes. Children cried, women screamed and so did some men. Others, ARP wardens mostly, tried to calm everyone down and prevent them from going outside. 'It's raining bombs out there. Stay where you are. Stay where you're safe.'

The boys stopped playing conkers. Stanley crept back to his mother's side, hiding his face beneath her arm. Turning her back towards the shelter entrance, Mary Anne hugged Daw and the baby tightly against herself with her free arm. If a bomb was going to hit them, it would hit her first. Daw shook and trembled, sobbing against her shoulder.

'I can't stand this,' she mumbled into her mother's coat. 'I can't stand it.'

'We'll be alright. I promise we will.'

Mary Anne turned frightened eyes over her shoulder. Carrying others with them, those panicking pressed against the shelter entrance. Heads disappeared in the crush. Mary Anne pressed her daughter's face more tightly against her own body, hoping that somehow she could protect her.

Suddenly the concrete roof trembled. Dust floated down in a milky haze, covering heads, stinging eyes and sticking in throats. A horror-filled hush descended, spreading through the concrete cloud.

Mary Anne closed her eyes. She wasn't one for church and praying, but war makes people dig deep. She offered up a silent prayer. *Please keep my family safe. If you take anyone, take me. Please take me.*

The sound of crashing buildings and the rumbling and shifting around them gradually ebbed away.

'They're going over,' someone said.

Someone broke into loud sobs. Others murmured prayers of thanks. A hushed sigh seemed to drift like the dust across the huddled humanity. Because someone else had died, because the chance of a bomb falling on them had passed and fallen elsewhere, a sense of contemplative silence descended. Those that had rushed for the stairs now pressed themselves against walls, their eyes staring as though seeing what might have been. Medical people in an assortment of uniforms tended those who'd been injured in the crush.

Two hours later, when the all-clear sounded, Stanley brought his head out from beneath his mother's arm. Daw lifted her gaze and looked around her with staring, scared eyes.

Fearing her daughter was on the verge of hysteria, Mary

Anne gathered up all her courage and helped Daw to her feet. 'Come on.'

Even though the air outside was thick with dust, it was easier to breathe than in the shelter. Daw looked for the baby's pushchair.

'Where's my pram?'

Mary Anne looked beyond her to where rescue workers clambered over a pile of rubble. The neighbouring air-raid shelter had indeed taken a direct hit.

'Those poor people,' she muttered.

'Are they blown to bits?' Stanley asked, his eyes wide with ghoulish interest and just a hint of fear.

Mary Anne didn't reply. 'Don't forget the bag.'

'Got it,' he said, raising it so she could see he wasn't lying.

Ambulance bells clanged and people shouted. A hose was being unwound from a fire engine. She failed to see a fire, but smelled the smoke. Somewhere, amongst all this dust, were buildings, people and her road back to the pawn shop. Mary Anne suddenly thought of the thermos flasks of tea they'd taken into the shelter. They'd been scared too rigid to drink it.

'We could have that tea now. It'll still be warm.'

Daw shook her head as she strapped Mathilda into her dusty and slightly bent pushchair.

'Not me, Mother. I'm off home.'

Home for Daw was above the corner shop owned by her husband's uncle and aunt. It was at the end of the street Mary Anne had once lived in with her family. Their home at number ten Kent Street was gone now, destroyed in a previous raid. Henry had been moved out to Aiken Street in Barton Hill on the other side of the river. Stanley had moved in with her at the pawn shop, though he did visit his father every so often, especially on Friday nights – not so much out of love, but more because of the fish and chips bought from the shop at the bottom of Avonvale Road.

There was no arguing with Daw. Mary Anne had decided years ago not to try. It was Daw's way. She was selfish, though she'd never admit to it. She was conservative and she refused to accept that Mary Anne's living with Michael would be for ever. She wanted things to be as they once were. Through her eyes they had been a cosy, loving family. The truth had been so different, but Daw would never see that.

Leaning heavily into the pushchair, Daw scuttled off, the slightly wobbly wheels squeaking as she trundled the pushchair over the rubble.

A well of emotion tugged at Mary Anne's heart as she watched the head of little Mathilda bob to one side, peering past her mother so she could see her grandmother.

'When will I see you again?' Mary Anne shouted after her.

Daw gave her a cursory wave over her shoulder, but no response. Mary Anne brushed a tear from the corner of her eye. Just dust, she told herself, but she knew it wasn't true. She loved little Mathilda, her first grandchild, and couldn't bear the thought of her growing up without recognizing who she was. Curtailing access to Mathilda was Daw's way of exacting punishment on her mother for splitting up with her father. It was never said in so many words, only hinted at, but Mary Anne knew.

Stanley tugged at the sleeve of her coat. 'You alright, Ma?'

'Just thinking,' she said.

It wasn't far to the pawn shop. Normally it would have taken only minutes, but today the world had turned upside down. There was rubble everywhere, and fire engines, ambulances and people in various uniforms were all rushing around.

Picking her way through the broken bricks and the twisted gas mains, she came to the alley that led out into East Street. The bag containing the Christmas things bumped against her legs. Stanley was carrying his in front, both arms wrapped around it. Despite the dust and rubble, a single tram had wound its way through East Street but had been stopped by the police.

Mary Anne headed in the direction from which it had come, craning her neck in an effort to see through the devastation and down the side street to the pawn shop.

A great cloud of black smoke blanketed the street exactly where the pawn shop was situated. With her heart in her mouth, she quickened her pace. Flames were licking upwards through the smoke. *No! Not the shop!*

She ordered Stanley to stay put.

'I'll go and look,' she said, piling her bundles against his dusty legs.

She ran towards the shop front.

'Oi! Where do you think you're going?' A policeman grabbed her arm. 'You can't go in there, love.'

'That's my shop!'

Round-eyed she stared to where Michael's business had been. The whole frontage was ablaze.

'What will he say?' she wailed, her hand over her mouth. 'What will he say?'

The shop was all they had and it meant a lot to him. Michael had inherited it from an uncle, who had inherited it from his father, who in turn had inherited it from his father. And now?

Men with dirt-streaked faces fought the flames. Steam mixed with smoke, its hissing sound obliterated by that of falling masonry. A brick chimney stack groaned and began to topple. Warnings were shouted. The policeman holding Mary Anne pushed her behind the waiting tram. More dust, black and acrid, joined the fetid air.

Another man wearing the uniform of an auxiliary fireman joined them. His face was soaked with sweat and grime. His nose was bleeding. He swiped at it with his sleeve.

'I'd like to get my hands on the bugger that did that,' he said grimly.

'You'd better hitch a ride on a Lancaster bomber then,' said the policeman.

The fireman shook his head. 'No incendiaries were dropped. It might have scored a hit, but I was hereabouts and didn't see or hear it explode.'

The policeman pulled a face. 'Could have been looters who started it. They can be mean like that. Light it up for the sake of it. Just arsonists at heart.'

Mary Anne looked disbelievingly from one man to the other.

The policeman met her look and shook his head. 'Not everyone supports the war effort. Some only support themselves.'

The fireman produced an incredibly clean handkerchief from his pocket, folded it in four and dabbed it at his nose. 'In these times you can never be too sure, but it's a possibility.'

Mary Anne closed her eyes and turned her face to the sky. Ash fluttered down, speckling her face. 'Now what do I do?'

'It's your place, is it, love?' said the fireman.

She nodded.

The policeman shook his head and tutted. 'Well it looks as though only the front of the old place has had it, but you can't go back in there, not for a good while anyway. Have you got any friends or relatives you can stay with?'

She shook her head. Her gaze drifted back to the smoking ruin that had been her home.

'The Sally Army is down there.' He pointed to a mobile trolley from which jolly-faced people were handing out tea and sympathy. 'They might be able to find you a bed. And just beyond them is the Red Cross and the WRVS or whatever. You could ask them.'

Numbly she gathered up Stanley and her things. In her mind she searched for solutions to her immediate problems. Immediate problems were all that she could attend to at this moment in time. Her first priority was to find somewhere to stay. Daw, her closest relative, lived on the corner of the old street above the corner shop. But she only had two rooms, hardly room to swing a cat. Overnight maybe? No longer than that. It wouldn't work, but for now it would have to do.

Henry also had a place. Stanley would have to go there, but Mary Anne couldn't. She just couldn't. The thought of living under the same roof as Henry, her husband, filled her with dread. The old memories resurfaced and wouldn't go away. Yes, she'd been told he never entered a pub nowadays; that he was a changed man. But still, deep down inside, she knew she could never trust him to stay that way.

'Come back when it's cooled down,' the policeman called after her as she walked away. 'There might be something you can save.'

She thanked him again.

'Before you go,' he said, lowering his voice and glancing in the direction of the fireman with the bloody nose. He beckoned her closer. 'Are you Harry Randall's mother?'

'Yes.' She was nervous about what he was about to say.

His voice dropped to just above a whisper. 'Well I didn't like to say in company, but could he 'ave done anything to upset certain people? You know, some of the dodgy types he got 'imself involved with?'

Admitting to herself that Harry was no angel had never been easy, and she certainly didn't comment on it to complete strangers. Nowadays she contented herself with the knowledge that he was serving his country. In her books that made up for his past delinquency. That was why her response now was curt and noncommittal.

'I don't know what you mean.'

The policeman winked. 'No. Of course you don't.'

Stanley did not welcome the news that he'd have to stay at his father's more or less permanently.

'It won't be for long,' she told him.

'He'll get drunk,' he said. His sour expression left her in no doubt as to how he felt about moving back in.

'No he won't, Stanley. Our Daw reckons he doesn't drink now. You heard her.' He shook his head, his eyes big and round as they looked up at her. His mother did her best to reassure him. 'It's true. Didn't you hear our Daw say so?'

'That don't mean it's true!'

'Just for a while, Stanley. Just until I can find us somewhere,' she said, walking on but not daring to look into his face and see his uncertainty.

The boy fell silent, dragging the carrier bag behind him now.

Mary Anne made an effort to be cheerful. 'At least we've still got the Christmas cake,' she said brightly. 'We'll all have a piece on Christmas Day.'

Stanley was unmoved.

Wishing the war was over, wishing the shop hadn't caught fire, she took Stanley around to his father's and then headed for Daw's.

If only Lizzie was here, she thought. But Lizzie, her second daughter, had left to join the Royal Army Service Corps. Somehow Mary Anne would let her daughter know what had happened. Somehow.

Three

Lizzie held up a large pair of khaki-coloured bloomers in disgust. 'I knew I should have joined the Wrens. Surely their knickers can't be anything like these! Just look at them. They're big enough to fit Nellie the elephant!'

Her friend Margot, an ebony cigarette holder delicately balanced between rich red lips, gave the offending articles a quick glance.

'Darling girl, you'll appreciate those bloomers in the depth of winter. Cut some arms just below the elastic and you can wear them over your vest.'

The suggestion wasn't without merit. Lizzie nodded approvingly. 'You've got a point.'

Folding the bloomers, she turned her attention to the other items, extras to those issued when she'd first joined up. Supply of army-issue female items was spasmodic to say the least. When a rumour did the rounds that extras had arrived, the girls swooped on the quartermaster's stores like a flock of hungry starlings.

'Any suggestions as to what I can do with these?' said Lizzie, her eyes popping at the stiffly starched canvas brassiere she held stretched between both hands.

Margot looked aghast and almost spat her cigarette from her mouth. 'My goodness! There are limits, my darling girl.'

Lizzie paddled one hand in a massive cup. 'Emergency shopping bags?'

'They'd make a pretty good horse blanket,' said Margot in her off-hand fashion. She immediately dropped her eyes back to the magazine she had spread on the bed in front of her. 'Big enough to fit this one here,' she said. 'Listen to this. Irish Hunter, seventeen hands. Suit experienced rider.'

Bessie Fitzpatrick, a red-headed girl from Tottenham in London, peered over her shoulder and shook her head. 'Nah! I got the experience, but he ain't my type. And seventeen 'ands? I get enough trouble with Irish blokes with two 'ands, let alone seventeen!'

It was obvious that Bessie was having a go at Margot, not that Margot appeared to notice or care. Lizzie had liked Margot straightaway, even though Bessie had called her stuck up.

'I thought you'd be friends, seeing as you both come from London,' Lizzie had said to Bessie when they'd first met.

Bessie had jerked her chin and tossed her head. 'Blimey, no! She's from Chelsea. That ain't London. Not real London. It's full of toffs. Just like 'er in fact.'

Lizzie had shrugged. 'I'm from Bristol. I wouldn't know about that, though we do have something like Chelsea. It's called Clifton and it's perched high above the Avon Gorge looking down on the city.'

'Nob Hill,' sniffed Bessie.

Bessie had been referring to a film of that name where the rich lived on the hill and the poor in the valley. She'd never viewed Bristol quite like that before, and despite Bessie she regarded Margot as a friend. Her accent and where she came from didn't matter. They got on well together.

The first thing they'd done when arriving at their training camp 'somewhere near Ipswich' was marching. Marching, marching and more marching – but that was after being issued with their initial items of ill-fitting uniforms. The girls did their best with what they were given, sorting things out among themselves. Big skirts were swapped for smaller ones, sleeves were altered and seams let out. Shoes were a problem; everyone acquired blistered feet.

Proper training meant learning about the vehicles they might end up driving. Some would end up driving trucks, some motorcycles, some cars and some might even get to drive ambulances. It very much depended on demand.

This morning, even though the girls were being flippant about uniforms, was a very important day. Today was assignment day when they were to be appointed to various transport pools around the country.

With nervous fingers, Lizzie buttoned and re-buttoned her jacket, polishing at an imagined speck on one of her bright, shiny buttons.

Margot closed her magazine, put out her cigarette and got to her feet. She began straightening her jacket, flattening it over her hips.

Lizzie caught her eye. 'You're nervous too.'

Margot hunched her shoulders in a huge sigh. 'Silly, I know, but I can't help it. I'm reminded of boarding school and being called to the headmistress's study for punishment.'

'Were you called there very often?'

A huge grin divided Margot's peaches-and-cream complexion. 'Quite a bit, actually.'

Lizzie nodded at Margot's wrinkled coverlet. 'Better smooth your bed before the Welsh dragon sees it.'

The Welsh dragon had tightly permed hair and protruding teeth. Lizzie couldn't help getting the impression that the imperfection was exaggerated, especially when Lieutenant Morgan snapped an order. 'Like they're going to bite you if you don't move fast enough,' she'd said to Margot.

Everyone stood to attention at the end of their beds, waiting nervously to hear what she had to say. She'd keep them waiting of course, drawing out the agony like the innards of a dead duck.

She went through the usual spiel, did the customary check of their beds, their lockers and even ran her fingers along the picture rail. Even when she rubbed her thumb and finger together, Lizzie knew she would feel no dust or grime. Everyone had made sure of that, polishing and dusting until their arms ached.

'Right!' she said at last.

The eyes of her charges glittered. Their breathing quickened. Their cheeks turned pink with anticipation.

The lieutenant's voice rang like an alarm bell. 'The notice giving details of your postings has been pinned up on the board. You will file there in an orderly manner. *Orderly*, mark you. You will not run to the notice board. Neither will you shout, scream, laugh or cry when you see where you are to be posted. Now . . .'

The Welsh dragon glanced at her wristwatch, scrutinizing the second hand, intent on prolonging the agony. Lizzie held her breath.

'Fall OUT!'

Stiffly, because they were trying so hard not to rush en masse, the girls filed down the avenue between the beds. Lizzie joined them.

'Randall! Fitzpatrick! Ponsonby-Lyle! Attention!'

The three did as ordered, snapping to attention, yet each wishing for their feet to be following everyone else.

Lieutenant Morgan stood before them, her thick legs braced to better support her stocky – tending towards fat – frame.

As was her nature, she yet again made them wait. Her neat grey eyes surveyed each of them in turn. She heaved her shoulders and took in a deep breath before she spoke.

'Well, ladies. You three have hit the jackpot. Not for you the rigours and responsibilities of keeping a truck or an ambulance on the road. Not for you the wearing of overalls for the riding of motorcycles. You three have been selected as drivers for important personnel. You will become part of the Lavenham pool. Each of you will be allotted to whoever needs you. Sometimes you will be seconded for only a day. Other times for longer. Now, collect your things. No need for travel warrants. A truck will take you to your new home.' She saluted. 'Good luck in all you do, ladies.'

'Somebody up there loves us,' said Margot, raising her eyes to heaven.

'Thank 'im for me,' said Bessie, whose impatience was obvious. Everything she owned was being pressed into her kitbag in double-quick time.

Lizzie was excited. 'I've heard you can end up as driver to some really important people. Imagine! One of us might end up driving Winston Churchill around.'

'I don't care who it is,' said Bessie, finally drawing her kitbag shut. 'Driving suits me a lot better than square bashing.'

Margot was more measured in her packing. Everything about her was methodical and calmly thought out. Even her complexion looked cool and smooth. Her hair was dark brown and permed into thick curls that never looked untidy.

Lizzie tucked her own tresses back around the length of old stocking she used as a base for the 'looped bun' lying at the nape of her neck.

At least it's not as unruly as Bessie's red mop, she thought to herself. Because she'd been rushing, wisps of redness burst like horsehair stuffing around Bessie's cap.

'Right. I'm off!'

Lizzie exchanged a quick smile with Margot before they followed speedily behind.

'We're moving like ballerinas,' Lizzie laughed.

Margot chuckled. 'What, with these shoes?'

They were each issued with cars that were roughly the same colour as their uniforms. Accordingly they set off for the transport pool on the other side of Lavenham. The weather was holding up well and it was daylight when they set out, following the route at a cracking pace despite the lack of signposts.

They trundled through the main street of a village where most of the houses were half-timbered and leaning against each other for support. All three pulled in outside a pub.

'I think this is Lavenham,' said Margot.

'It is Lavenham,' said Lizzie. 'I know it is,' she repeated, about to get back in her car.

'Really? How do you know that?' asked Margot, looking suitably impressed.

Lizzie pointed at a shop across the road. 'It says Lavenham Butchers above that shop.'

The other two looked over.

'Clever clogs,' said Bessie and got back into her car. Margot got back into hers and the three drove off.

The transport pool was on the other side of the town, based in what had been a series of stables set around a central courtyard. They were housed above the present-day garages in what had been the hayloft. A long, beamed room had been sectioned off into three small but separate rooms.

'Super,' said Margot when they first entered.

'Spiffing,' said Bessie in a mocking tone. 'It'll soon seem like home.'

'First things first,' said Lizzie. The other two watched as she sat down on her bed and eased off her shoes. 'It *is* home,' she pronounced, sighing as she lay full stretch on her bed.

Just two weeks after settling in and ferrying pretty ordinary army personnel from base to base and from one meeting to another, Lizzie was called into the office. The transport convenor was a hefty man of advancing years. He'd been brought out of retirement purely to run the unit.

'By some toff who thought we weren't up to it,' Bessie had snapped when they'd heard.

'You're to go and pick up a wing commander from the railway station,' the convenor said now. He gave Lizzie the basic details.

The day was bright for late autumn, all orange trees and blue sky. The sun shone but the air was fresh, not humid and heavy with dust raised from beneath the heel of the plough as it had been in the summer.

He gave her details of how to recognize him and told her that his name was Guy Hunter. 'You're to take him to his billet at Ainsley Hall. Your duties will be to drive him to airfields and suchlike. You're to make sure that he sees everything he wants. Is that clear?'

Reggie Stratfield was usually quite clear in his instructions, and never curmudgeonly. Today he was.

Lizzie thought about asking him what was wrong. Poor old chap. He was always being teased about his age, asked whether he'd ever fought beside King Arthur or Henry the Fifth. He'd always taken it in good spirits. Today he was not himself. Lizzie took the plunge.

'Is anything wrong, sir?'

One watery eye peered up at her from beneath a snowy eyebrow.

Before replying, he made a low, guttural sound, similar to a sleeping dog's growl.

'I just don't like foreigners!'

She didn't press the matter, presuming one of the Polish contingent had upset him in some way, but she brought it up that night at the local pub.

Bessie made a similar comment as before about seventeen hands when Lizzie mentioned the name Hunter.

'She's jealous,' said Margot, eyeing Bessie as she joined in with the group of soldiers having a singsong around the old piano.

'I can't think why,' said Lizzie. Bessie was fun, extremely popular with the rank and file.

'She's been ferrying local bigwigs around – or at least they're bigwigs during the week. The rest of the time they command the Home Guard.'

It still didn't explain anything. 'So?'

Margot rested her arm on Lizzie's shoulder. Lizzie smelled her expensive perfume. Everything about Margot was expensive. It got her noticed. That was how she knew the secret she was just about to impart.

'This wing commander is Canadian. Not too old either. Fingers crossed, my dear, and he could be Prince Charming.'

The wing commander's train was not on time. After waiting outside for over an hour, Lizzie got out of the car to stretch her legs. The sound of tinkling water led her to a small pond just opposite the railway station. The sound was made by a small brook tumbling over upright stones and into the pond. Some thoughtful soul – or perhaps everyone in the village – had provided a wooden bench on the grassy bank. At present it was bathed in some unseasonal sunshine.

Lizzie looked down at her feet. As usual, thanks to the heavy clumpers the army provided, her feet were killing her. Surely it wouldn't hurt to sit here a while in the fresh air? She checked the time on the station clock and strained her ears. The train was overdue and the track leading off into the distance was totally deserted. No, it wouldn't hurt to sit down.

Sighing with contentment, she sank on to the warm wood, undid her laces and slid her feet out of her shoes.

The sun was warm – too warm. The grass was cool and tickled her stockinged feet. All the early mornings and last night's visit to the pub had taken their toll. Her eyes closed and she drifted off.

Way off in the distance a wooden toy train was chuffing up a cardboard hill, its little whistle tooting just like a real one. Funny, she thought, how dreams can mirror reality, and somehow the two can fuse together as the sleeper begins to wake up . . .

The sun had gone in. At least, it seemed that way. A shadow had definitely fallen over her.

Drat! She'd fallen asleep. The train! The wing commander!

He was looking down at her, his eyes veiled as he scrutinized her feet.

'I'm sorry . . .' she began, all of a fluster. Suddenly she remembered to salute. Couldn't she be put on a charge if she didn't? she wondered absently. She shot up, saluted – and hit her toe on a stone.

'Ouch! Sir,' she said, wobbling slightly as she fought to carry out the formality while standing on one leg.

His expression remained implacable. No hint of a smile nor any sign of amusement in his eyes. His voice was as emotionless as his eyes. 'Put your shoes on and tidy yourself up. I'll wait in the car.'

Red faced she slid her aching feet back into their torture chambers, tidied her hair and straightened her tie and jacket. She noticed grass stains around her ankles, but there was nothing she could do about them now. Appropriate apologies ran through her mind. She opened her mouth to utter them the moment she got back to the car.

'I'm sorry—' she began.

'Never mind that,' he snapped, turning round to face her. 'Drive me to where I have to go.'

'Ainsley Hall?'

'Whatever.' He turned his face away to look out of the window.

Lizzie melted into her seat behind the steering wheel, her face red and her embarrassment total.

On the way to Ainsley Hall, the sun went in and the rain started. It pattered on the windscreen, pooled in ditches at the side of the road and leaked from thatched eaves.

She glanced in the rear-view mirror. Silent and still, her passenger gazed relentlessly out of the window. He'd said nothing to her and so far she'd said nothing to him. Would he report her for being improperly dressed? She bit her lip. It had been her plan to join up and see a bit of life, have a little adventure. And she'd been quite prepared to serve for the duration, but if he reported her . . .

What would be so wrong if I attempted to break the ice? she thought to herself. *Here goes!*

'Well. This is England. Raining again.'

She saw his head jerk round to face her. His expression was unchanged. His eyes were steely blue and his face was . . . She almost held her breath. He was handsome. No doubt about it.

She decided to try again, presuming he hadn't heard her properly the first time. 'I said about the rain, sir, and it being England . . .'

'Never mind the weather. Keep your eyes forward. Drive, don't talk.'

Her spirits nose-dived. Stratfield had told her that she was to ferry Hunter around for at least the next two weeks. She'd told herself she would still have plenty of spare time, that he'd tell her to take a half a day now and then while he did what he had to do. Now she wasn't so sure. He'd come across as demanding and, worse still, humourless.

He left her at the bottom of the steps leading to the arched doorway of Ainsley Hall after telling her to call for him at seven thirty sharp in the morning.

It was a forty-five minute drive back to base. The rain thundered down all the way, dripping from trees and dropping like metal shot on to the roof of the car. The shiny road helped to eke out the meagre gleam from the hooded headlights.

After parking the car, she first had to report in at Stratfield's office – not that it would be him sitting there after six in the evening; at night Sergeant Grimsby took over.

'I've got a message for you,' he said before she had a chance to head for the canteen. He handed her a written note. 'It's from your mother.'

He told her exactly what was written on the paper.

'Shop bombed. Have to find temporary accommodation. Will move in with Daw for now. Love, Mother.'

'Oh no!'

Her head began to ache. Poor Mother. The shop had become everything to her. She'd been looking after it for Michael and would feel guilty that it had been destroyed – as though she could have done anything!

She clutched the note, her head aching with increased tension.

'I wonder . . .' she said, leaning on the desk with both hands as she thought things through. 'Do you think I could have leave to visit my mother?'

Sergeant Grimsby opened the file in which he kept copies of the roster. 'I don't see why not. It all depends on whether your latest assignment wishes to swap to someone else, or insists on keeping you.'

'Can you phone him? He's at Ainsley Hall.' Her voice pleaded. So did her eyes.

Sergeant Grimsby took in her pretty face, the big eyes begging him to do something. He patted her hand. 'I understand, me dear. We all have only one mother. I'll ring right away.'

It seemed to take an age from him placing one digit in the first number to someone answering. After that he asked to be put through to the wing commander.

'Randall has asked for compassionate leave. You see her mother's been bombed out of her accommodation . . .' He paused to hear Hunter's response. Then she heard the click of the connection being cut.

Even before he said anything, Lizzie knew by his expression that the answer was no.

'He says plenty of people have been bombed out of their homes. Everyone has to manage. You're to report at seven thirty precisely.'

Quaking inside, she saluted, turned and shut the door behind her. Deep breathing did nothing to quell her fury. At the sound of footsteps, she turned her head. Margot was marching briskly along the corridor and looking pleased with herself.

'Guess what! I've done it. I've bagged myself a major.' On seeing Lizzie's expression, her own gleeful beam sagged and finally vanished. 'What is it? What's the matter?'

Lizzie explained. 'You know what,' she added, 'I was really enjoying this job until he turned up. Now I'm thinking of getting a transfer closer to home. And all because of Wing Commander Guy bloody Hunter!

Four

Daw was taking advantage of having her mother staying with her for a while. Mary Anne knew it but bit her tongue and said nothing. She enjoyed looking after her first grandchild. Mathilda was a joy, a little girl full of gummy smiles, coos and chuckles. Mary Anne looked after her while Daw did the queuing for rations, helped in the shop and also filled in a few hours at the air-raid warden's post at the end of the street. The main bugbear of living over the shop was having to sleep on the settee. She was getting older and her back was telling her all about it. Besides that, Daw had stipulated it could only be temporary.

'John's coming home at Christmas, Mum, and we do like the place to ourselves,' she said coyly. She was folding up baby clothes brought in from off the washing line and looked suddenly thoughtful. From experience, Mary Anne knew what was coming. 'Dad's got room. You don't have to commit yourself. I'm sure he'd let you take things slowly—'

'No!'

Mary Anne's response was sharp and loud – much sharper than she intended in fact. Mathilda jerked awake from her nap and began to wail.

'There, there,' said Mary Anne, and was about to pick her up but Daw pushed her aside.

'Now look what you've done,' her daughter snapped, cuddling the red-faced, yelling Mathilda against her shoulder.

Hiding her hurt, Mary Anne turned aside and began folding the washing Daw had left in a pile. It was becoming more and more apparent that her daughter was preventing her from cuddling Mathilda by way of punishment for leaving Henry her father. Daw wanted them reunited. 'It's where you belong,' she kept saying.

Her eldest daughter had never believed that her father had abused her mother. Harry and Lizzie had tried to convince her, but because she'd never seen it happen, as far as she was concerned it *hadn't* happened. Henry was benign in front of his children, clever at hiding what he didn't want them to see. But once they were alone, Mary Anne had known the darker side of his character.

The postman came just after Daw had left to do her fire-watching duty. John's uncle handed her the mail. 'There's one from our John,' he said, a gleeful look in his eyes. 'We've got one from him too. And there's two for you, Mary Anne. I expect it's your Lizzie and your Harry.'

'I expect it is.' She glanced at the envelopes before taking them.

Mathilda had been given her feed and was dozing when she got back upstairs. Mary Anne put John's letter behind the clock for Daw to read when she got home. She poured herself a cup of tea, scraped some margarine over a single slice of toast, and picked up her letters.

She read Harry's first and felt guilty for doing so, but she couldn't help it. He was her son and the most likely to get injured or killed even though he was 'doing something clerical', as he never stopped reminding her. She knew he was doing a little more than that, but realized he was trying to spare her worries. Harry had always been a caring son – an attribute he had not inherited from his father.

His letter was reassuring but guarded – just like the ones she'd had from Michael. She'd gone along to the burned-out remains of the shop and stuck a notice on what remained of the door advising of her forwarding address. She'd also managed to salvage a few things which were now stored in a lean-to shed behind the corner shop. The back half wasn't as badly damaged as the front, but the smell of fire damage was suffocating.

Lizzie's letter told her exactly what she already knew; that she couldn't get leave to see her for a few weeks yet. She wasn't allowed to say why – obviously because loose talk could betray secrets – but she did say that she wasn't enjoying the job as much as she had been.

But don't worry, Mum. Chin up. I'll be there when I can.

Mary Anne folded the letter and put it back in the envelope. Her eyes glazed over as she looked around the tiny room. The window was small, the curtains red and yellow. The wallpaper was speckled and scattered with red leaves. Daw had done her best with what she had, and at present she had more than her mother did. It was her nest, her little home, and Mary Anne was beginning to feel uncomfortable there.

She tried to persuade herself that she was just imagining that Daw was trying to get her back with Henry. She shook her head. Times were hard and living with her daughter wasn't easy. A few more days, that was all she could allow herself. And of course there was Stanley to think about.

After washing her cup and saucer in the tiny sink in the corner of the room, she dressed Mathilda and strapped her into the pushchair. Tying a sack full of things she'd rescued from the pawn shop – mostly old clothes she had no use for – she set out for a walk. The Red Cross shop in the high street would welcome the stock. From past experience, she knew they would also probably force some wool on to her, begging her to knit socks, mittens or balaclavas 'for our gallant troops'.

Parking the pushchair outside, she undid the sack from the handlebar and took it into the shop. A woman with wide hips and wearing some kind of uniform beamed at her as she entered.

'All donations gratefully accepted, my dear,' she said. Her no-nonsense attitude was well meaning but overpowering.

Mary Anne had expected the sack to be snatched from her immediately. But no, this was Gertrude Palmer. Of good family and name, Gertrude was a well known organizer. If anyone wanted a team of middle-class women to get things done, it was Gertrude who recruited and organized. What she lacked in height she made up for in width, carrying a stout bosom before her and an exceptional rear behind. Short hair clung tightly to her head. Her clothes were good quality but not fashionable. Like the wearer, they were neither fluffy nor frilly.

She called to someone at the back of the shop. 'Daisy! Come and take this. You and Edith can sort it and iron where necessary.'

She wrinkled her nose as she opened and inspected the contents. 'Ooow! Smells a bit burned.'

'My shop burned down during a raid, but I'd thought you'd still be glad of it.'

Gertrude's frown turned to a breezy smile. 'How very dreadful for you. Never mind. Daisy?' She turned to the volunteer she'd summoned from the back of the shop. 'Wash it first, then iron it. But be careful with the water and keep beneath regulations if possible. Two inches is quite adequate.'

Mary Anne hid a knowing smile. Gertrude had a will of iron when it came to rules and regulations. She could almost imagine her using a ruler to measure the depth of water in her bath before stepping in.

Before she could leave, Gertrude caught hold of her arm. 'Can you knit, dear?'

'Well, I . . .'

'Take this.' Gertrude handed her a brown carrier bag with string handles. 'Socks, mittens and balaclavas and the odd jumper wouldn't come amiss.'

'I'll do what I can.'

'Of course you will, dear. Bring them in when you can.'

Protesting was out of the question. Gertrude had already turned her attention to someone inspecting a black velvet hat with purple feathers.

Mary Anne smiled as she shut the shop door behind her – but not for long. Surely she had left the pushchair to the right of the door? Perhaps not. She looked to the left. No pushchair. No Mathilda. Panic gripped her. Dropping the carrier bag, she darted up and down the pavement, terror gripping her heart. She searched the length of the street, looked across the road, then walked up and down it between the morning traffic.

'Mathilda!'

Stupid! Stupid! Stupid! As if a baby could call back! *Where was she?*

She saw the policeman long before he saw her and ran towards him. 'Someone's taken my granddaughter! Please help! Please!'

'Now, now, madam. Calm down. Tell me it from the beginning.'

The policeman had kindly eyes and white whiskers – one of those called back in from retirement at the outbreak of war. She couldn't think straight. She certainly couldn't be calm.

Her legs must have suddenly gone weak because he seemed to grow taller. He caught her by her shoulders before she crumpled to the ground.

Having seen what was happening from inside the shop, Gertrude Palmer came to the rescue, holding a cane chair before her. 'Here's a chair. Sit her on this.'

The policeman obeyed. 'Now,' he said, 'tell me what happened. You say you left your granddaughter in her pushchair outside a shop.'

Mary Anne nodded.

'And which shop was this?'

Gertrude answered for her. 'This shop, of course. I saw her arrive.'

'Right. And at what time?'

'No more than twenty minutes ago.' Gertrude replied.

The policeman patted her hand. 'Now, don't worry, me dear. It could be just kids playing a prank. That'll be all it is. Leave it to me. I'll take a walk around and see if I can see her. If I don't find her, I'll blow me whistle and get some help.'

'Daisy! Edith! Henrietta!'

Gertrude was holding the shop door open. Her three assistants came rushing at her call.

'This lady has lost her granddaughter. She was in a pushchair—'

'A cream-coloured pushchair with chrome wheels,' Mary Anne interjected.

'A cream-coloured pushchair with chrome wheels,' Gertrude repeated. 'Now hurry up and find it. Whoever's taken it can't have got far. And run,' she added when it seemed as though they might only stroll. Her three assistants scurried off in three different directions.

'A nice cup of sweet, strong tea is in order.'

'I could do with one,' said the police sergeant.

Gertrude threw him a sour look. 'I was referring to this lady. It's her that's in shock.'

He looked crestfallen.

Gertrude partially relented. 'You're welcome to a cup, Sergeant, once you've found the baby.'

'Of course!'

He sounded as though he'd been fatally wounded, but he went to do his duty, striding off down the street, looking over the crowds for some sign of the missing pushchair.

'You'd better come inside, dear,' said Gertrude.

Gently but firmly, Mary Anne was taken back into the shop, the chair hanging over Gertrude's free arm.

Tea was poured from a steaming brown pot. After two sugars and milk had been added, the cup and saucer were forced into Mary Anne's shaking hands.

'Don't worry,' said Gertrude.

'I can't help it. I keep thinking the worst might have happened. Perhaps some woman who can't have children might have taken her. And then what do I do? What will my daughter say if that's happened?'

'It *won't* have happened,' said Gertrude. 'Just because a woman can't have children doesn't mean she steals them off the street. *I* certainly wouldn't.'

Gertrude's voice had softened. Mary Anne looked into the kind, grey eyes and instantly understood.

Gertrude smiled. 'Quite right, dear. I can see you've guessed.' She sighed. 'Percival and I were never blessed. But . . .' She straightened and slapped her hip. 'We both found other things in life to fill our time and take pride in. Helping those less fortunate than us, whoever and wherever they may be. That's our creed. Ah!' she said, looking suddenly straight at the window. 'My troop has triumphed. They've found her!'

Mary Anne leapt from her chair as the women and pushchair bundled into the shop.

'Mathilda!'

Her granddaughter was sound asleep, pink face against white cotton pillow.

'She was outside Reynolds, the biscuit shop,' said the woman called Edith, a lady with honey-coloured streaks in her hair and a twinkle in her eye. If anyone ever stood up to the overbearing Gertrude, she was the one most likely.

Mary Anne's attention was focused on Mathilda. She wanted to check her all over to make sure she was unharmed.

'She's fine,' said Edith, smiling up into her face.

'I can't believe it,' said Mary Anne. 'Did you see who did it?'

Edith shook her head. 'No.'

Mary Anne frowned. 'But why?'

The police sergeant had heard the news and joined them. 'Just kids,' he said with an air of having experienced the very worst of what youngsters could do.

She could do nothing but accept he was right. There was no other explanation.

Henry Randall dragged his pint mug towards him, lifted it up and took a long, deep draft. His hard eyes closed as he savoured the deeply satisfying taste of hops and barley. He took a breath, then knocked back the last mouthful. As he returned the glass to the bar, he licked the remnants from his lips then wiped his mouth with the back of his hand. The Lord Nelson was his favourite pub. It had a high ceiling and big windows. The bottom half of the windows was opaque, a mix of dimpled and coloured glass set in lead. The top half was clear and afforded quite a good view. The best view was of the Red Cross shop along a bit. Mary Anne was always in and out of the place. Knowing her she'd probably enrol as a volunteer before long. He smiled. Best thing she could do; easier than ever to keep tabs on her.

'A great pint, Jim,' he said to the ashen-haired man behind the bar. 'I'll have another.'

Jim took his glass and began to refill it. As he did so, his eyes wandered enquiringly to Henry's ruddy face. 'I thought you'd signed the pledge, Henry. Tea only. Teetotal!'

Henry shoved the money across the bar, his eyes fixed on the dark liquid pouring from the brass tap. 'A hard-working man deserves a pint or two.'

'That's three you've had, Henry.'

'And I've money for three more – maybe six.'

The landlord chuckled. 'I didn't think you being teetotal would last for long.'

Henry smiled. 'Well you know how it is with women, Jim. If it looks as though you are putting yourself out for them, they'll coming running in the end. They can't resist. It's a well known fact.'

Jim poured himself a half and joined him, elbows leaning on the polished mahogany bar top. 'I thought the best advice was to beat 'em and bed 'em.'

'That too,' laughed Henry, raising his beer in a toast. 'That too. Keep 'em guessing. Keep 'em on their toes, show 'em how frightening life can be and in the end they'll come running back!'

Five

That's one thing you can say about Patrick Kelly, thought Lizzie. *He writes a good letter on a regular basis, and they're always interesting.*

Her eyes followed his well-formed writing.

> *Can't tell you where they're thinking of sending me, but let's put it this way, I won't be needing long underwear. Rumour has it that I'll get some leave before I go. So be ready for me.*

Lizzie smiled. Patrick had willingly joined the Royal Air Force along with Daw's husband, John. He went on to say that both John and he were coming home on leave together. Her application for leave was already in place. She might not be able to have Christmas leave, but she had managed to get a few days before. She'd be sad to miss Christmas, but was glad the boys were getting the whole time off. They were the ones doing the real work and deserved to have a rest.

She folded up the letter and slid it into her breast pocket. As usual, she had picked Wing Commander Hunter up at seven thirty that morning. Since he'd arrived she'd been ordered to pick him up at the same time every morning. Each day, she'd open the car door for him, he'd tell her where they were going, and that would be it. He never indulged in small talk, never asked her how she was, and never mentioned what he was doing at each of the airfields or other places he visited. And she never asked. Since the time he'd refused her leave to see her mother following the destruction of the pawn shop, she had been as cool towards him as he was towards her.

She was presently sitting in the driver's seat, waiting for him to return from a morning briefing at a Bomber Command air base. The moment he got back to the car he would tell her where to go next. As they drove he would spend some time writing in a notebook. All they shared was the interior of the car. Meal times seemed not to exist for Guy Hunter, and so they did not exist for her. Although her stomach rumbled, she abstained and was therefore always starving by the time she got back to Lavenham. Margot would have saved her something from the mess, which she'd guzzle down before falling into bed.

The last base they were visiting today had an air of expectancy about it. Twilight was fading into night and the moon was rising over the tin roofs of the nissen huts. In the diminishing light, she could see people moving in the control tower, black figures silhouetted against the silvery sky. The blackout was total, and there was not even a Christmas tree light to see by.

A roar of engines had heralded the take off of bombers some minutes earlier. She wasn't quite sure why Guy Hunter didn't fly. Some Wing Commanders liked to keep their hand in, but he seemed more interested in writing copious notes, as though he were researching or planning something for the future. Quite possible, she supposed. Someone had to do it.

She got out to stretch her legs, paid a visit to the women's lavatories and had a quick word and a puff of a cigarette with a member of the ground crew.

'I wonder who'll get it tonight,' she said to him between grateful puffs.

'You mean besides us?'

'Most definitely.'

He pointed. 'Look at it. That's a bomber's moon. We'll give the enemy a bit of a pasting alright, but our boys had better watch it. The targets on the ground will be well lit up, but on the other hand, so will they.'

Lizzie put out her cigarette. 'I'd better be going.'

'You driving for that chap Hunter?' He made a clicking sound through the side of his mouth, as though he greatly approved. 'A real war hero. DFC, DSO and bar and God knows what else. Brought his plane in on one engine and didn't get out until his crew had. Carried one of them out on his back. Heck of a bloke. Canadian, ain't he?'

'So I understand.'

'You gotta watch these colonials, mind. They do like the girls.' He winked. 'I bet a pretty girl like you knows that already, yes?'

'No.'

A clock chimed on a far distant steeple, its sound easily heard over the flat East Anglian fields.

Lizzie glanced at her watch. 'Oh, shucks!'

After thanking her companion for the cigarette, she walked briskly back to the car. At no time did she break into a run. Hunter brought out the stubborn in her, doubly so now she was convinced he didn't fancy her. She'd gleaned something of his character. She intended getting back to the car before he did. The wing commander was a stickler for time and expected her to be standing there by the passenger door, waiting for him.

Tonight she was late. She prayed he'd been held up.

My prayers fell on deaf ears, she thought as she rounded the corner of a brick building. She saw a dark figure walking towards the car. He was bound to get there before she did. 'Oh, crumbs,' she groaned. A ticking-off was likely; some withdrawing of privileges, perhaps of leave.

Please, not leave! Her groan of frustration turned to teeth-grinding despair.

She badly wanted to get back to Bristol and see how her mother was faring. Living with Daw must be a nightmare.

Hunter was standing next to the car looking for her. She slowed and clenched her jaw. The nerve of the man; he was waiting for her to open the door for him. *Open the door yourself, you hopeless colonial!* she thought, but as usual the comment remained locked inside her head.

Maintaining an air of defiance, she opened the door.

'Lavenham,' he barked, sliding into the back seat.

He didn't look at her, but immediately got out his notebook and began scribbling.

What was in that notebook? What was he writing down?

She started the engine and headed back to Lavenham and Ainsley Hall.

On the way back to his billet, it was his habit to stop in Lavenham High Street. Every night was the same: park the car and wait for him. She'd watch him stride over the cobbles. He'd pause here and there, perhaps to admire one of the old, timber-framed houses, some of which leaned precariously against their neighbours. Eventually he would duck his head beneath an oak beam and enter the Swan, an ancient hostelry of bulging walls and a thick, thatched roof. Tonight was no exception.

Lizzie sighed and settled into the warm leather of her seat. Her stomach rumbled on cue. She wondered whether the Swan offered anything to eat. Some of these old inns offered bed and board. It certainly looked big enough to do so.

Hunter wouldn't like it if he saw her sneaking off, but she was starving! She surveyed the length of the old building. What if there were a back entrance where she could sneak in and ask for a hunk of bread and a wedge of cheese? Her stomach rumbled encouragement.

'Dammit!' she muttered under her breath.

She swung her legs out of the car, careful not to snag her army-issue stockings. They were thick and of the type grannies wore. What she wouldn't give for a pair of silk stockings, or even the new nylon range. Sheer luxury!

The street was deserted, the moon outlining the cobbles, houses and nearby church tower with a slim line of silver.

She moved cautiously along the front of the inn and around the side. Small windows looked out over a side garden and yard. There were dustbins and pig bins. The latter gave off the recognizable pong of food waste. The pigs had to eat. Nothing was wasted in this war.

A sliver of light showed from beneath the ill-fitting back door. No doubt the blackout curtain was a little short. She would point it out to them. They'd be much obliged and might even insist she stayed and ate something, she thought.

They did exactly that.

'What do you do then?' asked the landlady when Lizzie had got herself settled.

'I'm a driver. Mostly I just sit and wait.'

'For 'im in the bar?'

'Yes.' Her stomach chose that moment to churn like a tractor engine. Everyone heard it. 'I've had nothing to eat since breakfast,' she explained.

The landlady gasped. 'That's terrible. I shall be 'avin' a word with that man!'

'I'd rather you didn't,' said Lizzie, seeing her leave evaporating at the thought of it.

A little while later a plate of freshly made bread, local cheese and butter was placed in front of her.

'You get that down you,' said the landlady, and Lizzie instantly obeyed. She hadn't realized how hungry she was. Soon her stomach stopped rumbling.

'Something to drink?'

Lizzie swallowed the crust of bread she'd been chewing, aware that her lips were smeared with butter. 'Well, I wouldn't mind . . .'

Half a pint of pale-green cider was poured from a wooden barrel. Lizzie eyed the pea-soup colour with some misgiving and deftly took a sniff of it before she sipped.

She checked her watch. Hunter was a man of habit. Another ten minutes and he'd be back in the car.

'I have to go,' said Lizzie getting up from the wooden stool she'd been sitting on.

'Of course, me dear.'

'Can you settle my curiosity before I go?'

The landlady had a broad face that broadened further when she smiled. 'If I can.'

'What does he do in there?'

'Drinks two pints.'

'Does he meet anyone?' She'd thought perhaps that was why he insisted on being there by a certain time. She'd surmised that someone – a woman of course – might be waiting for him.

The landlady shook her head. 'No. He's a bit of a loner. Doesn't talk much except to order drinks and bread and cheese. Just like you, though 'e likes pickles as well.'

'He eats?'

Lizzie could hardly believe her ears. She was livid. The

blasted man ate and drank inside while she waited in the cold dreaming of her evening meal!

Anger warmed her cheeks despite the chill evening air. Grim faced, she marched back to the car, her fists clenched. She wanted to punch him – impossible of course, as it was probably a court-martialling offence. She must fix her thoughts on going on leave. She must!

She sat in the car seething, waiting for him to appear.

A small chink of light showed as Hunter opened the door and shrugged aside the blackout curtain. She got out and stood ready to open the rear passenger door.

Instead of getting into the car, he paused and looked directly at her. 'Are you feeling better, Randall?'

His question caught her off guard. 'Sir?'

'Your bread and cheese. Did it fill a gap?'

She felt herself blushing. He'd found her out. 'Yes, sir. It did.'

'That's fine, but just make sure your dining out doesn't interfere with your duties. I might have needed to leave quickly.'

This was too much for Lizzie. Suddenly she didn't care if she got put on a charge. 'Sir, I've had nothing to eat since six this morning. I might have got so faint you'd have to have driven yourself!'

She could see from his expression that she'd offered too much information. He hadn't asked her when she'd last eaten. She should know better than to give anything more than the basic facts.

'Is that insubordination I hear in your voice, Randall?'

She couldn't find it in herself to back down. 'No. Just information. An army marches on its stomach and I drive on mine. A little consideration wouldn't come amiss!'

The moment it was out, she knew she'd gone too far. Her stomach tightened so much, she was sure it was stuck to her spine. She waited for the consequences: a charge, loss of leave, perhaps even a posting to somewhere she didn't want to go.

The moon did something to his face. The firm jaw seemed to slacken, though it was hard to tell in such a light.

'I didn't know that.'

He got into the car. She shut the door and slid back into

the driving seat. In the rear-view mirror she saw him pause before reaching for his pen and notepad. His eyes met hers.

Lizzie considered what could happen if he did report her and the thought made her gulp. 'I apologize for being insubordinate, sir.'

'No need to. I was partly at fault – just partly, mind you. I assumed you use the mess.'

She noted that he didn't apologize.

'No, sir. I'm back too late. All the best is gone, and seeing as I have to pick you up early, I usually skip breakfast. I don't like eating that early.'

He nodded slowly as though he were thinking things through. 'My fault, but I figure I've made up for my shortcoming in more ways than one.'

Her response was out before she could stop it. 'Why's that, sir? Sorry, sir. I've got no business asking—'

'They charged me for your bread and cheese.' He dropped his eyes to his notepad. 'Drive on.'

'Oh!' She paused. 'If you'd allow me to pay you, sir.'

His head jerked up from his notes. He looked surprised. 'No need, Randall. No need at all.' His eyes returned to the paperwork.

Lizzie smiled. One up to her and no mention of her leave being postponed.

'Shall I see you in the morning, sir?'

'No,' he said, then got out of the car, walked up the steps and disappeared behind the heavy oak door.

Only the knowledge that she wasn't far from her bed kept her eyes open as she drove back to her cosy billet above the stables. But before she collapsed into bed she first reported to the adjutant.

'You're not required any more,' Charlie Grimsby said when she looked into his office.

'I'm not?'

'No. You must have blotted your copy book.'

Lizzie thought of the bread and cheese and smiled. 'I must have done.'

She left the adjutant's office still smiling. What did she care? She was going on leave in two days and was looking forward to it.

Six

'Mrs Randall!'

Mary Anne was ironing and Daw was folding pillowcases when John's uncle came hammering at the door. On opening it, she found him standing there restlessly, his eyes round with shock.

'Your things, Mrs Randall. They are thrown all over the place.'

Mary Anne rushed down the stairs and out into the yard. Things she'd rescued from the pawn shop – sheets, clothes and shoes – were thrown haphazardly all over the place. Fingers covering her mouth, she ran over the flinty yard. Whoever had done this had not been content with just throwing her things around. Footprints blackened by coal dust had trodden some items into the puddles. Although not quite ruined, everything would need laundering, which was a tremendous task given the number of things strewn around.

'Vandals,' said John's uncle, shaking his head as he patted her on the shoulder. 'Don't you worry. We will soon clean this up.'

'I'm sorry,' she said. 'It's my fault.'

He shrugged and spread his hands in the dramatic way he used daily. 'How can you be? It is us this is aimed at, me and my darling Maria. We are Italians. People around here know we are Italians and despite us living in this country for years, they see us as the enemy.'

'I'm so sorry.'

He shrugged again. 'It is not your fault. It is I who must apologize. These are your things.' He gestured at the ruined cottons, linens and tapestry prints.

Mary Anne began picking things up and a thought occurred to her. Only the family knew she'd rescued a little of the stock and stored it here. One thought followed another and her hands started to shake.

'Just kids all the same,' John's uncle was saying.

Auntie Maria, his wife, was less forgiving. 'Wait till I get my hands on them. I'll give them such a wallop.'

'Not kids.'

They both looked at her.

'Not kids,' she repeated, her voice trembling as much as her hands.

'Then who . . .?'

'I can guess who,' she said, lowering her voice.

They waited for her to enlighten them, but she did not do so. In her heart she felt a bitter anger. Henry! It had to be Henry.

He'd tried soft-soaping her to get her back, telling her he was a changed man and would never hit her again. She'd rejected every plea he'd made. Michael had made her happy, and with Michael she would stay.

'Look,' she said, holding up a white sheet complete with a size-ten boot print. 'Call this a child-sized foot print?'

No one met the accusation in her eyes. Even Daw, who continually fought her father's case, did not deny the likelihood that he could be responsible for this.

'Your father's quite capable of something like this,' said Mary Anne in a brief burst of accusation. White faced, Daw just shook her head.

'Wait till I see him,' her mother muttered into the sheet. Raising her head, her eyes blazing with anger, she repeated the same words to her daughter. 'You tell him that,' she said, more strident now. 'You tell him that I'll be round to see him. You make sure you do.'

Just then a series of firm knocks came from the shop door.

'We're closed,' Auntie Maria shouted in response, but the knocking continued.

She marched off, crossing herself and asking the dear Lord why she couldn't have some peace on her afternoon off. The knocking stopped and she wasn't long coming back. A big smile was spread all over her face.

'It's your Lizzie,' she said to Mary Anne. 'She'd gone by the time I got there, but—'

'Gone!' Mary Anne dashed past her, a satin slip – slightly muddy – fluttering over her arm.

'She's only down the road,' Auntie Maria called after her. 'She wanted to see the place where the old house used to be.'

Mary Anne heard. Although December had gripped the air with icy fingers, she felt warm. Lizzie was home. She could see her standing on the pavement, studying the bombed-out ruins of what had once been their home. Six houses had been hit that day, and theirs was one. Biddy Young's was another. Luckily no one had been in either of the houses. Only Mr and Mrs Crawford in number fifteen had refused to go to the shelter. They'd both been in their eighties; one bedridden and one hard of hearing. 'If Hitler wants me, he'll have to come and get me. I won't be up for any fighting, that's for sure,' old Mr Crawford had said.

Seeing Lizzie was like seeing a mirror image of herself, but younger, her slim body enveloped in an ill-fitting uniform. Mary Anne's heart skipped a beat. Her little girl had become a young woman and liable to make the same mistakes she had. She remembered Peter Selwyn Kendall, son of Lizzie's former employer, and prayed it would not be so.

'Lizzie!'

Lizzie turned round. 'Mum!'

They threw their arms around each other. Their affection was and always had been totally spontaneous. They had the same elegance, the same hair colouring – although Mary Anne's was a little faded with the years.

For a moment they stood silently looking at the bombed-out ruins.

Lizzie spoke first. 'It seems an age since we lived here.'

'I take it you went to the pawn shop first?' Mary Anne said wryly. She'd written to Lizzie telling her what had happened.

Lizzie nodded. 'The bus stopped there. It made me cry to see it. An incendiary, I suppose.'

'Apparently not, according to the fireman. He reckoned there were none dropped that night and put the blame on looters.'

Lizzie frowned. 'You mean they start fires deliberately?'

'I suppose so.'

She didn't mention what the policeman had said about Lizzie's brother, Harry. They both knew he had shady friends and moved in dangerous circles, but blaming those with no connection to their family lay easier on her conscience.

Lizzie looked into her mother's face. 'Have you told Michael?'

'Yes. He was very upset and is due leave, but says he's too busy to come right now. He's left me to do what I think best.'

'I see.' And Lizzie *did* see. She could see the barely concealed disappointment lurking in her mother's eyes. She had fallen passionately in love with Michael, enough to make her leave her husband for good. There was about a fifteen-year age gap between them, and Lizzie had always thought they'd surmounted that particular obstacle with ease. But had they? Was her mother worrying that Michael might never come back? That he'd found somebody else, perhaps someone younger? She decided it would be unwise to broach the subject. Let it be for now. Let everyone be happy. Smiling, she hugged her mother's arm close to her side. 'Well, go on, Mother. Tell me all the gossip.' Together they began to walk back to the shop.

'There's not much to tell – at least, not from around here.'

Lizzie detected the sudden nervous dip in her mother's voice. 'Has our Daw been on at you?'

Mary Anne shook her head. Her eyes met those of her favourite daughter. It was wrong to have favourites. She'd told herself that a hundred times. But it couldn't be helped. She and Lizzie were chalk and chalk. She and Daw were definitely chalk and cheese.

Lizzie's smile stayed in place, but lessened. 'There's something you're not telling me.'

'Well, she wants me out before John comes home on leave at Christmas. Only natural of course . . . And then there's our Stanley. I've got a lot of thinking to do.'

'Oh, Mum! You're not thinking of going back to Dad, are you?'

Mary Anne looked down at the ground.

Lizzie was flabbergasted. 'You're not!'

It was never easy to share inner thoughts and secrets, and very difficult when there were so few people to share them with. One thing they all knew and accepted was that her family came first.

She slipped back into the old habit of making excuses. 'I suppose I'm feeling a little down. Nothing seems to be going right just lately. I was brought up in a time when a wife was expected to stay with her husband no matter what.'

'Times have moved on,' said Lizzie, stressing each word like a school teacher determined to steer her pupil through the test. 'We're living in troubled times. People are grabbing happiness where they can, despite the consequences. You shouldn't be feeling guilty. Not now.'

Mary Anne studied her daughter, the steadfast eyes, the confident chin. *Who is this woman?* she thought. A fire burned in her daughter's eyes. Had it been there before and she merely hadn't seen it? Or was it new?

She turned away, not wanting to face the fact that Lizzie was very much following her own dictates. She wondered if there was another man.

'You're probably right,' she said, glad of the chill air on her face.

'Something will turn up – and anyway, will you really miss our Daw that much?'

'She's not the easiest person to live with.' It was a sad thing to admit to, but Daw could be a bit overpowering at times. 'I'll miss Mathilda though.'

'Of course you will.'

Mary Anne bit her lip. The thought of not seeing her granddaughter so often was the hardest thing to bear. She'd got used to doing things for and with her. The child was a joy, far more amiable than her mother had been at the same age.

Lizzie noticed. 'What else, Mother? You look worried.'

Arm in arm now, they stood before the house, sometimes looking at the tumbled bricks, and sometimes looking at each other.

'I'm not getting daft in my dotage – in fact I don't think I'm quite in my dotage yet – but the other day I took Mathilda out in the pushchair and I lost her. I left her outside the Red Cross shop whilst I popped in with some items they could make use of, and when I got back outside, she was gone. I found her, of course – or at least the ladies from the Red Cross found her. And then today . . .'

She went on to tell Lizzie about the shed being broken into and about the things she'd saved from the stock being found scattered and dirty all over the yard. Not to mention the shop being damaged beyond repair.

'And you think Dad did it?'

'Who else?' Mary Anne's expression darkened. 'I'm going round there to tackle him about it. I can get a tram to the centre and then another to Barton Hill.'

'There you are then. Fancy even considering going back with him!'

Girls turning a skipping rope parted as the two women passed by. The breeze blew colder, blowing Mary Anne's hair across her face. Her hand shook as she pushed it back behind her ear. Lizzie noticed it.

'Mum . . .'

'No comments about my nerves, please. Yes, things are getting to me. But I'll get through it. You just see if I don't.'

Lizzie withheld what she was going to say about her mother visiting a doctor or taking some rest. She certainly wouldn't get much rest living with Daw, that was for sure.

'What about moving in with Biddy? Doesn't she have a house to herself?'

Mary Anne shook her head. 'She did have. Apparently she had to move out to make way for a family that got bombed out at the beginning of December. They're asking a lot of people to double up and take people in. Biddy didn't want to stay there, so got moved into the ground floor rooms in the same house as your father. He's got the upper floor.'

Lizzie looked shocked. 'I bet me dad wasn't too pleased about that!'

'I doubt it too. I saw her the other day. She was visiting her sister down in the Chessels. She was telling me that she's got the downstairs rooms, and he's upstairs. She made a point of telling me that there was no funny business going on, mind you.'

Lizzie grimaced. 'Did she now! I wouldn't put it past her. I know she's your friend, but you know what a trollop she can be. Goodness. I wonder how long they'll be living there.'

Mary Anne shook her head. 'Who knows? Everyone has to make do with what they can get and crowd in where they can. Stanley's there too.'

She looked back along the street to the corner shop. Its windows were half covered with adverts for Fry's Cocoa, Cherry Blossom boot polish, and Colman's mustard. A mist was rising from The Cut and drifting inland along with its nefarious smell of stale mud and old drains.

'So you have to find somewhere else to live,' said Lizzie, following the direction of her gaze. 'What about Harry's flat?'

'Edgar's there.'

'Oh!'

The two women fell to silence. Both knew how it was with Harry, but it wasn't a subject they felt comfortable discussing – even with each other. Two men living with each other as brothers was one thing, but Harry and Edgar were closer than that, closer than friends.

Mary Anne turned to her daughter as a sudden thought occurred to her. 'Where are you staying, Lizzie?'

When Lizzie smiled, deep dimples appeared in her cheeks. 'Above the Lord Nelson in East Street.'

'That's opposite the Red Cross shop.'

'Is it? I suppose it is. I suppose you could come there with me. We'd have to share a bed of course, but it's better than nothing.'

'I'm going to have to do something – at least for the short term. Daw wants John and her to have their place to themselves. I can't say I blame her. We all need a place of our own. And then there's our Stanley to consider.'

Lizzie eyed her mother. The expression in her eyes was hidden, and yet she guessed what her mother was thinking.

'I won't offer you a penny for your thoughts; there's too many of them. Number one, you're wondering when or whether Michael will come back. Number two, you're considering moving back in with Dad for our Stanley's sake. You mustn't think like that, Mum.' Lizzie squeezed her mother's hand. 'Michael *will* come back. And you don't love Dad. You love Michael.'

Mary Anne raised her eyes and looked at her daughter. 'Is that enough? I've grown older since he's been away. He may have met someone, someone younger who doesn't have a grown-up family.'

Lizzie was adamant. 'No,' she said, shaking her head so vehemently that her hat nearly flew off. 'Don't even say that. He'll be back, Mother. He'll be back.'

Deep in conversation, they'd hardly noticed that they were stopped by the pile of rubble that used to be Biddy's house.

Both fell to silence, eyeing the upstairs fireplace on the party wall of what had once been the bedroom.

It was Lizzie who broke the silence. 'I suppose Daw's put the kettle on.'

'I expect so. She'll be glad to see you.'

It could never be taken as read that Daw would be pleased to see anyone, but Mary Anne told herself that it would be so. Two sisters together.

Lizzie's chatter returned to normal. 'I'm looking forward to seeing little Mathilda again. It seems an age since I saw her last.'

They turned and strolled back towards the little shop where the goods were spread out to make it look as though they had more in stock than was actually the case. They still had lots to talk about, but for the moment each was lost in thought. At last Lizzie said, 'Let me speak to Dad, Mum. I promise I won't lose my temper. I'll put things simply but honestly. Leave it to me. Don't go round there yourself. Promise?'

Mary Anne looked at her beautiful daughter. Unbidden, a terrible fear took hold of her – not fear of Lizzie getting killed or maimed in this dreadful war, but fear that she too might end up marrying the wrong man. Her long lashes brushed her cheeks. 'I'll promise you something as long as you promise me something in return.'

Lizzie laughed. 'If I have to promise, I will. Yes.'

'Promise me that you'll only marry a man who's good to you.'

Lizzie gazed at her mother, wondering what secrets she held that she had never told. Her father, Henry Randall, had treated her mother badly. And yet her mother was an intelligent woman, so why hadn't she married a man who was good to her? She decided not to ask any questions. Her mother's past life was her own, and she should talk about it only if she really wanted to.

You're taking the coward's way out, she told herself. But she wouldn't admit to that and other secrets, not to her mother. Instead her laughter was light and lit up her face. 'Never fear, Mother. I'll end up with someone safe and sound. I suppose Patrick's at the top of that particular list.'

Mary Anne sighed with relief. 'Good.' Patrick had endured an awful upbringing by a mother who'd had more men friends than hot dinners. Patrick hadn't had too many hot dinners at all. He'd grown up scrawny and scruffy, but Lizzie had become his friend. At the outbreak of war they became more than that. Patrick was good to Lizzie and in Mary Anne's opinion they were made for each other. This news couldn't have come at a better time.

All the same, why was Lizzie looking towards the mist rising from The Cut? Was there something in her eyes she didn't want her own mother to see? Mary Anne dismissed her concern. Her daughter had always been sensible. She wasn't the type to bring trouble home.

They both rubbed their hands together as they passed from the chill of the street and into the warmth of the shop. Cries of welcome reverberated around the back room as tea was poured and sandwiches and home-made cake were passed round.

Neither woman had noticed the lone figure watching them from behind the broken timbers of a bombed-out house. But he saw them and hated them for being a family, for being happy, and for having each other.

Seven

'Patrick, you look a picture.'

'In that case, Mrs Randall, I'm a failure. I was hoping I looked like a first-class aircraftsman!'

Patrick had come looking for Lizzie at the Lord Nelson pub after travelling up from a fighter station on the south coast. Like her he'd acquired a temporary room; unlike her, his lodgings were above a chip shop.

'Not that they've got much fish at the moment and not too many chips,' he said ruefully. 'Lovely smell though.'

In her son's absence, Patrick's mother had let his room out to lodgers and was making a pretty packet, an amount of money she had no wish to lose simply because he was back.

Not that he was too inclined to return to his childhood home anyway.

He found it funny that Lizzie and her mother were staying above a pub. 'Handy for getting home if you've had a few in the bar,' he said chirpily, his eyes following Lizzie's every movement.

Lizzie poked her tongue out at him as she handed him a cup of tea. 'Two days. That's all I've got, Patrick Kelly, so there's no time for me to get drunk. Well, not if you want to make the most of my company.'

His eyes sparkled as he grinned. 'I don't need to make any decision between you and a pint of beer. I know what I want.'

Lizzie blushed. 'Less of your cheek, Patrick Kelly.'

Her mother had returned to her sewing, pretending that the skirt she was altering had her undivided attention.

'Will you come with us to the pictures, Mrs Randall?' asked Patrick.

'I don't think so.'

'You're quite welcome. It's a cowboy film.'

She shook her head. 'Not my favourite kind of film I'm afraid, and anyway, I'm expecting our Stanley to call in.'

Patrick was far too polite to show his relief. All the same, she sensed it, and who could blame him? These two young people were serving their country. Both faced the possibility of being injured or killed – Patrick in the air, and Lizzie on the home front. Let them have their time together unchaperoned – no matter what they got up to.

'How's Stanley getting on?' Patrick enquired.

'Not too bad,' Mary Anne replied, 'though we'll all be happier when we've found somewhere to live.'

'Not easy,' Patrick said ruefully. 'Bristol had it bad enough in November, but you should see London.' He shook his head. 'The East End's a mess. I've occasion to go up there now and again, you know, stationed where I am.'

Lizzie had gone quiet, her eyes lowered as though the surface of her tea was incredibly interesting.

'How long before you leave?' she asked.

He shrugged. 'Thought we would have shipped out by now, but it won't be long. Mark my words, it won't be long.'

The three of them fell to an uneasy silence, but it didn't last long.

'Well! Better get going,' said Patrick, slapping his thighs as he got to his feet. 'If we don't get a move on, them cowboys will have shot all the Indians before we've even got there.'

Alone at last, Mary Anne let the sewing slip into her lap. Resting her head back, she closed her eyes and remembered how it had been in the Great War, the one they were beginning to call the First World War, because this, sadly, had turned into the second.

In her quieter moments like these, her thoughts went back to Edward, her first boyfriend. They too had felt that terrible urgency, the need to experience all life had to offer just in case it was about to end. For Edward it had ended at Cambrai. For her it had meant finding herself pregnant, 'disgraced'. Sent away before her time came, she had cried herself to sleep on her pillow night after night, wishing she and Edward had married first, but wishing most of all that he'd come back.

The child had been adopted. Her parents had dealt with all the details, but still there were rumours. Only a hastily arranged marriage would restore her respectability. She didn't find out until much later that Henry Randall had been paid to marry her. And at first they'd been happy. He'd worshipped her and nothing she could do was wrong. Trusting him to be magnanimous, she'd told him all about her secret sin, but his reaction was the opposite of what she'd expected. Overnight the caring husband turned into a jealous, cruel monster. The pedestal he'd put her on was pulled out from under her. Even so, she'd endured her punishment – for that's how she'd regarded it. She'd lived for her children – that was, until Michael came along.

She shook herself out of these maudlin memories, and took herself to bed for some much-needed rest. In the morning, she took the skirt she had mended over to the Red Cross shop. Gertrude immediately found a hanger for it and slid it on to a nail along with a few other skirts.

'You've done a nice job of that, dear. I'm sure some needy soul will snap it up,' said a joyful Gertrude, her voice reverberating around the crowded counters. 'Now, I've got a nice coat here that could do with altering . . .'

Huffing and puffing, she heaved a leopard-skin coat on to the counter. 'It's too long and a bit old fashioned. I thought that perhaps you could cut off the bottom and make it into a three-quarter length, and then make a pillbox hat with what you've cut off. I'm sure you can do it. Here!'

Before she had a chance to protest, the coat was almost plonked into her arms. 'I can't,' said Mary Anne.

'*Can't?*' Gertrude snapped, her face smothered in frown lines.

Mary Anne sighed. 'I'm afraid I haven't anywhere to live at present and I do have to spend some time finding somewhere. Perhaps then . . .'

Gertrude Palmer looked astounded, as though Mary Anne had slapped her on both sides of her face.

'Do you have a husband?'

Mary Anne found herself blushing. 'He's away serving with his regiment . . .' Her voice melted away. Michael had impressed on her that she mustn't go into too much detail about the fact that he worked as a translator, translating messages from German into English. He'd been born in England but raised in Germany. His mother and stepfather were presently in a camp on the Isle of Man. But that was another of their secrets and best not mentioned.

Mrs Palmer had small, shrewd eyes. Like a knife they cut right through to the crux of a matter. 'So where are you staying at present?'

'In a room above the Lord Nelson, but it's only for two days. My daughter's on leave, you see.' She stroked the fur flat. 'It's lovely though. I'm sure it would make a matching hat and coat, but . . .' She shrugged her shoulders. 'Finding suitable accommodation is very difficult.'

'Nonsense!'

The sharp voice made her jump. Gertrude didn't seem to notice.

'Depending on what standard of accommodation you happen to be looking for, there is no problem at all! I have just the thing. Come on. Follow me.'

Mary Anne did as ordered. It occurred to her that Gertrude might have been in the army herself at some time, or perhaps a matron in a field hospital. She certainly knew how to give orders and make people jump to attention.

Gertrude's sensible shoes clumped up an uncarpeted wooden staircase and eventually on to a small landing.

'That's the storeroom,' said Gertrude, indicating a room to her right. 'That's the usual offices,' she said, pointing ahead to a small bathroom. 'And this is one room, and this is the other. There's also an attic.'

She swung two doors open, one after the other. The first room was quite large with a bay window overlooking East Street. The other was smaller, its window overlooking the yard at the back.

'The kitchen's down in the shop, of course, but I'm quite happy for you to use it. Well? What do you think?'

Mary Anne realized that her jaw was hanging slack, but she couldn't help it. 'I think it's . . .' She shook her head and snatched at her throat. It was almost impossible to get the words out. She was so grateful, so overwhelmed.

Used to making snap decisions, Gertrude took her hesitation the wrong way. 'Well, if it's a little beneath you,' she said indignantly, 'most people would jump at it.'

'I think it's wonderful! I can't thank you enough . . .' She shook her head and couldn't stop her eyes turning moist. 'But there is one little problem I think I should mention. I have a son, you see. He's ten years old.'

Gertrude looked at her aghast. 'And he's living above the pub too? That's terrible!'

'No,' said Mary Anne, shaking her head. The right words rather than the truth tumbled from her tongue. 'I'd never allow a child of mine to live above a pub. He's staying with my husband— my husband's friend. It was all I could do for now.'

The lies came easily. Just little white ones, she told herself, knowing instinctively that Gertrude would not approve of her being married but not living with her husband. Her subterfuge worked. Gertrude showed unaccustomed sympathy.

'My dear, your son is welcome here. Make arrangements to move in as soon as you like.'

Feeling fit to explode, Mary Anne tried to say a simple thank you, but her emotions wouldn't let her. 'Mrs Palmer! Mrs Palmer! What can I say?'

She grabbed the ample woman and planted a kiss on her cheek. Gertrude Palmer's look of astonishment turned to discomfort as a tear tumbled down Mary Anne's cheek.

'There's no need to overreact,' she muttered.

It was odd to see Gertrude looking uncomfortable, suddenly aware that she had touched someone deeply.

Mary Anne smiled through her tears. 'Mrs Palmer . . .'

'Gertrude. Call me Gertrude.'

'Gertrude, I can't thank you enough . . .'

Faced with such sentimentality, Gertrude's gruffness returned. 'Think nothing of it. We needed a caretaker, what with all these looters around, and you're very good at mending and alterations. It's a very good arrangement to my way of thinking.'

'The only thing is,' said Mary Anne, wandering from the front room to the back and back again, 'is that all my furniture was destroyed in the fire.'

'Is that all? My word, I have a whole houseful of unused items in my old stable. You can take your pick of that. You'll find a bed, a three-piece suite and a dining set at least. I trust you can deal with curtains yourself – not that you really need them with the blackout curtains in place.'

Mary Anne touched the heavy serge required to hide the brightness of the room from enemy bombers. A smile radiated across her face. 'Oh, I think I can find something a bit more feminine to lighten things.'

Going to the pictures, walking, talking or going shopping, Lizzie and Patrick made the most of their leave. Money was tight, but walking was cheap. The shops in East Street were doing what they could to provide a little Christmas spirit. The big bombing raid of November had brought home to people just how bad this war could be. Old buildings that had stood for centuries had been turned to dust. Castle Street, the heart of the city's shopping centre, where courting couples had strolled on a Saturday night, had been totally destroyed. The smell of dust and destruction was everywhere, yet still people searched on bomb sites for valuables that might make their life a bit easier.

'You can't blame them,' Patrick said as they strolled past what had once been a large haberdashery shop.

'They're like rats,' said Lizzie, watching people clamber over heaps of rubble, digging to uncover anything that might be of use. 'What do they expect to find?'

'A silk ribbon for Christmas or a saucy garter perhaps; like I say, you can't blame them.'

What had once been shops were now unidentifiable heaps of rubble.

'Dangerous though,' Patrick added. 'There's old cellars beneath these buildings. Wouldn't take much to fall into one.'

They'd only taken a few steps when there was a loud rumble. A mountain of rubble suddenly disappeared in a cloud of dust. A woman screamed. 'Help! Help! My Charlie!'

But instead of helping her, people began running. Patrick grabbed a man as he tripped over a broken window frame.

'What's happened?'

The man sagged like a sack of spuds, his eyes round with fear as he looked up into Patrick's face.

'Her boy's fallen into the cellar.'

Patrick frowned. 'Aren't you going to help him?'

'Not bloody likely. The rozzers'll get called. I'm off.'

Wriggling like an eel, he struggled out of Patrick's grasp, his feet slipping and sliding on the rough ground as he ran off.

'Well, someone's got to go in there,' murmured Patrick, his eyes fixed earnestly on the dusty cloud. He was already peeling off his jacket. He handed it to Lizzie.

'Hold this.'

Lizzie caught it. 'Be careful,' she called after him.

Patrick held up a hand in a brief wave before his long legs were fording the hills and ravines formed by the broken building.

A woman running from the site tripped over and sprawled close to where Lizzie was standing. Lizzie threw the coat to one side and went to her aid. Lifting one shoulder she saw the blood pouring from where the woman's chin and nose had hit the ground.

'Can you get up?'

The woman staggered to her feet. She seemed dazed, her eyes unfocused.

Lizzie rummaged in Patrick's jacket and found his handkerchief. She flung the jacket back on to the ground and turned her attention to the woman's bloodied face.

A woman from a neighbouring house brought over a bowl of water. Lizzie wet the handkerchief and used it to wipe the blood from the woman's face.

'Can we sit her down?'

She helped get the woman to a stool, but when they tried to persuade her to sit down she began waving her arms frantically.

'No! Let me go.'

She hit out, the back of her hand slapping Lizzie's cheek. Lizzie fell face forward on to the rubble, grazing her face and spluttering in the dust.

'Well!' she said, raising herself with her arms. 'There's thanks for you!'

Dusting herself off, she got to her feet and looked round for Patrick's jacket. She frowned. Surely it should be there, not far behind her and close to the street?

It wasn't. She began to search, sure of where she'd placed it, but worried now, looking round at the gathered crowd.

'Has anyone picked up an RAF jacket?' she asked the onlookers.

No one answered. The mother of a young lad who'd just staggered off the site was dusting him off between clouts around his already red ear.

'That'll teach you to be more careful, my lad!'

Not once did she warn her son not to venture on to a bomb-site again. A sign of the times, thought Lizzie. No one had much, so who could blame them for rummaging for life's little extras?

Still, that didn't answer the question of the disappearing jacket.

'Has anyone . . .?' she began, but the crowd was swiftly diminishing.

The blowing of a whistle announced the arrival of the police. Four of them swarmed to where Patrick was helping a boy of about twelve. Both were covered in dust and blood was pouring from the boy's cut knee.

'Can you help?' Patrick called to the nearest policeman.

Lizzie didn't hear what was said. Craning her neck, she watched in shocked surprise as one policeman grabbed the boy and one grabbed Patrick.

'Yes, sir. We'll help you alright. All the way to the nick!'

Two policemen forced Patrick's arms behind his back, manhandling him over the rubble.

Patrick began to protest. 'But I haven't done anything!'

'Tell that to our sergeant,' said another of the policemen.

Lizzie stumbled towards him over the broken paving stones and shards of broken glass. She grabbed the policeman's arm.

'He hasn't done anything. Part of the building collapsed and someone was trapped inside.'

'We'll bear in mind all extenuating circumstances,' said the policeman in charge.

'I haven't been looting,' said Patrick, an amused grin on his face.

'You might not have been looting this particular building today,' said the policeman, 'but we have reason to believe you've been here before.'

Patrick almost laughed in his face. 'You're pulling my leg!'

'He wouldn't,' said Lizzie, pushing beneath a policeman's arm so that she was firmly wedged between him and Patrick.

'Is this yours?'

Patrick's jacket dangled from a hefty hand.

'Of course it's his,' said Lizzie, reaching out to take it.

'It's mine,' said Patrick.

The policeman snatched it back and slid his hand into a pocket. He smirked as he withdrew it.

The next bit happened like a dream. Perhaps it was instinct or the vague suspicion that this particular pile of rubble had once been a jewellery shop, but Lizzie guessed what he would find.

Her intuition proved right. A sparkling necklace dangled from the constable's fingers.

Patrick stared. 'That's not mine.'

'We know that, old son,' the constable spluttered. 'It belonged to G. H. Palmer and Sons, bespoke jewellers. You've had a shufty over this site before, 'aven't you?'

Patrick's amused expression melted into one of dazed confusion. 'No. I have not. In fact I've never seen that necklace before in my life.' He turned to Lizzie. 'Honest I haven't.'

Eight

Mary Anne felt a shiver run down her spine as she approached the front door of the house in Aiken Street. Of course she couldn't leave it to Lizzie to challenge her father. It was up to her to do that. But second thoughts about doing anything at all turned her legs to jelly. They'd feel a lot better if she turned away right now, but she would not back down. She had to face him.

She'd dressed in a green wool costume beneath a tan and green coat. Her hat was simple with a brim turned down over one eye. The look was conservative, the kind of look one adopted if going to visit a solicitor or a relative who was easily shocked. The last thing she wanted was to give him the impression that she was there on a social visit.

The road was long and lined on each side with flat-fronted terraced houses. Faces appeared at upstairs windows. Children stopped hopping over the hopscotch squares they'd drawn on the pavement, resuming their game the moment she'd walked past.

Number seventeen had net curtains at the downstairs window. They drooped and sagged on one side. Biddy had the ground floor. The lackadaisically hung curtains confirmed the fact. Neat décor and clean windows had never rated too high with Biddy Young.

Swallowing her nerves, Mary Anne walked the few steps to the front door and knocked. The sound reverberated inside a long, dark hallway perhaps, the floor tiled and bare of rugs.

She heard footsteps. They sounded lighter than she remembered. Her heart raced. Her legs shook.

The door was wrenched open.

'Mary Anne!'

'Biddy!'

Biddy's eyes swooped over her old friend, noting enviously that she still hadn't run to fat. She also noted the warm coat and fashionable hat she wore. Biddy liked clothes and would have liked those. Unfortunately Biddy was as round as a beach ball and her clothes didn't look good for long, mostly because she wore them until they were filthy.

'Come on in!'

Mary Anne nervously eyed the dark passageway behind her old neighbour.

'He's out,' she said, guessing Mary Anne was looking for Henry. 'He's on days this week, though not likely to finish until nine tonight. Come on. Come on in. I'll put the kettle on.'

Biddy led her to a reasonable-sized scullery. A green and white gingham cloth covered an old table. Two chairs were ranged either side of it.

'So, how was your sister?' said Mary Anne while taking in her surroundings.

'Oh, she's fine. At least she's still got her house,' she said.

'Shame it had to be you,' said Mary Anne.

'At least we're still alive. This might not be a palace, but it's home,' sighed Biddy. 'We've got a roof over our heads and there's a meal on the table – though that ain't much either. Oxtail stew and suet pudding tonight made with the leftovers of Sunday's dripping. Take the weight off yer feet.'

She gestured to one of the chairs. Mary Anne barely resisted the urge to ask for a duster before sitting down on the grubby seat.

'I'm so glad you came round. I've really missed you,' said Biddy between slurps of tea straight from the saucer.

Mary Anne sighed. 'Kent Street seems an age ago. And I miss my little business. What tales that old washroom could tell.'

Biddy laughed, her eyes diminishing to mere slits above her plump cheeks. 'A place to natter and come when you was a bit short. What would we 'ave done without you?'

Some would have survived and some poor souls would have starved or had their children taken away from them, Mary Anne thought, but she didn't have the heart to say so. No matter how poor they'd been, her old neighbours had been proud. It was all to do with self-respect and maintaining that there was always someone poorer – though God knew, it wasn't that likely.

'It wasn't always happy,' said Mary Anne. 'At least, not for me it wasn't.'

'Shame he wasn't in the bloody 'ouse when the bomb hit, I s'pose.'

'Biddy!' Despite everything, Mary Anne was shocked at her old friend's insensitive comment.

'Well let's face it, it would 'ave made fings easier for you, wouldn't it? And what if that lawyer comes back and gives you pots of money? Henry could make a claim on it as your legally married spouse.'

Biddy had reiterated everything about George Ford when

they'd met in East Street that day. Mary Anne repeated what she'd already said to her friend.

'I'm not the right Mary Anne Randall,' she said, and added wistfully, 'I only wish I was.'

'Will you ask him for a divorce?'

The question was sudden and unexpected. Mary Anne hesitated. 'Well . . . I'm not really too sure.'

She couldn't possibly declare to Biddy her fears that Michael might not return, but something else was making her pause for thought. Getting divorced was not a nice thing to do. Marriage was supposed to be for life. Even though she no longer lived with Henry, her status as Mrs Randall was difficult to discard.

Biddy's expression changed suddenly. 'Are you thinking of making a fresh go of things? You know – you and old Henry?'

'No. I am not. That's not why I'm here.' She set her cup and saucer down with great purpose. 'Some nasty things have been happening and I think Henry is responsible for them.'

Biddy's eyes nearly popped out of her head. She leaned forward. 'What sort of things?'

Mary Anne told her about Mathilda going missing and about the items she'd rescued from the pawn shop having been scattered around the yard.

'Two weeks ago next Saturday. I presume he got into the yard during the night – the back gate is never locked. Neither is the shed.'

Biddy looked away, chewing her lip as she thought things over. 'Now, let me see . . . When was it old Henry went to the tabernacle? I can't help but know his business, what with him having the rooms upstairs.'

'Tabernacle?' Mary Anne frowned. 'You mean *church*?'

'That I do. Church, not pub. Now there's a turn up for the books, don't you think?'

'That doesn't mean to say he's not responsible.'

'It does if two days ago he was off on a charabanc outing, driving the Bible-bashers to the seaside for the day. They went to Clevedon. Trouble was, they didn't have enough petrol to get back and had to wait until they could get some from members of the Clevedon tabernacle. Ended up sleeping in the church overnight from what he tells me.'

Mary Anne got to her feet. The news made her more nervous than ever. What if Henry should come home now and see her here. He might get the wrong impression.

'I have to go,' she said, her tea cooling on the table.

Biddy's face took on a pained expression. 'Oh, Mary Anne. Do you have to?'

Mary Anne picked up her gloves. 'Yes, I must. Look at the time. I don't want to miss the bus.'

'Wait for me. I'll fetch me coat and walk you to the bus stop. Hope they're still running. Shame old Adolf blew up the tram lines. I liked them better.'

On their way to the bus stop, Mary Anne made Biddy promise not to tell Henry that she'd called.

'I don't want him getting the wrong impression. Promise me, Biddy. Promise me as my one true friend.'

'Cross me heart,' said Biddy, making a vague cross shape across her ample bosom. 'I'll always be yer best friend. You know that, surely you do. It was me that sent that solicitor to you, after all.'

Mary Anne frowned. 'I don't know what you mean. The solicitor didn't find me. It was you who told me about the other Mary Anne Randall coming into that money.'

'Oh. Well, you'd think he would have made the effort to find you.'

'I didn't know you gave him my address.'

'Of course I did. I told you all about it that day in Bedminster, remember? Blimey, Mary Anne, he said your aunt had left you something in her will . . .' Biddy clamped a hand over her mouth. 'You ain't got an Aunt Maude, have you?'

'No, I haven't.'

'Oh, lordy!'

'Can you remind me of his name again?'

'Dead simple to remember. George Ford. That was it. Do it ring a bell?'

Mary Anne shook her head. 'No. It doesn't. He never came to call. I guarantee he didn't.'

'That's a shame.'

'Not really. I expect he realized he'd made a mistake and found the Mary Anne Randall who *did* have an Aunt Maude.'

'That would explain it.'

'Yes. Of course it would.'

Nine

Mary Anne accompanied Lizzie to Temple Meads station when her leave was over. Neither of them spoke very much; Mary Anne was still wondering about this George Ford character, and Lizzie was worried about Patrick. The police had arrested him for theft. His commanding officer down south would be informed and he might not get back to the airfield on time – if at all. In fact, he might well end up in Shepton Mallet Prison.

'I wish I didn't have to go back,' Lizzie said, clutching her kitbag before her and gazing to where the railway line glistened with rain.

Mary Anne tried to think of something positive to say, but it wasn't easy. 'It's a shame your people couldn't give you a few more days – compassionate leave they call it, don't they?'

Lizzie nodded and clenched her jaw. 'It's that damned Wing Commander Hunter. He's got it in for me. There are plenty of other drivers to take him around. He's just being awkward.'

'Never mind.' Mary Anne gave her daughter a hug. 'I'll pop along to the police station and see what's happening.'

'You promise?'

Lizzie's downcast expression tugged at Mary Anne's heart strings.

'I promise. And I'll let you know the moment I hear something.'

Amidst clouds of steam, Lizzie's train pulled into the station. Hordes of people in uniforms got off only to be replaced by just as many getting on.

'And write to me,' said Mary Anne, worried by the anger simmering in her daughter's eyes. Lizzie wasn't usually one given to anger or petulance; Daw was certainly better at the latter. Lizzie had a forgiving nature. She'd even visited her father, though in consideration for her mother's feelings she hadn't mentioned details.

Lizzie stepped aboard the train but remained leaning out of the window. Except for the worry in her eyes, she looked like a beautiful picture framed in the open window.

'Phone me. You've got the number. The office will come and fetch me,' she called out.

'I promise. I promise. I promise!' her mother called back.

Looking sadder than usual, Lizzie waved her last goodbye. Carriage after carriage slipped by until there was nothing left but clouds of steam and Mary Anne waving at nothing.

Worries about Patrick stayed with her all the way back to East Street. The night was drawing in. The shops were still open although their windows, usually bright with Christmas lights at this time of year, were blacked out. The streets echoed to footsteps and people chattering, excited despite the deprivations of war.

Mary Anne's nerves were on edge. At times she was sure she was being followed, but when she turned round, all she saw were dark figures against the greyness of dusk, hurrying home to escape the cold, just as she was.

What can I do about Patrick? she thought as she approached the Red Cross shop. So many bad things were happening in her life that she'd broken out in a rash, a redness on the backs of her hands that was slowly spreading up her arms.

People scurried ahead of her. Her eyes narrowed as she espied the shop doorway. Was someone standing there, watching her? A chill spread throughout her body.

Her steps slowed. Her heart beat faster.

She licked her lips and tried to speak. No sound came out. She tried again.

'Who's there?'

'It's me, Mrs Randall.'

After a while she recognized a familiar figure. Her steps quickened. 'Patrick?'

Despite her high-heeled court shoes, she ran the rest of the way.

'Inside, so we can see what we've got here,' ordered Gertrude Palmer. 'I'm not explaining things out here on the step.'

The familiar smell of mothballs and wet wool met them as

Gertrude pushed open the shop door. 'Now, where's that light switch?' she muttered.

The light snapped on.

Mary Anne found it impossible to return Patrick's amiable grin. She needed to know that things had been resolved. 'What happened? Are you free? Has everything been sorted out?'

His grin widened into a smile. 'I'm a free man. No case to answer. And I need a cup of tea.'

'Nonsense,' Gertrude interjected. 'You've already had one.'

'Another cup wouldn't come amiss.'

The two rooms above the Red Cross shop had lost their air of neglect. Two rugs of Persian origin and ancient years covered the floor of the room Mary Anne had decided she would live in. A third one, just as threadbare as the others, lay at the side of a brass bed.

A velvet-covered chaise longue – on which Stanley slept – lay in front of the living-room window and two armchairs sat on either side of a gas fire. Stanley hadn't needed any persuading to move back in with his mother.

Mary Anne turned on the gas and put a match to it. The pale pink glow slowly turned red.

Gertrude had followed them up the stairs. 'In case you're thinking I'm being nosy, this event involves me too,' she said.

Mary Anne wondered in what way she was involved, but held her tongue. Gertrude was the sort who only explained things in her own good time.

Without asking whether she wanted one or not, Mary Anne made her a cup of tea and listened as Gertrude explained.

'My husband owned the jewellery store across the road, so the police called him in to identify the object found in this young man's pocket. He called in here first so I took it upon myself to accompany him to the station, fortunately, as it turned out. My husband confirmed that the necklace was of no value; in fact it was merely a paste item he'd made for a lady customer – though "lady" might not be the right word,' she said with a sniff of her upper-class nose. 'That was when I was glad I had accompanied him, because I, dear lady, *did* recognize it as being in the shop only days previously. A one-time actress of dubious reputation had donated it. We won't go into how and why she has acquired a dubious reputation, only to say that it was good of her to donate. Anyway, Daisy sold that necklace on that very morning when it was found in our young friend's pocket.' Gertrude turned to Patrick. 'You did not pick it up where our purchaser had dropped it?'

'No. I'd never seen it before.'

Gertrude clapped her hands with delight. 'The plot thickens!'

'Just a minute,' said Mary Anne, frowning as she carefully picked over the details. 'How come the policeman looked in your pocket in the first place?'

'That's just it,' said Patrick, a slow guarded smile spreading across his face. 'The policeman was told to look in my pocket. He barely noticed the man who suggested it. I think he got a bit overexcited at the prospect of catching someone. All he remembers is that he was of average height, average looks and had no outstanding features whatsoever. Bland, I suppose you could say.'

Mary Anne shook her head. 'Why would anyone do that?'

Gertrude set down her cup. 'A prank?'

'At least I can get back to camp with a clear conscience and a clean copy book,' said Patrick, getting to his feet. 'I'll phone Lizzie from there. She'll be as relieved as I am.'

'I'm sure of that,' said Mary Anne.

He took his leave of them, explaining that he had to collect his kitbag from his digs above the chip shop on the way to the station. 'And thanks again,' he said to Gertrude and winked. 'You're a right sweetheart.'

Gertrude blushed like a young girl. 'Think nothing of it. I approve of honesty and all things traditional. I certainly do not approve of reputations being sullied by thoughtless tomfoolery!'

Although Gertrude's spine was made of stern stuff nowadays, and she was hardly the sort to blush easily, Mary Anne couldn't help but sense that she'd been quite a coquette in her youth.

The sound of Patrick's footsteps faded away and were followed by a short silence before footsteps sounded again, ascending this time. There was a short knock at the door before it was opened. The man standing there was dressed in civilian clothes, the brim of his hat pulled low over his eyes, hiding his face.

Slowly, very slowly, he raised his head and smiled.

'Marianna! The wanderer returns for Christmas.'

'Michael! Michael!'

Mary Anne felt the beat of her heart quicken. Such trials and tribulations had come into her life lately, and now, for the first time in months, she'd been called Marianna, the name he always called her.

Uncaring of Gertrude, she threw herself into his arms. He dropped the case he was carrying and held her tight. She took in the smell of him, the feel of him, the deliciousness of his lips on hers. Gertrude Palmer was almost forgotten, though not quite.

Mary Ann began to explain. 'This is . . .'

'No need for introductions, my dear,' said Gertrude, sliding past them to the open door. 'I know a husband when I see one, and a husband and wife need to be alone. I'll make myself scarce and see you in the morning.' She smiled. 'There's that lovely old curtain material you thought would make a nice skirt and bolero. I'm sure it would be snapped up.' She nodded to each of them. 'Goodnight to you both.'

Happy beyond words, Mary Anne did not attempt to explain the truth of her relationship with Michael. It was only the next day she realized beyond doubt that Gertrude would not approve of the unwedded couple living together. At the expense of losing her new home, the secret must be kept to themselves.

Ten

'Just because we're at war, don't mean to say we can't trim up for Christmas,' said Bessie. She was presently arranging some green leaves and berries in a jam jar on the window sill.

'Only in the canteen,' said Margot, who was sitting on the bed, her head covered in metal curlers. 'Rules are rules.'

The three of them were sharing a fruit cake that Lizzie had brought back from Bristol. Margot said something about it reminding her of boarding school.

'You two are breaking rules too. You're both sitting on your beds,' Bessie retorted.

Lizzie was rubbing her aching feet. 'Sometimes it's necessary. My God, I thought we'd left all this marching up and down behind.'

That morning had consisted of square bashing, square bashing and yet more square bashing.

The mess was being decorated with paper chains and, as if by magic, a Christmas tree had appeared. It was rumoured that it might have walked in from the forest down the road, but it was also accepted that just one wouldn't be missed.

'I don't think I'll be coming to this dance tomorrow,' said Lizzie. 'I bet you I'll draw duty and won't be able to go. It's just my luck.'

Margot smiled secretively and flashed her thick lashes. 'Well I know for sure that I'm going.'

'Major Bradley!' Bessie exclaimed, her broad smile dispersing freckles over her face. 'Personally I don't know which one to choose. I've got a whole troop of men wanting to take me.' She said it laughingly, but the others knew it was true. Bessie was bright, breezy and popular.

'One day there'll be a man you can't resist,' said Lizzie.

'But not yet. I'll let you know when I find 'im. Till then I'm out to enjoy meself.'

Margot raised a mocking eyebrow in Lizzie's direction. Bessie and her bevy of men continued to surprise her. She didn't exactly disapprove, but just didn't see the point of it all.

She turned her attention to Lizzie. 'No word from Hunter then, Lizzie darling?'

Lizzie shook her head. 'No. It seems he's fallen off the face of the earth. And it's all down to bread and cheese and a rumbling stomach.'

Margot laughed. 'A gentleman should always pay for the meal.'

'Even when he's an officer and she's only his humble driver?'

'There are no excuses,' Margot stated with an air of finality. 'And Cinders, you definitely shall go to the ball.'

'Yes,' said Lizzie. 'I've made up my mind.'

Perhaps it was the feeling of relief that Patrick had been

cleared of looting, but Lizzie yearned to celebrate, to enjoy herself in bright company, at least for an hour or two.

Later, only an hour before lights out, she was called to the adjutant's office.

'Orders from Wing Commander Hunter to collect him at seven thirty in the morning.'

She saluted the adjutant and said, 'Yes, sir.' After that she made her way to her bed. Travelling in wartime took far longer than in peacetime. Despite her youth, the journey to Bristol and back had taken its toll. The square bashing and recent training sessions hadn't helped either. And now the thought of Hunter . . . She slept well, though she couldn't help wondering where he'd been and, if he had been in England, why hadn't he called for her before?

At breakfast next morning the mess bubbled with expectation. Paper chains strung between hanging lampshades trembled each time the door opened and let in the winter darkness. Girls chattered and discussed who they were going to the dance with that evening. Others, the lucky ones who had Christmas leave, were discussing what they were doing once they got home.

Lizzie didn't have time for a decent breakfast. Half a cup of tea, a slice of toast and she was off. After signing for her car, she slid on to the cold leather, started the engine and headed for Ainsley Hall.

The crenellated towers and stark windows of the Tudor mansion stared blackly into the morning darkness. Dawn was only just beginning to turn the eastern sky from indigo to dark mauve. It promised to be a cold but fine day.

A flight of steps led up to the hall's entrance. An arched pediment frowned over a huge door of oak planks studded with iron nails. Usually Lizzie could see Hunter's impatient figure, blacker than the building he stood against, pacing up and down, his head bowed and a cigarette hanging from his hand. But there was no sign of him today.

She waited, unsure what to do.

The sentries posted at either end of the building did their pass by. Light shone through ancient windows and fell in diamond shapes on the frosted grass.

Finally the door opened and a figure emerged. She immediately got out of the car, standing to attention as she opened the rear door. The handle was icy beneath her fingers. It surprised her that the car had started at all.

'At ease, miss.'

It was not Hunter.

'The wing commander begs your pardon, miss, but says he is just finishing breakfast and, as the hour is early, would you perhaps care to come inside?' The man who addressed her so informally wore the insignia of a warrant officer.

Surprised by the invitation she blinked and slammed the door shut. Her feet crunched on the gravel drive as she followed the man up the steps.

The interior hall was panelled with oak screens. Lighter patches showed here and there where ancestral portraits might have hung, now stored for the duration of the war.

'You can sit here if you like,' said the man. 'I'll tell Wing Commander Hunter you're here.'

The smell of fried bacon and eggs wafted out into the hallway. Her stomach rumbled as she sat down. What was it about food that made her stomach do that? It had never been quite so vocal before the war. The less food there was, the more you craved, she decided.

'The wing commander asks if you'd like to join him.'

She looked up to see that the warrant officer had returned. She wondered if she'd heard him correctly.

'Would bacon and eggs be alright?' he continued.

Her stomach rumbled.

The warrant officer grinned. 'Sounds as though it would be very satisfactory indeed. Would you like to follow me?'

She *had* heard correctly, there was no doubt about it. The warrant officer led her to a table set close to a huge, lead-paned window. Wing Commander Hunter was tucking into a plate of bacon and eggs. He looked up when he saw her. 'Take a seat. Venables will get you a cooked breakfast. And toast, please, Venables. And more coffee.'

'Very good, sir.'

He held the chair out for Lizzie before taking the empty coffee pot and disappearing.

She rubbed her hands together and couldn't resist one last shiver. The room had raftered ceilings and was not that well heated, but was still in comfortable contrast to outside. And the smell!

Although she'd never had much response from him before, she felt obliged to make conversation. 'That looks good.'

'I thought you'd like some, and from past experience I don't think you eat enough for breakfast.'

She winced beneath his searching look, knowing he was referring to the bread and cheese he'd paid for at the Swan.

'That's very kind of you, sir.'

'An army marches on its stomach. That's true of any guy – or gal. You can't do a good job running on empty.'

She took in what he was saying and liked the way he said it. She'd never heard an American, except at the pictures, but the Canadian accent was very similar.

Up until now she had only really studied him through the rear-view mirror of the car. Now she was sitting opposite him and, bearing in mind that he was a senior officer and she mustn't appear rude, her eyes flickered between the room, the table and his face. She repeated the manoeuvre, all the time taking in something different about his features.

By the time she'd taken in his dark hair, his grey eyes and his wide mouth, the warrant officer had come back with her breakfast. A whole egg! A whole rasher of bacon and a shiny, deliciously greasy sausage. And bread, fried to golden perfection!

Just as she picked up her cutlery, her stomach rumbled. 'Pardon me.'

Hunter raised his eyes, but not his head. His eyes met hers and he smiled. 'Eat up, Randall. I like a quiet drive. You should know that by now.'

She didn't need him to repeat his order, but attacked the plate with gusto. Between mouthfuls of sausage and bacon, she sipped at coffee and nibbled buttered toast.

'When you've finished and have readied yourself, you can join me outside.'

He picked up his newspaper and stood up.

Fearing she might be remiss in her duty if she didn't, Lizzie started to stand up too.

'No rush,' he said in that honeyed voice. 'I need to fetch some notes from my office. Finish the toast. It's an order.'

'I will.'

By the time she had finished and gone out to the car, he was already sitting in the back seat.

'Sorry, sir,' she said, a little flustered that he'd beaten her to it.

'No need to be.'

'I expect the driver who covered for me didn't keep you waiting.' She didn't know why she said it. Not really curiosity, perhaps just a desire to keep open this channel of communication. Who knows, perhaps she would get to go to the dance this evening after all.

His response surprised her. 'I didn't have one. I wasn't here.'

She didn't know whether she sighed with relief or satisfaction, but she was glad no one had taken her place. It somehow made her feel special. She started the engine. 'Where to, sir?'

One of the airfields? she wondered. Or perhaps one of the radar stations, huge sentries of iron and radio waves guarding the east coast of England, giving advance warning that enemy planes were heading their way.

'London.'

'*London?*' she repeated, incredulous.

'London. Whitehall. War Department. I'll give you the directions when we get there.'

Eleven

Using only his fingertips, Michael smoothed away Mary Anne's hair from the nape of her neck. Warm as velvet, his lips brushed her skin. She moaned and flexed her spine, stretching like a cat luxuriating in attention.

'I love it when you do that,' she whispered.

'I love it when you do a lot of things,' he replied, his lips following the sweep of her shoulder.

She opened her eyes. It was still dark outside; she guessed it was about half past seven.

'I have to get up,' she said, swinging her feet to the side

of the bed. One foot ventured out from beneath the bedclothes, but retreated in response to the chilly morning air.

Strong arms reached across and hugged her close to his naked body. He was warm and all night she'd snuggled up to him, deliriously happy that her bed was not hers and hers alone.

'I've missed you,' he said and kissed her hair, smoothed it back and kissed her ear, her neck and her cheek.

'We can't stay in bed all day.'

'Why not? It's been so long.' His voice was deep and languorous, as sensually fulfilling as the fingertips that stroked her spine all the way down to the cleft between her buttocks.

'We have tonight,' she murmured, her voice, even to her own ears, seeming to purr with satisfaction. 'And the one after that, and the one after that . . .'

And then I'll be gone. The words were unspoken yet she felt their silence echo in her heart. Just a few days together and she must be grateful. Usually he wore the uniform of the Royal Signals Regiment, although he was part of no battalion or battle fleet. All he'd told her about his work was that he translated messages but as few people as possible must know this, hence arriving in civvies.

'I'm sorry about the shop,' she said.

He laughed. 'Why should you be?'

'I feel I should have been more . . . careful.'

'Careful about what?'

She couldn't answer.

He kissed her shoulder. 'Marianna, I know that people can be cruel for no apparent reason. It was not your fault.'

She finally managed to struggle – reluctantly – away from him. A little more persuasion and she'd gladly make love again. It had been so long – too long – since she had experienced the feel of his body against hers. Kisses and caresses mixed with the exhilaration of knowing what would come next. She'd revelled in the hardness of his thighs between hers, opening up like a flower welcoming his intrusion.

'I have to get up.' She slid from his arms, tiptoed to the window and peered out through a gap in the curtains. 'Gertrude and the others will be here soon.'

'Not in this room I hope. One woman at a time is quite enough,' said Michael, falling back on the pillow, his arms crossed behind his head.

'I've promised to make some more clothes from the odds and sods people have brought in. And there's knitting to unpick and re-knit. And things to mend.'

Since Gertrude's suggestion, it had become something of a challenge to make new things from old. She had found herself enjoying it. The women were good company and all kept in order by Gertrude Palmer, whom they openly termed 'The General'.

Michael lay in bed silently, his eyes half closed.

After washing in the small bathroom with the requisite minimal water, she came back into the bedroom. Michael had not moved. He seemed thoughtful, his eyes still hooded as though something was troubling him.

'Is something wrong?'

He shook his head. 'No. I was just thinking I might call in at the police station and get them to confirm what they told you.'

Mary Anne knew he was referring to the fire that had destroyed the pawn shop. 'It was a fireman who told me, not a policeman.'

He shrugged. 'I doubt it would make much difference. Anyway . . .' He swung his legs out of bed, stood and stretched.

Flushing but unable to tear her eyes away, Mary Anne studied his body. He was still young – younger than her. She questioned her own reasons for her involvement with him. Was it just because of his youth, his vigour, and also, of course, his kindness? Was their love just physical? Most of the time she believed otherwise; that theirs was a deep and lasting love, two people escaping from a cruel past. But sometimes, like now, she felt her age and worried how long things would last.

After the police had confirmed that the pawn shop had not been bombed but set on fire, Michael called round there to inspect the damage. *Perhaps I might also rescue a few items*, he thought. He soon saw that there was nothing to rescue. All that had been salvageable had already been rescued by Mary Anne or it had been looted.

Looking at the blackened walls, the supporting beams overhead, skeletal against the sky, a great sense of melancholy came over him. In the midst of a bombing raid greed had overruled fear.

'Nothing much left now.'

He turned round to see the policeman he'd spoken to at the station.

He nodded. 'They've taken everything.'

'They have now,' said the bobby. He lifted the front of his helmet so he could swipe at the redness it had left on his forehead. 'There was quite a lot of stuff here when it first happened. I was surprised having been on other looted sites. Looters take all they want, you see, then set fire to the place. Didn't look as though that much was taken. The cupboards were still full.' He jerked his chin in the direction of the glass-fronted cabinets in which most of the silver and jewellery had been kept. 'Them there,' he added.

Michael frowned. 'That doesn't make sense.'

'That's what I thought. Don't stand to reason. Yer missus came back and took what she could on the first trip. She came back a second time and course most of it were gone by then.'

Something glinted amongst the coal-black rubble. Michael's eyes narrowed.

'You shouldn't be going over there. That's dangerous,' shouted the policeman as Michael clambered over the shifting heap. Loose stones and grit tumbled out behind him. He slipped but managed to keep his balance as he grabbed at something gleaming in the dirt.

'What's that then?' asked the policeman.

Michael wiped the object against his thigh and then held it up. 'A crucifix. A silver crucifix.'

He recognized it as being an item Mary Anne had brought from her old washroom from where she'd run a small but thriving pawn shop of her own. Just as with this place, she'd sneaked back there after the house was bombed to see what she could retrieve. He vaguely wondered whether the beautifully modelled silver had brought bad luck to its owners. No, he decided. It was a holy thing and well crafted.

'I'll keep this,' he said.

'Certainly. It's yours anyway, isn't it?'

'Yes.'

Or someone's, he thought, but didn't know whose. Only Mary Anne would know that.

That night he showed it to her as they walked along East Street.

'It was John's,' she said. 'He pawned it so he could buy a ring for our Daw when they got engaged.' She smiled at it as she cradled it in the palm of her hand. 'It's Italian. I remember him telling me it had belonged to his mother. Both his parents were killed when he was a child. That's why his aunt and uncle took him in.'

'Has Daw heard from him?'

'He's coming home for Christmas. I've been invited to join them for Christmas dinner at the corner shop.'

'And Henry has also been invited.'

It was one of the things she hadn't voiced herself. The other thing was that Michael had not been invited.

He smiled wanly and squeezed her hand. 'Don't worry. I have to be back at my base before Christmas so I can't come anyway.'

'Oh well. Never mind.'

It hurt him. She could see it. But what could they do? That was the way it would always be, especially as far as Daw was concerned. Lizzie was different. So were Harry and young Stanley. They accepted that Michael made their mother happy. Henry had made her miserable and she'd had the bruises to prove it.

Young Stanley was with them now, roller-skating ahead of them on a pair of skates that Mary had told him were his Christmas present. She'd bought them in the Red Cross shop, and Stanley had seen her doing so, which was why he'd been given his present early.

'He's growing up,' said Michael suddenly.

Mary Anne shivered. 'As long as he doesn't grow up in time to serve in this war. Having one son and one daughter serving is quite enough.'

They walked on in silence, both lost in thought. Michael was first to speak. 'Did you notice how much was left in the stock cupboards when you went back to the shop after it was burned down?'

Mary Anne sighed heavily and frowned. 'I'm sorry, Michael, but I was so shocked, so devastated. I felt I'd let you down. One moment there was a shop, and next moment there wasn't. I felt terrible and barely noticed anything. I just gathered what I could.' She caught sight of Michael's frown. 'What is it?'

'I was wondering whether the fire really was started by looters. Why burn down a building still full of valuables?'

She shrugged. 'I suppose it doesn't make much sense. But what other reason is there? Who else could have done it?'

Michael's eyes clouded over as they often did when he was thinking of his past.

'Back in Germany they would not need a reason. Malice, sheer malice.'

Mary Anne shivered again just as Stanley fell over on his skates.

Twelve

Lizzie's mouth was dry. She'd never driven as far as London. There was some traffic, mostly army trucks and farm vehicles. The latter were usually pulled by a pair of Suffolk Punch, their golden rumps rolling from side to side, their breath steaming in the morning mist.

'Fine-looking animals,' Hunter said suddenly. He rarely spoke once they were in motion and took her by surprise.

'Yes. They are.'

'Big too.'

She wracked her brain for something to say. She'd always liked horses and remembered reading about them. The milkman who used to call at the house in Kent Street had been clued up on them too. He'd imparted information about them when he saw her smoothing the nag that pulled the milk cart.

'Apparently they're quite common in East Anglia. They're not as big as Shire horses but they're used because they don't have much feathering on their legs. The farmlands around here are flat and muddy. Hairy legs would pick up too much mud.'

'Better not go rolling my trousers up when I go walking across fields.'

'No. Best not.'

Lizzie glanced in the rear-view mirror. Had she heard right? Had he really cracked a joke? This was a surprise. And then he was admitting that his legs were hairy? She found herself blushing.

She felt slightly honoured in a strange kind of way. Her earlier aversion to him had ebbed slightly. It had something to do with the fact that he hadn't used another driver while she'd been on leave. The closed look had lifted. She found herself liking his face, wanting to study it that bit more.

'Did you find it easy to drive around yourself?' she asked. 'You know, seeing as we drive on the opposite side of the road to Canada?'

He looked surprised that she'd asked, and for a moment she thought he wasn't going to answer.

'What do you mean, Randall?'

She shrugged. 'Well, during the last few weeks – driving around – whilst I was on leave.'

'I wasn't here while you were on leave. I was on the other side of the Atlantic.'

'In Canada! I hear it's wonderful there. A really big country.'

The openness that had shone in his eyes now vanished. 'It is. Now perhaps you'll stop chattering and get on with your driving.'

His outburst was sudden and quickly passed, his attention returning to his notes. Lizzie seethed, wishing she'd kept her distance and been as unforthcoming as they'd both been at first. If that was the way he wanted it . . .

Acres of flat fields bounded the narrow roads beneath a wide sky. Two hours into their journey he tapped her on the shoulder. Surprised, she corrected the sudden jolt on the wheel and swerved back on to the left side of the road.

'Pull in here,' he ordered.

The road widened around a village green outside a thatched inn. Lizzie brought the car to a standstill behind the last of three army trucks.

'Home Guard,' she said, surmising that regular army would set up their own bivouac, not dive into a local pub.

'I think we need to stretch our legs.'

He strolled to the other side of the road and stood staring at a ploughed field. Lizzie followed him.

'Sir!' She saluted.

He turned round and kept his eyes fixed on her face as though not daring to let them drop.

'I wouldn't mind a drink, sir. If that's alright with you.'

He looked at her blankly. 'If you must.' He turned away again, his broad shoulders outlined by sky. The old Wing Commander Hunter had returned. Gone was the amiable generosity of this morning. Though still injured by his sudden mood swings, she decided to give it one more try.

'Would you like a drink, sir?'

'No.'

She left him there. The Home Guard mob greeted her cheerily and not with the usual ribaldry she could expect from regular soldiers. It was only to be expected, of course. Most of them were of retirement age.

She dared half a pint of cider and also requested a chunk of bread and butter. Once she'd devoured it, she went back outside. Hunter was sitting in the back of the car with his papers.

The rest of the drive was conducted in silence. Lizzie didn't mind. She felt refreshed, and by the time they got to London she was glad she'd had something to give her energy.

London bristled with war details. Barrage balloons floated like silver clouds and sandbags protected the entrances of tall buildings. The buildings in Whitehall towered over them, rows of blank windows staring out on the world.

The exterior of the building marked War Department was almost as drab as the rest of wartime London. Slinging her gas mask over her shoulder, Lizzie followed Hunter into the building.

He spun round so suddenly that she bumped into him, bouncing off his chest. 'You can go shopping,' he said to her. 'But only for one hour. No more.'

Shopping in London was amazing, she found. A lot of the shops were far too expensive for the likes of her – she'd need a year's rations to buy anything – but looking cost nothing and the hour went swiftly by.

Cheeks reddened by the cold air, she marched back to where she'd left the car. She'd calculated that if all went to schedule, she should be back at base in time for the Christmas dance. She wondered about mentioning it to Hunter, and decided she would.

But only if he were on time from his meeting, otherwise there was no point.

'Your car's been fuelled up, miss,' said the corporal outside the entrance.

'Really? I thought I had enough to get back to base, and besides there's a few petrol stations between here and there.'

'Perhaps the wing commander has other plans,' said the corporal.

There was something in the way he said it that made her think he was right. She was just about to question what he knew and wasn't telling, when Hunter appeared at the top of the marble steps. He strode down them quickly, his face as grim as when she'd left him.

'Croydon,' he barked as he slid into the back seat.

Croydon! 'I've never been there before,' she said haltingly, reaching for an army-issue road map before starting the engine.

'Good God, woman! Don't bother with that. I'll give you directions. We haven't got all day!'

His brusque manner stiffened her spine. She just about managed to sound respectful. 'Yes, sir.'

She'd looked long enough at the map to have a rough idea of where she was going. Each time he told her which way to go, her jaw tightened that bit more. And just when she was beginning to warm to him too. Well not now! Certainly not now!

The rest of the journey passed in silence except for him giving directions and one single attempt at normal conversation. He asked her if she was going home for Christmas.

'No, sir.'

'You've drawn duty?'

'Yes, sir.'

It was evening by the time they got to Croydon airfield and the grey winter light was fast sliding into darkness. Huddled buildings with flat roofs loomed ahead of them. Beyond were the indistinct shapes of aircraft. All were blurred by a seasonal mist.

For some reason that she couldn't explain, Lizzie's heart began to race. Apprehension clutched at her stomach. Something was about to happen, though she couldn't imagine what.

Get a grip on yourself, she thought.

'Stop here.'

She did as ordered. Ahead of them was the runway. He took his leave of her abruptly and without undue ceremony.

She lingered, amazed by what she was seeing. A large aircraft sat there, its propellers already turning. She looked for the customary RAF symbol on the side, but in its place was a large white star. Her eyes widened. The implications were enormous. Wing Commander Hunter wasn't merely flying *in* an American aircraft. He must be going *to* America. But why? What was going on?

Thirteen

It was three days before Christmas and two days after Michael had gone back to his posting that Gertrude came calling. She looked more serious than usual and was holding an opened envelope in her hand.

Mary Anne flung the door wide when she saw who it was. 'Gertrude. How lovely to see you. Do come in. Can I get you a cup of tea?'

Gertrude's grim-faced expression did not improve; in fact the straight, thin lips became even straighter.

'No. What I've got to say I can say here.'

A cold fear clutched at Mary Anne's stomach. Her gaze dropped to the letter. 'What is it? Has something happened to someone?'

Her first thought was Harry, but then she noticed the envelope was plain brown with no official insignia. It was not a telegram. Her knees almost buckled with relief.

'No,' said Gertrude, her mouth snapping shut. 'Except that I have been seriously misled. You have been dishonest with me, Mrs Randall, and I am not best pleased.'

Mary Anne frowned as she shook her head. 'I don't understand.'

'This letter arrived at my house this morning. It is from a

person stating that the man who's been staying here these last few days is *not* in fact your husband!'

Mary Anne felt the blood rush to her face. What she'd feared all along had actually happened. But had Henry sent the letter? How dare he!

'I can explain, Gertrude . . .'

'*Mrs Palmer* to you!'

This was the side of Gertrude Palmer that Mary Anne had hoped never to see. An upholder of tradition and Victorian values, Gertrude was not the sort to be persuaded that sometimes – just sometimes – such things were acceptable.

Mary Anne was lost for words. She knew what was coming – and yet they'd been so careful. But someone had betrayed them.

'I'm afraid you'll have to go, Mrs Randall. I do not countenance lewd behaviour on any premises under my jurisdiction.'

Mary Anne was shocked, but refused to take it lying down. 'If you'd known my husband, you would have jailed him for violence!'

It was a well-known fact that Gertrude Palmer sat as a magistrate. No doubt she'd had plenty like Henry before her in her time.

'That is not the issue here,' Gertrude said between clenched teeth. 'The man you had in your bed was not your husband. It is not seemly. I cannot allow it.'

There was nothing for it. Mary Anne set her jaw and folded her arms. She would not be humbled. She'd had too many years of that. 'How long will you give me until I can find something else?'

'One week. That is all.' She turned to go, but paused. 'Here,' she said, thrusting the envelope forward. 'You might as well have this. I am informed of the circumstances. That is all that matters.'

Mary Anne took the letter. Her hand dropped to her side as though it weighed the same as a sack of coal. She had no wish to read it. There was nothing to be gained.

'What about Stanley?' she murmured, but it was too late to implore. Why hadn't she done so at the time? *Stunned*, she thought, *I was stunned*. But she would go round to Henry again, she determined. She would try and catch him in and give him a piece of her mind. Alright, so he hadn't been around when the pawnshop had caught fire. Perhaps it really had been looters and her imagination had merely been working overtime. But he *could* have written this letter.

She opened the envelope and looked at the writing. She frowned. Henry could barely sign his name, and even that was in a squiggly hand. This writing was neat and rounded. The grammar was tight and the sentences went straight to the point. She crumpled it in her hand and left it sitting on the table. There was no point in moping over what had happened. She had to find somewhere else to live. Her eyes misted as she looked around the room. It had been such a short, sweet stay.

The job of doing alterations and making good clothes from old ones was taken from Mary Anne. When she went through the shop, Edith was bent over the old treadle sewing machine. Defiant of Gertrude Palmer, it was she who glanced up and called out best of luck. Gertrude threw her a warning look. Edith just glared back at her.

Outside Mary Anne took a deep breath of fresh air. Tonight promised to be frosty. *And soon I'll be homeless*, she thought dejectedly as she turned left out of the shop doorway.

'Mary Anne!'

She stopped and looked round. Edith was running towards her, one hand holding on to her hat.

Edith was small and easily looked up into Mary Anne's face. 'I wanted you to know that I don't think you're a scarlet woman. I know there are sometimes circumstances beyond our control. I told Gertrude that.'

Mary Anne smiled weakly. 'I wish I could believe that she'd listen.'

A sudden movement made her look over Edith's shoulder. Gertrude was leaning out of the shop doorway, her face as dark as a December night.

'I think you'd better get back here,' she said.

Edith was adamant. 'Look, we're volunteers! You don't pay us or own us. We can do what we like and speak to who we want.' Edith's uncharacteristic vibrancy lessened as she turned back to Mary Anne. 'Where are you going?'

'To find somewhere to live.'

'Do you know who wrote the letter?'

Mary Anne shrugged. 'At first I thought my husband wrote it, but the handwriting . . .'

'Perhaps he got someone else to write it. Some people are

better at writing letters than others. I'm not terribly good myself. My sister Cissy usually writes mine for me.'

Mary Anne stared into the distance. There had been something vaguely familiar about the writing. Did Stanley, her youngest son, write like that? Anger boiled inside her. How dare Henry do that? How dare he get Stanley to write for him! But what about Biddy Young? She could write; perhaps it had been her.

'I hope you find somewhere,' Edith said and patted her hand. 'Good luck.'

Mary Anne made a sudden decision not to go to where Henry was living, but to seek him at work. Henry worked as a taxi driver. His usual pitch was outside Temple Meads Station. *That*, she decided, *is where I'll find him.*

The cabs were lined up alongside the colonnade. Nudges and sly whispers were exchanged as the drivers eyed her approach. She couldn't see Henry's cab and presumed he was out on a fare. She paused, nervously considering what she would say. The gathered cabbies recognized her and divided into two camps; not physically with their whole bodies, but in their eyes. Some simmered with hostility, others with conjecture: if she was sleeping with one man who wasn't her husband, why not another?

They're shameless, thought Mary Anne, veering away at the last minute from the leering smiles, the secretive winks.

She headed into the station concourse and bought herself a platform ticket. She'd wait there if she had to. No doubt Henry would be told her whereabouts by one of his colleagues.

A ticket collector doffed his hat as he punched her ticket. She blushed and hurried on. Age had enhanced her looks. She had an elegance about her she had not owned in her youth. She'd been pretty, yes, but lots of young girls are pretty. Few women grow into elegance.

She sat on a bench. The smell of soot lay heavy in the air. Trains screeched and belched as they pulled in and out of the station with uncommon regularity. Uniformed men and women got on and got off, all going somewhere, all having been somewhere.

Glancing up at the station clock a while later revealed that she'd been there for half an hour. Henry had to be back by now. She passed back through the barrier, informing the ticket collector that she was just going out to see if her son had arrived.

'But I will be back,' she said lightly, flashing him a smile.

He promised not to charge her for another platform ticket when she got back. He doffed his hat again.

Just as she was approaching the wide entrance to the station incline, she saw Henry coming the other way. Her nerves tightened at the sight of him. The sites of old injuries throbbed anew as though warning her not to trust him, not to forget what he'd done.

His face brightened when he saw her. 'Mary Anne!'

Despite her anger, Mary Anne felt that old nervousness taking hold of her. She clasped her hands together over the handle of her handbag. She wanted to run, but she also wanted to fight.

He eyed her quizzically. 'Nash and the others told me you'd come in here. Are you going somewhere?'

'I came to see you about this.' She thrust the letter at him.

He frowned as he took it and spread it open. His eyes flickered between the letter and her. 'You know I can't read too well,' he said gruffly and thrust it back to her. 'What does it say?'

'Do you get our Stanley to write letters for you?'

'Sometimes he writes out my daily log for me.'

The daily log was where Henry recorded his fares and fees for the day. Someone in the family had always written it out for him. Stanley was now the only one who stayed with his father on a regular basis.

'What does it say?' Henry asked her again.

Mary Anne took a deep breath as she pushed it back into her handbag. 'It slanders my name.'

He didn't say anything, merely jerked his chin as though he understood exactly what she was saying.

'Have you heard from our Harry?'

Mary Anne was taken aback. Father and son had never seen eye to eye.

'He writes to me quite regularly.'

It was true. Like Michael he was based in England and did top-secret code-breaking work. Harry wrote regularly to his mother but not to his father. 'What's the point?' he'd said in his letters. 'He wouldn't read them.'

Henry's eyelids flickered as though he were censoring his

thoughts before voicing them. 'Did you ever hear from that lawyer bloke? I wouldn't give 'im yer address, but I think that busybody friend of yours did.'

She shook her head. 'Unfortunately, I think I was the wrong Mary Anne.'

Henry studied his feet as he spoke. 'Understandable I suppose, seeing as yer family did have a few bob.'

Having no wish to bring up the past, she turned away. Her family had been reasonably well off. Henry had never had trouble with that – not until later, not until she had trusted him.

'This damned war,' he said suddenly. 'I suppose the Yanks will come in when it's all but over!'

She didn't look back. 'I have to go.'

He didn't ask her where she was going and she wouldn't tell him she was homeless. He'd only offer for her to stay with him and she wouldn't do that. She *couldn't* do that.

'I still want you back, Mary Anne, even though you 'ave been living with yer fancy man,' he called after her.

Mary Anne bristled. 'Don't call him that,' she shouted back.

'Get going then, and good riddance! Yer no better than yer friend Biddy Young. She's got a fancy man too. Calls on 'er once a week when the young 'uns are at school – to 'ave a cup of a tea and a chat, she says. But I think we both know what that means don't we? Eh? Yer both tarred with the same brush, and that's the truth of it!'

His loud voice followed her down the incline to the main Bath Road. She winced at the sound of it, hating him saying those things. She wasn't like Biddy! She wasn't like Biddy at all!

Fourteen

Daw's husband John had been lucky enough to get leave for Christmas and was making the most of it. Running a corner shop had some advantages for his Auntie Maria: she'd made a cake, cooked a chicken and had made a plum pudding from fresh plums pickled back in October. The custard was sweetened with a mix of honey and sugar saved over weeks from the rations. The flour used in the cake and pudding was boosted with breadcrumbs. The chicken had been reared from a little yellow chick bought the previous Easter.

Mary Anne sat on the opposite side of the table to Henry. Every so often he tried to catch her eye, but she made sure he didn't. She could tell he had hoped for reconciliation. His merry expression turned morose. The corners of his mouth sagged with disappointment. His eyes followed the sherry bottle and the brown ales being passed around the table. He kept boasting that he had abstained for nearly a year. She didn't believe him and her worst fears were realized when she saw him sip at a glass of sherry, then down it in one go.

She felt hot suddenly and excused herself. 'I'm just going out back.'

The air outside was crisp and cold, the ground still covered with last night's frost. She took great gasps of it, glad of the chill reddening her cheeks and clearing her head. Could she – dare she – go back in? Although her dress had long sleeves, she shivered. The door to the yard suddenly squeaked open.

'You'll catch your death standing there, Mother.'

'Harry!'

Her big son wrapped her in his arms. 'Merry Christmas, Mother.' He kissed her.

'Harry!'

She stroked his cheek, noting the extra hard lines that hadn't been there when he'd gone away. His eyes looked deeper. Perhaps his thoughts were too.

'I didn't know you were coming home.'

'It was a last-minute thing,' he said as they strolled arm in arm back into the house. The warmth and the smell of roast chicken hit them. 'That smells good,' he added. 'What's the chance there's some left for me?'

'There's bound to be. John's Auntie Maria is Italian, remember.'

Mary Anne jerked at Harry's arm, stopping him just short of the living-room door. 'Your father's in there, mind. And he's just broken his pledge to be sober.'

She saw his features tighten, his eyes fix on the closed door. 'You're not back with him?'

'Of course not. I was invited to Christmas lunch, and so was he. It's a family thing and one way to make the rations go further.'

Harry's expression was unchanged. 'I don't think this is a good idea. He'll start on me, and then that'll ruin it for everyone.'

Mary Anne didn't argue. 'Wait here. I'll make my excuses and get my coat. You wait down in the yard.'

He nodded and whispered a brief agreement. She waited until he was out of sight before opening the door.

'I've got a bit of a headache. I think I'll go home. Do you want to come, Stanley?'

Stanley stopped stuffing a second helping of plum pudding into his mouth and shook his head. 'I haven't had me cake yet.'

Mary Anne smiled to herself. Stanley was a typical boy and stronger than he used to be. *Strange things happen in war*, she told herself.

John's auntie insisted she take some food with her. 'We must not let it go to waste,' she said while wrapping cake and pudding in greaseproof paper and setting a pie dish filled with roast chicken and vegetables in the bottom of a brown paper carrier bag.

Daw wasn't too disappointed that her mother was leaving early. John was home and she wanted time with him.

Henry got up from his chair and leaned on his knuckles. 'I'll see you out.'

Mary Anne was instantly filled with alarm. 'No need. I can manage.' But Henry insisted.

John's Uncle Guido helped her into her coat. Henry looked put out, but she couldn't help that.

Shouts of 'Merry Christmas!' sounded in the passageway behind her. Suddenly, so did the patter of small feet.

'I've changed me mind,' Stanley shouted. 'I've got me cake.' He waved a paper bag.

Mary Anne breathed a sigh of relief. At least she wouldn't be left alone with Henry, though Stanley wasn't that much of a deterrent. All she hoped now was that Henry would go back inside before seeing Harry; that way a quarrel might be avoided.

Attempting to swallow the lump in her throat, she stepped out into the yard. The air seemed even colder than before. She told herself that was what was causing her to shiver so intensely. Her fear lessened suddenly when she saw there was no sign of Harry. He was outside. He had to be.

Before she could make for the exit, Henry grabbed her arm. 'I got half a bed if yer interested.'

She smelled the sweet sherry on his breath. She pulled away. 'I'm going home.'

'You ain't got a home. Not a proper one.'

Mary Anne struggled. 'Let me go.'

The light of perverted enjoyment shone in Henry's eyes. 'Yer still me wife, Mary Anne. I've still got me rights and I could drag you with me and no man would dare to stop me. D'you know that? No man could stop me!'

'Let go of me mum!'

Henry had forgotten his youngest son. Stanley's small fists pummelled his father's side. His feet kicked Henry's shins. Henry yelped and bent to protect his limbs from the well-aimed blows.

'You beggar! You little beggar!'

Stanley grabbed his mother's hand. 'Quick, Mum. Come on!'

Mary Anne glanced over her shoulder. Henry had staggered and tripped against the steps leading up to the attic storeroom and was lying flat on his back.

Harry stepped forward just as she slammed the solid gate behind her. Stanley's face was a picture, his eyes popping out of his head. But before he had a chance to shout his brother's name, Mary Anne slapped her hand over his mouth.

'It don't sound as though me dad's too happy,' said Harry, looking bemused and taking her arm as they hurried along.

Mary Anne grinned. 'Well at least he's taking it lying down. He's been at the sherry.'

Once they were out of earshot, Stanley wanted to know everything Harry had been up to.

'Did you kill any Germans?' he asked with an exuberance that left Mary Anne worrying what he would grow up to be.

'Not directly. In a way I prefer to think that my work *saved* lives.'

'Are you a spy?' Now Stanley was almost bursting out of his skin with excitement.

'Not quite. And stop asking me questions. It's all very hush-hush. I mustn't talk about it.'

Stanley wasn't to be put off that easily. 'You can tell me.'

Harry stopped suddenly, catching hold of Stanley's shoulders and spinning him round and bending down so they were face to face. His voice was only a little above a whisper. 'If I tell you what I do, we'll both be in trouble. We'll both be traitors, see, and you know what they do to traitors, don't you, Stanley?'

Stanley gulped and his jaw fell open.

Harry made a gun shape with his hand and aimed it at Stanley's chest. 'Bang!'

Stanley just gaped at his brother. He swallowed. 'Crikey!'

Harry slapped his brother on the back. 'Come on. Let's be going.'

Mary Anne smiled at her sons' antics. She loved them both. She'd specifically not asked too much about Harry's war work, but knew it was to do with crosswords and code-breaking. Stanley was less circumspect, but Harry's response had given him food for thought. He was quiet for a while.

Mary Anne exchanged a smile with Harry, who winked. 'Think I nipped that one in the bud. Now, Mother,' he said, gripping her arm, 'tell me what the matter is. And don't say "nothing". I can see it in your face.'

Stanley chose that moment to climb on to a low wall running alongside Victoria Park. Mary Anne was about to call him back, but Harry stopped her. 'Let him have five minutes of fun. My car's around the corner.'

Mary Anne's eyes opened wide. 'You've still got your car? How are you managing about petrol?'

Smiling, Harry tapped the side of his nose.

That was Harry. When hadn't he had supply sources? She wondered if he was still involved in the black market, but then asked herself how he could be. He usually wore the uniform of the Royal Corps of Signals, but she knew he was doing more – much more – than that. Strangely enough the posting must suit him. He'd always been secretive, living on the edge of a shadowy world which she knew nothing about.

'So,' he said, lowering his voice. 'Tell me what you've been up to.'

She'd written to him about the pawn shop being burned

down and the implication that looters rather than a bomb were responsible. She'd also told him about living with Daw.

'I knew that wouldn't last,' he said. 'But the rooms above the Red Cross shop sounded nice.'

Mary Anne turned her head to watch Stanley kicking at the few leaves still lying in the grass. Even the park keeper had gone off to war. The iron railings had gone the year before, taken to be melted down to make Spitfires and warships, they'd said. Donations of pots and pans had also been called for. There'd been none left in the pawn shop. Everything was gone.

'The world looks neglected,' she said suddenly.

Harry looked puzzled. 'Never mind the world. What about you?'

'Michael came home just before Christmas. He stayed for three precious days.'

She knew Harry was studying her expression, trying to read what was going on inside in case she should lie – which of course was highly possible.

'And then?'

It all came out about Michael staying and Gertrude receiving that letter. She'd never been good at keeping secrets – even years ago, when she'd told Henry that her parents had paid him to marry her because she'd had a baby and her fiancé had not returned from the Great War. Henry was no great catch, but he'd been proud to marry her. He hadn't known about the baby, of course, but they'd been happy and she'd thought she could trust him to rise above petty recriminations. He had not. Her honesty changed him. Her life was never the same again after that. But she'd kept the two truths from her children – the truth about why she'd married their father and also his violence towards her. Bruises could be hidden.

'So now I have to look for somewhere else to live.' She sighed. 'It's not easy. There are plenty of others needing somewhere too.'

She felt Harry's eyes on her, more contemplative than before. 'So who wrote the letter?'

She shrugged. 'Your father. Who else? He may have got someone to write it for him. I don't know for sure. I did think our Stanley might have written it for him, but it was too well crafted for a child. It had to be an adult.'

They both watched Stanley swinging on a low-hanging tree branch.

'It could have been our Stanley. Have you asked him?'

Mary Anne shook her head. 'No. The boy's gone through enough. We've all gone through enough.'

'You're protecting him again.'

She shook her head. Stanley had been a sickly child and she'd almost lost him to TB. But he'd pulled through. She'd never been able to stop mollycoddling him. It was something inside, something that warned her he must always be protected or she'd lose him. She wasn't prepared to do that.

Harry suddenly took hold of her arm again. He shouted out to Stanley. 'Come on, our Stanley. We're off now.'

Stanley came racing back. Twigs and leaves clung to his pullover and his bare knees were smeared with mud.

'Where are we going?'

Harry pointed him to where a small black Austin sat at the kerbside. It was the only car in the very long street that bounded the park. Harry's eyes searched the empty street. No police. No questions. He was glad of that.

Mary Anne sat next to her son in the front seat. Stanley fell into the back, lying full stretch on the navy-blue leather.

'Cor! Wait till I tell my pals about this,' he cried as he caressed the thickly padded upholstery. 'No one in our class has got a car!'

As they drove away from the kerb, Mary Anne eyed her son sidelong. 'So where are we going?' She kept her voice low so Stanley would not hear her. Harry replied in similar fashion. He smiled in that long, slow way of his, the way that made his mother almost fall in love with him – like she had on the day he was born.

'Look, Mum. How about moving into my flat with Edgar?'

Mary Anne tried not to fluster. The flat was the first place to come to mind on the day the pawn shop was burned down. But she knew it wasn't empty.

'I couldn't. He's your friend. I wouldn't want to intrude.'

She couldn't bring herself to say "lover", just as she hadn't been able to go round there in the first place.

'Mum, it's my flat, not his. I can have anyone in there I like. I can chuck him out if I wish.'

'Would you?'

He shook his head. 'Edgar belongs there.'

Mary Anne nodded. 'Yes. I know that. How is he by the way?'

'Well enough when I left him.'

The flat was in a large old building close to St Nicholas Market. Its large Georgian windows looked down over the river towards Bristol Bridge. In peacetime the view had been one of the hustle and bustle of a busy city. Castle Street, Wine Street and those around it had thronged with people on a Saturday night. Now there were just ruins where Tudor houses had rubbed shoulders with those of a later age. All had gone up in flames back in November.

The flat itself reflected Harry's personality. The décor was a tasteful blend of neutral tones, everything from coffee cream to vanilla.

Edgar rose from a leather chair to greet them. He held both Mary Anne's hands and kissed her on each cheek.

'Mary Anne. How lovely to see you.'

She felt funny being called by her Christian name by a boy who was almost young enough to be her son. Edgar oozed with the confidence of someone twice his age.

He tried to greet Stanley in the same manner, but the youngster sidestepped his embrace. Edgar managed to land one kiss on Stanley's cheek. Stanley's response was to grimace as he wiped it off.

Harry quickly explained the situation. 'My mother has nowhere to live. I've invited her to move in here.'

'Then she must. I insist.'

Edgar's sincerity touched Mary Anne's heart and brought a tear to her eye. It swiftly disappeared with his next comment.

'But we don't have room for the boy.'

The two young men locked eyes. Mary Anne could not read the look there, but she knew they were agreed. There was no room for Stanley.

Mary Anne read that look. 'I shouldn't have bothered. Stanley! We're going.'

Harry barred her way out. 'Mum. This flat has one bedroom only. And children aren't allowed. At least give it a try for a few days. Our Stanley can go back with his dad.'

For some reason it hurt to hear Harry refer to Henry as Stanley's dad and not his own. Blood was thicker than water after all.

'I'll drive you back to yer dad's in the car. Alright, our Stanley?'

Stanley's face lit up. What was living with your mother compared to driving in a car?

'I'll make up a bed in the cubby hole,' said Edgar.

'I'll put the kettle on,' said Harry.

Mary Anne followed. The kitchen, just like the living room, was crisp and clean – chic as they would have said in her day.

'Are you sure Edgar doesn't mind?' she asked.

Harry looked directly into her eyes. 'Mum, he *can't* mind. This is my flat. But, saying that, whatever feelings Edgar shows are totally genuine. I won't see my mother on the street and neither would he.' He smirked suddenly. 'Or at my sister's come to that. Daw can be irritating at the best of times. I couldn't live with her, that's for sure.'

Mary Anne smiled.

'And don't worry,' he said as he spooned the tea into a cream china pot. 'I've still got contacts. I'll find you a place of your own for you and our Stanley. OK?'

'OK?' she asked, bemused by the unfamiliar word.

'It's American, Mum. Don't you ever go to the pictures?'

She sighed. 'I used to, but not for a long time.'

He fell to silence as he placed everything onto a tray.

Stanley appeared in the doorway. 'Got any biscuits?'

Harry reached into the cupboard and brought out a packet of shortbread. 'Someone where I'm stationed gave me them for Christmas.'

Mary Anne wondered who. She hoped it was a girl, but she wouldn't ask him. She'd wait for him to tell.

'I think this war breeds evil,' she said suddenly.

'You could be right.' He frowned heavily, like he did when he was thinking deeply.

'It's very likely that Dad did write that letter. Has it occurred to you that it might have been him who started the fire? He can be a vindictive old sod when he wants to be!'

The thought had occurred to her, of course, and she told him so. 'People change in wartime. Some band together and pull together. Others pull for themselves or make mischief for others, as though it's some form of entertainment. Like that business with the necklace in Patrick's pocket. That couldn't have been your father. We'd have seen him.'

Harry nodded. 'You could be right.'

Mary Anne shook her head and smiled sadly. 'Even when a sudden bit of luck did occur, it turned out not to be for this particular Mary Anne Randall.'

'What do you mean?'

Mary Anne told him about the lawyer who'd called on Henry. 'Henry didn't send him to me because he knew I didn't have an Aunt Maude. Would have been nice if I had; I wonder how much she would have left me?'

Harry took the tea on through. 'You should have said that you did have an Aunt Maude. Wouldn't have hurt.'

'That would have been dishonest,' said his mother. 'Besides, I never saw the man. He went to your dad's place. It was Biddy that told me.'

'Never mind,' said Harry. 'If you had been the right woman, he would have come calling, wouldn't he?' He turned to his younger brother. 'Grab some biscuits, Stanley. I'll get you back to your father before it gets dark.'

Stanley didn't wait to be asked twice before cramming half a packet of shortbread into each hand.

'Won't be long,' Harry said with a smile.

Something about the way he said it made Mary Anne start.

'I'll have a fresh cup when I get back,' Harry added, catching sight of his mother's expression.

Stanley's feet clumped noisily down the stairs behind him. Once outside, he wasted no time in clambering into the front passenger seat. 'Are you going to stay and talk to Dad for a while when we get there?' he asked.

Harry stared at the road ahead. He was clenching his jaw hard enough to break.

'Oh yes,' he said, more so to himself than to his little brother. 'I'll be doing that alright.'

Fifteen

Harry's jaw clenched the moment he entered Aiken Street. He knew his father for what he was and could not accept that anything had changed. His worst fears were borne out as he stepped over the dull brass threshold. If his mother had been living here he would have seen his face reflected in its polished surface. As it was, the only woman living in this house was Biddy Young and she'd never been too keen on housework.

But it wasn't neglect of the front step that filled him with foreboding. The sound of drunken laughter and the smell of strong stout wafted out to meet him and Stanley. His concern was not for himself – he'd seen the look on his brother's face. Stanley had adjusted to the fact that his parents lived apart. That adjustment had gone quite smoothly, simply because Henry Randall had stayed on the wagon. All that was about to change.

A long passageway ran from the front door to the back of the house. In front of him were the stairs leading up to his father's rooms. These houses were all pretty much the same, built for the working poor in the last century and little improved over the years. Harry could almost find his way up the stairs in the dark. To his right was the front room his father used as a bedroom; behind that the living room and the settee where Stanley slept when he stayed. At the very end of the passageway was the scullery.

The interior walls were brown gloss and the lino underfoot cracked with wear. The smell of damp and grease increased with each footstep.

The sound of raucous singing came from the end of the passageway. Stanley stopped. His pale complexion paled even more. Round-eyed he stared, his feet seemingly nailed to the spot.

Harry understood. He patted his brother on the shoulder. 'Go get your things. You can stay at my place with Mum.'

Stanley didn't hesitate.

Harry passed the sound of slamming drawers and cupboards as Stanley packed his pullovers, trousers and favourite things. Harry guessed this would include the roller skates he'd been given for Christmas. It was the only thought that brought a smile to his face.

A female voice joined in his father's singing. They both sounded drunk. Harry's features hardened when he saw them. His father and Biddy Young were dancing. They were doing some kind of reel, her arm linked into his and twirling around. Their other arms were outstretched, their free hands clutching a bottle of brown ale.

'Wish me luck as you wave me goodbye, not a tear, not a fear, make it gay . . .'

They saw him and came to a staggered stop, leaning against each other yet still in serious danger of toppling over.

Henry had trouble focusing and even more trouble balancing. His mouth stretched into something between a smile and a sneer. 'We was just 'aving a little drink.'

Biddy, her face paint-smeared and her clothes in disarray, leered at him as though she were twenty not over forty. 'After all, it is Christmas.'

Harry eyed them with contempt. 'My, my. But you two certainly suit each other. You,' he said, pointing at Biddy, 'reckon you're my mother's friend. And you,' he said, now pointing an accusing finger at his father. 'Why she ever consented to marry you, I'll never know!'

His father's attempt at a smile now curled into a cruel sneer. 'You!' he shouted, attempting to jab a finger at Harry's shoulder, but missing and falling against the sink. 'You! You bloody queer! That's what you are! Bloody queer! Sooner mince around and make yerself look nice than be a real man and get yerself bloody shot. Best thing that could happen that is; getting yerself bloody shot.'

Biddy heard nothing. She'd slumped on to a chair, her fat chin resting on her ample breast. She was snoring.

'Listen to that,' said Harry, pointing at the snoring Biddy. 'Sounds like a pig. Suits you down to the ground. Both pigs together!'

Wild-eyed, Henry Randall staggered a few steps closer to his eldest son. Spittle bubbled from the corner of his sagging mouth.

Harry stood unafraid, determined to fight his mother's corner, and if that meant hitting his father to the ground, then so be it. His fists clenched instinctively. He was ready to do whatever was necessary.

'So I'm a pig, am I? Then that makes yer mother a sow, does it?'

Harry barely controlled himself. His eyes glittered as he shook his head. 'My mother's far from that – but you! Just look at you. Drunk again. So will poor old Biddy here get a beating when she wakes up? Just like the ones you used to give my mother?'

'Your mother!' His father spat on the floor. 'You talk about 'er as though she's the bloody Virgin Mary. She weren't no virgin when I married 'er, that's fer sure. She was soiled goods. Soiled goods that I was paid to marry, though I didn't know that at the time.'

A cold chill mixed with Harry's anger. He gripped his father's shirt collar and hauled him up so that his heels were raised from the ground. He stood only on the soles of his feet and his face was turning swiftly red. But Harry didn't care. He would defend his mother to his dying day – even against his own father.

'You vindictive old bugger! Pretending to want her back when all the time you've been hounding her. It was you sent that letter, weren't it? You old sod!'

'Get off me.'

Harry began to shake him like a terrier with a rat. 'You did it! You slandered her good name! Go on! Admit it!'

Although his father's face was red as a beetroot as he tried to catch his breath, defiance burned in his eyes. 'I didn't write no letter and I didn't get nobody else to write it either.'

'You're lying!'

Henry Randall's sneer was so ugly Harry felt a great compulsion to slap it from his face.

Henry carried on. 'Yer mother's family didn't tell me the whole truth; didn't tell me she'd already been soiled and 'ad a nipper.'

Harry felt the colour draining from his face, felt his arms trembling and his fingers tightening around his father's throat.

'You're lying!' Even as he said it, he asked himself why his father should lie. So many young men had dashed off to the Great War and died in the mud of Flanders. His mother wouldn't be the first to have been left in a difficult predicament.

Relishing the uncertainty in his son's face, his father chuckled. 'There you are! Didn't know you 'ad a big brother, did you?'

A brother! The statement seemed almost monstrous, but the effect was instantaneous. The hands gripping his father's shirt collar loosened. No longer having the benefit of Harry holding him up, Henry Randall crashed into a chair. His head tipped to one side, his mouth gaped and he laughed mockingly before his eyes shut and he began to snore.

Stanley tugged at his sleeve. 'Can we go now?'

Harry looked down and saw the round blue eyes staring up at him imploringly. He ruffled his little brother's hair. 'Of course we can. Well, you can't stay here. Have you got everything?'

Stanley nodded.

It wasn't until they were in the car and he'd started the engine that something struck him. Stanley had averted his eyes from his father and Biddy. He wondered how long the drinking had been going on, how long his father had been living a lie. There was nothing to be gained by asking Stanley about it. *Best he should forget*, he thought to himself. *Best to just get on with his life*. But how could you forget your father? His mother was a different matter. He could understand what had happened. That's how things were back then and they weren't that different nowadays, though he sensed things were changing fast. But there was one other nagging concern that he couldn't yet come to terms with. How would he deal with the brother he'd never known he'd had, and where was he? What was he doing now? Would they ever meet?

Sixteen

On Valentine's Day there was a dance being held at the old guildhall in Lavenham and Lizzie was determined not to miss it.

Work had been pretty routine for the past few weeks since just before Christmas when she'd taken Wing Commander Hunter to Croydon. She'd ferried a few VIPs around and some had been cheeky enough to ask her out. One of them had succeeded. Flight Lieutenant Warren had been acting as escort to a party of visiting dignitaries. The party had consisted of civil servants, all bowler hats and smelling of ink. Their complexions had been pasty white, feeble in comparison to the fresh-faced Warren. Once the dignitaries had been handed over to senior officers, Warren had sought her out.

She was excited about going out, but that excitement was mixed with guilt when she received a letter from Patrick. As befitting Valentine's Day, the letter contained one of his verses.

If I should die tomorrow, think only this of me,
That even with my dying breath, my words would be for thee.
If I should die tomorrow, shed not too many tears,
But hold the joy of how we lived, and love me through the years.

'Gosh, that's sad,' said Bessie, reading it over Lizzie's shoulder.

Margot read it too. 'It's honest.' She sighed. 'Live for today. Tomorrow may never come. That's what he's saying. What do you think, Lizzie? He's your chap.'

A vision of scruffy Patrick, dragged up by a harlot of a mother, was the first thing that came to mind. He'd always followed her around, and she'd liked him. On joining up he'd turned into a very fine young man. She knew how he felt about her, and she'd felt the same about him – at least she thought she had.

'Things are different in wartime. Where would we be if it had never happened?'

'I would have been a debutante.' Margot was holding a pale silk dress against herself and admiring her reflection in a mirror. 'Uniform or civvies?'

It was obvious from the tone of her voice what she wanted the answer to be. But there was no choice.

'Uniform!' shouted the rest of the girls in unison.

The order had been given. Uniforms must be worn to the dance – the top brass insisted. It was all about having pride in what they were doing, and showing the civilian population that they were professional at all times.

Lizzie was touching up her lipstick. It was red and her mother had given it her for Christmas.

They all snapped to attention when the hut officer entered. She looked straight at Lizzie. 'Randall. I know you've got a pass, but I've been ordered to tell you anyway. That Canadian chap, Wing Commander Hunter, is flying into Croydon. He's asked that you be there with a car. If you're dead set on going to this dance, I can get someone else to fetch him. It's up to you.'

'Isn't it nice to be wanted?' said Margot – under her breath of course because they were all standing to attention.

Although her heart had been set on going to the dance, Lizzie hesitated before answering. At first she'd considered the wing commander a bit of a cold fish. For a long time all he'd done was stare out of the car window, deal with his paperwork, and respond curtly to any attempt at conversation. Why should she jump at the chance to pick him up from the airfield? And yet, for one fleeting moment she considered exactly that.

'If there is someone else, Sergeant . . .'

'That can be arranged, Randall. At ease.'

A sigh of relief ran through them all. Muscles relaxed and the chatter returned to the usual subjects. Bessie was flashing her engagement ring.

'Do you like it?' she asked Lizzie.

Lizzie gave it a cursory glance. 'I've already told you, Bessie. I think it's smashing.'

'So do I,' crooned Bessie, admiring the tiny diamond for the umpteenth time that day. She'd flashed it at least a dozen times to anyone who would stop to look. She sighed. 'Won't be long now before I'm married and out of all this. No more uniforms. No more getting up at the crack of dawn.'

'Lucky you,' said Lizzie. 'Though just because you're engaged doesn't mean you get to leave here straightaway. I heard there are some married women who've opted to stay on, or been ordered to stay on . . .'

'Not me! I won't be staying.'

There was something in Bessie's tone that made Lizzie look at her. The girl from Tottenham had a complexion that erred towards pink; at present it was red, bright red. Never had her eyes sparkled as they did now, as though she were holding in a secret that was aching to get out.

Just as Lizzie was about to ask why she was so excited, a message came saying that Bessie's chap, Arthur Frayling, was waiting for her outside.

'Gotta rush,' she shouted, flinging her greatcoat around her shoulders.

Thoughtfully, Lizzie watched her go. Bessie was always a ball of energy and full of saucy comments. But this excitement, this aura of expectation, was something new.

'Rule fifty-seven,' said Margot.

Although Lizzie had an inkling of what that might mean, she asked Margot to explain.

'She's in the pudding club. You heard what she said. She was adamant that she'll be out of here shortly and that, my dear Lizzie, is the quickest way. The fact that she is only engaged and not married is beside the point. And don't deny that was the question you were going to ask. I can see it in your eyes.'

It was true. Bessie's Arthur might be all for getting engaged, but it didn't mean he would see it through. Margot again voiced her own thoughts.

'Arthur's sowing his oats now, but will he stick around when the bun starts to rise?'

Lizzie looked away from Margot and folded her arms. 'I'm sure he will. He seems a very nice boy.'

Margot made a humphing sound. 'They're all very nice boys. But that doesn't mean they stick around, especially in wartime.'

The sound of a truck driver blowing his horn told them that their transport to Lavenham had arrived. In peacetime their journey would have taken no more than twenty minutes. In wartime, with no headlights, no signposts and a full load of giggling girls on board, it took closer to forty.

Blackout curtains screened the interior of the guildhall from enemy aircraft. The girls picked their way over the slippery cobbles, voicing their approval for heavy shoe leather. High heels would have been suicidal. Despite having to wear uniform, the smell of face powder pervaded the ancient hall.

Flight Lieutenant Warren was already inside, one of many blue uniforms amongst just as many – probably more – khaki ones. She saw him peering through the crowd. He smiled when he saw her.

'So glad you could come,' he said and took hold of her hand.

'There was nowhere else to go tonight.'

'Super! Care to dance?'

The music was provided by a local quartet who only seemed to know waltzes and foxtrots. They had a few dances and a few drinks, and her escort played the gentleman – until the few drinks became quite a lot.

'I like dances that bring people closer,' said Reggie Warren.

'So I notice,' said Lizzie as her bosoms brushed against his chest. She readjusted her stance, just enough to leave an inch or two.

'Shame you couldn't wear a silky dress,' said Reggie. 'Like her over there.' He pointed to a curvaceous blonde in a slinky satin dress. 'You can see every curve. Bet her partner can feel them too.'

Despite the thickness of her uniform, she felt a hot hand run down her back and land on her bottom.

'Can't feel much through this,' he said laughingly.

Lizzie bristled as he attempted to raise her skirt, cupping his fingers into her flesh.

'Don't do that!' She pushed herself away from him.

He laughed. 'Lizzie, sweetheart . . .'

She pushed her way through the laughing, dancing, happy couples. She didn't need to look over her shoulder to know he was following.

Someone grabbed her arm as she bustled through. It was Bessie and Arthur, entwined like bindweed climbing a fence.

'He's nice,' said Bessie, a wicked twinkle in her eyes. 'If I wasn't already spoken for, I wouldn't throw him out with the rubbish.'

Lizzie ducked away, presuming he wasn't following her.

Someone shouted at her to watch the light as she headed through the door. It slammed behind her. She found herself leaning against the old building, feeling the patterns in the plasterwork beneath her fingers. To one side the old bottle glass of the ancient windows glimmered with frost. The stars were out. It wasn't completely dark but dark enough.

Her breath was steam. All she could think about were the feelings Reggie had aroused in her. There had been an element of revulsion, but also one of guilt. The guilt was that surely she should be keeping herself for Patrick. Didn't everyone, especially her family, expect her to marry him?

The revulsion was only with herself. She'd actually *enjoyed* his groping fingers. It had been so long since the days when she'd worked for Mrs Selwyn Kendall and had sneaked off with her son, Peter, on Wednesday afternoons when the shop was closed. They'd made love in the back of his car. She'd felt so swanky to be riding in his car and being seen with the likes of him. Not that they went out much as such, they just met to make love – at his convenience.

You were a willing partner, she said to herself under her breath. *You liked it*. She watched her breath turn to steam, taking the words away into the blackness.

A couple came out of the main entrance, a splash of momentary brightness falling over the slippery ground. She sidled along a bit further into the darkness so they couldn't see her. Unaware they were being observed, they kissed and she heard the rustle of disturbed clothing.

'No,' she heard the girl say. 'Don't do that.'

In the dim light she could see the couple grappling, the girl pushing away the intruding hand beneath her skirt. There was a flash of white thigh as the skirt was pushed higher.

She heard the young man say, 'Come on. There's a war on.'

'Yes, and she's the one fighting it.' Lizzie bit her lip. The comment had slipped out before she'd had chance to stop it.

The young man – a soldier judging by as much of his uniform as she could see – turned in her direction. 'Oi! Who's there?'

The girl took advantage of the situation and escaped, the door closing noisily behind her.

The soldier's shadow fell over her only a second before he did. His features were disfigured by what little light there was. He was far from happy.

'Nosy cow! Like watching, do ya?'

Lizzie took sidesteps, feeling her way along the wall with the flats of her hands. 'I was out here first. I didn't know you were going to come out and start that nonsense right next to me, did I?'

'Well now you 'ave, what you gonna do about it?'

She sensed by the way his body was looming over hers that he had his own ideas about what she should do. She made a movement as if to leave. 'Excuse me. My boyfriend will be looking for me.'

Reggie Warren was hardly her boyfriend, but he was a good enough excuse. She tried to sidestep round the man blocking her way. He sidestepped too, countering her move.

'Let me pass.'

'Fair exchange is no robbery. Your bloke can 'ave that frigid cow that's just gone back in, and in exchange . . .' In the dim light, she fancied he licked his lips.

'Let me pass.'

'Not likely!'

He was so much bigger than her and when he lunged, wrapping his arms around her, it was like being hugged by a bear.

His lips were hard and cold upon hers and somehow, as he held her, one hand dropped on to her rump, tugging at her skirt. Cold air licked at the bare flesh above her stocking tops. She struggled for all she was worth, but his arms were huge and strong, his hands everywhere at once.

She tried to bring her knee up, to hit him where it would really hurt.

'Naughty,' he snarled, wrapping a huge hand around her neck and lifting her so that only her toes remained in contact with the ground. 'Do that again and I'll . . .'

Suddenly he was yanked backwards. Coughing, spluttering and clutching at her throat, Lizzie fell backwards too, hitting the wall of the building behind her before sliding to the ground. Her head swam. Her eyes closed. It was like being under water; she was out of breath and trying to get to the surface.

In her bleary state she heard a single, sickening thud, then a groan.

As she started to come to, she became aware again of a shadow falling over her. A hand reached for her. She hit it away.

'No! Leave me alone!'

'Randall? It's OK. He's out cold.'

The voice was familiar. As her reopened eyes adjusted to the darkness, she recognized the features of Wing Commander Guy Hunter.

Seventeen

'A letter for his dear mama,' said Edgar as he came into the kitchen holding a handful of post. He handed Mary Anne a single letter, keeping the rest for himself.

Mary Anne stopped stirring the leek and potato soup she was making and looked at the handwriting. Definitely Harry. This was the first letter she'd received from him in over a month. The thought turned her mind back to the last time she'd seen her son, when his leave had ended. She remembered clearly what she had said – something about her always standing in railway stations since the start of the war. She'd also remembered stamping her feet against the cold.

Harry had said something noncommittal like, 'That's wars for you.'

He had said very little indeed that day. Mary Anne had eyed him worriedly. Something had changed between them. So far she hadn't come right out and asked him what the problem was – if there was one. Perhaps she was imagining it.

It was a week after that when Stanley blurted out the truth. He'd come in upset because someone had stolen his roller skates. He blamed his father then went on to tell her the reason why he suspected him.

'It's Dad!' he wailed. 'Harry called him a pig 'cos he was dancing with Mrs Young and drinking again. I was there. I saw it all.'

After seeing him on Christmas Day, it came as no surprise to Mary Anne to be told that he was back on the booze. To be told that he'd been dancing with Biddy was a little harder to swallow.

'Are you telling me the truth?' she'd said, bending down and shaking him by the shoulders.

Everything about that day had come tumbling out. Harry

had sworn Stanley to secrecy, but the young lad, not quite eleven, couldn't keep it in – not once he was questioned by his mother.

Mary Anne had immediately taken pen to paper. Late at night, a time when she could think straight and there was no one else around, she sat down and wrote an apology and an explanation to her eldest son. At the same time she did the same to Daw and a third letter to Lizzie. They all had to know. What point was there in doing otherwise? And so she'd explained about Edward going off to war, leaving her in the family way, and then how she'd been sent away to give birth, and forced to give the baby away and marry an oblivious Henry.

After turning the gas off and taking off her apron, she made her way to where a handsome wickerwork chair caught the light from the window. Fearfully, she prodded the paper until the letter lay in her hand. Merely unfolding it sent shivers down her spine. Her heart was in her mouth.

The letter contained three paragraphs. She read through quickly, finally returning to the second paragraph, the most important of all.

> *It felt strange being the eldest son one minute, and the next being the second son. A few words describe how it was: cheated, abandoned, unloved, untrusted. All of those words count towards my feelings, but when I wrote them down and reread them again and again, only one word described my behaviour – selfish. It was selfish of me to react as I did, not to think how you must have felt when Edward did not return. I cannot even begin to imagine how it must have felt to give your firstborn away. You have loved and lived through all our growing pains, never condemning us for what we had grown into – me most of all.*

Lizzie had already written back telling her about her friend Bessie who was pregnant and engaged. A wedding date had been set before the bridegroom got his marching orders. She said little about having a sibling she'd known nothing about, except to say that there would probably be a lot more women left in that state if this war went on for much longer. She could say little about what she was doing, but just enough to let her mother know that she was doing fine and had met some very interesting people.

> *Before we know it, thousands of American troops will be over here as well. Imagine the birth rate when they arrive! I've met a Canadian, but that's not quite the same thing is it. But he's very nice.*

Strangely enough, those few words were enough to worry Mary Anne. There was so much that could not be said and her thoughts turned to Patrick. Patrick loved Lizzie. She was in no doubt about that. Lizzie hadn't really said anything in her letter about being enamoured of this 'very nice' person. In fact all she'd said was that he was *nice*. That was what fuelled Mary Anne's imagination.

Suddenly wearied by all the disturbance around her, she lay her head back against the cool leather and closed her eyes. Everything was so unsettled. With the exception of Stanley, her children were scattered to the four corners. Of course Daw wasn't that far away, but there had been an atmosphere between them ever since Mary Anne had left her father and set up home with Michael. Daw liked the world around her to be at peace with itself. She easily turned a blind eye to things she didn't want to see – hence she had never accepted that her father had acted violently towards her mother. She never would.

Behind her closed lids, she dreamed of the day when she would have her own home again. Michael would be in it and so would her children.

Her son's flat was exquisite, but although Edgar was kindness itself, she was not at home here. It was too crisp, too clean, without the gathered clutter of a lifetime – of more than one person's lifetime.

A frown creased her forehead as she thought about Henry. She'd been right not to believe that he'd changed. The thought of what might have happened, of the life she would have returned to, sent a shiver down her spine.

If only, if only . . . It would be so easy to break down and cry, but she couldn't. She had Stanley to consider. He hadn't always been a healthy child. He still needed looking out for and she knew from experience that he wouldn't rely on his father.

She remembered one terrible time when Henry had been brutalizing her in the privacy of their bedroom. He'd ripped at her clothes and taken her forcibly and in a bestial fashion. Only they hadn't been doing it in private; Stanley had been watching from the doorway.

The sudden clump-clump of Stanley climbing the stairs brought her back to the present.

She could see from his pained expression that something bad had happened.

'I took off me roller skates so I could play football with me mates. Brian was going to be in goal because he's got his leg in plaster and he can block the goalmouth, so I put me skates behind him. And someone took them! Someone took them!' He looked and sounded totally distraught.

Mary Anne sighed. 'This war. It's making saints of some and sinners of others.'

Stanley looked at her in disbelief, not quite understanding what she was saying. He screwed up his face and rubbed his hand through his sweaty hair. 'Why are so many bad things happening, Mum? Is it me dad doing it all?'

Mary Anne's answer caught in her throat. Many bad things had happened, but were they really down to Henry? Or were some of the things – like mislaying Mathilda in her pushchair – purely coincidence?

She got up from the chair. 'We'll go out and look for them. Someone might have picked them up by mistake.'

Deep down she knew there was little chance of finding them, but she had to do her best for her son, just as she tried to do her best for all her children. She'd spent years trying to please Henry, but all to no avail. Michael had been her departure from living for others, but there were still occasions when they took precedence.

They passed Edgar on the stairs. He had a flower shop not far from Eastville bus depot. He was young but had a bad heart, one reason why he did not participate in very strenuous war work, but instead ran first-aid courses and rolled bandages for the Red Cross.

'Good evening, Mrs Randall. I've brought you these.' He handed her a bunch of snowdrops and crocus.

Mary Anne bent her head to smell them. 'That's very kind of you, Edgar. They're lovely, really lovely.'

He looked from mother to son. 'Are you going out somewhere? If you are, I can put them in water for you until you get back.'

'That's very kind of you. Someone's taken Stanley's roller skates.'

Edgar sighed. 'A sign of the times. You wouldn't believe what people get up to in the blackout. I'm surprised more people don't get murdered. And the thieving!' He rolled his eyes dramatically as he took back the flowers that he'd only just given her. 'I'll deal with these.'

The door had slammed shut, so she left him rummaging for his keys. 'Oh no! I've lost them.' He continued to hunt in each pocket.

Mary Anne stopped and turned round. Stanley tugged at her sleeve. 'Come on, Mum. It'll be dark soon.'

'Just a minute,' said Mary Anne. 'I've got my key handy.'

Edgar continued to mumble and search his pockets, his right hand diving from one side to the other, his left holding on to the bunch of flowers.

'We won't be long,' Mary Anne called to him over her shoulder as she followed Stanley down the stairs.

Twilight was fast turning into night by the time they were out in the street. Fifteen minutes or so and total darkness would descend.

They searched where Stanley had been playing football and asked the few people still out and about whether they'd seen anyone carrying such objects. No one had.

Finding them was always going to be a fruitless task, but Mary Anne couldn't let Stanley know that. She was determined to do her best, to make up for . . . The thought came unbidden into her head, yet she knew beyond doubt that it was always there. She was always trying to make up for the fact that she'd taken up with Michael. She'd run bleeding and battered from Henry and fallen into Michael's shop doorway. It had been months before she'd seen Stanley again. The guilt had never quite gone away, and yet Stanley showed no sign of condemnation – on the contrary he had seemed to accept the situation totally.

A thick fog began to descend. What with that and the

blackout, it wouldn't be long before they couldn't see their hands in front of their faces.

Mary Anne put her arm around Stanley's shoulder. 'I'm sorry, pet, but we have to go back. This is hopeless.'

With slumped shoulders, his hands slung hopelessly in his pockets, Stanley dragged his feet all the way back. Darkness came down like a thick blanket. Mary Anne firmed her grip around Stanley's shoulders. A few feet apart and they wouldn't see each other at all.

Southern Mansions, where Harry had his flat, had an apron frontage of black and white tiles and pillars on either side of the door. The white tiles gave them some idea of where they were. Mary Anne kept looking downwards ahead of her feet. The tiles must be here somewhere.

Just as she spotted the small white squares, the door ahead opened. Someone rushed out, almost knocking her over. Still clinging to Stanley, she gasped as the figure swept past. She narrowed her eyes in an effort to see who he was and where he was going. It was useless. The blackness swallowed him as though he'd never existed.

'Quickly,' she said to Stanley.

There was no obvious reason for them to ascend the stairs at break-neck speed, just an inner feeling that something was badly wrong.

'Wait here,' she said to Stanley once they were on the landing. He didn't argue for once, perhaps because her fear was apparent on her features.

The door to the flat was open. Light should have fallen out on to the landing, but it didn't. All was darkness.

Heart racing, she stepped inside.

'Edgar?'

'Here.'

His voice quivered from the direction of the sideboard, but she couldn't see him. She reached for the light switch. Edgar was crouched against the front of the sideboard. Blood was streaming from the side of his head.

'Oh my God!'

She raced for the bathroom and ran a scrupulously white flannel beneath the tap.

'Who did this?' she asked, dabbing at the cut in his temple.

'A very masculine man, no doubt. It's nothing new, but at

least he didn't call me Nancy Boy or any of the names I've been called in the past.' He gave a weak laugh. 'I quite expected him to. But he said nothing. That was what was so strange. He just came up behind me, punched me in the kidneys and hit me over the head.'

'A robber!' said Stanley, his eyes shining with gruesome excitement. 'He saw us go out and thought nobody was here!'

Mary Anne glanced around the apartment. No drawers or cupboard doors hung open, the tasteful watercolours still hung on the wall and the elegant porcelain and silver candlesticks still graced the mantelpiece.

'It doesn't look as though anything is missing.'

'He wasn't here long enough for that,' said Edgar, wincing as he shook his head.

It was then she noticed something poking out from beneath his ankle. She reached forward and picked up his door key. 'At least you found your key.'

'No. I didn't find it. He let himself in with it. And I didn't drop it, Mrs Randall. I *know* I didn't.'

She frowned.

Stanley's eyes shone like they did after a visit to the pictures. 'He stole it when you weren't looking. He knew where you lived and planned to break in and take all your money . . .'

'Stanley!'

'But Mum and me foiled him. We came back and—'

'Stanley! That's enough.'

'But it's exciting . . .'

Mary Anne gave him a good shaking. 'This isn't a Saturday-morning serial at the pictures, Stanley. It's for real. Edgar's been hurt. We need to call the police.'

Edgar became agitated. 'No! No. Don't do that.' He looked sheepish suddenly, his eyes full of sadness. He lowered his voice. 'You know what they're like with blokes like me.'

'That's silly,' said Stanley, reanimated now his mother had let go of him. 'We could tell him about that man we bumped into outside. We could describe him.'

Mary Anne felt goose bumps break out all over her body. The man they'd bumped into had been in such a hurry he had almost knocked them over.

'Stanley's right. We did bump into a man, but it was dark.'

Suddenly Edgar grabbed her hand. 'Please. Don't go to the police. I'll be alright. Honest I will.'

He winced as she helped him to his feet, coughed and wiped his mouth with the back of his hand. His fist was spattered with blood.

'You should see a doctor. You said he hit you in the kidneys.'

Edgar shook his head emphatically. 'No. I'm alright.' That weak laugh again. 'It's just one of life's little troubles.'

'Can I ask you something?' said Mary Anne, a sudden thought crossing her mind. 'Do you get these little troubles when Harry's around?'

A warm smile spread across Edgar's face; admiration for Mary Anne's son shone in his eyes. 'Never. Harry has powerful business partners – if you know what I mean.'

Mary Anne nodded. It wasn't often she admitted, even to herself, that Harry was not quite as upright and honest as she would have liked him to be. She wouldn't be wearing new stockings and eating brisket on Sunday if that was the case. Harry knew people and some of them were downright dangerous to know.

Eighteen

The bell above the shop door jangled as Mary Anne entered. Daw was behind the counter sorting out ration coupons. She looked surprised and also less than happy to see her mother.

'Busy then?' said Mary Anne as brightly as she could.

Daw frowned and held her head to one side. 'I wasn't expecting you.'

Mary Anne shrugged and held on to her smile. 'I haven't seen Mathilda for a while. I expect she's grown.'

Daw nodded. Her lips were tightly pressed together and she was having trouble meeting her mother's eyes.

It had been a few months since Mary Anne had last seen

her granddaughter. The thought of holding that soft little body sent a thrill through her own.

'If you're busy I can take her for a walk in her pushchair.'

Daw jerked her attention away from the coupons. 'And lose her like you did before?'

Mary Anne's mouth fell open. She hadn't told Daw about what had happened. No family member had done so, because no family member knew.

'Who told you?'

'Never mind who told me,' said Daw, her tone totally devoid of warmth.

A sick feeling came into Mary Anne's stomach. 'Can I see her?'

'She's asleep,' Daw snapped.

Mary Anne hung her head and a tear squeezed out from the corners of her eyes.

'Daw, I haven't seen her for quite a while. I'm really missing her.'

Daw glared. 'And you think I should consider your feelings?'

And this is my daughter, thought Mary Anne, eyeing the dark hair and eyes. Henry's daughter, her father through and through.

Just as Mary Anne turned to go, the shop door was pushed open. A woman in a tweed coat went straight to the counter demanding a piece of cheese and waving her ration book.

At the same time John's Auntie Maria came through from the living accommodation at the back of the shop with Mathilda in her arms.

'Ah, Mary Anne,' Auntie Maria cried, her round, dark features creasing with joy. 'Look,' she said, turning to the cherubic child in her arms. 'It is your grandmother.'

'I'll take her,' snapped Daw even though she was halfway through serving the woman with cheese.

'You carry on,' said Auntie Maria in her firm, unflappable manner. 'I want to talk to your mother and Mathilda wishes to see her grandmother.'

Mary Anne almost cried with joy as she took the child from the warm woman's arms. For some reason, Daw rarely contradicted John's aunt and uncle; perhaps it was because she lived on the premises. Whatever it was, Mary Anne had no intention of looking a gift horse in the mouth.

'Come on my sweet,' she said to Mathilda, cooing in her ear and kissing her cheek. Carrying the child in her arms, she followed Maria into the back of the shop.

Behind the counter, where the till tinkled with coins and the bacon slicer took up most of the room, was the cosy living room where they'd eaten their Christmas dinner.

Knitted cardigans and smock dresses hung drying on a line suspended above nuggets of glowing coke. The mantelpiece was high and decorated with a length of red chenille trimmed with matching bobbles.

Maria went into the kitchen to put the kettle on. 'I wanted to have a little chat with you,' she called over her shoulder. 'I think Daw is being led astray.'

Mary Anne heard her but was too engrossed with her granddaughter to fully take in what exactly Maria had said. The big blue eyes and the winning smile had captured her full attention.

'What was that you said?'

Maria repeated it and added, 'I've tried to reason with her, but she's having none of it.' Maria shook her head. 'It is not right that a daughter should be that way with her mother.'

As the words began to sink in, Mary Anne's attention was diverted from the lovely child she held in her arms and she had to ask Maria to repeat herself again.

Maria sighed and took a sip of her tea. 'I was saying that Daw is being influenced by some "friend" who is saying that you have a bad reputation and should not be bothered with. She says that not content with living in sin with one man, you are now living in sin with another.'

It was like being socked in the jaw – and she'd had some of that from Henry in her time so she knew how it felt. In fact this was worse. Daw was so different from her other daughter, Lizzie, but she'd never been downright vindictive. And yet, if what Maria said was to be believed, she was being so now.

'That's not true! I'm living in Harry's flat. She knows Harry has a flat he shares with his friend, Edgar. And Stanley is there with me. He can swear that I'm telling the truth.'

Maria tutted and shook her head. 'Daw tends to pick the bits of truth that she wants to believe. When she sets her mind on something, nothing anyone else says can make her change it.'

'Just like her father.'

'So I understand.'

'And yet this friend is influencing her judgement. I'm surprised.'

Between sips of tea, Maria took down the baby clothes from the line, folding then caressing each item to flatness.

'This friend seems a right know-all and I for one do not like this person even though I have never met them.'

Mary Anne sighed deeply. 'And I suppose this friend told her I'd lost Mathilda that day.'

'I suppose so.'

She frowned. 'But who is this friend?'

She ran through all Daw's old friends in her mind. School friends, friends in the same street, friends where she'd worked in the tobacco factory; all different characters, but were any of them nasty?

'I can't believe this,' said Mary Anne, shaking her head. 'Who could it be?'

Maria spread her hands, palms upwards, her shrug signifying that she did not know.

'I tried asking her, but she was very closed about it. Said it was none of my business. I've got a feeling he may be an air-raid warden.' She patted Mary Anne's hand. 'Up until this war started, this world was ruled by men. I think it will be different once it is over. Us women are entitled to live a happy life. I understand what you did and why you did it. Visit me on those days when I look after Mathilda when Daw attends the First-Aid Centre. It is cruel to try and separate you from your grandchild. I will not have it.'

Eyes brimming with tears, Mary Anne kissed the top of Mathilda's head and thanked her good fortune for the likes of John Smith's Auntie Maria.

'I should go,' she said.

Maria raised both her hands and signalled that Mary Anne should sit back down. 'Not so quickly. How about we go for a walk in the park? It's windy out, but it's dry.'

Mary Anne jerked her head towards the door dividing the living accommodation from the shop.

'What about Daw?'

Maria's face lit up with childish wickedness. 'Wait a moment.'

She got up, opened the door just a crack, and peered through. Noiselessly, she shut it again.

'She's still serving Mrs Draper. The woman takes forever to make up her mind, and even once she's bought all she wants, she watches like a hawk as you cut out her coupons. Come on. Wrap up the baby. The pram's out the back. I'll get my coat.'

Mary Anne couldn't help giggling as the two middle-aged women ran along the pavement away from the shop, the child chortling with glee as the pram bounced over the kerb and on to the cobbles.

Victoria Park was not as it used to be. The smell of turned earth and growing vegetables had replaced the smell of pre-war flowers, but the trees were still there, the first buds of spring bright green on their branches. Men in navy-blue dungarees were digging or watering fresh green vegetables. Even children were helping out, picking sprouts or using a trowel to pull weeds from around the precious plants.

The fresh air was exhilarating and John's aunt chatted merrily about times gone by and what Italy had been like when she and John's mother were children.

'But that was before the war,' she sighed. 'It is far behind us.'

As Mary Anne pulled Mathilda's blanket a little higher around the cherry-pink face, a thought occurred to her.

'I think I have something that used to belong to your sister – perhaps to you too.'

'Oh?' Maria eyed her quizzically.

'Yes,' said Mary Anne, and went on to tell her about the time John had come to borrow money against a silver crucifix that she'd guessed had belonged to his mother.

'He'd wanted the money for Daw's engagement and wedding ring. I gave him the money but never sold the cross on. I couldn't do it somehow. I kept thinking that one day he might want it back.'

'You have this?' said Maria, her eyes shining.

'You remember it?'

Maria clapped her hands together. 'Of course I do!'

'Michael found it in the ruins of the pawn shop. I still have it.' She turned and looked with gratitude into Maria's dark eyes. 'You've been so kind to me. You must have it back.'

Maria's eyes brimmed with tears. 'It is a pleasure. I cannot thank you enough.'

They sat on a park bench. Mathilda was sitting up, observing everything with unusual interest.

'She's a lovely child,' said Maria.

Mary Anne murmured a reply. Her eyes were elsewhere, her attention caught by a man in a trench coat walking along the path at the side of the bowling green. She fancied he had been staring at them.

Nineteen

Lizzie and the wing commander had been travelling between airfields, 'co-ordinating events' as Hunter liked to call it, when he'd spotted a dog fight in the distance.

Streaks of white vapour trail criss-crossed the sky as the Messerschmitt and the Spitfire locked horns above the English countryside. In their midst was a low-flying bomber, the bone of contention between the two.

Hunter got out a pair of binoculars. Lizzie shaded her eyes with her hand.

'They're chasing the bomber.'

'Correction,' Hunter said slowly. 'The Spitfire is chasing the bomber. The Messerschmitt is trying to protect it.' He paused, mouth slightly open, eyes glued to the binoculars.

'Damn!'

'Is he down? Have the Germans got him?'

'No.' Hunter sounded surly. 'There should be more up there protecting him. We need more planes. More men.'

His voice drifted away. The bomber flew overhead, the German in hot pursuit, determined to protect his charge. The RAF Spitfire harried him all the way.

The planes flew some way distant. There was a staccato

burst of gunfire, and then a plume of white as one plane hit the earth. It was hard to tell which one. For a moment they both stood there, each wrapped up in their thoughts.

'Well,' said Hunter. 'That's it. There's nothing we can do. Ground forces will deal with it now. Let's find a pub.'

'I hope the pilot's safe,' said Lizzie, the gearbox making a crunching sound as she pushed the stick into first gear.

'I hope he is too. Good pilots are hard to find – and so, may I point out to you, are good gearboxes. Treat it gently, will you?'

Lizzie smiled. 'Yes, sir.'

Things between she and Wing Commander Hunter had changed since his knight-in-shining-armour act outside Lavenham guildhall. He'd taken her to a village pub afterwards and bought her a brandy to steady her nerves.

'I should have put him on a charge,' he'd said at the time.

Lizzie had gulped at the brandy and nodded. 'Yes sir.'

'I should have put you on one as well.'

'Me?' She'd stared at him in amazement. 'What are you saying? That I was partly to blame?'

'Of course you were. It wouldn't have happened if you'd come to collect me as I'd requested.'

That was when their relationship had changed. His eyes had twinkled when he'd smiled. He'd made her feel like a very weak-kneed Scarlett O'Hara to his rakish Rhett Butler. His smile was like that. His looks were even better. What was it about blue eyes and dark hair? Such a contrast. And that voice, that husky sound from deep down in the throat, allied with an accent that was American and yet at the same time not quite American.

He'd walked her back to the dorm that night and told her he'd made arrangements for her to be billeted at Ainsley Hall.

'For my convenience,' he'd said with a smile.

Her heart had fluttered like a butterfly trying to escape a glass prison. Convenient for her as his driver, or for something else entirely? And of course, she would miss Margot and the others.

There was no point in protesting; at least, that was what she told herself. The plain fact was that she had no compunction to protest. Wicked though it seemed, the war was proving to be an adventure. Where would she be now if not for the war? Someone's wife? A mother? Or still in service and seeing Peter Selwyn Kendall on Wednesday afternoons?

The pub they found today was called the Robin Hood.

'Do you think he drank here?' asked Guy, scanning the bar as if half expecting the outlaw of Sherwood to be sat sipping a beer.

Lizzie laughed. 'Possibly. I shouldn't have thought it's changed much since his day.' She took off her cap and slid on to the seat of a high-backed oak settle that was scarred with age. It was hard to tell exactly what was burning in the huge inglenook fireplace – logs mostly – but fuel being hard to come by, it could be peat and even dried cowpats, judging by the smell.

'So,' he said, returning with two halves of farmhouse cider. 'Tell me about yourself.'

The boldness of his look made her blush and lower her eyes.

'There's not much to tell. I mean, where do I start? In my childhood, with my parents?'

'If you like. Tell you what, let me tell you about mine. My father is the manager of a canning factory in Hamilton, Ontario – that's just a spit and a hop from the Great Lakes and the border with the United States. My mom used to be a nurse, but she stays home now. She's collected a menagerie of animals over the years and they take up most of her time. The nursing experience comes in handy – you know, pregnant pussy cats and chickens with ingrown toenails.'

Lizzie's jaw dropped. 'Chickens haven't got toes.'

'True,' he said, grimacing after taking a sip of the greenish liquid which seemed to be laced with splinters of wood and apple pips. He lowered his voice. 'Is this really for drinking or should you be cleaning the car with it?'

Lizzie giggled. 'Farmhouse cider is always strong and rough. It's the way they make it. I've heard some grim stories regarding the ingredients. Really grim!'

He eyed her enquiringly. 'Like what?'

She shook her head. 'You wouldn't want to know.'

'Try me.'

'Rats!'

'You're kidding!'

'No. It's said to add flavour if a rat falls in.'

He'd only just taken another sip. With a rueful expression he put it back on the table and pushed it away.

'I think I'll pass.'

Like two adolescents they made faces and spoke in quiet whispers. Lizzie couldn't believe the difference in their relationship since they'd first met. He'd been cold and standoffish; she'd reacted by putting his attitude down to class, rank and his being foreign. Did being a Canadian count as foreign? She supposed it did in some quarters, but to her Guy Hunter was becoming far from foreign – in fact he was getting too close for comfort.

'Do all the animals have names?' she asked now.

He nodded. 'Milly, Molly and Mandy.'

She laughed, recognizing the characters from much-loved childhood books.

He talked a lot about the lakes, the forests and a trip he'd done to Niagara.

'Thunder falls. That's what it should be called,' he said. 'The sound of the water tumbling over the rocks is deafening.'

'It all sounds wonderful,' she said, her imagination racing with visions of high mountains, vast lakes and wide blue skies. He told her of the snow in winter, far deeper than even Scotland ever had.

'This land is too flat,' he said, jerking his head towards the tiny windows to the flat expanse of fields, ditches and sky.

Not for the first time in her life, Lizzie was mesmerized by a man from a different background than she.

But this is different.

The affair with Peter was in the past. She wasn't really sure that Peter had considered himself better than her, but his mother certainly had. It had taken a war, a blizzard and time apart to open her eyes to the truth. The other obvious difference between Peter and Guy was that the former had hidden away rather than join the armed forces. Guy had already been a flier; he'd told her so and his rank was emblazoned on his uniform.

'And you? Is it flat where you come from?'

She lowered her eyes and fiddled with her glass as she thought of her home town. Row upon row of red-brick terraces, the chimneys of W. D. & H. O. Wills, the soap factory, the trams rattling along East Street where the buildings blocked out the light. In her mind's eye she hurried along past the shops, over Bedminster Bridge and up Redcliffe Hill.

'We have a lot of historic buildings in Bristol – or at least we did until the Luftwaffe dropped bombs on it. A lot of the buildings were black and white and dated from Elizabethan times – nearly five hundred years ago. But there are still a lot of old buildings clustered around St Mary Redcliffe Church. It was the favourite church of Queen Elizabeth the First, you know.'

'Was it really?'

She paused. Was that mockery she detected in his voice? She looked into his eyes. It seemed that he was looking at her with great interest. A sudden spark seemed to ignite between them and history had nothing to do with it.

'I think we should see each other socially,' he said, the timbre of his voice turning her legs to jelly. 'We work together. Why not play together?'

Never in a month of Sundays would she ever have envisaged something like this happening. It was like being struck by lightning – not that she ever had been, but there was always a first time. And this was it. She was sure of it.

'We're both far away from our families,' Guy went on. His smile was wide and warm. 'What's the harm in going for a picnic or a pint?' He grimaced suddenly and tapped a brawny finger at the remains of his drink. 'Unless you're drinking this stuff,' he said with a grin.

Lizzie's gaze stayed fixed on his fingers, especially his ring finger. There it was, a band of gold that she'd never noticed before, a blatant declaration that he was married and had no business meeting her socially. Her spirits took a dive. Then the old wartime mantra came back to save them.

But we could be dead tomorrow.

There were considerations, but she shoved them to one side. Her mind was made up. Their eyes met. His smile lessened, becoming almost quizzical as though he too were asking himself a question and deciding on the best reply.

'Yes. I'm married. I'll make no bones about it.' He looked down at the table top before taking her hand in his. 'This war is set to get worse. Who knows where we'll be one year from now. The lives of thousands of people are in my hands. I need some kind of solace. If you allow me to lean on you, I'll allow you to lean on me. Do you agree?'

'I'm engaged,' she blurted suddenly.

It wasn't quite true, but in a strange kind of way, she was meeting him halfway. They both had other lives, other people who figured strongly in them. But they'd been thrown together. Here, in this place, there was just the two of them.

'But I think we both need someone,' she said.

He nodded and reached for his glass. 'Let's drink to that,' he said, forgetting just how potent – and disgusting – the cider tasted.

Lizzie took a gulp and made a face. They'd both swallowed too much of the strong brew and ended up spluttering and laughing at each other across the table top. Suddenly, he leaned across and kissed her on the forehead. 'Champagne next time.'

Taken by surprise, she stared at him, her face warm and red from the fire. 'I've never drunk champagne.'

'Then it's about time you did.'

Lizzie's new billet at Ainsley Hall had wooden shutters on the inside, a window seat and the most glorious furniture she'd ever seen. A large number of the rooms most suited for office space had been stripped of valuable furniture. Except for the attic rooms that had been turned into dormitories, the bedrooms had been left intact.

Her mouth had dropped open when she'd seen the four-poster bed, the heavy coverlets and the tapestries hanging on the panelled walls.

'You should see it,' she said to Bessie when they met up in the mess back at base. 'It's big enough to sleep a family.'

'Or just two people,' said Bessie. 'That's nice, isn't it?'

She didn't sound as though she really thought it nice. In fact she sounded very gloomy.

It wasn't instinct or insight that prompted Lizzie's conclusion as to why Bessie was acting this way. It was just a guess – the right one as it turned out.

'It's Arthur isn't it?'

Bessie nodded and buried her face in her hands. The pancakes on her plate dulled as they cooled. Wartime flour wasn't quite what it used to be – a bit like them really, she supposed.

Fearing he'd been shot down or bombed, Lizzie reached for her friend's hand. 'Oh, Bessie. I'm so sorry.'

Bessie shrugged.

'Is he . . .?' She looked to Margot for explanation. Margot rolled her eyes and regarded Bessie as though she were the daftest person she'd ever met. 'Married,' she said with an air of finality.

'Married!' Lizzie could hardly believe it. 'Oh lordy!'

'I tried to tell you, Bessie. I told you I'd heard rumours,' said Margot.

Bessie looked at her with blazing eyes. 'Oh, yes! You told me! You told me he already had someone. But you didn't tell me he was married!'

Margot shrugged. 'I hardly thought a man who proposed getting engaged and therefore married had already tied the knot. I just said I'd heard rumours. Anyway, why didn't you ask him yourself? Why get in the family way first then ask questions afterwards?

Lizzie remained quiet. She told herself that it wouldn't happen to her. She also told herself that she was going into this arrangement with Wing Commander Guy Hunter with her eyes wide open.

Margot followed her outside. 'I prefer smoking outside,' she said on seeing Lizzie's look. 'I'm not prying. Honestly I'm not.'

'I didn't say you were.'

'Good.'

Margot leaned against the wall behind her and lit up. The smoke rose blue and curling like a gradually drawn-out spring.

'So what's with your wing commander? Is he married?'

Lizzie nodded but couldn't bring herself to meet Margot's silently asked question.

Margot sighed. 'My major isn't and I'm afraid we're going to have to do the obvious. We're going to get married. You're the first to know.'

'Oh, Margot, I'm so happy for you,' said Lizzie, throwing her arms around her neck.

Margot grinned and for the first time ever, Lizzie saw her cheeks turn blush pink. 'And I'm not pregnant,' Margot added.

Lizzie's gaze drifted back to Bessie. 'What do you think she'll do?'

Margot shrugged. 'What can she do? Her chap's done a double cross. It's his poor wife I feel sorry for. She could divorce him, I suppose, but then there's the stigma. People tend to point one out. But then, it won't be the last marriage to break up before this war is over.'

No, thought Lizzie. *Probably not, and although I should go to Guy and stop this right now, I can't. I'm drawn to him. I want him and there is nothing I can do about it.*

Something about what Lizzie was thinking must have showed in her expression. 'You know what's going to happen, don't you?' said Margot. 'You're going to fall in love and you're going to want him to divorce his wife and marry you.'

'Of course I won't.'

Margot sucked on her cigarette holder, silently holding Lizzie's faltering gaze.

That night she dreamed she was at a double wedding where there was only one groom and two brides. One of them was her. The other was Guy's wife. She woke up tangled in the bedclothes, like a moth caught in a web.

Her guilt went with her to breakfast. There was a letter awaiting her from Patrick. If anyone was going to make her feel guilty it would be Patrick. She'd promised him so much. Half of her still wanted to hold true to that promise. The other more curious half wanted to tread an unknown and more dangerous path. Only time would tell which one she would choose.

Twenty

Mary Anne jerked upright in that state between sleeping and waking, when the line is thin between what is real and what is not.

Her first thought was that someone had shaken her shoulder and was standing over her. One glance at the curtains billowing into the room and the open window swinging on its hinges and reality reasserted itself. The nightmare was broken, though the shadowy figure that followed her in daylight still lingered somewhere at the back of her mind.

Satisfied she was definitely in the real world, she got out

of bed and crossed the room. The bedroom lino was cold beneath her feet and the breeze from the window pleasantly crisped the film of sweat that covered her body.

Once the window was closed she got back into bed. Pulling the green satin eiderdown up to her chin she gazed at the lampshade and the black shadow it threw across the ceiling. Turning on to her side she heaved the eiderdown even higher, closed her eyes and wished Michael was still here and that the war had never happened.

Everything will be all right in the morning, she told herself. *Get to sleep.*

She finally fell asleep and slept fitfully, semi-alert in case the dream returned.

In the morning she had butterflies. She eyed her reflection in the bathroom mirror, alarmed to see that her expression confirmed what she felt. The fine brows were arched and the brown eyes were luminous – a little excited, a little afraid. She knew very well that both the nightmare and the butterflies were left over from an unhappy marriage when apprehension had developed into something more, an intuition that was always right and always frightening.

'Were you having a nightmare?' Edgar asked at breakfast as he ladled porridge into three dishes. He'd given up the big bed to her and Stanley and had moved into the smaller box room. Edgar was kindness itself.

'Did I shout out?'

'Yes!' said Stanley.

Mary Anne frowned at him. 'So where were you?'

'I slept on the settee out here. Don't you remember?'

His mother rubbed at her eyes. She was so tired of lying awake, worrying about everything and anything. Her immediate concern was still about living somewhere safe. She'd thought that here in her son's flat would have been safe enough. Now, since Edgar had been attacked, she wasn't so sure.

She took a spoonful of porridge and sipped at the tea Edgar had poured out for her. 'This is very good of you,' she said. 'But I still feel I'm an inconvenience.'

He looked quite shocked. 'Of course you're not! You're Harry's mother!'

It amused her to hear him say it in that way, as a daughter-in-law might say it to her husband's mother. She wondered if the similarities were more obvious when the two of them were alone. She wouldn't ask. The social taboos were still in place. What they did together physically was still a crime. Overall she would prefer not to know.

She took another spoonful of the porridge, wondering at how he managed to make it taste so sweet with sugar being so scarce.

'That was lovely,' said Stanley, his spoon clattering in his dish. He glanced at his mother and Edgar, and then swiftly, before anyone had time to object, he gripped the dish with both hands and licked it clean.

His mother swiped the pristine dish from his hands. 'Now off to school. I'll see you in the morning.'

It was Friday and he would be staying with his father tonight. At first he'd protested that he wouldn't stay there any more – some childhood memories were too difficult to overcome – but the promise of a regular fish and chip supper had swayed his loyalty. To his credit, Henry resisted the drink on a Friday night. Mary Anne had instilled in Stanley that should his father succumb to the beer, he was to come home straight away or knock at Biddy's door. Not that Biddy was much better than Henry nowadays. From what Harry had told her, she was enjoying herself, having a stout or two of an evening and entertaining gentlemen callers. But she wouldn't see Stanley mistreated, in that at least Biddy was above board.

Mary Anne straightened Stanley's tie, patted his collar flat and smoothed his jacket. He was using Lizzie's old bicycle to get to school. It was a fair distance, but everyone was putting themselves out at the moment, even the children.

'Another cup of tea?' asked Edgar.

She nodded, wrapping both hands around the warm china. She found herself wishing for time to fly by, for this war to be over, for things to be calmer. Most of all she wanted Michael home again.

'Why do you think that man was here the other night?' she asked Edgar.

'I told you why.'

'Will he come back?'

'Possibly. Harry says I'm to get in touch with some friends of his if he does. They'll sort it out.' He raised his eyebrows.

Mary Anne didn't need him to explain what he meant.

Edgar caught her frowning. 'Anything wrong, Mrs Randall?'

Her hand trembled as she tucked a stray wisp of hair behind her ear. 'I'm not sure that it was you he was after.'

He waited for her to continue.

She gulped down her fear and listed all the things that had happened. 'First there was the pawn shop burning down, then there was Mathilda going missing, then Patrick being framed for looting, then a letter being sent to the Red Cross shop. After we came here, Stanley's skates went missing and you got attacked. And all in a period of a few months. Is that enough?'

Edgar frowned. 'If they're not coincidence, then who's responsible?'

Mary Anne shook her head. 'I don't know. All I worry about is that if I'm right, what might this person do next? Murder us in our beds?'

'So that was the reason for the nightmare?'

She nodded.

The sound of the post falling through the letterbox made her start. Edgar fetched it.

'Two for you,' he said, his face beaming. She thanked him and mused that he got almost as excited as she did when her children or Michael wrote.

The first was from Michael. An increased workload and sickness amongst staff meant he wouldn't get leave for a while. *Perhaps not until May . . .*

May! Another month. She sighed, her heart momentarily lifted by the words he wrote. The fact that he'd held this same piece of paper she was reading was strangely comforting, but nothing could compensate for his physical presence. She looked up, catching a glimpse of herself in the mirror hanging above the sideboard.

'You look gorgeous. Not a day over twenty-one,' said Edgar as if reading her thoughts.

She laughed. 'Go on with you.'

The second letter was from Patrick. She smiled as she began to read, anticipating that he'd included one of his poems. Patrick was one of those people greatly moved by their positive emotions such as love and happiness. He never wrote about sad things. But there were no poems and as she read on she began to understand why. He said he'd written to Lizzie telling her he was being posted abroad, but had received no reply. He asked Mary Anne whether she had heard, if everything was alright, if Lizzie was well. He also stated that he hoped to have leave in late summer.

It wasn't difficult to read into what he was really saying. *She hasn't written. Is there anyone else?*

Mary Anne frowned and stroked her cheek thoughtfully. She too had wondered why she'd received no letter from Lizzie. Deep down she knew that Patrick was right to be concerned. Lizzie was sometimes drawn to the wrong kind of man.

Edgar interrupted her thoughts. 'We've got kippers for tea tonight.'

'That's nice.'

She didn't ask him where they'd come from. Like Harry, he had a black market line to those in the know. Not all the supplies coming into Bristol Docks went to legitimate suppliers. That was how Harry could afford this place.

'I'll be off now,' said Edgar. 'I'm late already.'

Edgar was lucky enough to have an assistant to open and run his shop for him so could afford not to get in until ten if he liked.

'Got your day all planned?' he asked her.

She fingered the letter from Michael, feeling the crispness of the thin paper and finding that today it just wasn't enough to raise her spirits. A greater closeness was needed. She wanted him home before May.

'I'm going out shopping. I'll pick up some greens if I can. This afternoon I'll write some letters.'

After he'd gone, she washed the dishes, washed herself then put on her hat and coat. The weather was warmer, but she still had to make do with the brown tweed and black hat she'd worn all winter. Most of her clothes had been destroyed in the fire, but today she would go to the burned-out ruins one last time.

The black buttons on her coat were big, square and reflected the spring sunshine. She took a tram to Redcliffe Hill and walked from there, carefully averting her eyes as she passed the Red Cross shop. The women helping out there were a good sort and were doing a good job, but Gertrude was overbearing at times. She could make them very miserable indeed if she had half a mind to.

The front of the pawn shop had been boarded up so she went through the alley and around the back. The damage wasn't so bad at the back. The single tree in the centre of the yard was bright with buds. Its branches waved in the breeze. She fancied it was waving at her and smiling, welcoming her back.

Silly, she thought and turned her attention to the back of the building. The windows had also been boarded over, but the back door was still in situ and locked. She took the key out of her handbag.

The scullery was dark and smelled of blackened wood and plaster. The linoleum floor she'd once swept and polished was covered with dirt. She felt her way to the front of the living room and the corner cupboard. The smell was worse here, but the corner cupboard was still there, though its surface crumbled beneath her fingers.

Kneeling down, she ran her hands over the lower door until she found the smooth roundness of its china knob; gave it a tug and yanked the door open.

Something scuttled past her foot. She gasped. A mouse? Never mind. Mice couldn't harm you. Leave that to humans!

Amazingly, the interior of the cupboard was undamaged. Her fingertips ran over the top shelf and touched Michael's precious record collection. Her heart leapt with joy for his sake. Something of his uncle's *had* survived. She dropped her hand to the floor of the cupboard. As with the top shelf, nothing was missing. She found the box she was looking for, opened it and got out a candle and matches.

Her hand trembled as she lit it. Holding it aloft, the meagre flame flickered in a draught. A lump came to her throat as she beheld the blackened walls. In the corner the metal springs of the chaise longue hung on to what remained of its frame. Her gaze lingered. She remembered recuperating there after Michael had found her collapsed on his doorstep.

Scuffling and the sound of something tumbling down attracted her attention. A cat ran out from beneath the stairs. It disappeared through a gap in the floorboards, probably down into the cellar and out through the broken coal hatch.

The ground floor of the shop was open all the way to the rafters. The door to the front bedroom was still shut, just as she'd left it. Anyone stepping out would fall and break their neck.

Glass crunched underfoot as she made her way into the shop. The counter was still intact, though its mahogany top was a little scarred by the heat. The rest of the shop was totally devastated.

The wire cages protecting the most valuable items were twisted and bent. Charcoaled frames were all that remained of the glass-fronted cupboards. Smashed china and glass covered the floor. The strange thing was that the remains of watches and bits of silverware poked blackly through the debris. Why?

The answer was not long in coming; Michael was right. Whoever had started the fire wasn't interested in the goods stored here. It couldn't have been looters – and if it wasn't looters, who was it?

Twenty-One

Guy Hunter's life was a round of War Ministry meetings and airfield inspections. 'Call me a liaison officer,' he said when Lizzie asked him what he actually did.

She gained a little insight one day on a visit to an aerodrome. They'd driven straight into an enemy attack, and the sky above them was black with enemy bombers. They'd been caught in the melee and had been forced to take shelter in a deep trench protected by sandbag walls.

Running on her way to the trench, someone had shouted out that WAAFs and other women should go to their own shelter.

Guy had pushed her onwards. 'There's no bloody time for social niceties!'

The noise was ear-splitting. Lizzie cowered low, her tin hat fallen over one eye, her fingers in her ears. Guy's thigh brushed against hers and his hand was pressing on her back, pushing her downwards.

Murmurs of fear and anger eddied around her. Someone prayed. Someone sang in a very shaky voice.

The sound of fire bells succeeded that of the 'all clear'. Those who had survived crept from hiding and into a fiery hell.

Great plumes of black smoke billowed up into the sky from damaged hangars and buildings. Plumes of lesser density –

but far more worrying given the scarcity of airworthy planes – rose from the few fighters left on the ground.

'As if the lack of pilots wasn't bad enough,' muttered Guy.

Narrowing his eyes brought them into sharper contrast with his outdoor complexion. Someone could feel fear when he looked like that, Lizzie thought.

No one was given time to feel sorry for themselves. A staff sergeant bent over close by, spewing up whatever he'd had for breakfast that morning. A colleague asked him if he was alright.

Guy barked out an order. 'Of course he's OK. Now come on. Put these bloody fires out.'

The staff sergeant's reaction was instant and unexpected. His eyes glared with a mix of fear and anger. 'OK? *OK?* Don't you use no American terms here. The Yanks ain't in this war, late again like they were for the last lot.'

The wing commander's reaction was just as instant and just as unexpected. He grabbed the man by his jacket collar and dragged him to where the propeller of a burning Spitfire had been blown off to within feet of their shelter.

'Do you see that?' Still hanging on to the man with one hand, a very angry Guy pointed at the twisted piece of metal. 'That propeller's travelled a long way. Do you know that? It states its place of manufacture. Detroit, USA. So don't be so quick to condemn, Sergeant. Open your eyes and you might learn something!'

'Can you help here?' someone called out.

Lizzie turned to see a line of stockinged legs sticking out from beneath a tarpaulin. She ran over to where WAAFs were dealing with their dead, her thoughts in turmoil and her nerves taut.

'One of the women's shelters scored a bad one,' said a corporal with smudged cheeks and a ripped skirt.

Sometimes when she'd been asked to help out with things, Guy had intervened. Today he'd come into his own. He was now directing operations, asking questions about how many planes they had, how many pilots were still up, how much fuel there was, how many were dead . . . Too many.

The only damage to the car was a smashed headlight.

'Well that's something we don't use much anyway,' she said, sounding much more confident than she actually felt.

Guy was subdued. His jaw was set in a grim line. He was forthright, businesslike and obviously considering the day's events. Well, she decided, if he was being strong, then she must be likewise.

Dirty, tired and feeling as though she were made of brittle glass and would easily shatter, Lizzie got behind the wheel of the car. As darkness fell they began the drive back to Ainsley Hall.

The night was moonless and her head began to ache with the effort of driving through such absolute darkness. The one headlight they had left, muted as it was with black paint, made a poor show. Coming on top of such a frightening day, it wasn't long before the cracks began to show.

Losing track of the road, one wheel bounced on to the grass verge and just as quickly bounced back off again.

'For God's sake, woman! Watch where you're going!'

It was all too much. She jammed her foot to the floor. The car stalled.

'Don't yell at me!'

Falling forward on to the wheel, she burst into tears, her shoulders shaking in the aftermath of all that had happened.

She didn't see his reaction, the concern in his eyes and the guilty expression. She knew nothing until he had opened the car door and dragged her out into his arms.

He caressed the nape of her neck as she cried against his shoulder. 'I'm sorry, Lizzie. Now go on, cry. Let it all out.'

The tears were bad enough, but the trembling was worse, as though she'd been dipped in ice and only just pulled out.

'I'm due for some leave this weekend,' he said gently, kissing her ear. 'I think you are too.'

She was in no fit state to refuse his offer; her emotional state had become far weaker than her body. That night she lay in bed thinking about it. All the old conventions seemed to be breaking down. People were not daring to look beyond the here and now simply because tomorrow might never come. *So grab your happiness while you can* – was it Bessie that had said that? She didn't remember, and anyway, it didn't matter. Whatever she decided to do was up to her, but in the meantime she must find time to write, though carefully. Before putting pen to paper she would lock her feelings deep inside. Nothing about her relationship with Guy Hunter must show, as only time would tell where their relationship would lead.

The following day she got a letter from Margot saying that Bessie had now gone home.

> *Whether she'll keep her little bundle or not, I don't know. She did talk about having her adopted, but was undecided. She asked me to forward you her address and that of the nursing home she's booked for the big event . . .*

Tottenham. Bessie had gone home to Tottenham. Lizzie added the address to the back of her diary. When she got time, she'd write. Funnily enough it was going to be easier to write to her than to her own mother – and as for Patrick . . .

Twenty-Two

Stanley had only just left to cycle over to his father's when the brick arrived.

Edgar was working late at the flower shop; business had been slow due to the weather.

Mary Anne considered drawing the blackout curtains but decided to wait until dusk had melted into night. Although the lights of the city were long extinguished in order to hide its existence from the German air force, Mary Anne liked looking out. Before the war, lights from streetlamps, houses and advertisements had made the city glow. Now everything was grey. At twilight the sky too was grey, though a lighter shade than the chimney stacks sticking up into it. At ground level the streets heaved with bombed shops and offices, which were all that remained of Castle Street, Wine Street and the other old streets at the heart of the city.

The bombing of November 24th had been swift, heavy and frightening. The one thing in its favour had been the day of the week: Sunday. The shops had been closed. Only those unfortunate enough to live above them had been injured or killed. Hundreds would have been killed if the raid had come on a Saturday night when the shops were open till ten and people promenaded up and down the street.

A slight movement in her peripheral vision caught her eye. Someone had ducked into the bombed remains of the insurance offices at the end of the street. She glanced over her shoulder at the sound of the front door being opened, then returned her attention to the street. She looked to where she'd thought someone had been standing. There was nothing there now; just weeds and rubble.

She turned away, a ready smile on her face for when Edgar stuck his head around the door.

'Good evening,' he said, impeccable as always in a dark suit and tie.

Before she had a chance to answer, a brick came flying through the window.

'God, aren't the bombings enough?' she shouted.

She fell on to her knees, her hands clasped as though in prayer on the sofa in front of her.

Edgar crouched near the door through which he'd just entered, staring at the window. 'The bastards!'

He said it low and with feeling, his eyes glaring with hatred, or was it sheer anger?

Mary Anne stared at him open-mouthed. He saw the silent questioning in her eyes.

'They know Harry,' he said, as though that answered everything. Then with surprising swiftness he got to his feet. 'I have to go out.'

Mary Anne stared at the brick and the broken glass, too shocked to move.

He paused before leaving. 'Will you be alright?'

Her neck seemed stiff, too stiff to nod, and her chin trembled when she finally managed it.

'I won't be long. I'll get this sorted,' he said. 'Lock the door behind me.'

She didn't know how long she stayed staring at the brick, her knees aching on the hardness of the floor. Like notes made on a calendar, a diary of events was scrawled across her mind. The man who'd hit Edgar over the head, the feeling of being followed, and now this.

A nerve ticked beneath her right eye. Her shoulders began to tremble. She wanted to shout for Michael, but Michael was too far away. And where was Stanley?

Gone to his father's. Of course he was.

Her eyes went to the clock on the mantelpiece. How long since he'd been gone? How long till he got back? *Tomorrow*, she thought. *Stanley will be back tomorrow.*

But at least he wasn't here when the brick came through the window. Be thankful for that, she told herself. He was with his father enjoying himself. Everything would be alright.

Twenty-Three

Stanley closed his eyes and took a deep breath. 'Hmm!' he murmured. His stomach rumbled in response. One sniff of the fish and chip shop at the bottom of Avonvale Road and he'd come to an immediate stop. Besotted with the delicious aroma, he was unaware at first of the three boys leaning against a wall.

'Are you gettin' some?' one of them asked, his fingers travelling along the handlebars to the bicycle's battered bell.

'Nah,' said Stanley making ready to push off. 'Me dad's already got some warming in the oven. Hmm,' he murmured again, enjoying the envious looks on the three boys' faces. 'Can't wait to sprinkle on the salt and vinegar. Lovely!'

A gangly boy with holes in his pullover leapt towards him, shouting at the top of his voice. 'Yah! Yah! Yah!'

'Get 'im! 'E's ridin' a girl's bike!'

Stanley knew the rules. He was trespassing on foreign territory, but was too fast for the likes of them. Pushing off swiftly, he was soon pedalling hell for leather down Marsh Lane, laughing all the way. *He* was the one going off to eat fish and chips at his dad's, not them, and he'd enjoyed making them jealous. Not many got a treat like that nowadays.

The door to number seventeen was open when he got there.

'Dad!' he shouted as he wheeled Lizzie's bicycle into the

narrow passageway. He sniffed the air, expecting the unmistakable aroma of his supper to be drifting along from the kitchen. But there was nothing; just the dank smell of mouldy wallpaper and mouse droppings. He frowned. Perhaps his dad had forgotten to put the gas on.

His stomach gurgled with a mix of worry and hunger as he headed to the end of the passageway. The kitchen was at the back of the house, an added-on protrusion just like the rest of the terrace. Even in broad daylight the kitchen was gloomy. One window and a door opened on to the back yard. There was a deep sink and a wooden draining board in front of the window, a wooden cupboard next to that, some shelves above it and a gas stove sitting on thin enamel legs.

He sniffed again. Still nothing.

There was a bit of bread and a tiny piece of cheese on the side. The cheese rind was a mottled shade of green. The bread had a greyish tinge. He broke off a piece, fingered it, but threw it back down. This wasn't what he'd come here for and he was angry. Not for the first time in his life, his dad had disappointed him.

Overcome with anger, he strode back along the passageway. The stairs were to his left. The door to Biddy's front room was to his right. He paused, listening to the muffled snatches of conversation and laughter. Probably entertaining one of her fancy men – or perhaps her husband was home. Then he remembered her husband had been killed at the docks a while back, though not from the bombing. Apparently he'd been drunk and fallen into the water ten minutes after the pubs had closed and just before an air raid. Nobody had had the time or the inclination to pull him out.

Stanley pressed on, clumping his way up the stairs so his dad would hear him coming and know he wasn't well pleased.

He thought he heard the rattle of a doorknob from downstairs and someone say his name, then a man's muffled voice.

He knew it wasn't his father; the loud snores coming from behind the bedroom door led him to Henry Randall. The old familiar smell of stale beer accompanied the sight of his father lying prone on the bed, his bottom lip quivering with each noisy breath.

Stanley shook his father's shoulder. 'Dad! Where's me supper?'

His father grunted – like a pig, thought Stanley, clenching his jaw as well as his fist. If only he was older . . .

'Dad!' He dared to shake him again, even though he knew – he'd seen – what he was capable of when he was drunk.

'Dad!'

Again nothing.

'Right. I'll give you a Joe Louis,' he muttered. Harry had told him all about Joe Louis, the Brown Bomber. He'd shown him pictures from a boxing magazine. Stanley clenched his hand into a tight fist, drew his arm back like a spring and punched him hard. A calloused hand shot out and grabbed his throat. Bleary eyes flashed open.

Stanley gasped for air, his mouth opening and shutting like a goldfish.

His father blinked. The bleariness in his eyes was replaced by recognition, then outright alarm.

'Stanley!' The hand fell away.

'Stanley,' he said again, struggling from the bed. 'I'm sorry, lad. I was dreamin'. I didn't know it was you. Come here, lad,' he said, reaching out. 'I won't hurt you.'

Stanley began backing towards the door, his eyes fixed on his father's bloated features. Seeing his fear, his father smiled and modified his voice. 'Now come on, lad. I woke up with a start. Never fear.'

The soft voice did nothing to stop Stanley walking backwards.

Henry tried again. 'I'm sorry, lad. I wasn't expecting you. Did you want something in particular?'

'Yes,' said Stanley, backing towards the door. 'Me fish and chip supper! It's Friday.'

Henry slammed the palm of his hand against his forehead and groaned. 'I knew there was something.'

He made as if to rise, but swayed a bit and then fell back on the bed, hitting his head on the wall as he did so. Yet again he was out cold, mouth open, legs at a twisted angle.

Stanley eyed him warily. Was he going to get up? He didn't move. Padding over to the bed on tiptoe, he looked down at him, his heart racing. Was he dead? How did you tell if a person was dead? *Perhaps if I stuck a pin in him*, he thought, and looked around him.

Although the furniture was sparse and second-hand, the

room was neat. He went into the front room. A huge old sideboard complete with a back mirror stood against one wall. He opened the drawer, searching for a pin. Needlework boxes contain pins, he reasoned. But men didn't do sewing and mending, he decided after a fruitless rummage. He slammed the drawer shut.

There was nothing else for it. Biddy would have a needle. It would probably be rusty and used to pick her teeth or darn her stockings, but it would have to do.

Just as he was about to go downstairs and interrupt Biddy and her man friend, the sound of snoring resumed from the bedroom. Disappointed about the fish and chips but glad he wasn't going to get blamed for killing his father, he closed the door and set off back down the stairs. He did it quietly, unwilling to explain anything to Biddy.

A man was standing outside Biddy's parlour door. The man was wearing a khaki trench coat fastened with a belt and buckle. The brim of his brown trilby was tilted slightly forward, casting a shadow over his eyes.

The man smiled. 'You're Stanley Randall, aren't you?'

There was something about the man's smile, the shape of his chin and the sound of his voice that put Stanley at ease. His features glum with disappointment, he nodded vigorously.

'You don't look too happy, old chap. Has someone done something to upset you?'

Stanley nodded again. He'd had it in mind to be miserable all the way home to his mother, and not to speak to anyone until he'd told her all about it. She'd be sympathetic and find him something to eat, but it wouldn't be fish and chips. Those fish and chips meant such a lot to him, the big treat of the week, and his father had let him down. But now here was this man, taking an interest in his misery.

'My dad forgot to get me fish and chip supper.' He didn't add that he'd probably spent his supper money in the pub. He was too ashamed.

'Oh, that's a great pity,' said the man. 'You must be absolutely starving!'

Stanley's belly chose that moment to make its emptiness known.

'Ah!' said the man, a wider smile revealing his shiny white teeth. 'It seems that you are.'

To Stanley's great surprise, he brought a ten-shilling note out of his pocket. 'Here,' he said. 'Get yourself some supper.'

Stanley's eyes were as round as soup spoons. Ten shillings was far too much for fish and chips. Half a crown would have been more than enough.

'You don't have to spend it all at once,' he said, as if reading Stanley's mind. 'Keep some for emergencies or to treat your friends.'

Stanley licked his lips as he slowly reached for the money.

'Just one thing,' said the man, his fingers tightening on his half of the note. 'You mustn't tell anyone I gave you this. You know what grown-ups are like; they'll start asking awkward questions when there's no need to. Do you promise?'

Stanley nodded. 'Yes.'

'Say it.'

'I promise.'

The man fingered the brim of his hat, bending it that bit lower. 'It'll be our little secret,' he said. 'If your mother asks, tell her your father gave you the money, and if *he* asks . . .'

'He won't. He's drunk.'

The man nodded knowingly. 'Grown-ups aren't as perfect as they make out, are they, Stanley, especially parents. We don't choose our parents, do we? We get what we're given so to speak.' He patted Stanley's shoulder. 'I understand how you feel, Stanley. I had the same problems myself.'

The man looked at the boy and the boy looked back. They were both silent for a moment as each weighed up the other. The man spoke first. 'I'm always around. I'll make sure I watch out for you. Never fear.'

Stanley stared up at him, not sure what to say.

'When you can't get what you want from grown-ups, you come and see me. I'll make sure you get what you deserve. Is that understood?'

Stanley nodded. He hadn't a clue who this man was, but he liked what he said.

'Go on,' said the man with a jerk of his head. 'Get your fish and chip supper.' Suddenly his hand shot out of his pocket. He held a warning finger before Stanley's face. 'But tell no one. Do you hear me? Tell no one.'

Stanley had no trouble in agreeing to the condition. As he prepared to remount the bicycle, he watched the man walk off down the street. He took big strides and didn't look to right or left. Once he was out of sight, Stanley thought he heard a car start up. Anyone who flashed ten-shilling notes around *had* to be able to afford a car, he decided.

The boys that had been hanging around the chip shop earlier were still there, faces pressed against the steamed-up windows, their scruffy clothes flapping around their bony frames.

Stanley had no intention of waiting for his supper one moment longer. Pulling his bicycle on to the pavement, he made straight for them.

'Right! Who fancies a fish and chip supper and a bottle of Tizer?'

Three surprised, pale faces jerked round to face him.

'You offerin'?'

'Yeah! Me dad gave me a ten-bob note to get rid of me.' The lie rolled easily off his tongue.

'Cor! Wish my dad would give me that when 'e wanted to get rid of me,' exclaimed the gangly lad, his mouth already hanging open.

'Wish I 'ad a dad,' said another miserably.

The four of them piled through the chip-shop door in a conjoined mass, lining up at the counter, their sticky fingers leaving marks over the chrome trim.

'It's only fishcakes and chips tonight,' said the fat lady behind the counter.

The boys didn't care. Once they'd been served, they went outside making themselves comfortable on the pavement, their backs against the wall.

Not a word was spoken until the newspapers containing the fishcakes and chips were licked clean.

'I'm going to join the army when I grow up,' said one of the boys. 'Look. I've got a gun.'

He pulled out a cap pistol and pulled the trigger. The cap sparked and gave off a sharp twang. *Not really like a gun at all*, thought Stanley.

'That's not real,' said one of the others. 'This is real.'

Stanley had noticed earlier that the boy's trousers dragged down on one side. Now he saw the reason. His eyes opened wide.

'Wow! Where did you get that?'

The boy smirked proudly. 'My granddad brought it back from the war.'

'Can I hold it?' asked Stanley.

The boy eyed him warily before passing it over. 'Only for a minute, mind.'

'No one can be in our gang unless they've got a gun,' said the third lad. He brought out a gun carved from wood and painted to look real. 'You'll have to get one if you're going to join our gang,' he said to Stanley.

'Right,' said Stanley, his eyes following the real gun as he passed it back to its owner. 'I'll get one.'

'It's got to be a real one,' said the boy with the saggy trousers as he returned his grandfather's gun to his pocket.

Stanley nodded. 'It will be. I've got a friend who'll get me one, you just see if I don't.'

His mother was taping over a window pane when Stanley got home. 'I didn't do it,' he said on seeing the bits of glass brushed into the dustpan.

'Of course not,' she said abruptly.

He accepted her brusqueness and didn't ask any more questions; just in case one of his pals was responsible and his shilling a week pocket money might come a cropper. She didn't ask him why he was home.

Puzzled, he watched as she locked and bolted the door, pulled the blackout curtains and sat shivering with her cardigan wrapped tightly around her. Suddenly, as though drawing back from somewhere, she turned on a smile and tried to look brave. 'Did you enjoy your supper?' she asked him.

'Yeah!' he exclaimed with total honesty. 'It was the best ever!'

'Right. Well, seeing as you're home tonight, you can have a bath. The geyser's working again and there's a bar of Lifebuoy in the soap dish.'

Stanley groaned. 'Aw, Mum! I 'ad a bath last week.'

'Had! The word is "had", Stanley. It has an "aitch" at the beginning. And baths should be taken at least once a week.'

Stanley baulked at the thought. 'Mr Churchill says we 'ave to save water.'

'Have, Stanley. And yes, Mr Churchill did say that we have to save water, but he didn't say it meant that Stanley Randall and other boys shouldn't wash and take a bath occasionally.'

'I don't like this house,' Stanley said as his mother manhandled him to the bathroom.

'Only because it's got a proper bathroom,' said his mother.

Stanley grimaced, wishing they could go back to a house with a tin bath hanging on the back wall. Trust Harry and Edgar to have an indoor one. Bath night could be put off if it was raining, no one wanting to fetch the bath in. But here there were no excuses.

Once he was in the bath, she began tidying the clothes he'd thrown on to a chair. The remaining change from the ten-shilling note fell from his pocket and rolled across the linoleum.

She frowned as she picked up the florins, the sixpences and the shillings. 'Where did you get all this?'

Stanley was about to tell the truth, but suddenly remembered the stranger and his promise.

'Six shillings from me dad.'

His mother raised her eyebrows. 'He gave you that much?'

Stanley decided to elaborate on the basic lie. 'He said that the people on the church outing gave him a big tip and he wanted to share it with me. He thought you might need a shilling or two to buy a few extra things.'

Mary Anne raised one eyebrow in a singularly surprised fashion. Perhaps Henry had turned over a new leaf after all.

Stanley was in bed when Edgar tried his key in the lock at around eleven. He knocked at the same time.

'Everything alright?' he asked. A draught of cold air came in with him. Mary Anne turned up the gas.

'Yes.'

Edgar rubbed his hands before the fire's glow. 'Would you like a cup of cocoa?'

They sat sipping cocoa and talking about what had happened until around one o'clock.

'I think someone is definitely stirring things up for us,' said Edgar. 'A few of Harry's friends are looking into it. They think they know who's responsible.'

He looked up at her quickly, then lowered his eyes. She sensed he'd been going to mention Harry and his connection with the black market, but hadn't been sure just how much she knew.

'I do know what Harry was up to before going away,' she said.

Edgar looked her in the face. 'You know about the nightclubs?'

Nightclubs?

'Yes.' She nodded curtly, as though she were telling the truth.

Edgar sighed. 'What with this war, they're certainly coming into their own. You can't imagine the mix of uniforms on a Saturday night. The trouble is that with Harry being away, there's a few trying to muscle in.' He shrugged his narrow shoulders and pushed his spectacles back up on to the bridge of his nose.

Mary Anne was intrigued. Harry had never mentioned anything about nightclubs. She couldn't help but want to know more.

'How many nightclubs does he own?'

Edgar almost laughed. 'He doesn't own them; he's merely got a certain interest . . .'

He stopped, his features freezing as he realized the truth. 'You didn't know.'

She held his gaze. 'About him being involved in night-clubs?' She shook her head. 'Tell me.'

He glanced nervously between the milky surface of the chocolate and her face. 'I don't think . . .'

Mary Anne pointed in the direction of the broken window pane.

Edgar nodded. 'As you know, your Harry can take care of himself. He's handy with his fists. So he got a bit of a reputation for sorting out the rough stuff. A few of the night-clubs knew him anyway through the fags he got from Wills's and sold via contacts. Anyway, gangsters were muscling in on the nightclubs and Harry was asked to help them out, so he did. His price was always a cut of the take, and then one club owner, Randy Kirkwood, made it legal and gave him a proper share complete with the paperwork. There's some that reckon Harry pulled the wool over Kirkwood's eyes and that what he took was their share. Of course, with Harry going away it's left to me to sort things out, and I do,' he said, rubbing his bloodied knuckles. 'Drive me out and the coast is clear. That's their game. That's what they're up to.'

'What else are they likely to do?'

He shrugged. 'Anything.'

Later that night Mary Anne lay in bed mulling it over. She told herself that Harry was not a true criminal; he didn't kill people, he didn't rob banks. On the other hand it was obvious that he'd made some very dangerous enemies.

The room was in total darkness thanks to the blackout curtains. Even so, she stared up at the ceiling, narrowing her eyes as though seeking a pinprick of light through the darkness. If only Michael were here . . . But he wasn't. She hadn't heard from him for weeks. Yet again the doubts resurfaced, made more intense by the darkness. Worries that had been manageable by day turned into ogres at night. She'd never considered a time when Michael wouldn't be there, but anything was possible. The old habit of living for everybody else seemed the only right and proper thing to do. Michael had been an indulgence; the real world was catching up with her, and as if that weren't enough, there were Harry's friends to consider.

These people were frightening, and although the flat was very comfortable and central, she had to think of Stanley. But where could they go? She squeezed her eyes shut but could not blank out the notion that there was only one place really open to her.

Her sense of foreboding was like an anvil resting on her chest. If she stayed here things might get very nasty, and she couldn't think only of herself. She had to consider Stanley.

She rolled over on to her side, her tears staining the pillow. In the morning she would write to Michael telling him to find someone else. In the evening she would go round to see Henry and offer to come back. Although unpalatable and liable to cause heartbreak all round, she had no other alternative. She had to forget about herself, about being happy. To do that she had to forget about Michael.

Twenty-Four

Wing Commander Guy Hunter had been patient with Lizzie's nervousness and her mumbled horror on seeing the legs sticking out from beneath the tarpaulin.

'Here,' he'd said, hugging her against his shoulder and giving her a clean handkerchief to cry into.

That, she decided, was the moment that she fell in love with him. All reason had fled. The staunch arguments for resistance became trivialities.

On Friday he told her to stand down.

'I have to go to London on Monday,' he said grimly. 'And I know you could do with some rest and recreation. It was quite an ordeal.'

She nodded. Her stomach rumbled. She'd been unable to eat anything the night before and this morning at breakfast was no better.

'You look pale,' he said. 'You need some fresh air. We're both due leave. Didn't we agree that only yesterday?'

Standing straight, hands behind her back, she picked out the memories of the morning before the bombing and the sight of the dead girls.

'Yes, sir. We did.'

'Stop the "sir", at least when we're alone.'

'Yes.'

'Call me Guy – but only when no one else is around.'

She nodded. 'Yes. I will.'

He flicked at some papers lying loose on his desk, gathering them up into a folder. 'Now go and pack your things. We're taking the slow boat to London via a little place called Shotley.'

Lizzie felt her face growing hot with embarrassment. *A hotel?* Separate rooms, she hoped.

Guy read her concern. 'Don't worry about what people might say. We're staying in private accommodation. It's got two cabins and two beds. You need a rest. We both do.'

She wasn't in the mood for guessing games, so didn't quiz him on their journey.

The salt smell of sea air and the screech of gulls sounded overhead. Lizzie's spirits lifted. She began craning her neck for a glimpse of the sea. Ahead of her she could see flint-built cottages and wooden-framed houses lining a road leading to the beach.

'Left here,' he said suddenly.

They turned into a narrow lane where spring flowers speckled the grass verges with yellow, pink, blue and white.

'And left again,' he said.

They turned at a sign saying 'Brian's Boathouse' painted in faded green on what remained of a small wooden dinghy.

'Park over there.'

She followed where he pointed, chickens squawking as they scattered before the turning tyres.

'This is it.'

She looked round for a hotel, but saw only a boat.

It was moored alongside a wooden jetty in an inlet on the River Orwell.

'I bought it from a man who took it to Dunkirk,' he explained, eyeing the boat with undisguised pride. 'He decided he never wanted to go to sea again. You can't blame him really. It couldn't have been pleasant motoring into the shallows in those conditions. It was sheer luck he didn't get blown out of the water.'

'It's lovely,' said Lizzie. The truth was, she knew nothing about boats, but she studied it as though she did.

She judged it to be about forty feet long, made of wood and more generally termed a gentleman's motor yacht. It had a wheel house standing proud of a teak deck. Its hull was white, relieved with stainless steel stanchions and a broad mahogany toe rail.

Guy took their bags, threw them aboard, and then turned to help her on. Lizzie shivered.

'Are you cold?' he asked as he took out a key.

'A little.'

He smiled. 'Never mind. You'll soon be warm. I'll turn on the gas and rustle up a cup of tea. OK with you?'

'Lovely.'

The inside of the boat was surprisingly cosy. It had a small stove for heating and cooking.

'I keep mostly tinned stuff,' he said, opening and shutting cupboards as though food was of the utmost importance.

She stood watching him, aware that his action was based on nervousness more than hunger.

'Why have you brought me here?'

'I told you. We both need a change.'

'You're out to seduce me.'

'Don't be silly.'

'You can stop pretending.'

'Pretending? What do you mean?'

'You can stop pretending that you're intent on cooking up a meal. Anyway, I'm cold, not hungry. I want to be warm. I want to be cosy.'

He stopped what he was doing. The strong face was soft with surprise and a hint of indecision. The wing commander – the organizer – looked unsure of what to do next.

'I'm cold,' she said again, wrapping her arms around herself and holding his eyes with her own.

'Are you sure?' he said softly.

She nodded.

Falling into his arms was easy. Falling into bed was just as easy. *It's only afterwards that things will get difficult*, Lizzie thought. But for that moment they were in a world of their own. There would be time for guilt afterwards – tomorrow or the day after that.

His voice had deepened to a brandy-brown rasp as his hands explored her body. He was slow and gentle, almost as though he supposed it was her first time, which, of course, thanks to Peter, it was not.

Anticipation had covered her body like a smattering of dew before the sun sucks it dry. His thighs were rough against hers, his loins applying pressure, easing off and applying again as he eased into her.

His hair fell over his forehead. She licked at his chin as he moved above her, relishing the hardness of his body against hers.

'Don't ever regret this,' he said between deep, captured breaths.

His eyes held hers. At first she considered it an odd thing to say. Later she would understand.

The cabin was dim, but a small porthole let in enough light by which to study his features. He buried his face against her neck, the rhythm of his movements breaking up as he began to lose control. A similar sensation travelled over her body, throbbing and pulling him inwards until they finally shuddered to a nerve-tingling halt.

They lay replete, studying each other's features, touching each other's hair, each other's lips; each other's throat.

'You have lovely hair,' she said, coiling a loose lock around her finger and drawing it into her mouth. 'I think it was your hair I fell in love with first,' she said languorously. 'Though it might have been your eyes.'

He had a relaxed smile and his eyes were half closed. 'You don't sound too sure. Now I know beyond doubt that it was your feet I fell for first.'

She laughed. 'My feet?'

He cupped her face with one hand. 'That first day you were lolling on a bench with your shoes off. I saw your feet before I saw the rest of you.'

'That's hardly the stuff love songs are made of – "I fell in love with your feet!"'

He frowned and tried to look grim, though a smile flickered at his lips. 'Then the songwriters and poets of this world need to look at feet more closely. Surely there's at least one who's moved by the sight of a girl's wriggling toes? Come on. Think of all the poems you've read. There must be one.'

Mentioning poetry brought Patrick to mind. He was the only poet she knew, the only poet whose work she'd read without having to, simply because she enjoyed it. The guilt came too, and Guy saw it.

'You knew a poet?' His voice softened.

'Yes. A friend.'

He ran his fingers down the length of her spine. 'Do you still hear from him?'

'Sometimes,' she whispered.

She flexed her spine, surprised at how quickly she was becoming aroused, wanting him all over again.

'Is he . . .?'

'Shush,' she said, placing her fingers over his lips. She didn't want to hear this; she didn't want to be reminded that she and Patrick had had something of an understanding.

'Make love to me again,' she said, kissing him.

Much later, food was again suggested.

'Tinned beef, tinned beans, and fresh bread,' he said, handing her the cans from the cupboard.

She heated up the food on a small gas ring while he buttered the bread and laid the table.

'You're very domesticated,' she told him.

'Practice,' he said with a smile.

She eyed him knowingly. 'That's what I thought.'

Once he'd realized what he'd said, his smile melted. 'Yes. I'm married, but . . .'

Lizzie had a great urge to put her hand to her heart. Had it stopped beating? She held her breath as she waited for him to continue, aching to hear the words that came after the 'but'.

'We got married just as war was declared. It was kind of a spur of the moment thing. Since then we've both realized that marrying was a mistake. So now we aim to do something about it.'

'I see.'

He passed a plate to her. She filled it with the contents from the saucepans.

'You know you're not just a passing fancy,' he said, the fingers of his free hand encircling the nape of her neck.

My, it feels so delicious! Of course she wasn't just a passing fancy. She closed her eyes, wanting this moment to go on for ever. Never mind food. Never mind anything. All she wanted was him.

She waited for him to say the word she wanted to hear.

'We're going to get a divorce.'

Lizzie refrained from sighing but a great sense of relief swept over her. He had said it.

The whole car-driver unit had been transferred to Ainsley Hall and Lizzie was again sharing a room with Margot. As she tiptoed across the cold floor in the early hours of Monday morning, Margot's head popped up.

'You're back.'

She rolled over and switched on the light. 'My, you look rosy faced. Did you have a good weekend with your brother?'

The question took Lizzie off guard. 'What?'

'You told me you were off to see your brother.'

Margot adopted a searching gaze when she guessed she wasn't being told the truth. Her eyes darkened as she focused thoughtful attention to the shifty way Lizzie tried to collect herself.

'Have you got something to tell me?'

'Of course not,' said Lizzie, shaking her head.

Margot propped herself up that bit more. 'Well, I've got something to tell you. Bessie's had a miscarriage, poor thing, and lo and behold, the silly girl contacted her ex and suggested that they get back together.'

'She's willing to forgive him?' Lizzie was a little surprised, but if Bessie cared for the chap that was her business.

'She was indeed. Unfortunately his wife wasn't.'

'His *wife*?'

'That's right, my dear girl. Our Romeo had a wife that he forgot to mention. Not that I'm that surprised. A virile man can suffer severe memory loss when there's no wife to rein him in.'

'You make men sound like horses,' said Lizzie as she began to unbutton her jacket.

'Absolutely, darling,' said Margot with a wry smile. 'Stallions. They're all stallions.'

Lizzie felt Margot's eyes following her around the room, but refrained from meeting her enquiring gaze. Her whole body was tingling in the aftermath of Guy's lovemaking. Yes, he had a wife, but as he'd told her himself they'd married in haste at the outbreak of war and now they wanted a divorce.

'Well, I say, that's not army issue,' said Margot once Lizzie was stripped down to her underwear. She was wearing a soft pink bra and French knickers that Peter had given her, taken from stock at his family's haberdashers and ladies' outfitters.

They were far skimpier items than the army was ever likely to issue. She bent her head so that Margot wouldn't see her blushing.

'I brought them with me.'

'They're very delicate.' Margot's eyes continued to follow her with the kind of scrutiny usually reserved for only the best from Harrods. 'Difficult, I should think, when you're in a bit of a hurry.'

Lizzie folded her blouse and put her jacket on a hanger. 'Difficult? Why do you say that?'

Pulling the bedclothes more closely around her, Margot began to settle back down. 'Because you've put them on back to front.'

Lizzie gasped and slumped down on the end of her bed.

'Are you sure there's nothing you'd like to tell me?' asked Margot, peering at her from over the bedclothes.

Lizzie groaned. 'Oh, Margot!'

Margot sat up, the bedclothes pulled up to her chin. 'Come on. Tell me all about it.'

Lizzie covered her face. 'I'm a fool. I'm a bloody fool!'

Margot didn't contradict her but sat silently, waiting for her to explain. Margot was a good listener and knew when to keep mum.

Their eyes met, not so much in mutual understanding, but as though they knew the time was ripe for secrets to be shared.

'I think it was the way he looked at me over undrinkable cider that finally swayed me. And his voice, of course.'

She held back on the more intimate details, like the way his voice dropped an octave lower when aroused, or the way he'd driven the car that day, one hand draped casually over the wheel.

Margot eyed her silently.

'Am I a fool?' Lizzie asked her.

Margot thought about it for a moment. 'Yes,' she said at last. 'You are. But then, you're not the first and you won't be the last.'

'Don't ask me not to see him again.'

'I won't. You must please yourself.'

'I will,' said Lizzie with a firm thrust of her chin. 'I love him and he says he's getting a divorce.'

'Fine,' said Margot, tucking a strand of escaped hair back into her hairnet and snuggling back down.

'You don't sound as though you believe him.'

'Of course I do, darling. And by the way, Patrick phoned.'

'Patrick? What did you tell him?'

'Exactly what you told me, that you'd gone away for the weekend with your brother.'

The tingling that had lasted until she'd got into bed suddenly vanished. Whatever happened she had to keep Patrick away from Harry, at least until she'd had a chance to straighten things out.

Twenty-Five

Michael read the letter from his Marianna more closely and more often than he did the German transcripts he was expected to translate. His brows furrowed in a deep frown and the fact that he hadn't heard the command to fall in brought him to the attention of Major Swinburn, Head of Section.

Even when the major's shadow fell over him, his thoughts were still in Bristol.

'Are you with us, Maurice?'

Michael looked up and blinked.

The major smiled like a snake with lockjaw. 'Bad news from home, Maurice?'

Michael slid the letter back into the envelope and the envelope back into his pocket as he got to his feet. 'Just a personal matter, sir. I'm sorry.'

The major rolled his shoulders and jerked his head forward until their noses almost touched. 'You will be!' he snarled. 'Now salute, you Kraut bastard. Salute or I'll have your stripes.'

Michael didn't want that to happen. Recognizing the quality of both his work and his leadership, he'd been awarded a corporal's stripe a few months after arrival. He'd been complimented on his dedication to duty, sometimes working until late in the night to get a job done. A few of the others in his unit were also of German extraction, though none had got caught up in the tide of events in Germany as he had. Nowadays he felt ashamed for having loved uniforms so much; perhaps it would have been different if he'd confined his obsession to Boy Scout uniforms, but in Germany things weren't like that. One uniform had led to another. Eventually he'd found out what that uniform had stood for.

The major was not his favourite person and the major's feelings were likewise. There was something about the major's whispery-thin moustache, the light blondness of it, the mean amount of hair above an equally thin set of lips.

The translation unit was attached to the Bletchley Park complex. Harry, who had always been good at crosswords, worked in the code-breaking department and they sometimes met in the canteen.

Harry greeted him jovially, but his smile vanished once he noticed Michael's grave expression and the letter clenched in his hand. Michael did not protest when Harry took the letter from his hand and read it.

He shook his head and eyed Michael across the table. 'She can't be serious.'

Michael shrugged. 'Absence does not always make the heart grow fonder. Sometimes it breaks things apart.'

'But to go back with my father?'

'For the family's sake, she says.' Michael shrugged. 'I suppose I can understand that.' He hid his face in his hands. 'Damn Hitler! Damn Churchill! Damn the bloody lot of them!'

Harry glanced nervously around him. 'Steady on, mate. You can damn Hitler all you like, but don't let anyone hear you doing the same to Churchill. You'll be hanging from a gallows before you know it.' Harry laughed as though it were a huge joke.

Michael couldn't bring himself to laugh. 'I have to see her,' he said, his blue eyes meeting those of the son of the woman he loved.

The laughing stopped. Harry eyed Michael thoughtfully. Her mother deserved this man and this man really did love his mother.

'Can you get any leave?' he asked, his expression serious now.

He sighed heavily and shook his head. 'There's too much going on at the moment.'

'I know,' said Harry. 'What with a war at sea and people sick with the flu. This winter was very cold.'

The two men exchanged the same conspiratorial look; the Bletchley nod as some people called it. Each knew what was going on in radio chatter and coded messages, but only their own small part in it. Exchange of information between sections was not encouraged.

'How about I write to our Lizzie and get her to visit?'

'You would do that?' Michael sounded surprised.

'Why not? She can only say no, and I doubt she'd do that. She likes you. We both like you.' Harry leaned forward. 'You're the best thing that ever happened to my mother. I don't care about the details, only that she's happy.'

Michael managed a weak smile. 'Thank you.'

Harry and his mother understood each other better than most. Neither condemned the other for the way they were. Only his father had done that, but Michael was something different. Harry liked the man and could understand why his mother had fallen for him and left his father. His father was a different matter. There was no love lost between father and son and never would be.

Harry had a feeling he knew what was coming.

'If I can't get leave and Lizzie won't go to see her, I'm going AWOL.'

Harry shook his head. 'No. You'll be in deep trouble.'

'I have to do something.'

'Look,' said Harry, raising one hand in a halting gesture, 'leave it to me. I've had letters too. There's been some trouble at my place, but I can get things sorted out.'

He didn't impart to Michael just how worried he was. Edgar had written explaining things. Harry was surprised. He hadn't expected any disagreement from those he used to do business with. If he got a chance to go home, he'd sort out the lot of them – and not with kid gloves either. Hard fists were all the toe rags understood.

He frowned as he walked back to the hut where he broke codes down into their intrinsic parts and built them back up again. Just as he got back to his desk, someone came to him saying he had a telephone call. He frowned. He didn't know that many people with a telephone. He followed the young woman who had called him. She was engaged in similar work to himself.

'In here,' she said curtly. 'And don't be long.'

He cradled the receiver until she'd closed the door. As he raised the phone to his ear, his gaze settled on a wall chart spotted with pin heads and pencilled lines.

'Hello?'

'Harry! It's me!'

It was Edgar and he sounded not so much excited as pleased with himself.

'I've had a phone put in, Harry. I've missed you.'

The advantage of being able to contact home much more quickly than by mail was not lost on Harry, but there were drawbacks.

'Edgar, you can't phone me here. They don't like it, old son.'

'I had to phone you, Harry. So many things have been happening, I thought you should know.'

'So Ma told me in her letter.'

'Someone's out to get us.'

Harry didn't disagree with his statement, but he wouldn't run scared. He was Harry Randall and had a reputation to maintain.

'Put Mum on,' he said.

'She's not here.'

'Where is she?'

'Gone!'

Gone! He guessed where she'd gone but had to hear it said, just in case he was only surmising, just in case he told Michael the wrong news.

'She was worried about the boy. She didn't want him getting hurt,' he explained.

Feeling sick inside, Harry returned the receiver to its cradle. It was now imperative that someone go home to see what was going on, and if he couldn't get Lizzie to go, then he'd have to go himself – with or without permission.

He put in a request for compassionate leave, but to no avail.

'No one can be spared,' said the same gingery-haired major who hated Michael's guts.

Sensing there was menace behind the Signal Corps uniform, he was less aggressive with Harry, but he was also turned down.

Sending letters was strictly controlled when there was a big job on. Permission had to be sought, so Harry did just that.

'I need to send a letter or two. Do I have your permission for that?'

The major paled before the insistence in Harry's tone. He didn't dare refuse him. 'I should think so,' he said.

That night Harry wrote to Lizzie, stressing his concern about their mother. As an afterthought he also wrote to Patrick. One of them would go. He was sure of it.

Twenty-Six

'Here. Have another.'

Henry Randall eyed the old clock ticking away on the wall behind the bar. He licked his lips, tasting the residue of the last pint on his tongue. He'd had three pints already – or was it four?

'I should be gettin' on 'ome,' he said, not too convincingly.

The tall young chap beside him prodded the brim of his trilby with two fingers, sending it sitting further back on his head.

Henry rubbed at his bleary eyes. Where had he seen this bloke before?

'You're too late, Henry. It's already being poured.'

Henry eyed the mahogany-brown beer dribbling like treacle from a polished brass spout. He licked his lips again. How long had it been since he'd drunk beer as only real men can drink; pint after pint after pint? He answered his own question. Since *she* had gone away to live with that German bloke.

The man standing beside him noted his grimace and inwardly smiled. He had a lot in common with Henry Randall. Here was a man who found it difficult to forgive anyone anything – a bit like himself. He just needed a bit of coaxing to bring the violence to the surface.

George Ford was good at altering his appearance – not with false beards or moustaches, just subtle differences like the addition of spectacles, the shaving of eyebrows and the application of chalk to add pallor to his complexion. With growing satisfaction, he watched as Henry reached a shaky hand across the bar. The hand faltered.

'I shouldn't,' said Henry, folding his fingers back into his palm.

'Of course you should!' The man in the trench coat gave him a slap on the back. 'Haven't you been working hard all day? A working man deserves to enjoy himself once in a while. Anyone who says he shouldn't deserves a good beating.' In order to emphasize the point, he slammed his right fist into the palm of his left hand. 'A quick jab in the ribs wouldn't come amiss. Women should know their place. That's what I say.'

'Aye,' said Henry, his face darkening as his mind recounted all the slights he'd endured. 'You're right. You're too bloody right!'

Henry had been taken aback the day Mary Anne had appeared on the doorstep with a few belongings and Stanley at her side. They'd stared at each other for what seemed like minutes but must have only been seconds before one of them spoke.

Taking a deep breath, Mary Anne had asked if she could come in. 'But only if you want me to,' she'd said. 'Your son and I have nowhere else to go.'

Henry's legs had turned to jelly. This was the day he had dreamed about, and here she was, standing on the doorstep asking to come back.

Biddy was out. He'd had the house to himself and suggested they go upstairs into his own rooms. One room was set out like a parlour, and he used the biggest of the other rooms to sleep in, with the box room for storage – not that he had that much to store.

Stanley shuffled his feet impatiently, his eyes darting back to the front door and the street beyond. Boys were playing marbles and swinging from rope tied to the crossbar of a lamp post. Others were playing cricket and all of them were having fun. His face was a picture of happiness when his mother told him to go outside and play.

'Your father and I have things to discuss.'

Their discussion had been stilted but it was agreed that they would try again. He'd asked her whether she'd told the pawnbroker – Michael, she corrected him – that she was going back to her husband. She'd nodded. He'd wanted to reach out and smooth away the tightness of her jaw, but he stopped himself. He'd not wanted to appear too affectionate, too willing to let bygones be bygones. And why should he? Wasn't he the innocent party, the legal spouse left in the lurch?

Their first few days together had proved just as stilted as their conversation. He'd been disappointed. He'd wanted it to be so much more; he'd especially wanted them to sleep together again, but she'd refused.

'Not yet,' she'd said in that soft voice of hers. 'I'll sleep on the sofa for now.'

'Not yet,' he muttered in the pub now as his glass was refilled. 'Not yet, she says! But a man has needs. A man has rights. She's me wife after all. She's me wife,' he repeated.

The man at his side expressed sympathy. 'Quite right, Henry. Love, honour and obey; that's what a woman's supposed to do. And if she doesn't obey, you have to deal with it. It's hard, but it's the truth. It has to be done.'

* * *

'That bike's too big fer you,' shouted one of the gang of boys who hung around the bottom of Aiken Street. 'And it's a *girl's* bike!'

'Better than none at all,' Stanley shouted back at them.

Wobbling but cycling gamely onwards, Stanley headed for number seventeen feeling excited, confused, but also a little nervous. His mother would want to know what was in the carrier bag dangling from the handlebars. That in turn would lead to questions about where he'd been and who he'd been with.

'Just say I'm a friend,' said the man with the khaki eyes. 'And call me Joe. Now remember our plan.'

Stanley's blood surged with excitement. Of course he'd remember the plan. He couldn't join the local gang if she discovered what Joe had given him.

Mary Anne wiped her hands on her apron and narrowed her eyes. The brown paper carrier bag hanging from the handlebars was making Stanley wobble more than usual. There was something disconcerting about his demeanour, though she couldn't put her finger on what it was. She'd start with the carrier bag.

'What's that?' she asked as he came to a rubber-scorching halt.

Usually he would have grinned and opened the bag, keen to share his good fortune, but he was strangely reticent. 'Nothing for you,' he said, far too cheekily for Mary Anne's liking. She grabbed his shoulder as he attempted to push past her.

'Not so fast, young man.'

'Let me go.' He wriggled and screwed up his face.

'Stanley, you are not going inside this door until you show me.'

The ill-tempered frown remained as he begrudgingly took the carrier bag from the handlebars and opened it.

Mary Anne peered inside. She didn't know what she'd expected to be in the bag but it certainly wasn't a pair of roller skates. The sight of them confused her. 'They look like yours.'

Stanley sniffed. 'They are mine. This bloke found them.'

Mary Anne frowned. 'A man? What man?'

Stanley looked away from her and shrugged. 'Just someone.'

Rarely did Mary Anne consider her children were lying, but Stanley was. She was certain of it.

'So where did he find them?'

Stanley continued with his evasive manner. 'I don't know, but he said there's loads of criminals back round where we were living. He said—' He stopped suddenly.

Mary Anne frowned. 'Go on, Stanley. What else did this man say?'

Her youngest son stood like a block of wood, his eyes carefully averted from his mother's face, and Mary Anne didn't like it, she didn't like it at all. Stanley's attitude, on top of everything she'd been through these past few months, suddenly became too much to bear. Grabbing his shoulders, she brought her face down to his level and gave him a good shake.

'Don't you dare keep secrets from me, Stanley! Don't you dare! Now tell me. What did he say to you?'

Her eyes were blazing and her loud voice took Stanley by surprise. The bike went crashing against the wall. Wide-eyed, Stanley stood with his fists clenched at his side and whispered so quietly that she didn't catch what he said. She asked him to repeat it. 'Now,' she said, just when it looked as though he might change his mind.

'He said that it was your fault we were living in a place like that. He said women couldn't be trusted to do things right without a proper man around!'

Mary Anne stared at him. All the hurt, all the anger of most of her married life erupted in one swift slap. Stanley's face reddened. He looked shocked, but he didn't cry and didn't answer back.

'Now pick up that bike and get inside,' she shouted.

Stanley's eyes went to the brown carrier bag. 'My skates . . .'

Mary Anne pointed to the dark passageway inside the front door. 'Inside!'

Tears stinging his eyes, Stanley did as ordered, leaving the bicycle leaning against the wall just before the stairs.

'Now go and wash your face and hands,' ordered Mary Anne, though not so stridently. She regretted raising her voice the moment Biddy Young's parlour door opened and her fleshy face peered out.

'Your Stanley up to no good then, Mary Anne?' She said it with a knowing smile. Her youngsters had made a career out of being no good. The youngest had only just started work and had already been sacked for thieving.

Mary Anne was in no mood to take any criticism, except perhaps from herself.

'No fancy man tonight then, Biddy?' she asked, glancing beyond Biddy to the scruffy room.

Biddy's pleasure at hearing Mary Anne lose her temper was soon wiped from her face. 'I haven't got one – not one you'd call a fancy man as such. He just pops in when he's passing by. I expect he's busy at the moment.' Her features sagged as though she were storing lead in the corners of her mouth.

Mary Anne didn't need Biddy to tell her that the 'fancy man' hadn't called for quite a while, that perhaps he'd tired of Biddy's blowsy company.

Sensing Biddy needed to unburden her woes, Mary Anne relented and offered what any friend would. 'Do you fancy a cup of tea?'

Biddy wiped her fingers across her nose. 'Not really.'

'I've got biscuits.'

Biddy brightened immediately. 'Lucky sod! Where did you get them then?'

Mary Anne smiled and tapped the side of her nose. 'That's for me to know and you to guess at.'

They settled into the kitchen at the back of the house. Mary Anne noticed that Stanley's tea – bread, margarine and a scrape of plum jam – lay untouched on the table.

Biddy noticed it too. 'Don't your Stanley want his tea then?' The legs of the chair closest to the plate scraped noisily along the floor. Food was Biddy's big passion, a far bigger passion than men. Wartime rationing was sheer torture, though you wouldn't think she went without much judging by the rolls of fat resting on her thighs.

Mary Anne concentrated on lighting the gas beneath the kettle. Her palm still stung with the aftershock of slapping Stanley's face. She was filled with remorse, more so because Biddy had heard everything.

'So how's the family?' she asked as she carefully portioned spoonfuls of tealeaves into the pot.

'They're all fine,' said Biddy, her face filling out as she

smiled. 'My boys look 'andsome in uniforms, even if I do say so meself. My Alf would 'ave been proud as a peacock to see 'em.' At mentioning Alf, Biddy dabbed at the corner of one eye with a grubby fingertip. 'God rest 'is soul.'

Biddy went on to relate what her boys were up to. One was in the navy, one in the army, the latter having been rescued from Dunkirk.

'They was the bravest lads of all at Dunkirk,' she went on. 'And so was them in their little boats that came to rescue them. If it hadn't been for them, my Cedric would be no more than bleached bones on a baking beach.'

Mary Anne didn't inform her that Dunkirk was just across the English Channel and therefore the temperature wasn't much different from England. Instead she poured the tea.

'Still, it gets a bit lonely with only me youngest at 'ome,' said Biddy, her attention momentarily diverted to Mary Anne prising off the lid of the biscuit barrel. 'And I do miss my Alf.'

'Of course you do. And I bet you've got more than one admirer lining up to take his place,' said Mary Anne, offering her the open biscuit tin. She gritted her teeth as Biddy took two, then dived in and took another two.

Biddy tittered like a silly girl. 'Well there was one. He was a lot younger than me, mind you, but he told me he liked mature women, and anyway, he didn't think I looked old enough to have grown-up sons.'

Mary Anne almost choked. If she'd had biscuit crumbs in her mouth, she would have spattered them all over Biddy. Instead she managed to hide her amusement behind her teacup and took the tiniest sip possible.

Biddy sighed. 'I think he must have been posted. He was in aircraft engineering, you see. Could have been sent anywhere at a moment's notice, he told me. Very important war work, you see.'

Mary Anne asked when she'd last seen him.

'About a week before you got here,' said Biddy. 'Shame that.'

She makes it sound as though I've got something to do with it, thought Mary Anne. 'Never mind,' she said, hiding her feelings behind a watery smile. 'As you said, he was doing important war work and was bound to go sooner or later.'

On dunking the last biscuit and sucking it dry, Biddy's attention returned to the biscuit tin. Mary Anne pretended not to notice her interest, and slammed the lid on and returned the blue and white barrel to its shelf.

Biddy sighed heavily, whether due to her lost love or the loss of the biscuit tin, Mary Anne couldn't be sure. She was just about to ask the name of the man who had stolen her heart when she heard Henry shouting from the passageway.

'Here comes your lord and master,' muttered Biddy and got up from her chair. She paused before leaving. 'How's he been?'

Mary Anne raised her eyes to meet those of her old friend. She wanted to say that she felt as though she were at the beginning of a race, waiting for the starting wire to spring into the air. Only it wasn't a starting wire; it was Henry's temper simmering just beneath the surface.

The door flew open. Henry stood there, his face flushed and his eyes blazing. The stink of beer wafted from his breath and his clothes.

'Who gave him those bloody skates?'

Mary Anne got up and took the dirty cups and saucers to the sink.

'They're his own. He lost them but someone found them and gave them back to him.'

'I suppose the Kraut bought them for him! Bloody stupid idea. If I catch 'im skating in the house again, I'll take them off 'im and chuck 'em in the river!'

Mary Anne knew better than to answer. Trying hard not to quake with fear, she turned her back on him, concentrating on pouring boiling water on to the crockery. She added a handful of soda crystals.

Biddy eased towards the door, giving a nervous wave once she'd got there. 'I'm going now, Mary Anne. I'll see you tomorrow,' she said in a sickly, scared voice, her eyes flitting between the two of them before dashing out the door. Henry reached out and slammed it shut.

He paused for a moment, admiring the curve of his wife's back, the way her buttocks swelled beneath the simple cotton frock. His eyes lingered there.

'A hard-working man is entitled to a drink,' he slurred,

swaying slightly as he made his way across the kitchen to the sink.

Before she had time to step aside, he'd slapped his hands on her hips, groaning with satisfaction as he slammed his groin against her behind.

'Let me go!'

The rim of the sink dug into her stomach. His fingers dug into her hips as he scrabbled at her dress.

'You're me wife,' he muttered, his blood rushing to his groin despite the drink. It had been so long – far too long.

Mary Anne stopped struggling. What had she expected him to do? She'd kept him at bay for a few days only. His talk about being teetotal and churchgoing had some truth about it, but deep down she'd known he wouldn't keep to it. Henry regarded himself as master in his own house. What he wanted, he got. She'd come back of her own free will. He could do as he liked.

She closed her eyes, both hands clasping the kitchen tap as he bent her over. She felt his hands groping at his flies, closely followed by the hard heat of his erection.

Please let it be over quickly! she silently prayed.

The back of her dress became bundled around her waist. The elastic waistband of her knickers strained around her thighs. Goosebumps raced over the expanse of bare flesh. The heat of his loins was on and in her, his hands squeezing her breasts.

He groaned when it was all over, his breath hot against her neck. 'You're me wife,' he said once he'd done up his fly buttons and she'd rearranged her clothes.

He fell immediately into a drunken stupor, sprawled in a brown chair. The old springs moved in time with his snoring and horsehair stuffing pushed through the holes.

She stood completely still, looking at him. *He's only taken a husband's rights*, said a small voice in her head. *He hasn't hit you*.

No. He hadn't hit her. She'd seen the joy in his eyes when she'd appeared on the doorstep that day. To her surprise, he'd been accepting of the terms of her return, the request that he give her time to readjust.

'I'll come to your bed when I'm ready,' she'd said.

With uncharacteristic enthusiasm, he'd agreed to her terms.

So why after just a few days had he returned to some of his old ways? And how long before she had bruises to hide and cuts to blame on the slip of a bread knife?

Perhaps she'd have stood things a little longer if it hadn't been for Stanley.

Her youngest could be relentless about the fish and chips he so enjoyed. It was hard asking him to do without because of the rationing. But still he carped on. One night when Mary Anne was rolling a precious piece of pastry for a pie, the tension boiled over.

Henry came in smelling of drink. Stanley was on him in seconds. 'Dad, I could really do with some fish and chips. I'm starving. Have you got a shilling, Dad? A sixpence would do.'

Mary Anne could see trouble looming. Gone was the cheery disposition Henry used to adopt in days gone by. Back then it was only her to whom he'd shown his darker side. Now she was afraid for Stanley.

'Stanley. Leave your father alone. He's been at work all day.'

'No he ain't! He's been in the pub!'

Out of the mouths of children . . .

No sooner had the thought occurred to her than Henry grabbed Stanley by the shoulder of his pullover, swinging him around like a rag doll. 'I'll teach you, you little . . .'

Mary Anne stepped between the two of them, tugging at Henry's arm and pushing Stanley backwards. 'Leave him alone!'

He raised his hand. She raised her rolling pin, her eyes blazing with an anger Henry was not accustomed to.

'Stanley! Get our things. We're going.'

She could not believe the strength of her voice, her tight grip on the rolling pin. She held Henry's attention as she never had before.

'We're going,' she said firmly and knew she certainly would.

Upstairs Stanley stuffed everything they'd brought with them into two bags. Reaching beneath his bed he brought out his secret object given him by the man in the trench coat. He'd done as the man had said that day, tucking it beneath his pullover, the roller skates diverting his mother's attention.

Carefully rewrapping the item in a pair of trousers, he placed it at the bottom of his bag. Finally, after a few layers of underwear and pullovers, he covered it with his skates.

He paused. How about taking one more look at it? The temptation was too much. He couldn't resist. Silently he unwrapped the cloth from around the barrel and laid the gun in his hand. It was real; he was sure it was real.

At the sound of his mother's footsteps racing up the stairs, he quickly returned the gun to its hiding place. He didn't need it – at least not yet.

Twenty-Seven

Lizzie and Guy managed to sneak another two days aboard the boat. The rain was drumming on the roof like a thousand fingers.

Lizzie lay next to Guy, cosy beneath the bedcovers. Both were looking at the ceiling, as though concentrating their minds might make it stop. Guy had checked the tanks and found a little fuel, enough for a small trip, but the weather had put paid to all that.

'Doesn't it ever stop?'

'Never mind,' she said, snuggling against him, relishing the scent of his skin in the aftermath of sex. 'We can go again when the weather breaks.'

'In the summertime?'

Lizzie laughed. 'This is summer.'

'You could have fooled me.'

She stroked the tufts of unruly hair growing at his temples. The rest of his hair was quite straight and dark. The tufts were blond and wavy, swirling over his brow.

'I'd like to live on a boat someday,' he said, a faraway look in his eyes and a dreamy note in his voice.

'This boat?'

'Why not?'

Lizzie imagined herself living on a boat with him. It wasn't quite what she'd had in mind. The boat could accommodate two quite comfortably, but what if there were more than two; three perhaps, or even four? She couldn't help voicing what was in her mind.

'There's only room for two. Any more than that and it could be extremely crowded.'

He shrugged. 'That's OK. Visitors would have to manage.'

Lizzie lowered her eyes and rolled away from him on to her back. 'I wasn't talking about visitors. I was talking about a family, when your divorce comes through and you remarry.'

'Oh, yeah. Yeah,' he said. 'Sorry, honey. I wasn't thinking about that.'

The drumming on the roof intensified.

'Where would we live?' Lizzie asked him. 'Here or in Canada?'

'Canada of course.'

He hadn't asked her for a preference. There would be no discussion. He was Canadian and had no intention of living anywhere else. In one respect the prospect of living in a foreign land excited her. But what about her family? Her feelings were too big to keep inside. 'I'd miss my family.'

'You'd get used to it. I'm missing mine – my parents, that is.'

The flat way he said it surprised her. If she wanted him it would have to be on his terms, that was clear. She pushed away the sudden comparison between him and her father. Guy wasn't at all like her father. He didn't drink so much as her father, and he wasn't hot tempered. On the contrary, he could be quite cold at times – *but only in response to insubordination*, she reminded herself and was reassured.

The sound of gentle breathing told her he'd fallen asleep. She looked at him sleeping, the dark lashes resting on the high cheekbones. He had a dimple in his chin – quite a deep one. She smiled as she poked her small finger into it. He murmured something but didn't open his eyes.

'I'm going to have a cigarette,' she said.

'You don't smoke,' he murmured and rolled over on to his side.

She couldn't blame him for being tired. He was continually flitting about the countryside and from one country to the next. He'd never fully explained what his trips back and forth to America were about, except that when he was there he travelled up to see his parents in Canada.

'When time allows,' he'd said to her.

'Do you visit your wife too?' she'd asked him.

'Only when my lawyer tells me to get my tail up there and sort a few things out.'

He'd kissed her afterwards and made her feel warm all over. Confirmation that the separation from his wife was proceeding stopped her enquiring about his war work. He was in charge of squadrons, took part in operation planning, but still there was something else, something he was loath to discuss.

Don't worry about it.

Wrapping his jacket around her nude body, she tiptoed across to where he'd left a packet of Camel cigarettes sitting on the table. She slid one out, looked for a lighter but saw none.

It must still be in his pocket, she thought.

She reached into the pocket of the jacket she was wearing. Her fingers touched the lighter. She drew it out. A piece of paper came with it and fell to the floor.

The letter was written on sweet-smelling paper, the sort that had disappeared within months of the war starting.

She hadn't meant her eyes to fall on the signature – or perhaps subconsciously she had. The insecurity of loving another woman's husband had never quite gone away, even though he assured her that he and Pamela – that was her name – were in the throes of getting a divorce.

Curiosity got the better of Lizzie. Carefully the letter was unfolded and flattened. Her heart skipped a beat when she saw the signature. For a brief moment she thought about refolding the letter and shoving it back into Guy's pocket, but it was too late. Her eyes were already scouring the words. There was nothing in this letter about a divorce. Quite the opposite – the woman was calling him *darling*! She'd signed off *Your affectionate and ever loving Pamela*. Guy had said their divorce was amicable, but this amicable?

Guy stirred. Like generations of 'other women', she couldn't bring herself to believe what she'd read and certainly couldn't tackle him, not at this moment. Not until she'd had time to think about things.

Twenty-Eight

In response to Harry's letter, Patrick Kelly knocked at the door of the house in Aiken Street. After receiving the letter, he'd phoned Harry to ask if he'd seen Lizzie. He'd also told him about the letter he'd received from her saying she'd fallen in love with someone else but asking if they could remain friends.

'I suppose I was expecting too much,' said Patrick with a careless laugh. 'But I would have liked to see her, just to get things clear in my head.'

It had been obvious from Harry's tone that he wasn't fooled. Patrick was hurt. Lizzie was the girl he'd always loved. She'd never commented on his scruffiness or the fact a whole regiment of 'uncles' visited his mother on a regular basis. She'd treated him with respect and they'd grown close – but apparently not close enough.

Harry had gone quiet, though Patrick could almost hear his sharp mind ticking away on the end of the phone.

'Are you still there, Harry?'

'Yes, mate, and I've got a plan.'

That was why he was here knocking on the door of Aiken Street. Harry had explained that his mother was having a string of bad luck – small things, some of it, but the pressure had become such that she'd had no alternative but to move back in with his father. He'd asked Patrick to check things out.

Patrick recalled how easily Harry had slid back into the familiar Bristol dialect.

'Michael Maurice can't get leave, and if someone don't go and sort things out, he's likely to end up in big trouble. With him living in Germany all they years, they'll be saying he's a spy or somefing. I wrote to ar Lizzie telling her to go home and see what was happening. So with a bit of luck – kill two birds with one stone, eh?'

Heart in his mouth, he leaned close to the door and listened. The door was thick and heavy, but he could hear a heavy tread on creaking boards. Henry Randall perhaps?

Swollen with years of weathering, the door stuck, shuddered, then creaked open.

'Bless me! If it ain't Patrick Kelly. Looking for Lizzie, are you?'

He'd hoped to see Lizzie in the doorway. Biddy Young was as dissimilar to Lizzie as anyone could be. She was fatter than ever, her hair still dyed to near whiteness and her make-up applied with a trowel.

'Yes I am, Mrs Young. I heard from Harry that she was likely to be down here visiting her mother. When's she back?'

Biddy's jowls made a flapping sound when she shook her head. Her red lips tightened like a wrinkled rosebud.

'Ooow, she's not 'ere, Patrick. She came just as Mary Anne and young Stanley were packing their things and moving out.' She jerked her head towards the stairs behind her. 'Henry Randall's back in his old ways. They was halfway down the street last night when Lizzie came along and caught 'im raising his hand to her mother. She gave 'im a mouthful, I can tell you. Shouted at 'im and called 'im all the names under the sun. I should think the whole street heard.'

Biddy could not have known it, but hearing her talk that way about Lizzie made him proud. In the past she'd stood up to those who'd shunned his company and criticized her being friends with him. Now she'd stood up to her father. She was gutsy and his heart overflowed with love.

'Do you know where they've gone?'

Biddy looked peeved. 'They wouldn't tell me where they were going. Can't understand why, I'm sure. I mean, me and Mary Anne go back a long way. We was neighbours in Kent Street and I was a very good customer of 'er little business. There weren't a week gone by when I didn't 'ave something to pawn. Still,' she said with a derisory sniff, 'if she don't want to share 'er secrets, I suppose that's up to 'er. Want a cup of tea, son?' she asked, her face suddenly brightening.

Patrick declined. He had no intention of spending the morning listening to Biddy's gossip. Mary Anne probably had a very good reason for not telling Biddy where she and Lizzie were off to and he could easily guess what it was. The whole street would end up sharing the secret – and that included Henry.

'She won't go and stay at Daw's if she can help it,' Harry had said.

All the same, with no clue of where else she might be, Patrick made his way to Kent Street.

The street had changed but the shop had not. Six houses had been destroyed in the bombing on the night of November 24th. Patrick felt compelled to walk past the shop and inspect the bombsites first. All that remained was a gaping hole and mounds of rubble where weeds thrived and dirty-faced children played cowboys and Indians.

'Bang! You're dead!'

Patrick stopped and looked at the two sets of kids firing pretend guns at each other. He felt a sudden surge of dismay. Wasn't a real war enough for them? *They're just kids*, he reminded himself. *You did the same yourself not so long after 1918*. He turned away and headed back towards the shop, his thoughts doing a backward flip again at the sight of it.

The same enamel signs adorned the blank wall at the end of the building and beneath the shop windows, advertisements for Colman's mustard, Cherry Blossom shoe polish and Sunlight soap.

The brass bell above the shop door jangled as he pushed it open. Daw was wiping the bacon slicer. She looked up, a smile fixed on her face ready to welcome a paying customer. Her face dropped when she saw who it was.

'Patrick. Home on leave, are you?'

No 'good morning'. No 'nice to see you', he thought.

'Yes. I was wondering whether you'd seen Lizzie. I heard she was home.'

Daw pursed her lips and went back to wiping off the sharp teeth of the circular blade. 'Well you know more than I do. I've had no letter from her for ages.'

'Oh! When did you last write?'

The question seemed to take her unawares. Her mouth formed a childish pout as she looked at him. 'When have I got time to write letters? I've to help in this shop, I do air-raid duty and I've got a kiddie to look after.'

He nodded as though he understood and sympathized. The

truth was he thought her self-centred. She'd never been any different and, if anything, she was getting worse. *Poor John*, he thought.

'I'm sorry to have troubled you. Any idea where your mother might be?'

She shrugged. 'Out shopping? Perhaps Dad knows.'

'No. She's left . . .' The moment those first few words were out of his mouth, he knew he shouldn't have said anything.

Daw's eyes flashed with anger. 'What are you saying? She's left him again?'

'I . . .' Patrick was stumped for words.

Lizzie had once told him that Daw should be an actress. 'She's good at putting on an act,' she'd said. At the time he hadn't been sure of what she'd meant, but he certainly knew now.

Daw rested the back of her hand against her forehead. 'Oh, my poor father! Left alone to fend for himself. After all he's been through!'

Patrick found himself wanting to laugh. The dramatic attitude was bad enough, but Lizzie had also told him the truth about Henry Randall.

'I'd better be going,' he said.

She didn't ask him to let her know her mother's whereabouts; neither did she offer him a cup of tea. It didn't matter. He was here on a mission and was determined to follow it through.

He went back to the digs he'd got himself above the Red Cross shop in East Street. The woman in charge reminded him of the flight sergeant he'd run into on first joining the RAF. On reflection he'd decided that even Flight Sergeant Derrick would have crumpled beneath her superior gaze.

'You may have a key,' she'd said.

He couldn't help standing to attention when she looked him up and down.

'Should you go out at night, I would prefer you to come through the back door. We have a lot of valuable merchandise here, and although you look an honest kind of chap, I don't know you from Adam. So, back-door access only! Is that clear?'

'Definitely worse than Sergeant Derrick,' he muttered once she was out of earshot.

Harry had suggested he check with Edgar to find out exactly

what had happened. 'If he ain't home or at the flower shop, get hold of him at the nightclub.'

The Black Cat nightclub was pretty central and preferable to seeing Edgar at home or at the flower shop. Even so, he didn't want to see Edgar either. He tolerated Harry and even liked him, though mostly because he was Lizzie's brother. If he hadn't been he would have steered well clear. He couldn't help it. That was the way things were, especially in the services; poofs were barely tolerated.

A big man with a broken nose and a cauliflower ear wanted to charge him five shillings to go in.

'I just want to see Edgar Williams,' he said.

The big man's eyes were blue and unmoving, like a dead pig's.

'What about?'

'It's personal. A family matter,' he added quickly on seeing a trace of contempt creep into the big man's eyes.

'You related?'

'Distantly. If you could tell him Harry sent me.'

'Harry?' The big man's expression changed immediately. 'Why didn't you say so!'

Even though he was presently away serving his country, Harry was paid due respect; there was no calling him 'queer', 'poof' or 'bent'.

Waving a meaty paw, he gestured someone over. 'Vince,' he said to the thin man in spectacles. 'This gent wants to see Edgar. Is he in?'

'Yep,' said Vince. He led Patrick into the bar area and pointed. 'There he is.'

Edgar was wearing a blue jacket and pale checked trousers. He looked spruce, sprightly and incredibly confident.

'Edgar?'

Edgar looked puzzled as though he were trying to place the face.

'Patrick Kelly. I'm an old friend of Harry's. I think you know he was worried about his mother.'

Edgar's face flooded with realization. 'Yes. Yes, he was. Please,' he said, pushing a stool forward. 'Take a seat. Would you like a drink?'

Patrick accepted a small beer.

'Now, what's happening?' Edgar asked once they were both

sitting and out of earshot of other customers. 'I knew she should never have gone back to Harry's dad. Has he hurt her again?'

Patrick shook his head and took a sip of his drink. Raising his eyes he noticed the mirror at the back of the bar. Curious eyes beyond his reflection were turned in their direction. He pushed aside concerns about what they might be thinking. He was here on a mission. He needed to know what had been going on first hand.

'I don't know for sure whether he has, but I think the threat was there. When I went round neither Lizzie nor her mother were there; an old friend told me they'd moved out last night.'

'Oh, Lord!' Edgar made a mournful face.

'So you don't know where they might be?'

Edgar shook his head. 'She was getting nervous about this and that. We had an intruder in the flat, then there was the time Stanley's roller skates went missing, and me getting beaten up. She couldn't cope with it, poor love. She thought somebody was after her.'

Patrick glanced briefly at Edgar's fresh-faced complexion. 'Why did she think that?'

'Because something bad happened each place she went.'

'Have you had any more problems since?'

Edgar shook his head. 'Harry seemed to think that the Truman gang had something to do with his mum getting so much hassle, but I checked them out. Like us they've got their beady eyes on other things besides nightclubs. The black market is thriving. Everything's got a price and there's a fortune to be made. Food and silk parachutes are a safer market than this game.'

Patrick frowned. 'So you don't know where they are?'

Edgar shook his head. 'No. Sorry.' He was thoughtful for a moment. 'Do you think I should ring Harry and let him know she's gone missing?'

'I wouldn't advise that. He's got enough on his plate,' said Patrick, rising to his feet. 'Leave it with me. Once I've found her and know she's safe, then you can pick up the phone.'

He left Edgar having agreed to that. Now what? He walked along the blacked-out street, the sound of his footsteps ringing on the cobbles. A light drizzle started to fall, tickling the nape of his neck, sending goose bumps down his spine. He turned his coat collar up. There was no let up to the darkness, not the merest glint of light shining through a chink in a curtain, not a star, not a headlight, not a line of light seeping from beneath an ill-fitting door in those places where buildings were left standing.

All around him were the results of bomb damage – lilting walls and gaping doors and windows lined with blackness. The smell of dust rose with each droplet of rain. Rank weeds watered by rancid water rustled in the wind.

He fancied he smelled smoke and turned to face it. For a brief moment he thought he detected a sudden light in the bombed-out ruins on Castle Green overlooking the river. This was the area that had borne the brunt of the bombing on November 24th. Buildings that had stood for centuries had been pounded to dust. The lower basements were still intact, a haven for those with no roof over their head or no way of paying for one. The smoke was from their cooking fires. He could even smell what they were cooking. Heaven help the homeless on a night like this.

Before the war and the blackout he might not have noticed smells or heard things so clearly. Moonless nights meant depending on other senses rather than sight.

The sound of a tram alerted him to the fact that he'd strayed out on to the rails. Luckily trams were noisy things. It didn't matter that its windows were boarded up so no light could escape. He heard it before he saw it and was able to get out of the way in time.

That night, once he was back above the Red Cross shop and had made himself tea and toast, he got Lizzie's letter from out of his pocket. He fingered it, tracing around its folded edges. Did he really want to read it again? He turned the light off, walked to the window and drew back the curtains. Rooftops, spires, towers and cupolas were coal black against an indigo sky. The clouds were beginning to disperse. A ray of moonlight searched the sea of blackness just like the beam of the searchlights that sought intruders. He knew all about what it was like flying up there. He'd heard all the stories from his pilots, the giddy knights whose steeds were called Spitfire and Hurricane. But tonight he wasn't pondering the bravery of young men not yet twenty-one and dying for their country. He was thinking of Lizzie. Where was she? he wondered. And was she with her mother or with someone else? He didn't know, but he cared, he cared very much indeed.

Twenty-Nine

'Mother, you can't stay here,' said Lizzie, scrutinizing the dismal surroundings with a look of dismay. 'It's a mess!'

'This is where I've been happiest,' said her mother.

'You didn't tell me it was as bad as this.'

Mary Anne pretended she hadn't heard and looked away.

She'd told her daughter that the rooms above the burned-out ruins of the pawn shop were liveable.

Lizzie eyed the smoke-damaged walls and blackened windows. Grit and broken glass crunched like ground bones beneath her feet. *This is dismal, dirty and about to fall down, hardly a happy home*, she thought. She was about to voice her opinion, but her mother got there first.

'It's also where I feel safest,' she said.

Lizzie couldn't argue with that. She wanted to hit her father, to shake him into a different man. Impossible, but anger could make you wish for the impossible when times were bad.

She followed her mother, grabbing Stanley every so often when he looked like destroying things further; ripping at ragged curtains or stomping on a piece of glass.

The two bedrooms at the back of the house were intact. The downstairs rooms, including the kitchen, were in a sorry state but the sink and water supply were still working. The most redeeming feature about the place was that it had an indoor bathroom upstairs, a luxury by anyone's standard. The front of the building had sustained the worst damage, and nothing remained of the shop front, which was now open to the sky. The main bedroom on the upper floor no longer existed. All that remained was its door opening on to nothing but a void; quite a drop to the ground.

'Better keep this locked,' said Lizzie.

'The lavatory still works,' said Stanley after he'd used it.

'So does the sink,' said his mother, grabbing his shoulders and wheeling him back in the direction he'd just come from. 'Wash. You've got soot all over your face.'

'I had a wash last night,' he wailed.

'That was yesterday. You weren't playing with soot yesterday.'

Lizzie grinned. 'Nothing changes.' Her expression turned serious. 'Look, are you sure about this, Mum?' she said, her arms folded purposefully as she addressed her mother. 'We can still take a room above the Lord Nelson.'

Her mother shook her head. 'That's hardly a home, and it's expensive.'

Lizzie looked down at the floor. 'I could pay.'

'No you couldn't.'

No. She couldn't. But she'd had to offer.

'I don't want you to tell anyone where I'm living,' said Mary Anne suddenly.

Lizzie raised her eyebrows. 'No one?'

'Tell only those people that need to know. No one else. And that includes our Daw. She has friends . . .' She shrugged. 'Someone's been making things bad for me . . .' Her voice trailed away. She closed her eyes and held the back of her hand against her forehead. 'Oh God! Am I going mad?'

Lizzie fought down the sickness within. It was as if a veil had fallen from her eyes. She was still her mother, yet this woman before her had changed immeasurably since Lizzie's childhood. She found herself dividing that change into two parts, and the first time she'd noticed change was when her mother had moved in with Michael. The years had fallen away; she'd seemed like a girl again. But this time she looked tired, thinner, haunted even. The last word was perhaps the most fitting, but also the most frightening.

Stanley swivelled from the waist like children do when they're watching adults and feeling nervous about things they don't quite understand.

Lizzie's first inclination was to shout at him to go outside and play, but somehow she didn't want to bear this alone.

She purposefully moderated her tone so as not to sound as worried as she felt. 'Do you think Father is doing these things?'

'I did at first, but then he was sometimes at work when

they occurred.' She swallowed and threw back her head, opening her eyes as she exposed the whiteness of her throat. 'I think it's Routledge. He was in the army with your father, but he was also the caretaker appointed to look after the shop just before Michael arrived.' She was about to tell Lizzie that Michael had found Routledge entertaining a young prostitute in his uncle's bed, but remembered that Stanley was listening. She chose her words carefully. 'Michael caught him abusing that trust and threw him out. He swore revenge.' She shrugged. 'And with Michael away . . .'

'Have you actually seen this man?'

'No.'

'What about going to the police?'

Mary Anne laughed nervously, her shoulders shuddering at the thought of it. 'They'd probably lock me up – and I don't mean in the cells.' Her expression was forlorn. 'Don't let them do that, Lizzie. Believe me, I'm not mad. Someone really is making life difficult for me.'

There had been so much Lizzie had been going to tell her mother, but not now, not after seeing her and hearing all this. It would be too much to bear. 'You're right about this place,' she said, forcing herself to sound bright and breezy even if she didn't feel it. 'This is your place. Yours and Michael's place.'

From then on the mood brightened. There was much to do, but both women, and even young Stanley, went light-heartedly about their work.

'We'd better get a meal on the go now I've found these,' said Mary Anne, sighing with satisfaction on finding a set of willow-patterned china in a cardboard box at the bottom of a cupboard.

She also found a black and white gingham oilcloth to set over the table. A quick wipe and the table was ready for laying. But cooking a meal wouldn't be quite as easy, as Lizzie was quick to point out.

'The gas pipe is probably fractured so we can't use the stove.'

'What's for dinner?' asked Stanley, wiping his wet hands down his shirt. 'I've washed,' he said to his mother before she had a chance to ask him. 'Even behind me ears.' Obligingly, he bent his head, tugging each ear forward in turn.

'Hmm,' said Mary Anne after close scrutiny. 'They look clean enough. If you want dinner I need you to gather some wood and some coal from the coal house out back. The gas supply's been cut off. We'll have to use the range and the range needs wood and coal.'

Stanley did as he was told, the prospect of getting dirty all over again incredibly appealing.

'There's plenty of wood to burn,' she said to Lizzie. 'There's bits of our best furniture, some of it over a hundred years old, all half burned already. Seems a shame to chop it up, but there . . .' She shrugged.

Lizzie found an undamaged saucepan, filled it with water and began helping her mother chop vegetables and the bit of scrag end ready for the pot. As they chopped out of Stanley's ear shot, Mary Anne told her daughter about her father getting back on the beer and threatening to thrash Stanley.

'Daw wouldn't have believed me and I didn't want to go back to Harry's place.' She also told her about Gertrude and the letter she'd received about she and Michael not being married. 'So there was nothing else for it,' she explained. 'It was here or nowhere.'

Soon the fire was glowing and an earnest joviality accompanied their endeavours, both women making an effort to rise above their own personal worries – Mary Anne's that Michael would never come back, and Lizzie's that Guy would not keep his word to divorce his wife.

'I have to keep my spirits up for Stanley's sake,' said Mary Anne.

'Me too,' said Lizzie, 'but also for you.'

It was easy to lie, far easier than Lizzie had supposed. She couldn't – she wouldn't – burden her mother with her own problems. Sadness and admiration jockeyed for position as she watched her mother making do, pretending that the happiest place she'd ever known was unchanged. It took great courage to do that, she decided, but breaking point could never be that far away. She would not say anything about Guy, his wife and their relationship. She would not tell her about the latest development and ask for her advice. Her mother had enough to cope with.

'Just look at our hands,' said Mary Anne, holding her hands palms outwards.

'I like black hands,' said Stanley. 'You can belong to the Black Hand Gang if you've got black hands.'

Mother and daughter laughed. 'Is that all we need to belong to a gang?' said Lizzie.

Stanley scowled. 'No, stupid.'

They all had black hands. Lizzie dotted a blob of dirt on her brother's nose. Stanley laughed at first, but then had second thoughts and swiped at it with the back of his hand.

'I'm not washing again,' he exclaimed. 'Not until tomorrow. Can I go out to play now?'

His mother answered. 'Yes, but be back by dark. And come in the back way. I don't want anyone to know we're here. Alright?'

'I'll be quiet as a mouse.' Glass scrunched beneath Stanley's feet as he ran out the back door.

'Quiet, my foot!' Mary Anne exclaimed.

She watched her youngest son scramble over the rubble out in the back yard. The walls surrounding the yard were still standing. So was the back gate. She was thankful for that. It gave them some privacy and the fact that there was a sign outside saying 'Dangerous Building' would keep nosey parkers at bay.

Her gaze returned to the single sapling that had withstood the blast of the bombing, the fire and the freezing temperatures of the last winter. Spring buds were blossoming into summer. It made her feel better.

'Yes, I think we'll be safe here,' she said, mostly to herself though, of course, Lizzie was within hearing distance.

To her surprise Lizzie made no comment. It wasn't like her second-oldest daughter to be so quiet for so long. Instinctively, she presumed something was wrong. She turned away from the window. Lizzie didn't meet her enquiring eyes that were as thoughtful and as beautiful as her own. Arms folded in the defensive way she'd adopted of late, she was plucking at her bottom lip, head bowed, brow furrowed in thought.

'Did you hear what I said?'

Lizzie's head jerked up. 'Of course I did.'

'There's no need to snap.'

'I'm sorry.' Lizzie sighed deeply. She went to her handbag and got out a cigarette.

'Since when have you smoked?' her mother asked.

'It's the war. It's making me a bag of nerves,' said Lizzie, slipping the cigarette between her lips while she rummaged in her bag for her lighter. The lighter was sleek and silver, shaped something like a bullet. A Streamliner, Guy had called it when he'd given it to her. It flashed brazenly and had an air of ostentation about it, even of guilt – just like her really.

Mary Anne pretended that the fire needed stoking. 'I don't think you should smoke,' she said, bending before the range to prod the coals with the poker.

'I'll do as I please.'

The retort was hasty and unexpected, and the second within a few minutes.

Mary Anne straightened and looked at her. There was a certain tension in her daughter's eyes that hadn't been there before. It worried her, but for the moment she'd hold her tongue. If Lizzie had something to tell her, she would get round to it in her own good time.

'I'm sorry,' said Lizzie, her expression full of remorse. She rubbed at her forehead and closed her eyes. 'I'm tired. It was a long journey and the train was slow. I didn't mean to snap.'

Mary Anne said nothing, but buttoned her cardigan and hid her glorious hair beneath a turban tied at the front. Her hair had been a dark honey-blonde in her youth. It still held most of that colour although it was less vibrant than it used to be.

'I'm going across to the Red Cross shop. I used their address when I was last there. I think they'll agree to let me use it again for my letters. It's just a precaution,' she added.

Lizzie nodded but still seemed distracted.

'Why don't you go and lie down?' said Mary Anne.

'Yes. I might do that.'

It was good to get out into the fresh air. Despite the bomb damage, the lack of colour and the shabbiness of people making do, the atmosphere was uplifting, because it was May and the sky was blue.

Mary Anne cut through the alley into East Street. Butterflies were doing cartwheels in her stomach at the thought of entering the shop again, but it had to be done. *Asking Gertrude Palmer a favour has to be more frightening than going to meet the King*, she thought to herself. *But she can't refuse me this*, she decided as she approached the art deco frontage of the Red Cross shop. The doorbell tinkled an unidentifiable tune as she entered. The butterflies perched with folded wings the moment she saw Edith behind the counter. Not much more than five feet tall, the poor woman was almost buried behind a pile of donated clothes; everything from fox furs to gentlemen's combinations. Edith's deepset hazel eyes lit up at the sight of her.

'Mary Anne!'

She came out from behind the counter, clasping her close with bent, arthritic fingers as though she were her long-lost daughter, even though they were roughly the same age. 'I'm so pleased to see you.'

With a jerk of her chin, Mary Anne indicated the mountain of clothes. 'It seems you're in danger of being buried alive.'

Edith made a face. 'We're short on seamstresses willing to carry out alterations for nothing. They'd sooner get a job sewing uniforms or in a munitions factory and get paid for their war work. I told Her Majesty that when she insisted you leave the flat. I told her she'd regret it, but . . .' She waved her arms like a courtier about to take a bow. 'You know how it is. A queen expects to be obeyed.'

'I must admit, I did enjoy the work,' said Mary Anne.

Hope widened Edith's eyes. 'Are you available?'

Mary Anne thought quickly. 'Yes, I am as a matter of fact.' Gertrude would not refuse her help, would she?

'Gertrude will be relieved,' said Edith as if reading her thoughts. 'Especially if I make it sound as though it's all her idea. I wouldn't dream of telling her I told you so.' She winked like a young man would, saucily as though they were sharing a naughty secret. 'But you know, and I know.'

Mary Anne felt as though a ton weight had fallen from her shoulders. She'd been worried about asking if she could use the shop for her mail. Now the way was open, so she went ahead and asked.

'Of course you can,' said Edith. 'There's a few people round here do that for one reason or another. Some of them have been bombed out like you and haven't yet found anywhere suitable to live. Some of them . . .' She paused and lowered her voice, her eyes fluttering sidelong as though not wanting to be overheard. 'Someone has letters sent here that don't come from her husband.' She winked. 'If you know what I mean.'

'I see.'

A vision of Michael flashed into her mind; Michael and her not being married had been the reason she'd been evicted from the flat above the shop in the first place.

Her thoughts must have showed on her face. Edith patted her hand. 'Never you mind. I'm in charge of that side of things. People can still send each other letters, can't they? I'll arrange things right away.' A wistful look came to her face. 'I used to get a lot of letters during the Great War, you know. I didn't get any after 1916.' Her eyes turned misty. 'But I kept the ones he did send. I keep them tied up with a purple ribbon.'

'I see. So you never married?'

'Oh yes. I married after the war when I came out of the VADs – I was a volunteer nurse, you see. But I left him over there. He was a French lieutenant. I bandaged his wounds.' She leaned closer, her voice dropping to a whisper. 'We did a lot of things together. He was already married, but you know what foreigners are like. He didn't think it was wrong, and I didn't either. There was a war on . . .' Her voice drifted away along with her precious memories.

Edith's revelations had been quite surprising. The woman was so human, and no doubt she would have offered more of her life story over a cup of tea, but Mary Anne's attention had already drifted through the doorway to the room at the back of the shop. She saw a flash of blue uniform heading for the back door. The height, the way he moved and the outline of his face as he turned slightly confirmed who he was.

'Patrick!'

He turned abruptly, his long legs striding swiftly and assuredly towards her.

'Mrs Randall! Here you are! Where have you been? Where's Lizzie? Where are you staying?'

She shook her head and held up a hand, begging him to halt.

'One question at a time, Patrick.'

'Harry sent me to find you. He was worried.'

'I can understand that, but there was no need to be. I was going to write to him as soon as I was settled. See?' She brought out the letter she'd written only that morning. 'It's short and sweet but it explains everything.'

Patrick's face was flushed. He looked past her into the shop, seeking the one person he wanted to see above all others.

'Where's Lizzie?' he asked.

Mary Anne hesitated. It wasn't that she was worried about divulging her address to Patrick; Edith was out of earshot. Earlier she'd had the feeling that Lizzie was holding something back. Now Patrick was looking apprehensive, as though something unexpected had happened, something he hadn't been prepared for. And Lizzie, she decided, was at the bottom of it.

Thirty

'I think you should go to the pictures, Lizzie. Have you told him you will?'

Lizzie was washing the dishes while her mother wiped. Patrick had joined them for a meal, and Mary Anne was taking advantage while Patrick had gone to relieve himself.

'I told him I'd think about it. I thought you could do with a hand here.'

'I can manage. There's nothing here that can't wait. It's been a mess for months so another few days aren't going to make that much difference.'

She stole an unseen glance at her daughter. Lizzie was looking down at each cup, each plate and each saucer she cleaned as though she might wipe the pattern off if she weren't careful. Mary Anne looked back to the hot water but kept up a perpetual series of glances in the hope of seeing her daughter's eyes in order to gauge what she was thinking. Soon she decided there was nothing for it but to be direct.

'Are you keeping something from me, Lizzie?'

Lizzie jerked into instant alertness as if she'd been woken from a dream. 'No. Of course not. Whatever makes you think that?'

Her retort was accompanied by a nervous laugh. Mary

Anne was not fooled. She decided to mention the only other love interest Lizzie had ever had. 'Have you seen anything of Peter?'

'That creep! Not since I caught him hiding in the attic. I heard he got posted to North Africa.'

Mary Anne smiled wryly and raised her eyebrows. 'Well that's a bit different from Canada. A bit warmer too.'

'In more ways than one, from what I hear on the news,' Lizzie added.

Their faces creased with amusement. Peter's mother had told everyone that he had enlisted and been posted to Canada on a training programme. With the help of his mother, Peter Selwyn had actually hidden in the attic in order to avoid enlistment. Lizzie had caught him out.

'That was more than a year ago,' said Lizzie, overcome with sudden nostalgia. She stopped wiping and looked out the kitchen window, catching glimpses of back yard brick and drooping buddleia.

'Eighteen months or thereabouts,' said her mother. She too stopped scrubbing at the pot and thought of the happy days of her first acquaintance with Michael. Bleeding profusely from an impending miscarriage, she'd collapsed on his doorstep. He'd taken her in and done everything Henry, her own husband, wouldn't dream of doing.

Lizzie sensed where her mother's thoughts were heading. 'Has Michael heard from his parents?'

Mary Anne nodded. 'They're quite alright. They're still on the Isle of Man, but they hope not for much longer. The powers that be are trying to sort things out. Hopefully they'll get sent to another camp on the mainland. There are no houses for them, but at least they'll be able to move around freely. It won't be a prison camp like on the Isle of Man.'

The sound of the flush being pulled preceded Patrick's arrival.

'Perhaps if you don't go to the pictures, we can have a little talk,' said Mary Anne, eyeing her daughter knowingly. 'Something's obviously worrying you.'

'Of course it isn't,' said Lizzie as she finally set the plate she'd just wiped on to the pile for putting away. 'Whatever makes you think that?'

'You've wiped that same plate four times, put it down on

the pile four times, and picked it back up again four times. Have you finished wiping it now?'

Mary Anne glanced over her shoulder at Patrick. Her heart went out to him. His hands were in his pockets, his eyes were fixed on the floor and his jaw was clenched in a straight, rock-hard line.

'I think our Lizzie has decided she's going to the pictures with you,' she said.

He lifted his head and his face brightened. 'Is that right, Lizzie?'

'You bet,' she said with the jolliest smile Mary Anne had seen on her daughter's face since she'd come home.

'No heart-to-heart talk with Mother tonight,' murmured Mary Anne, a smile playing around her lips.

Patrick looked worried again and addressed Lizzie. 'Well if you really want to have a chat with your mother . . .'

'Oh, no,' said Lizzie, untying and tossing aside her apron. 'I'd love to go to the pictures with you.'

'Can I come?' asked Stanley, who was busily scraping the saucepan of the last vestiges of stew.

Lizzie had been about to say no, but thought better of it. 'I suppose you can. What's playing?' she asked Patrick.

Patrick's disappointment that they wouldn't be going alone was obvious. 'I dunno,' he grumbled. 'It might not be a U. I think it's an A.'

'That's alright,' whooped Stanley. 'If it's an A certificate, I can get in with you two.'

'I'll get my coat,' said Lizzie.

Mary Anne closed the blackout curtains after they'd gone and lit the candles. The glow of the coals in the range turned the dirty walls to rose and the flickering flame of the candles added a frieze of dancing shadows.

They'd cleaned the room and the old dining table enough for her to start unpicking and re-cutting some items on which Edith at the Red Cross had asked her to work her magic.

The light wasn't really good enough for her to see by and after a while she rubbed at her eyes, leaned back in the chair and dozed in front of the fire.

Patrick gave Lizzie his arm. Together they walked silently with Stanley skipping around in front of them, rabbiting on about Zorro and his flaming sword of freedom.

'So,' said Patrick once he'd plucked up the courage to face the truth. 'Who is this new sweetheart of yours?'

Lizzie lowered her eyes. 'I couldn't help it, Patrick. I was his driver and it just happened. We were working together.'

'And ended up sleeping together.'

'I didn't say that!' Lizzie's retort was hot and the blood rushed to her face.

'I'm sorry. I shouldn't have said that.'

Lizzie sucked in her lips as she considered what she could say. There was nothing really. Somehow Patrick had stumbled on the truth. 'It's alright.'

They'd reached the doors of the Town Hall Picture House. The queue for the one and sixpenny tickets was already moving forward. They tagged on to the end of it, Stanley first, proudly stating the fact that he was paying for himself. He counted out some pennies and threepenny bits that Patrick had given him.

'I thought we were engaged,' said Patrick suddenly after paying for their tickets.

'I'm sorry I gave you that impression.'

'I thought it was more than an impression. I thought it was fact.'

The darkness of the theatre hid her guilty expression. Patrick was speaking the truth. She *had* promised him a lot and now she'd gone back on her word. 'I'm sorry, Patrick. But I want a better life.'

'The sort of life Peter, that other geezer, could have given you – if he'd been willing.'

'You've no right to say that!'

This time he didn't say sorry. Neither did she pursue an apology. His comment hit too close to the truth. Peter, her employer's son, had led her on, toyed with her and made her believe he loved her. She told herself that Guy wasn't like that, that he really loved her and would get a divorce – especially now, when she told him her news.

'You've got to promise me that you'll say nothing to my mother – or anyone else for that matter.'

'Of course not,' said Patrick.

People already seated rose so they could squeeze through to their seats. Pathé News was on, reporting about events in North Africa. There were cheers for the Eighth Army and jeers for captured Italians.

Lizzie was glad of the darkness and the need to be quiet.

Once they were seated, Patrick whispered into her ear. 'I'll always love you.'

Fixing her eyes on the screen, she pretended she hadn't heard. But she wasn't watching the film; she wasn't really there at all. She was wishing the time away, wanting to be gone from Bristol and back in East Anglia. Despite Harry's entreaties, she wouldn't have come down at all if Guy hadn't been forced to go away.

'I'll be back as soon as I can,' he'd told her. 'We'll sort things out then.'

She'd believed him totally, but now a tiny seed of doubt was starting to grow. *No*, she thought to herself and cut it off at the root, *Guy will be there for me*. She must believe that.

To Lizzie the film that was billed as being just over an hour long seemed more like three hours. Her eyes were fixed on the screen but she wasn't really seeing it. At last the film finished and the National Anthem was played. The patriotic majority stood and waited patiently; the few who were less than patriotic raced for the exits.

Stanley chattered about the film all the way home, a fact that went a long way to bridging the silence that had descended between his sister and Patrick.

'I'm going to be like Jimmy Cagney when I grow up.'

'You won't,' said Lizzie. 'Mum won't let you.'

Stanley continued to skip sideways along the pavement making rat-a-tat-tat noises from the pretend machine gun he was using.

Both Patrick and Lizzie walked along with their hands in their pockets, heads down. It was a clear night and darkness had only just fallen. The sound of gunfire sounded in the distance.

'Swindon. Or Gloucester,' said Patrick.

'Hmm.' Lizzie made no real comment. At least the bombing wasn't here. At least they were safe for the moment.

They walked along the street at the back of the old pawn shop, not needing to cut through the alley from East Street. Streaks of brightness behind ragged purple clouds formed a dramatic backdrop for a forest of chimneys, broken roofs and floating barrage balloons.

The street was empty, the last kids having been called in

long ago for supper and bedtime. A trail of smoke rose from the blackened stump of what remained of a chimney above the pawn shop. Another pillar of denser, blacker smoke rose in the proximity of the back yard.

'Hello! What's going on?' Patrick frowned and quickened his pace.

Lizzie heard the concern in his voice. 'What is it?'

As they came level with the gate, it jerked open. A figure in a trench coat came flying out, almost knocking them over.

Patrick grabbed him.

'Hey! What are you up to?'

'Mother!' Lizzie ran into the back yard, Stanley right behind her. What she saw there filled her with terror. A fire had been set against the back door. The old paint was already blistering, which was causing the smoke.

'Smother it,' shouted Patrick, still grappling with the man in the trench coat. 'Smother it!'

Lizzie grabbed a damp sheet from the line. 'Quick, Stanley. Spread it over the fire.'

Considering his age, Stanley was quick to act. Bravely he grappled with the edges of the sheet, fastening them over the fire with bits of brick and stone. His face was creased with concern, his eyes narrowed against the stifling smoke.

What remained of the smoke turned from black to white and steadied from toxic plumes to drifting mist. The damp sheet had done its stuff.

Lizzie pushed past it and unlocked the door, shouting for her mother as she ran inside. Stanley picked up the leg of a chair on his way out to join Patrick. Holding it with both hands, he raised the weapon over the man's head. His jaw dropped open when he saw who it was.

The man struggled and attempted to get up. Patrick rolled him over on to his back, pinning him to the floor by pressing one knee into the small of his back, his hands pinned to the dirty ground.

'Run and get a copper,' he said to Stanley. 'Tell 'im this bloke was trying to set light to a building with your mother inside.'

Stanley's eyes flashed with anger. 'Can't I bash 'im first?'

'Do as you're told. Get a copper.'

Stanley dropped the chair leg, started to run off, then picked it up again and set it down at Patrick's side. 'If he struggles, give it to 'im.'

Patrick couldn't resist a grin. Wasn't that a line from the film? He looked up. It was darker now the fire had been put out, but he saw two figures, Lizzie and her mother, standing at the back door.

'I've got him,' he called out. He saw Lizzie put her arm around her mother. Wanting to reassure them further, he called out again. 'It's all over.' He wasn't sure, but he wanted to believe he saw Mrs Randall's shoulders relax. He hoped so. 'Enough of these shenanigans,' he said to the man squirming on the ground. 'The coppers will know how to deal with you.'

Mary Anne finished relating the list of mishaps to the policeman – most of which it seemed could be laid at the door of George Ford.

The policeman – a bluff, no-nonsense sergeant with a veined and bulbous nose rapidly turning to purple – was considerate and patient. Every so often he licked the end of his pencil before scribbling in his notebook.

Mary Anne was pleased to see him take her so seriously. She'd half been expecting him to think her just a hysterical woman, bombed out of her home, with no husband and children all flown the nest except for the youngest. Stanley was proving himself a hindrance to the proceedings. He was still imagining himself as Jimmy Cagney. It didn't help matters that he kept firing at the sergeant with his pretend machine gun until Lizzie shooed him out.

The sergeant asked if she'd met George Ford before. She shook her head. 'No.'

'We've taken your husband down to the station and questioned him. He claims that this George Ford was an attorney at law seeking to inform you of an inheritance – from an aunt who doesn't exist, according to him. Is that right?'

Mary Anne nodded. 'So my husband told me.'

She was tempted to ask why they'd taken him down to the station but presumed she knew the answer to that already. She too had blamed Henry for the series of mishaps, but who was this George Ford? Had Harry upset one of his shady friends? But why pick on her? Partly to steer any blame away from her son, she mentioned Routledge, but only cautiously. She refrained from mentioning her relationship with Michael except to say that she was looking after the shop in his absence.

'Mr Maurice upset Routledge. Mr Routledge got very angry and threatened to have his revenge.'

The police sergeant sipped at the cup of tea he'd been given before making a note. He frowned. 'And you're certain you don't know this man?'

'Absolutely sure.'

Brushing biscuit crumbs from his tunic, he struggled to his feet. 'Ta very much for the tea, Mrs Randall. Much appreciated.'

'Think nothing of it, Sergeant. I have to say I'm relieved he's been caught. I can't understand why he hated me.'

'Who knows,' said the sergeant. 'But rest assured, we're asking questions and making enquiries about this George Ford. We'll let you know if we find anything out.'

Mary Anne thanked him and showed him to the door.

'I think he was a nutcase,' Patrick said to Lizzie on his return.

'No. That doesn't make sense. Why pick on Mother? No,' said Lizzie, shaking her head. 'Dad put him up to it, the vindictive old sod!'

Stanley heard her swear and gasped. 'Wash your mouth out, Lizzie Randall.'

Lizzie grabbed him by the shoulders. 'Little brothers should be seen and not heard. Besides that, they should be washing their face, brushing their teeth and getting to bed.' She steered him towards the bathroom as she said it, pushed him inside and shut the door. 'And don't come out till you've had a good scrub.'

Patrick was sitting on an old chair, elbows resting on his knees, his hands clasped before his furrowed brow. He looked up as she came back in. 'Lizzie. Can we have a talk?'

'This is hardly the time, Patrick,' she snapped.

He couldn't have taken a slap in the face more badly. Despite herself, her heart went out to him. She'd let him down. A dark mood had descended on her. How would her affair with Guy Hunter end? Happy ever after was what she wanted, and even though he'd assured her that they would be together, she remembered Bessie and was frightened.

Thirty-One

Mary Anne bounced Mathilda on her lap. Every so often she glanced up at Daw. Should she tell her what had happened? Half of her said yes, the other no. The old-style Mary Anne, the one who lived for her children rather than herself, said yes. After all, Daw was as much her daughter as Lizzie was, and Lizzie already knew everything.

'I've got something to tell you,' she finally said.

Daw was being her usual reticent self, folding washing and testing the iron she'd placed on the gas ring before slamming it on to a sheet and ironing like mad. She hadn't been at all happy to hear that her mother had left her father again.

Mary Anne took the plunge and told her about the man at the back of the pawn shop. 'They took your father in for questioning too, though they let him go,' she said, still bouncing the baby, and glancing at Daw to see her reaction, but Daw was her characteristic self. She slammed the iron back on to its stand.

'How ridiculous! Dad wouldn't do anything like that. He wouldn't dream of harming any of his family. I've told you before, Mother, I refuse to believe it.'

Although Stanley appeared to be totally engrossed in a piece of home-made cake, really he was all ears. 'He beat me!'

'Liar!' Daw shouted, loud enough to make the baby jump and burst into disgruntled yells.

'No I'm not,' he shouted back. 'I'll show you.' He swiftly tucked up his pullover and tugged his shirt out from his trousers. 'There,' he said, turning round and exposing his back.

Both Mary Anne and Daw fell to silence. Fine red wheals covered his back.

Mary Anne fought to find her voice. When she spoke there was a cold righteousness to her voice that hadn't been there before. 'When did he do that?'

Stanley turned round, his shirt tail still hanging over his backside. 'Last week, just before we ran away.'

She handed the baby to Daw, crouched down in front of her son and clasped his shoulders. At the same time she tried hard to stop her hands shaking. 'Why didn't you tell me?'

Her voice trembled, but she forced herself to sound calm. Stanley had been sick in the not-so-distant past. She didn't want to chance it happening again. He mustn't be upset.

Stanley's huge blue eyes looked at her soulfully. 'I didn't want to upset you, Mum. You 'ad enough on yer plate.'

Mary Anne was beside herself. 'Oh, Stanley! And there was me thinking I'd rescued you before anything happened!'

Swiping his nose with the back of his hand, he held his head at a cocky angle. 'I can protect myself now. I'm a member of the Barton Hill Gang. I'll shoot anyone who hurts you, Ma.'

Smiling through her tears, she smoothed his hair back from his forehead and sniffed back a tear. 'My brave little soldier.'

His grin spread from ear to ear. 'That's what I am, Ma. A soldier.'

Looking quite put out at the chain of events, Daw tugged Stanley's arm. 'So what did you do? Dad wouldn't have beat you unless you'd done something really wrong.'

Stanley frowned at her. So did Mary Anne. 'I saw him coming out of the pub with that man, Mr Routledge. They were laughing together. I told him he shouldn't be drinking 'cos me mum wouldn't like it. Mr Routledge said I was in need of a good beating. He kept saying it to me dad over and over again. "Don't take that lip. Spare the rod and spoil the child. Spare the rod and spoil the child" he kept saying, over and over and over again . . .'

Mary Anne could hardly believe what she was hearing. 'Hardly a reason for beating him like that!' she exclaimed. 'Or do you still defend your father?' she asked Daw. 'The police think this George Ford character could be a spy or someone who's escaped from a mental institution. Either way, they think he's quite dangerous, but clever – very clever. They're trying to find out the truth.'

She waited for Daw to speak on her father's behalf as she always did. On hearing no response, she turned to look at her. Although Daw was in the habit of hiding her feelings behind a tightly controlled mask, this time something had slipped.

She was hugging Mathilda to her breast. The baby was screaming with dismay, but still Daw stared into the distance, seeming not to hear the child at all.

'Daw?' Still with one arm around her son, Mary Anne eyed her daughter quizzically. Daw didn't seem to be listening.

'Daw,' she said again.

Her eldest daughter jerked herself back to the present. Her mouth was open as though she'd been about to speak, and yet she seemed unable to utter a sound.

Mary Anne frowned. 'What is it? Is Mathilda alright? Is there something you want to tell me?' She mentally checked off everything that might be wrong.

'George Ford. He said he was a friend of Dad's,' she said quietly. 'I met him when I was fire watching. He was a fire watcher too. At least, that was what he told me. He was so nice to talk to.'

Mary Anne gaped at her. 'Was George Ford the friend you mentioned a while back?'

Daw nodded slowly. 'I thought he was. He seemed so friendly, so caring about my welfare and the sort of person you could unload your troubles on.'

Her mother sank into a chair as the picture became clearer. 'You mean that, when he asked, you told him everything about your family. Is that right?'

Daw bit her bottom lip and the glitter of self-belief left her dark brown eyes when she nodded.

Mary Anne hid her face in her hands and shook her head. It was tempting not to drop her hands from her face ever again. What was happening to her family? At first she peered out through the gaps in her fingers. Once she'd got her thoughts into some order, she dropped her hands. It occurred to Mary Anne that Daw was now showing more concern for her family than she had for years.

'Mum, I'm so sorry . . .'

Mary Anne shook her head. 'You're not the only one. This George Ford was determined to destroy my family, it seems. But *why*?'

The question was to stay with her for the next two months. Living in the ruined pawn shop was strangely satisfying, though she missed Michael constantly. She had written to him after leaving Henry for the final time, resolving never to doubt their relationship again. His letters were still sporadic and she devoured them like dairy cream the instant they arrived.

Harry came home on leave and managed to repair a few windows and build new walls. The smell of blackened timbers persisted, but at least the old place would be cosier for the winter. While summer lasted, great swathes of sunlight warmed the rooms by day and turned them red at sunset. Mary Anne sat with her eldest son on the old chaise longue, staring out the window with their arms around each other.

'We're like rich people on the *Queen Mary* watching the sun go down as we cross the Atlantic,' said Mary Anne wistfully.

Harry's arm tightened around her shoulder and he kissed her hair. 'There are only troops on the *Queen Mary* these days.'

'How sad. I'd like to take a trip on her one day.'

'After the war,' he said, hugging her close. 'When the world's at peace and you're juggling another grandchild on your knee.'

Mary Anne sighed. 'I keep asking Lizzie about her beau, but she doesn't let on. She says she'll be off abroad before very long, but won't say where she's going. I'll worry about her, of course, but . . .'

Harry felt her shrug beneath his arm. He wanted to say to her that it wasn't usual for women drivers to go abroad into a battle zone, but he kept his mouth shut. Lizzie's letters had been few and far between of late, but now she was saying that her posting was so top-secret that she wouldn't be able to send any at all. Had his beloved mother noticed that Lizzie was sending conflicting stories? It seemed strange to him, but he wouldn't tell her that. She had been through enough. All he wanted was for her to be happy.

Thirty-Two

Lizzie threaded a piece of elastic through her skirt's button-hole and around the button. 'Breathe in,' she muttered to herself.

The waistband fastened – just. There was no full-length mirror in the room she shared with Margot and Annabelle, a new girl with sleek blonde hair and a confident manner. She and Margot had hit it off right away. Lizzie had felt left out at first, but was now glad of being left alone a bit more. They still spoke but although Margot made comments about her putting on weight, she didn't dwell on the subject. 'Stodge and more stodge,' she had said, referring to their daily diet.

Lizzie had joined in with her own comments about suet pudding and potato pie. Once Annabelle was in the room, her presence seemed to fade into the background.

Margot came into the room just after Lizzie had secured her skirt. She brushed briskly at the front of it as though she were only removing crumbs, not flattening it over her stomach.

'I've got leave. Isn't that marvellous?' she said, adopting her happiest voice as she ran a red lipstick around her mouth.

Margot stood wavering by the closed door. 'I suppose you're off with Wing Commander Hunter this weekend.' There was something about her tone of voice that stabbed at Lizzie's heart. She controlled the sudden shaking in the hand holding the lipstick.

'That's right.'

There was a beat or two of silence before Margot said, 'Have you told him yet?'

Lizzie felt her heart beating harder. 'Told him what?'

Margot was standing beside her now, her expression serious, her eyes intent. 'You can't fool me, Lizzie. That skirt is too tight for you. And don't tell me it's purely suet pudding. It's a pudding alright, but not a suet one.'

Lizzie spun round on her. 'It's none of your business. It's between me and Guy.'

'Of course it is. So what does he say about it?'

Lizzie reached for her gas mask and her handbag. 'It's none of your business,' she repeated.

Once outside the door, she regretted snapping at Margot. She stalled, her hand remaining on the door handle as she tried to decide whether or not to apologize. *No*, she thought. *If I do that I'll break down and tell her everything, just as Margot told me all about Major Bradley when they split up.*

'He's not terribly good in bed, darling,' she'd said. 'I need a more physical man, truly I do.'

The word romance rarely came into Margot's conversation, but Lizzie found her amusing and valued her friendship.

It was two weeks since she'd told Guy that she was pregnant. They'd been on the boat. The day had been beautiful, the red russet of an early autumn glowing against a blue sky. Mornings had been crisp and fresh; the evening sky streaked with a salmon-pink sunset. So romantic, she'd thought. The time was ripe to tell him. But he'd just stared at her, a look of total incomprehension on his face.

'Are you sure?'

She caught hold of his hand, pressing his palm against her stomach. Feeling a sudden flutter, he winced and withdrew it.

'That's . . . amazing,' he said.

The look in his eyes had changed immediately. The old shielded look came back to worry her. She'd told herself that he merely needed time to get used to the idea.

'You'll have to bring your divorce forward,' she said, laying her head against his shoulder and hugging him tight.

'I'll certainly have to make some plans, for sure,' he'd said.

They'd been busy during the last two weeks, back and forth to London, acquiring more and more paperwork as they went. During this time they'd only managed to snatch a couple of hours alone at a pub or parking the car while they took a breath of fresh air.

'Things are hotting up in the east,' he'd said when she'd suggested they take a room in a hotel and sleep together. He'd frowned as he'd looked into the distance, as though he were seeing a far worse war looming than the one they'd experienced so far.

'Will the Americans get involved?' she'd asked, more by way of conversation than anything else. This war was the reason they'd met, yet its importance lessened with the growth of the child within her.

'Could be.' He looked at her strangely then, unnerving her. Sensing he wasn't comfortable with the subject, she grasped an excuse from thin air.

'You've got a lot more paperwork,' she'd said as though that were the reason she'd mentioned the Americans.

The sky clouded over suddenly. Lizzie shivered.

'We'd better go,' Guy said.

She'd picked her way back over the grass verge, her shadow falling ahead of her. Suddenly she'd realized he wasn't with her. She'd stopped and looked back to see him, hands in his pockets, head down as he kicked thoughtfully at a clump of bright-red poppies.

She was thinking of this incident now as she made her way to his room on the first floor of Ainsley Hall.

'Randall!' Lizzie saluted Sergeant Pauline Cropper, a good-natured young woman with a country complexion and a broad bosom. 'Adjutant wants to see you in his office.'

'Yes, Sergeant.'

A freckly ginger-haired girl came out of the office just as Lizzie was about to knock. The adjutant saw her and beckoned her with a crooked finger.

'Come on in, Randall.'

Lizzie saluted and stood to attention.

The adjutant sat back in his chair. 'At ease, Randall. Take a seat.'

The queasiness of her condition intensified. Since when had the lowest in the pecking order been offered a seat? Something was up. A whole range of tragedies funnelled through her mind. Had something happened to Guy? To one of her family? Or was it something really mundane, like being posted elsewhere? She would refuse, of course. She had to be here for Guy. She was his girl, his own driver, and he was getting divorced so he could be with her.

The adjutant sighed and rested his clasped hands on his substantial belly. 'I'm sorry to inform you of this, Randall, but you're being transferred to a non-sensitive unit dealing mostly with the transport of medical supplies and suchlike.'

She asked him to repeat what he'd said. He did so, but even then she couldn't believe it.

'You're insinuating that I'm a security risk?'

The adjutant eyed her over the top of his horn-rimmed spectacles. 'Not me, Randall. The wing commander.'

She felt as though her body, her limbs, right to the tips of her fingers and toes, had been turned to ice. This was total betrayal! Her greatest fear had been realized.

'There must be some mistake!' she cried.

The adjutant raised his eyebrows, peering at her over the top of his glasses. 'No. There is not.'

Her stomach churned and the child seemed to turn with it, the living weight easing from one side of her body to the other. 'But Wing Commander Hunter said that I was to drive for him and him alone.'

'The wing commander requested that he be reposted to the Far East. I believe that he and his family are to be stationed in Singapore.'

'His family? His parents are going to Singapore?'

'His wife and children, Randall. I believe he has four children and another on the way.'

'Yes, of course he has another on the way, and I'm the mother!' The thought screamed in her brain but did not make it to her tongue. For now and for a long time to come, she would be drowning in hurt. He had four children. He'd lied. How could he do this to her?

She gulped back the hurt, though was certain it showed on her face. 'Sir, I hope you don't mind me asking, but why do I have to be transferred to a non-sensitive unit?'

The adjutant gave his stern look again. 'Wing Commander Hunter felt you were asking too many questions about his work. He thought it better that you were reassigned to a less vulnerable situation where asking too many questions wouldn't do too much harm. But I must warn you, Randall, your behaviour will be monitored. Be like Dad. Keep Mum. OK?'

It was as though the blood had drained to her feet and flooded from her toes. He saluted. She was expected to return his salute, but her legs turned to jelly as she got to her feet. She slumped back down in her chair, then made a second attempt and crumpled to the floor.

She awoke in a world of white. Slowly the whiteness turned to cream. A hospital screen surrounded the bed she lay in. She heard voices outside. Someone was asking a question. Someone else was answering.

'I'll see if she's awake.'

A round face framed by a crisply starched head dress appeared from behind the screen.

Cool fingers circled her wrist. 'How are you feeling?' At

the same time as asking her the question, the nurse studied the minute hand on the fob watch hanging from her breast.

'I'm fine. I think. What happened?'

'You fainted. Understandable, given your condition. Five months gone and nobody noticed. I'm astounded.'

Lizzie closed her eyes and tried to recall where she'd been when she'd fainted. Or was that all a dream? Had the adjutant really told her that Guy, along with his wife and four children – and another on the way – were being posted to Singapore?

'You have a visitor,' said the nurse, interrupting her thoughts. 'I'm only supposed to allow close family to visit you, but he says he's your fiancé, so on this occasion . . .'

Lizzie's heart thudded against her ribs. It was all a dream – of course it was!

'He's here?'

The nurse smiled. 'I'll let him in. No doubt he wants to make sure that mother and baby are doing well.'

Lizzie glowed with happiness. Guy had come back – no, he'd never gone away. It was just a dream.

'Alright, Lizzie?' said a familiar voice – but not the one she wanted to hear.

Lizzie's smile froze on her face. The nurse brought Patrick a chair. He looked brown and healthy, a tan left over from an assignment abroad.

'Ten minutes only.'

'I won't tire her,' he said cheerfully, his teeth blazing white against his brown skin. His smile wilted away once he'd studied Lizzie's look of surprise. 'I'm sorry. I can see you were expecting someone else. Perhaps I should go.'

Lizzie squeezed her eyes shut, but the tears trickled out anyway.

'I take it he's left you.'

She gulped. There were no words, only emotions sitting like lead in her chest. Patrick loved her. Of that she had no doubt. She knew what he was thinking, knew what he would say if she confirmed the facts.

'The baby should have a father,' he went on, and looked sheepish when he said it. 'I love you, Lizzie. I'll marry you. I'll give the little 'un a home.'

Eyes squeezed shut, lips quivering with silent sobs, Lizzie

shook her head. Her misery was history repeating itself, yet she couldn't tell Patrick that. Her mother had told her about the child she'd given away following the death of her sweetheart in the trenches. Henry Randall had married her, unaware of the child's existence. Trusting him to understand, her mother had told him the truth. From then on Henry Randall's true character had come through. The blame was always there. She couldn't go through that; it would be like letting her mother down and Mary Anne Randall had quite enough to worry about.

'No,' she said, shaking her head. 'That wouldn't be fair. It's my life and my mess. I won't ruin things for you.'

He glanced around him before leaning forward and whispering, 'I'd tell your mother the baby was mine. She wouldn't have to know anything else.'

'No, Patrick. I won't do that, and I don't want Mum to know. You must promise . . . promise me you won't tell her.'

'But . . .' He'd been about to say that her mother would be worried, but the look in her tear-filled eyes stopped him. She looked scared, as though some ghost was only inches from her pillow. 'I promise.'

'Do you believe that the same sin can run in families?'

He frowned, flicking at the corner of his eye as he thought about it. 'I couldn't say. I suppose it's possible – like red hair and green eyes can be passed on, so perhaps behaviour and making the same mistakes can be, but there again . . .'

He'd been about to say that he was nothing like his mother, but presumed he was more like his father, though of course he couldn't say. He'd headed for new horizons years ago.

Lizzie interrupted him with a question. 'You're still posted abroad?'

He nodded. 'Yes.'

She thought carefully but swiftly before asking him a favour. 'I want you to say you've seen me in the same location as you're stationed and to send them my love. Will you do that?'

He hesitated to answer, wondering what she was planning, but finally said simply, 'I will.'

'Good.' She closed her eyes again.

Patrick felt an ache in his guts that wouldn't go away. He

wanted to help her in any way he could. He didn't care if it was wrong, didn't care that he was lying. If that was what Lizzie wanted, that was what he would do. But what would she do about the baby? He had to ask her.

Her eyes flicked open suddenly and she pushed herself up on to her elbows. 'There's a girl I used to know who left the unit because she was pregnant. She'd booked herself into a place where she could have the baby without anyone knowing, though she ended up telling her parents, but she wanted it adopted. It turned out that she didn't need it in the end, but if you can get hold of Margot, she'll get the details from the girl.'

'And until then?'

Until then. She fell back on to the pillows, thoughts falling into place one by one. 'Until then I'll be here.'

'I mean, where will you be until you have the baby?'

'I'll find somewhere to stay until then.'

'Is there anything I can get for you?'

She fixed her eyes on the top of the screen surrounding her bed, almost afraid to look into his eyes in case she agreed to everything he offered. 'My friend Margot. Can you ask her to come in and see me as soon as she's got the address?'

Thirty-Three

Michael swept into the Red Cross shop, past Gertrude Palmer who opened her mouth to say something but didn't get the chance. The customer she was serving was demanding her full attention.

'These bloomers were my mother's best ones, but I'm sure you'll make good use of them,' said the mousy woman in the pillbox hat. Determined to assist the war effort to the best of her ability, Gertrude plastered her smile back on her face.

'Of course we will,' she said absently.

Mary Anne stopped cutting the hem off an evening dress and dropped the scissors when she saw him. She was dreaming, surely she must be dreaming!

'My,' said the woman, her attention diverted by the sight of Mary Anne and Michael embracing in the middle of a pile of second-hand clothes. 'What a delight! And what a home-coming! I believe every one of our serving men should get a welcome home like that. Don't you?'

'Of course,' said Gertrude through a thin-lipped smile.

'Come,' said Michael. 'We're going home.'

'But I've work to do.'

Michael indicated the neat pile of what had been car blankets, thick enough and good enough to make into winter coats. Someone who used to drive out regularly in the draughty old-fashioned cars had brought them in. 'Is this more mending?'

'Alterations,' said Mary Anne. 'I'm making them into winter coats.'

'I'll carry them home for you.'

He swept the lot up beneath one arm, kitbag beneath the other and even managed to open the door to the street. Her face covered in smiles, Mary Anne followed on behind him.

Edith and the others smiled knowingly as she passed. Even Gertrude's stiff countenance softened.

'Lucky you,' whispered Edith, her bright eyes sparkling through the wrinkles. Mary Anne blushed.

'I haven't had a chance to change the bed,' said Mary Anne as Michael swept her into their old bedroom. Lavender polish and a glass vase full of Michaelmas daisies helped overcome the residual stench of burned walls.

'But I've managed to get some cream distemper for the walls,' she explained, but her words were stifled with kisses. He peeled off her clothes as she rubbed her tear-stained cheek against his stubble. When had she started crying? She couldn't recall. She didn't care. Michael was home.

'Why are you crying?'

'Because you're home.'

'Perhaps I should go away again?'

'No. Oh, no! It's been so long,' she said, driven to greater hunger by the smell of his body, the hard feel of his chest against hers.

Making love with Michael made it seem as though he'd

never gone away. There was a musical symmetry to the way their bodies moved together, like playing a familiar tune on a long-lost violin. The notes were the same, finely tuned and echoing through their bodies and into their minds.

She arched her back when he kissed her breasts. She ran her hands over his arms, reacquainting herself with the shape and tone of his muscles. The union was swift and passionate, intense and yet sensitive, a prelude to more sustained love-making to come.

They lay tangled in the sheets afterwards, a fine sheen of sweat glistening on their naked bodies. He ran his hand over her shoulder, her ribs; the indentation of her waistline and the sweeping curve of her hip.

He kissed her forehead, her nose, her cheeks and her lips. He kissed each breast, ran his tongue down to her belly button and into her loins. He kissed the inside of each thigh before returning to the pillow where he lay, replete, gazing into her eyes.

'I have missed you.'

She snuggled closer, still wiping tears of happiness from her eyes. 'At times I thought I would never see you again.'

'But you've received my letters?'

'Yes. But they were so few. I received letters from your parents too. They said they were well and that you were well. The censor doesn't allow much else.'

'You have no need to worry about me,' he said, cupping her face with one hand. 'It was you we needed to worry about. This man – this George Ford – who is he?'

She shook her head, her hair soft and gold against the pillow. 'I don't know.'

'No idea at all?'

She shook her head more vehemently. 'Michael, I've wracked my brains. I don't know who this man is. The police said he escaped from a military mental hospital, the sort where men go who've been affected by battle – shell shock and such-like.'

'I understand. I have heard how battle can change men for ever.' He lay back on the pillow, one arm bent beneath his head, her head resting on his chest. 'Harry is home too. You had a letter?'

'Yes, I did, at the same time as yours. I was going to get

everything nice for you, the walls painted and new flooring laid before you got here.'

He laughed. 'I will paint the walls. Harry will help, I am sure.'

'I can't wait,' she groaned.

'And Lizzie? Have you heard from Lizzie?'

'Yes. As you know, she's been posted somewhere top secret so can't write as often as she used to and can't get any leave at all. She said it's all very hush-hush. Goodness knows when I'll see her again. She thinks Christmas. Patrick sees her sometimes and passes me a message – you know, "don't worry, Mum, I'm OK." OK!' She smiled. 'Funny how that word – if it is even a word – has entered our language from the American movies!' She laughed.

Michael laughed with her, but his thoughts were elsewhere. There were rumours that the Americans would enter the war before very long. Intercepted messages between Berlin and Tokyo were becoming more and more difficult to decode. Something top-secret was happening and it worried him. Lizzie worried him more. She couldn't be telling the truth about her new job. Apart from sections like his, there was no limit as to how many letters she could write; the content was what was important. And no leave until Christmas, she had said, but Christmas was still three months away. He thought about mentioning this to his beloved Marianna, but thought better of it. She had been through enough. He was home, but only for a short while. They would make hay – and love – while the sun shone.

Harry was also home on leave. He came round that night, bringing Edgar with him. The table was laid with bread, along with a little butter and jam given to Mary Anne by Edith.

'I have a plum tree in my back garden,' Edith had explained.

Mary Anne had been amazed. 'Where did you get the sugar?'

Edith had winked far too wickedly for a woman of her age. 'It's a secret.'

Mary Anne was proud of her white tablecloth. She'd got it back in September 1939, just after war broke out. Mrs Riley, the woman who'd pledged it back then, was dead now. Even the laundry room from where she'd run her pawn-broking business was gone, destroyed in a single night by a single bomb. The tablecloth had also survived the bombing of Michael's pawn shop. It was as white as ever, having been taken to the shelter each time there was an air raid.

'Fruit cake!' cried Edgar, holding a large tin above his head. 'I made it myself.'

Stanley was first in the queue.

'Where did you get the sugar and the eggs?' asked Mary Anne, her eyes wide with amazement.

Edgar tapped the side of his nose. 'Harry told me this was to be a celebration, and I duly obliged with a celebratory cake.'

Mary Anne noted the yellowish remains of a bruise on Edgar's cheek. 'That George Ford certainly knows how to knock a man out, doesn't he?'

'So who is he?' Harry asked his mother.

'We don't know. The police told me he was released from a military mental hospital. That's all we know about him.'

Stanley shoved his plate forward. 'A big slice, please.'

Laughing and talking, Mary Anne cut the cake into large portions.

'Is your other daughter coming round with the little one?' asked Edgar.

Mary Anne shook her head and hid her feelings. 'No. She has fire-watching duty.' The truth was that Daw did not approve of Harry's relationship with Edgar, which she deemed 'unnatural'. Her mother had not tried to persuade her.

The fruit cake was moist and accompanied with bread and margarine, baked apple slices and treacle. Mary Anne kept a quarter of the cake for the following day and with Stanley's help took the dishes down to the kitchen.

While they were gone the three men started talking.

Michael lay back in his favourite leather chair, his eyes half closed. 'So this nutcase – why did he do it?'

Harry was sitting with his elbows resting on his knees. He was frowning and staring at the old black range. Edgar was inspecting a child's winter coat Mary Anne had fashioned from an old car blanket.

Realizing he wasn't going to get an answer, Michael got up from his chair. 'I will go and help Marianna.'

'That was rude,' said Edgar.

'No it wasn't. I just didn't want to hurt him.'

Edgar raised his fine, ginger eyebrows. 'Hurt him? In what way?'

'Nothing.'

'Don't give me that, Harry. If it's nothing, then you wouldn't have that troubled expression. Tell me.'

Harry took a deep breath. 'I've been making enquiries. I couldn't say anything in front of Michael because I didn't want to upset his feelings, but I think that George Ford is my half-brother. My mother's sweetheart was killed in the trenches but he'd left her pregnant. The child was given away and she was forced to marry my father.'

'So you think he sees himself as the victim of a terrible injustice and is taking it out on your family?'

'Something like that.'

'So why don't you ask your mother about it?'

With a swift flick of his wrists, the blanket coat was neatly folded and placed back on the pile.

'I don't know if I've got the nerve. It's personal.'

'It happened. There's nothing to be ashamed of.'

Harry jerked up and glared at him. 'I'm not ashamed!'

'You're embarrassed. Your mother won't be. You'll see. Ask her, then we'll see if I'm right.'

Michael chose that moment to reappear. 'Stanley has just nipped out to play cowboys and Indians in the street. Marianna insists I go find him and get him back.'

'Do you want me to go with you?'

Michael smiled. 'No need. He will no doubt be with the other rapscallions shooting at each other on a bombsite.'

Harry waited a minute or two after Michael had left before getting to his feet. 'Alright,' he said to Edgar. 'I'm off to wipe dishes – and ask a certain embarrassing question.'

'You'll cope,' said Edgar with a toss of his head.

Harry glanced back at him before leaving. Edgar had picked up a pair of scissors and an uncut blanket. No doubt by the time he got back another jacket ready for sewing would have joined the others in the pile.

The sight of his mother washing the dishes moved Harry. Her soft auburn-gold hair shone like a girl's as it fell across her face. Unlike some women in their forties, she still had a waistline, high breasts and a trim bottom. He wondered what she would say if she knew what he was thinking. He smiled. She'd be pleased, he was sure of it.

She turned her head as she realized he was standing there. 'Harry! You didn't need to come down. I've almost finished.'

He leaned on the draining board and folded his arms. 'I was thinking about this George Ford character. Was he very old?'

'No.' She shook her head and stopped wiping a plate as she thought about it. 'I think he was probably just a little older than you.'

'But you don't know him?'

'No.'

Harry prided himself on being able to hold his own in any kind of company. He'd never felt nervous in his life, but he did now. He shifted his weight from one hip to the other as he sought the right words – if there were ever any right words for something like this.

'You wouldn't have known him years ago? As a child, perhaps?'

His mother gave him one of her sidelong searching looks, the one that begs the question, 'What have you been up to?'

'No,' she said, looking puzzled, almost hurt.

This is the time to take the plunge, Harry decided. Taking her hands in his, he looked deep into her eyes. 'Mum, could he have been the baby you gave away all those years ago?'

His lovely, respectable mother suddenly appeared very small, very feminine and very pale.

'No,' she said, her voice not much more than a sigh. 'No.'

He knew she was telling the truth and told Edgar so later.

Stanley came dashing back up the stairs before Michael did. Michael was frowning when he got back. He looked up to the landing as the door to Stanley's bedroom slammed shut.

'I think that boy is up to something.'

'He's a boy. Of course he is,' said Harry.

'It was such an obvious solution,' Harry muttered to Edgar as they drove back to their flat. 'Too obvious, perhaps, though I would have thought she might have considered it a possibility. After all, he would have changed his name and his looks would have changed after all this time.'

'Or there could be a more obvious reason why she *knew* for sure that George Ford was not the child she gave away.'

Harry slowed the car to allow a man and woman to cross the road. Edgar was a wonderful person, but he could sometimes act a bit superior. You had to draw the conversation out of him.

'Alright, Edgar, I know you're dying to tell me. Why is my mother so sure that George Ford is not the baby she gave away?'

'Simple,' said Edgar. '*Both male and female did he create . . .*'

'A girl?' Harry's jaw dropped as Edgar stated the obvious.

'A girl.'

'But I was sure . . .'

'And even if your mother did refer to her firstborn as a boy – which of course you're not sure about – do remember that people like to cover their tracks . . .'

Thirty-Four

'I knew you'd look after her, Mother, so I brought her straight over.'

Mary Anne was about to say that she did have work to do, that a pile of garments for mending and alteration were waiting on the table. But one look at darling Mathilda and harsh words about being put upon and taken for granted melted away.

'John's coming home. I'm going down to the station to meet him.'

'I'll take you for a walk,' Mary Anne said to the smiling child once Daw had trotted off to please herself.

The weather was turning colder, coal was becoming scarcer and the advent of Christmas was causing headaches. There was nothing to buy in the shops and everyone was looking to 'make do and mend' or pass on Christmas presents from years before. Old fur coats were being made into teddy bears, velvet evening gowns into golliwogs and old underwear into dolls' clothes. Bits of wood were being carved into wooden trains and cars for the boys. Women dreamed of silk stockings, though there was precious little hope of them coming into the Red Cross shop.

Mary Anne pushed her little granddaughter all the way along East Street and up Redcliffe Hill. The old faggot and pea shop on Redcliffe Hill was doing what it could with minimal ingredients, but vegetable stew was more readily available than meaty faggots.

The elegant lamp posts hung dull and unlit and the church spire was silent; no bells would be rung until the war was over. Like many others, Mary Anne wondered when that day would come.

By mid-afternoon the light was beginning to fade. Shops that would normally be blazing with light now pulled down their shutters. The blackout was total, the streets murky and miserable.

She was just approaching the Red Cross shop and about to cross over the road to the alley when someone waved at her.

'Mary Anne! You've got a visitor.'

She strained her neck, hoping it was Lizzie arrived home unexpectedly and looking for her. She'd said nothing in the single letter she'd received about coming home, and it had been so long. Patrick had written to say he'd seen Lizzie and that Mary Anne was not to worry, but that wasn't the same as seeing her in the flesh.

'This way,' called Edith, still waving.

'I can't leave Mathilda here,' said Mary Anne, as the anxiety of losing her months before still gave her nightmares.

'Bring her in, dear,' said Gertrude, her broad face peering over Edith's head.

The two women helped her manhandle the pram. There was something urgent and excitable about the two middle-aged women as they bundled Mary Anne and the pram through the door. Something was going on.

'Close that door and pull down the shutter, Edith. Hurry up.'

Edith did as ordered. The shutter rattled into place. The other shutters were already drawn halfway down the windows.

The sound of a switch being clicked was instantly followed by the meagre light of a 25-watt bulb.

'This lady wishes to see you, Mrs Randall,' said Gertrude. She deferred to the lady mentioned with a sweep of her arm, almost as though she were royalty.

The other occupant of the shop was sitting on a bentwood chair, one stockinged leg crossed elegantly over the other. She was wearing a flattish black hat with a half face veil speckled with sequins. Her shoulders shifted inside a glossy mink coat. Gloved fingers drew a fine ebony cigarette holder from a blood-red mouth.

Mary Anne almost curtsied. She may not be royalty, but this woman certainly wasn't from Bedminster.

At first the woman's eyes settled on the baby. 'She's lovely. What's her name?'

'Mathilda. She's my granddaughter.'

The woman gave her a long, enquiring stare. Mary Anne squirmed. Who was she? What did she want?

Turning away from Mary Anne and the baby, she cast her glance sideways at the other two. 'I'm sorry to be such a bore, but do you think we could have some privacy?' Her voice was commanding, but disarming. She had the air of someone who knew how to give orders without people taking offence. She knew how to get the best out of people.

She hasn't come across Gertrude Palmer before, thought Mary Anne, and almost said so out loud.

To her great surprise, Gertrude locked the front door. 'You stay here and have your little chat,' she said in the most ingratiating tone Mary Anne had ever heard her use. 'Edith and I will trot out to the kitchen and make ourselves a cup of tea. Would you like one?'

'Not for the moment,' said the elegant woman. 'Perhaps later.' The confident expression and the air of self-assurance melted like snow. The true colour of the woman's complexion seemed to seep through the expensive make-up. She tilted her head back so she was looking up into Mary Anne's face. For a while she seemed to study her features, almost as if she were seeking something familiar. 'Perhaps you should sit down,' she said, indicating the old stool to the side of the counter.

Perplexed as to her visitor's identity, Mary Anne dragged the stool across the floor, scratching the linoleum as she went.

But she wasn't looking at the floor; she was studying the woman's features just as intently as the woman had studied hers. Inside she trembled. One look at the woman and she knew – she just knew.

But Mary Anne showed no outward sign of guessing her visitor's identity. She stayed calm as she made herself comfortable. 'What did you want to see me about?'

The woman stubbed out her cigarette in a glass ashtray. Even that was a sign that Gertrude had been impressed. She usually only handed out tin ones for everyday use.

The woman hesitated. 'My name is Elizabeth Ford. I'm George Ford's wife.'

Setting aside her initial guess at the woman's identity, Mary Anne sat deadly still. Had she heard right? That wasn't at all what she'd expected the woman to say.

'You're George Ford's wife?'

'Yes, I am. The police came to call and told me what had happened. We've been searching for George for some time now. He had a breakdown after Dunkirk. He hasn't been the same since. It's almost as though what was positive before his ordeal has now become negative, and vice versa. Poor George.' She said it softly, her eyes gazing down at the floor.

'I don't quite understand what you mean,' said Mary Anne, jiggling the pram as Mathilda started to stir. 'Have you come here to apologize, or say he didn't do the things he did?'

'No. I just wanted to explain . . .'

Mary Anne jumped to her feet. She recalled the relief she'd felt when George Ford had been apprehended. She'd been surprised that she'd felt no anger, no need for revenge. But now this woman had come here and everything she'd held down was bubbling to the surface.

'If you're asking me to forgive him, don't bother. He burned down my business. He caused problems with my husband. He even stole my granddaughter! What do you mean about negative and positive?'

Mrs Ford hung her head. Her earrings blinked with diamonds. 'I think you need to know a little about me, Mrs Randall. I had a very happy childhood. I had everything money could buy except for one important thing: I was an only child. I was surrounded by wealth and privilege, but no family. I had always fretted about it. George had promised me that one day he would find my real family – or at least, my real mother. You see, Mrs Randall, like a lot of babies born after the Great War, I was adopted. I told George that it didn't matter and he understood that. My adoptive parents had loved me in their own way. But George was never the same after Dunkirk. Everything seemed to go topsy-turvy. He was put in a military mental institution but he got out. I'd previously told him the basics of my true parentage. He made enquiries. Those enquiries led him to you.'

Through all this Mary Anne had remained silent. She'd known it the moment she'd set eyes on the woman; she knew who she looked like.

This was not how she'd expected things to turn out. Years ago she'd dreamed of meeting up again with the child she'd given away, but knew it would be impossible in reality. Henry would never have allowed it. Was this perhaps a dream?

'Well!' she said, looking away, pretending that jiggling the pram and the sleeping Mathilda demanded her full attention. 'Well . . .'

'I suppose it's a bit of a shock.'

Mary Anne squeezed her eyes shut and fought to control her feelings. The pain of giving her child away had clawed at her heart for years after the event. Even before and after her marriage to Henry, her parents had forbidden her to mention it. 'Best forgotten, soonest mended,' they'd said. What a stupid statement. Her heart had never been mended simply because she had never forgotten.

Her eyes met those of Elizabeth Ford and she knew immediately that this was her daughter – Edward's daughter. She had the same eyes Mary Anne had fallen in love with all those years ago.

'George was an intelligence officer,' Elizabeth continued.

'That explains a lot.'

'He knows how to get information.'

'You look like your father.'

Elizabeth beamed. 'Do I?' She got up and picked up the small mirror that women used when they tried on second-hand hats. 'It's nice to know that I'm looking at some resemblance of him each time I look into the mirror.'

Mary Anne made a concerted effort to understand and get control of her feelings. In her dreams she'd thrown her arms around her long-lost daughter, perhaps even rescued her from a cruel orphanage. But this woman had not suffered deprivation of any kind. Well groomed, confident and at ease with her lot, there was nothing she lacked as far as Mary Anne could see.

'I'm sorry for what happened, Mrs Randall, but George is not himself. He's back in hospital now and receiving more treatment. Such a shame. He had such good prospects and we had made wonderful plans for our future. Such is the nature of war. It has been the biggest blot on my life.' She held out her hand. 'Well, goodbye. It's been quite a pleasant experience to meet you face to face after all these years. But let's face it, we both have our own lives, our own family connections and our own circle of friends. We move in different worlds. I won't trouble you again.'

Silently Mary Anne took the hand that was offered. She remembered the tiny fingers she'd held before Elizabeth was given away. This hand was so different to the one she remembered and the woman was so different to the one she'd imagined, the one who would fall into her arms and cry with her over all the lost years.

'Goodbye,' she said, forcing some firmness into her voice.

'Goodbye, and yet again, my sincere apologies.'

The shutter rattled and the blackout curtain fell over the door as it would at the end of a play. Mary Anne blinked away tears and covered her eyes. If only she'd had the courage to hug that woman, but how could she? She was totally self contained, totally in control and she most definitely belonged to another world, one in which the likes of Mary Anne had no part to play. If her heart had been only partially broken when she'd given her baby away, it was now totally shattered.

East Street was busy with women queuing up for whatever goods were available in the shops. The rule was that if you saw a queue you joined it. Elizabeth Ford did not join queues; she had a housekeeper who did that. She also had a maid and a gardener. The latter grew fresh vegetables in a handsome walled garden behind Lechley Manor, her husband's home.

Looking straight ahead of her, she made her way to the taxi she'd paid to wait and drive her back to the railway station. Recognizing gentry when he saw it, the driver got out quickly when he saw her coming and saluted as he opened the taxi door.

'Back to Temple Meads, madam?'

'Yes.'

She sat back against the smooth leather upholstery and stared out at the blackness. There was nothing to see, but in her mind she was imagining how her visit had affected the woman who had given birth to her. She had told her most of the truth, but she had not told her how bitter she had been towards the woman who had given her away. All her life, from the moment a spiteful cousin had told her the truth, she had felt a bitter resentment. Only George had known her true feelings. He'd never acted upon them, telling her that it was best to forget and get on with her life. 'She must have had her reasons,' he'd said. 'And now we have each other, and there's no way I'm ever going to desert you.'

George had meant what he'd said, and yet he *had* deserted her, though in a way she could never have anticipated.

At Dunkirk he'd been trapped in a bomb crater beneath a layer of bloodied corpses. He'd had to hide there for three days, the enemy only yards away. The French Resistance had found him, got him in some sort of shape and back to a hospital in England. That was when they'd found out that he'd been affected mentally.

And now, through his illness, she'd found her mother and she was still shaking from the experience. She'd never expected her natural responses to be so strong. Perhaps she would have come away unaffected by the meeting if her mother – her true mother – hadn't mentioned that she looked like her father, Edward, who'd been killed in the trenches. That's when it came to her how much they'd both suffered, and how much suffering she was likely to go through in future. It would take years for George to recover.

The cold self-assurance she'd presented to Mary Anne Randall began to crack. She took out a powder compact from her handbag, dabbing at the smears of mascara staining her perfect cheeks. There was no saving the exquisitely applied paint and powder. The façade finally cracked. With slow, stiff movements, she wiped the make-up from her eyes and the lipstick from her mouth.

The taxi driver glanced at his passenger in the rear-view mirror. 'Are you all right, madam?'

Elizabeth sniffed. She thought about the two pieces of

crocodile-skin luggage she'd brought with her. They were driving up the incline towards the entrance to the railway station when she made her decision.

'Driver!' She tapped on the glass partition. He stopped the car before sliding it open.

'Yes, madam?'

'Take me back to the Royal.'

'Yes, madam.'

She had made up her mind. She would stay a few days. First she would collect her muddled emotions. It was like having a deep well inside, and her emotions kept surfacing – sometimes muddied, sometimes clear. She needed time to think things through, time to decide whether she really could walk away and forget her real mother existed or whether they could make amends.

Thirty-Five

Hospital sounds echoed off the arched ceilings and bare walls. The ward reminded Lizzie of Cheddar Caves, except that caves didn't have electric lights suspended on the end of impossibly long wires.

During the night she'd woken to the sound of rain pitter-pattering against the window. If she hadn't opened her eyes she could almost have believed she was back on the boat, lying against Guy's warm chest and wishing the rain would fall harder.

On opening her eyes, the cosy memory was replaced by the stark reality of being left in the lurch. The nursing sisters were pleasant enough, but the ward sister – a woman with cast-iron curls and a square chin – eyed her with disdain. 'You young women,' she said. Inconsequential words, but what wasn't said had more meaning. The scorn was there for her to see, like grey ash misting the warmth in her eyes.

Breakfast was bread and margarine with a teaspoonful of

marmalade, plus a cup of weak tea. Pretty poor fare, not that Lizzie was very hungry. The empty feeling encompassed her heart as well as her stomach.

As she lay there she planned for the months ahead. Somehow she would keep the secret from her family. She trusted Patrick not to say anything. When the time came she would sign the necessary documents and once that was done and dusted, Guy and the memento he'd left her with would vanish from her mind. She would wipe the stain from her memory too and make a vow that she would never fall for that kind of man ever again. What had she been thinking? Why hadn't she seen he was a slightly older mirror image of Peter Selwyn Kendall – braver, of course, but from a similar background all the same?

Yes, she thought, closing her eyes and snuggling back beneath the bedclothes. Wing Commander Guy Hunter would be consigned to history. Afterwards she would join the Wrens, just as she'd always promised she would. The problem was how she would manage up until the birth. She couldn't stay here and she couldn't go home. Accommodation was expensive, but she had to survive somehow until going to the nursing home. It was Margot who solved her problem.

Visiting time was from seven until eight o'clock in the evening. So far only Patrick had visited. Now a nurse took the screens from around her bed.

'There's no need,' Lizzie protested. 'I'm not expecting anyone.'

'Sister's orders,' said the nurse. 'She likes everything to be uniform. Either screens around everyone, or screens around no one. Other people are expecting visitors, so I'm afraid you have to fall in with the plan.'

Lizzie sighed and purposely turned her head away, preferring to stare at the vast expanse of evening sky rather than the trickle of visitors padding nervously across the ward.

The shuffling and muffled voices were rudely interrupted by the sound of high heels smartly striking the floor. Who dared breeze into the ward with such determined steps? Lizzie's spirits soared.

Margot made a uniform look elegant despite the coarse fabric, the abundance of buttons and lack of style. Out of uniform she resembled the models in a glossy magazine. She was wearing a fitted navy-blue jacket over a slimline skirt. The jacket had a white collar. Her handbag and shoes were navy blue and white and she wore pearls around her neck and in her ears. Heads turned from all around the ward. French perfume titillated the air like the wings of a scented butterfly.

Lizzie's spirits scurried all the way up the light wires to the arched ceiling.

'Margot! I didn't know you were coming.'

'No problem, my darling,' she said, planting dry lips on each of Lizzie's cheeks before pulling up a chair and crossing one silky leg over the other. 'Patrick told me everything and I took the initiative from there.'

Lizzie sank back against the pillows. 'Margot, what a bloody fool I've been.'

'Yes,' said Margot. She took out her cigarette holder and silver case. In response to a look of condemnation from the ward sister, she put it away again. 'Is she the sergeant-major here?' Margot asked.

'You could say that.' Lizzie beamed. Things were getting better already!

'Right,' said Margot, brushing invisible flecks of dust from her jacket. 'I took the initiative and got in touch with Bessie. It seemed the sensible thing to do, seeing as she made arrangements for a similar scenario. By the way,' she said suddenly, 'do you know she's now a mother? Isn't that amazing, especially seeing as that man of hers wanted nothing to do with the first child! Well, that's Bessie for you!'

Lizzie couldn't remember quite who Bessie had ended up with, and what was more, she didn't want to remember. She was ashamed to admit it, but being compared with Bessie made her feel cheap and common.

'You're not the same, of course,' said Margot, as though reading her thoughts. She patted her hand with one white-gloved hand. 'You mustn't think that way. The past is behind you now. Look towards the future. Promise me you'll do that?'

Lizzie promised. 'Yes, yes. I will. But it isn't easy.'

'No. Getting in the family way was the easy bit,' said Margot. 'Anyway, let's get down to the reason I'm here. Bessie booked herself into a nursing home. She told me that it's run by the Salvation Army, but is very clean and there's no charge. It's a registered charity, apparently. They look after you and arrange the adoption once it's all over. Here's the address,' said Margot, handing her a slip of paper bearing her personal monogram.

'Lovely paper,' said Lizzie, her thumb tracing the raised lettering as a lump came to her throat. Strangely, she carefully avoided studying the address. Not now. Not yet.

Margot eyed her knowingly. Her voice, usually so cut-glass, so self-assured, now softened, just like a mother soothing her baby. 'I'm not fooled, Lizzie. You don't care tuppence about the paper. Look, I can only guess how you're really feeling, and it's OK to let it out. And if you want to shout and swear that all men are animals – especially RAF bigwigs – then, sweetie, feel free to do so.'

Lizzie stiffened and bit her lip. The tears would be hot on her cheeks if she let them fall. But she wouldn't. She had to maintain her self-control. 'It takes two to tango.'

Margot sighed. 'You're very brave.'

'No. I'm very scared. I've been a fool. I should have learned from my mother's mistake. Something similar happened to her.'

Margot raised one finely plucked eyebrow. In a certain light she resembled Marlene Dietrich – confident, blonde, pale-faced and dark-eyed. She didn't ask what Lizzie meant by her comment. Lizzie wouldn't have answered if she had.

'I take it from my mission to Bessie that you don't want your parents to know about your fall from grace. And you don't want to marry Patrick?'

'It wouldn't be fair. He's such a sweet man and although at one time we did talk about getting engaged, I couldn't do it now.'

'Why not?'

'Isn't that obvious? The baby isn't his.'

Margot shrugged. 'So? It happens in the best of families.'

'I wouldn't want to tie him down.'

Margot shrugged again. 'It's your decision, but it's a damn good offer.'

Lizzie shook her head. 'I can't.'

In her heart of hearts she was still half hoping that Guy would come walking into the ward carrying a huge bouquet. In her more logical moments she knew it was only wishful thinking, a dream from which she must wake up. Where was he now? she wondered. Still in Singapore with his wife and children, she supposed.

'So!' said Margot, crossing one silky stocking over the other. 'I take it you've been lying here planning what to do next. Am I right?'

'Yes. The nursing home can be arranged?'

Margot nodded. 'I checked.'

'I'm going to join the navy afterwards.'

Margot grinned wryly. 'Do that by all means, my dear, but do watch out for the admirals. They too have wives and children and are away from them far longer than wing commanders.'

Lizzie could have been insulted by Margot's comments, but instead she smiled at the cutting joke. Margot's satirical comment was merely intended to amuse.

'I think I'll avoid top-brass officers from now on.'

'I'm glad to hear it.' Margot studied their surroundings with disdainful eyes, her thick eyelashes sweeping her cheeks. 'Well, you can't stay here for ever, my sweet, and you can't arrive at the nursing home until the optimum moment. Have you considered where to stay until then?'

This was the question that had been unsettling Lizzie for some time. 'I don't know.'

Bits of pale lemon wool had transferred from her bed jacket to the turned down sheet that covered her. Lizzie picked at them thoughtfully. Hotels and guest houses were too expensive. She could ask Harry if he knew of anywhere, but that would mean letting him into the secret. She'd already asked Patrick; he didn't have a clue but badly wanted to do something to help.

'I could ask a few of my mates,' he'd said.

She'd declined his offer, fearing he would interpret her acquiescence as a sign that she might marry him. She cared for him deeply, but surely love was what she'd experienced with Guy – or had that been merely passion?

'I've got a place,' said Margot. 'I call it my bijou getaway, my little place in the country where I can be myself rather than Margot Ponsonby-Lyle. It's near Stowmarket, which isn't a million miles away from here, so I can visit you quite regularly – an added bonus if ever there was one.'

To Lizzie it felt as though a ton weight had fallen from her shoulders. Her face relaxed, the muscles down her back stopped feeling as taut as a bow string. She almost leapt across the bed.

'That's wonderful! Oh, Margot, how can I ever thank you enough?'

Margot winked one dark eye and pursed her red lips like a femme fatale from a 1920s movie. 'There is a certain proviso, my darling Lizzie.'

Lizzie waited, half expecting her to say that she could only stay there for two weeks a month.

Seeing her anxious expression, Margot laughed. 'Don't look so worried, darling. I require no rent, the accommodation is clean and the house could do with a full-time resident to warm it up, so to speak. The first proviso is that you use the second bedroom, a charming little pink and white room up under the eaves.'

'It sounds wonderful.'

'Slow down, darling. The second proviso is far more important than the first. You'll have to put up with me using the main bedroom when I need to.' She winked again. 'It has a four-poster with a lumpy mattress, but it doesn't stay lumpy for long with two bodies rolling over it. My chap's quite a hunk and helps me flatten it now and again. How's that with you?'

'Very generous. I can never thank you enough.'

Relieved to have somewhere to stay, Lizzie didn't immediately enquire who else was rolling over the lumpy mattress with Margot. She had a bolthole to stay in until presenting herself at the nursing home and that was really all that mattered.

Thirty-Six

'It's small, but pretty,' Margot said on the day she collected Lizzie in an army staff car and took the road to Stowmarket.

Margot was telling nothing but the truth. The cottage was thatched wattle and daub, with thick beams supporting a low ceiling. An ancient range, its brass handles polished by Margot's 'little woman from the village', provided hot water for cooking and heating. As winter approached, the little woman's husband brought apple and elm logs to burn in the huge inglenook fireplace. He also trapped rabbits, a welcome addition to anyone's diet.

'Your secret is safe with me,' said Margot, 'as long as mine is safe with you.'

Margot's secret was Owen, a PT instructor from Cardiff. He spoke with a Welsh accent, sang in the bath and had iron-hard muscles.

'What he lacks in mental agility, he certainly makes up for physically,' murmured Margot on the first weekend she brought him to the cottage.

'With those muscles, he could flatten a lumpy mattress all by himself,' Lizzie commented. She'd just seen him doing physical jerks out on the front lawn, muscles as thickly knotted as tree roots protruding from the confines of a tight white vest.

'But not so much fun, darling,' whispered Margot. She licked her lips.

Lizzie saw the hungry look in her eyes, surmising it had nothing to do with the mince and onions being stewed for lunch. She'd probably looked at Guy in the same way at one time, wondering what the likes of him saw in a girl like her. Her mother would have warned her. She wondered about Margot's mother.

'Do your parents know about him?' she asked Margot.

'Good grief, no! Pa would fetch a shotgun and Ma would have a fainting fit. There's no commitment between us – perish the thought,' explained Margot with a flourish of manicured fingernails, French perfume drifting from every movement. 'It's purely a physical thing. Being with someone physically helps me forget there's a war on. After the war I'll probably marry an ex-major from the Guards with a job in the City – a stock-broker or a Swiss banker. He'll be rich, I'll be a dutiful wife and although he might not be much in the physical department, I'll put up with it. After all, I'll still have my memories.'

Margot sounded totally convinced of how things would be, as though a map had been drawn with a straight path that she would dutifully follow. In a way Lizzie was saddened by it. What about poor Owen? How did he feel about the affair?

They were two lovely people from opposite ends of the social spectrum, and yet in a strange way they suited each other. But then, opposites attract, she thought – just like her and Guy.

Owen seemed nice and was well put together. He was very keen on keeping fit, getting up early and doing physical training in the garden most mornings. Margot on the other hand rarely came down to breakfast before nine.

Lizzie took her friend a cup of tea in bed when she came to stay. Four visits down the road she suggested Margot get up and join Owen out on the lawn.

'It's not civilized,' she'd told Lizzie, her voice muffled beneath the bedclothes. One eye blinked open. 'Besides, I had all the exercise I needed last night.'

'Margot, you are incorrigible!'

'But fun,' murmured Margot, retreating back beneath the bedclothes. Lizzie laughed and went back downstairs.

She fried a little streaky bacon for breakfast, and set out toast, butter and marmalade. Both the bacon and butter came from a nearby farm and was brought in by Margot's 'little woman' who turned out to be called May Letherby.

Lizzie glanced out of the small kitchen window. Owen had finished his morning exercise and came in wiping at his naked upper torso with a towel. His muscles rippled and bulged beneath his skin. Feeling her face redden, Lizzie picked up the spatula and attacked the sizzling bacon.

'There's mushrooms as well as an egg today,' she said, scooping both on to their plates. 'Mrs Letherby came across the mushrooms in the field on her way over.'

She stopped herself from gabbling on that Mr Letherby kept chickens, and that the bacon had come from a pig killed and cured some weeks before. Officially, it should have been reported to the Ministry of Food, but this was one little piggy that the Letherbys had kept for a private market.

Owen beamed and sniffed the air. 'Champion!'

Shrugging himself into his shirt, he pulled out a chair, straddling the seat as though he were mounting a horse.

Lizzie sat down too. She picked up the teapot. 'Tea?'

'Let me,' he said, his mouth full of bread and mushrooms. He took the pot from her and poured. 'You're in a delicate condition, luvvy. No sense in lifting anything heavy when I've got the muscles to do it for you.' His smile was as broad as his accent. She thanked him and, between mouthfuls of breakfast, she asked him how long he'd been in the army.

'Five years now. I'm what you call a career soldier, you see. That's why I'm not fighting overseas. I'm wanted here, to use my experience to lick men into shape. They're so green some of them, you see. Greener than a valley in springtime!' Suddenly he nodded at her belly. 'Marge tells me the father ran out on you.'

Marge? Margot never allowed anyone to call her Marge. *'So downmarket, darling. Makes me sound like a girl from a cotton-mill town.'*

Lizzie felt her face reddening. 'She had no business telling you that.'

'She tells me a lot of things. Sometimes she tries to hold back, but I've got a way with her, you see.'

'Oh, you really think so?' snapped Lizzie, slamming down her knife and fork. 'You've got big muscles. And that's all you've got and that's the only reason she bothers with you. There's no commitment. She told me that herself!' Her eyes blazed. She wanted to stab him with her look.

A slight smile played around his lips. 'Is that what she told you then?' His voice was as gentle and as rhythmic as a song. His eyes twinkled with untold secrets. He leaned closer, so close that she could smell the fresh sweat glistening on his chest and shoulders. 'Mark my words; me and Marge will spend the rest of our lives together. She might not admit it just now, but believe you me, that's the way it will be.' He gestured again at her stomach. 'I didn't mean to insult you. We all need a bit of passion in the midst of all this bloodshed. I understand if you don't want to talk about it. I apologize. Have to say though, it makes me ashamed to be a man when others of my gender treat women like that.'

Accepting that Guy Hunter had lied to her was never easy. Night time was the worst; it was when she was alone and darkness fell that she remembered how it had felt to lie in his arms. That was also when she felt jealous of Margot and her Owen. She never challenged Margot that the relationship was anything but physical. Only time would tell who was telling the truth. In the meantime she fended off letters from her mother. It was hard enough going through this by herself, harder still ignoring the fact that her mother would be worrying.

On one of Margot's weekends with Owen, she was burning the last of the autumn leaves on a bonfire at the edge of the vegetable garden. Margot had already phoned to say they were coming. 'And we've got a surprise for you,' she'd added.

There was no point in asking Margot what the surprise might be; she was terribly good at keeping secrets.

The sound of a car engine made Lizzie raise her head. The sun was bright but low in the sky, seeming to hang by a thread above the wide, flat landscape.

She shielded her eyes, aware that her cheeks were prickled red by the cold. Her hands were cold inside some old leather gardening gloves she'd found. Her stomach muscles were aching; she wouldn't admit, even to herself, that strenuous exercise could bring on a miscarriage, though she'd heard it could. She just carried on with whatever she wanted to do, just as she would once the child was born.

Margot's car appeared, framed by thorny branches and rose-hips forming an arch above the white wooden gate. The weak sun glinted on the car windows. Two figures were in the front – Margot and Owen of course – and another sat in the back.

She squinted, trying to make out who it was – definitely familiar, she decided; definitely male. The sudden shifting of her stomach was only partly due to the growing baby, as at least ten per cent was apprehension at Margot's 'little surprise'.

Crisply efficient and smiling broadly, Margot closed the car door behind her. The figure from the back seat got out and joined Owen, the two men chatting amiably, though Patrick's attention – for that was who it was – kept straying to her.

'My dear,' said Margot, her lips barely brushing Lizzie's cheeks. 'You are in need of good company and I—'

'We,' Owen corrected her.

'It was our shared opinion that you needed good friends around you and Owen and I cannot always give you our full attention.'

'Because we're too wrapped up in each other,' added Owen, at the same time hugging Margot tightly to his side with one arm.

Margot untangled herself from Owen, took Patrick by the elbow and dragged him forward. 'So who better?'

Patrick fiddled with his cap, turning it this way and that as he fought to decide whether he'd done the right thing by coming here.

Lizzie couldn't make up her mind whether she'd ever found Margot insensitive in the past. A sneaking suspicion that she was being manipulated wouldn't go away. *Margot is clever, and don't you forget it*, she told herself.

'This is going to be a marvellous weekend,' Margot declared, sliding her arm into Owen's. Together they headed up the garden path, the dried leaves of winter foliage rustling against their legs as they passed.

Together Lizzie and Patrick watched them go, neither quite ready to say what was on their mind.

Patrick got in first. 'I'm sorry. I don't want to intrude. I did tell Margot that, but you know how she is.' He paused, waiting for her reaction. 'I'll go if you don't want me here.'

She didn't answer at first. It wasn't easy to ask herself in the space of a minute exactly how she felt about him staying, though one practical question did spring to mind.

'I don't know where you'll sleep,' she blurted.

Patrick's cheeks flared the colour of the rosehips hanging languidly by the gate. 'She said I could have the settee by the fire.' He hung his head for a second. 'I'll be warm there.'

Damn Margot! Didn't she know that Patrick staying would make her feel awkward, guilty and every other negative emotion she could think of? The answer was obvious: yes, of course she knew! That was the whole purpose of this visit, wasn't it? To get her to accept Patrick's offer of marriage and keep the child.

The prongs of the rake dug into the ground as she thought things through. Her first inclination was to send Patrick packing. That would teach them!

'Let me finish this.' She let him take the rake from her hands and watched as he meticulously raked up leaves and twigs embedded more deeply in the soil.

She folded her arms. 'I thought you were going abroad again.'

'I was, but then, what with the Americans getting involved, plans got altered.'

'Did you want to go back overseas?'

'What young chap doesn't want to see the world? But then I didn't think it was so important any more. There are other things more important than seeing the world, and anyway, I've seen a fair bit of it so far.'

He glanced up at her. She didn't need him to tell her what or who was more important; she could see it in his eyes.

'There,' he said, shaking the last of the leaves on to the bonfire. 'All done.' He turned to face her. 'Shall I stay, or shall I go?'

She pursed her lips and swayed from side to side. 'I'll make us a cup of tea. I might even find a slice of carrot cake.'

'Carrot cake?' Patrick looked surprised. City people never came across cakes actually made from carrots.

Lizzie laughed. 'May makes cakes from anything that's plentiful – even turnips.'

He looked faintly sceptical. 'I'm not sure I'm going to like this.'

'Oh, you will,' she said, her voice lighter now she'd made the decision that he could stay.

'I expect Margot's already got the kettle on,' he said, nodding towards the square of amber light that was the kitchen window.

Lizzie, a light smile playing around her lips, shook her head. 'I doubt that very much.'

Just at that moment a sudden movement at the bedroom window drew their attention. The curtains were being drawn – and in broad daylight. Unlike the kitchen, the bedroom windows did let in enough light to see by. But Margot and Owen were after privacy, not daylight.

'I see,' said Patrick. 'Looks like the tea and cake is for us alone.'

Once inside, Lizzie pulled off her gardening gloves, took off her heavy coat and Wellingtons and reached for the kettle. The kettle was big, black and made from cast iron. Originally made to cater for a whole family plus a few farmhands, it was heavy even when only partially filled.

'I'll do it,' said Patrick, taking it out of her hands.

'I'll cut the cake.' In the end she laid out cold rabbit as well as the cake.

'Parsley,' she said on seeing Patrick pick at the green bits.

The sound of creaking bedsprings sounded from the ceiling above them.

'It's a four-poster,' said Lizzie as though that alone explained the series of squeaks.

'Should we leave anything for them?'

She shook her head. 'I doubt they'll want feeding until morning. Tuck in. Eat all you like.'

Patrick did as ordered. 'Tastes good,' he said after swallowing the first mouthful. 'Your mother will be surprised when I tell her how well you're eating up here.'

Alarm made her prickly. 'You haven't told her, have you? I will never forgive you if you have.'

He looked hurt and shook his head, placing the rabbit bones on the edge of his plate. His voice was quiet, considered. 'No. Of course not. You should know me better than that.'

'Thank goodness!'

She couldn't bring herself to say anything more substantial to him. If she did it might give him hope. Up until now she had been strong, determined to go through with this and come out the other side unchanged. To carry it through she had to remain strong, untouched by any pressure from her family. If her mother ever found out about the child, she'd persuade Lizzie to keep it.

'I don't want to end up in the same circumstances as my mother,' she said to Patrick. 'I don't want to marry a man purely to save my reputation. Once this is over the child will have a good home and will never know or care that I ever existed.'

'If that's what you want,' he said. He fell to silence, pushing bits of meat around his plate as though he'd lost his appetite.

Watching his reaction made her feel bad, and she didn't want him to think badly of her. The feeling was new, or at least she thought it was, but didn't friends always think well of each other? Wasn't that what friendship was all about? The urge to make amends, to rebuild his opinion of her, was intense. There seemed to be only one way of doing this. She fingered her piece of cake, breaking off small bits that didn't find their way to her mouth until she'd made the decision to explain.

The steady squeal of the bedsprings continued above their heads. Another illegitimate baby in the making? No, Lizzie decided. Margot was too fly for that.

'You never knew your father, did you, Patrick?'

'I remember him only vaguely – or I think I do. I can never tell with Rosie.'

Rosie was his mother, though he could never quite bring himself to call her that now he was a man; it was his reaction to a neglected childhood.

'You know my father and you know my mother. You also know Michael.'

Patrick nodded. 'Michael's a nice bloke even though he is foreign.'

'But not my father. Henry Randall is not so nice, is he, or hadn't you noticed?'

Patrick speared a piece of rabbit with his fork. 'I've noticed he likes a drink.'

'My mother's sweetheart died in the trenches but left her pregnant. She had the child adopted and was forced into marrying my father. It was the worst thing she ever did – marrying my father, I mean.' She leaned forward, her wide eyes looking directly into his in an effort to emphasize all she was saying, all she was feeling.

'She married him and began to trust him. She trusted him so much that she told him about the child she'd had adopted. That was when he took to the drink and began to treat her badly – very badly. He was very careful to hide his behaviour from us, but I began to suspect. It was our Stanley who opened our eyes. Poor lad was sick a lot when he was younger and kept from school a lot of the time. He saw it all. Shocking for a boy of that age.'

Patrick frowned. 'But surely things would have been different if your mother had kept the baby.'

'Not without a husband. She did the right thing in finding the child a home. What she did wrong was to marry my father just to save her reputation. Men can change once you marry them.'

Patrick looked down at his plate and dropped his fork. 'Oh. I see. You think I might turn into a monster like your father.'

She shook her head. 'No! That's not what I mean. What I mean is that marrying you and foisting someone else's child on you is unfair. Don't you see that?'

It had been some time since the last creaking bedspring; now it started up all over again.

Patrick raised his eyes to the ceiling. 'It doesn't matter who you are or what you are if you love one another. Nobody's perfect. We all fall off the straight and narrow now and again.'

'Have you fallen off the straight and narrow, Patrick?'

He looked perplexed rather than guilty. 'I'm not perfect,' he said enigmatically.

* * *

The weekend turned out to be better than expected. In the daytime moments when Margot and Owen could be roused from the four-poster bed, they sat in front of the fire, talking, drinking dandelion wine and eating more of the rabbits shot by May's husband. A walk to the White Hart pub resulted in green cider. A poker was thrust into embers falling from a burning log and held there. Once it glowed red hot it was thrust into the cider, sizzling and sending the aroma of apples drifting to the rafters.

'I still want to marry you,' Patrick said to Lizzie as they walked back through a field stiff with stubble. 'Will you at least think about it?'

Lizzie sighed. 'I can't promise anything, Patrick. Leave it a while. I'm so mixed up at this moment in time.'

They plodded across the field while Margot and Owen raced ahead of them like greyhounds, keen to get back to the cottage and the four-poster bed.

A cloud of crows rose from the trees ahead of them, cawing and shrieking in continual argument.

Patrick suddenly asked her the question she'd often asked herself. 'Your mother must wonder what happened to that child.'

'I suppose she does.'

'Have you ever asked her about it?'

Lizzie shook her head. 'No. I expect she did at first, but not after all these years. The child accepts the adoptive parents as their own. It's best that way.'

Patrick was silent as he helped her over a stile. The air smelled of wood smoke and the promise of frost. 'And yet you think she would persuade you to keep your child. What makes you think that?'

'If I told her right now, she'd let her heart rule her head. Once it's all over – if she ever does find out – she'll understand that I'm being sensible.'

'And that's your final decision?'

'Yes!' she said, her resolute tone meant to leave him in no doubt of her commitment to this plan of action. 'That is my final decision.'

The threesome left the cottage on the Sunday evening, and Lizzie was again left to her own devices. She watched the car until it disappeared into the winter mist that hung in waves over the low countryside.

Despite her initial reluctance to welcome Patrick's presence, she found herself missing him. It had been a good weekend. She had stated her case and Patrick had accepted her decision. She told herself that she was doing the right thing, that her mother would agree – that is if she ever found out.

Nothing would sway her, or so she thought – that was until she received another letter from her mother. She read the first paragraph, stopped, took a deep breath and read it again. The unexpected had happened and suddenly a fine filigree of cracks began to appear in her plans.

Thirty-Seven

Elizabeth Ford stayed in Mary Anne's mind for a long time after she'd left. While she was sewing, helping in the Red Cross shop or looking after Mathilda, two separate visions – one of a baby and one of a grown, elegant woman – floated and then merged in her mind.

They were sitting in the back room of the shop; Edith was unpicking ancient cardigans and knitting them into socks, hats and matching scarves. Mary Anne was trimming a broad-brimmed funeral hat with a tiger-print silk scarf.

Edith's eyes still sparkled but age was catching up with her. Her tear ducts ran constantly, leaving sticky trails at the sides of her eyes. She dabbed them with a folded-up handkerchief and blew her nose with another kept solely for that purpose.

'A penny for them,' Edith said, taking a break from knitting to dab at her eyes.

Mary Anne sighed and put the hat down on the table, smoothing the brim with both hands. 'I was just thinking that we can never quite escape our past.'

'Very philosophical, my dear, but quite right. What we do in early life forms our future and who we are.' She fell to silence. Mary Anne sensed her keen eyes were studying her, seeking her mood before disclosing her thoughts. 'That young woman the other day; she meant something to you?'

Mary Anne played with the ends of the tiger-print scarf. Should she be honest? And what answer would *be* honest anyway?

'I think so.'

'I know so,' said Edith softly. 'I could see it in the eyes, you see. My mother always said I had the knack of seeing what people were really feeling just by looking into their eyes.'

'I didn't know it showed that much.'

'It did, my dear. But I wasn't really referring to you. Your emotion was obvious, but so was hers. That lady of the manor exterior didn't fool me for one minute. I've known plenty like her in my time, their feelings hidden behind an expensive façade.'

From the very first time she'd entered the shop, Edith had been something of an enigma. She even had the measure of Gertrude Palmer.

'She's been a Girl Guide all her life,' Edith had explained with a sly smile. 'Absolutely loves uniforms and giving orders. I heard tell that she'd wanted to be head girl at the public school she attended, but was pipped at the post.'

Mary Anne had looked at Edith in amazement. 'Edith, you know everything about everyone.'

When Edith had smirked her face lit up like a schoolgirl's. 'Don't let these wrinkles fool you. I'm the same age as Gertrude.' The smirk turned into a wide grin. 'I went to the same school,' she said mischievously.

Mary Anne burst out laughing. '*You* were made head girl?'

Edith nodded. 'Just imagine me. Black stockings, gymslip and hockey stick. I may be small, but I kept them in order.'

Edith's questioning eyes now met Mary Anne's, shaking her out of her reverie. 'Yes,' she said. 'Elizabeth Ford does mean something to me.'

'And you mean something to her. As I told you, I saw it in her eyes. Did I ever tell you about my Frenchman?' Edith sighed and her eyes adopted a faraway look as she dragged back the memories. 'I was already a widow of mature years, but that didn't matter to him. He was so attractive, and when he spoke in that wonderful accent—'

'Perhaps another time,' said Mary Anne abruptly. She got up from her chair and proceeded to prepare a pile of work to take home with her. 'Look at the time. I'd better be going before our Stanley gets home from school.'

It wasn't quite true; Stanley wouldn't be home for another fifteen minutes, but if she didn't get out Edith would soon know all her business and she didn't want that.

'I won't be seeing you tomorrow,' she shouted over her shoulder. 'I'm going round to our Daw's. John came home last night and I thought I'd go round and say hello.'

Edith's eyes were steady and wise. She waved one slim hand in farewell. 'Goodbye, Mary Anne. I'll tell you more about my secret love, my *très joli* Frenchman tomorrow.'

That night Mary Anne dreamed of the day she'd given Elizabeth away and awoke mopping her tears with the sheet. No one could have known, not even her parents, but she'd actually chosen the name Elizabeth herself. The baby had been handed over nameless, but the new parents had chosen the same name. Perhaps it was something to do with the marriage of the Duke of York and Lady Elizabeth Bowes-Lyon – the present King George VI and Queen Elizabeth. Their daughter too was called Elizabeth, just like Mary Anne's first daughter – just like her third daughter too, though she always insisted on being called Lizzie. It didn't really matter. The truth was that Elizabeth Ford's visit had left a gaping wound where Mary Anne's heart used to be. She had a great urge to make amends, to explain that she'd been forced to give her daughter away. *But she doesn't want anything to do with you*, said a voice in her head. It hurt, but she had to face up to the truth.

The next day she washed her face in the old enamel bowl, patted it dry and eyed her complexion in the mirror. Her skin was healthy and her eyes shone with a brittle brightness that hadn't been there the day before.

She addressed her reflection. 'Today is a new day. You must put the past behind you and look ahead. Michael is depending on you. So is the Red Cross for that matter,' she muttered, thinking of the pile of alterations waiting to be done.

Daw looked sour when she opened the door just after midday. John was slumped at the table, his head in his hands. Mathilda was asleep in her pram.

'I'm off out,' said Daw, tying a headscarf beneath her chin. 'I've got shopping to do. Not that I'm likely to get much, but seeing as someone came home and ate every last bit of bread we had . . .' She threw an even sourer look in John's direction.

'Oh, God. Give it a rest,' he murmured from behind his hands.

Reluctant to interfere, Mary Anne went straight to the pram and looked down at her granddaughter. 'Well at least someone's content,' she said softly.

'I'm off,' said Daw without a backward look. The door slammed behind her. Mathilda twitched but did not wake.

Mary Anne took off her brown felt hat that had a red trim. Her coat was of the same brown and was checked with thin strips of red and white. Two weeks ago it had been a car blanket; now it was the best coat she owned.

She turned to John, who had now emerged from behind his hands. 'Have you had anything to eat?'

'No.' He shook his head. 'She's not too pleased with me. I came in after having a few beers with the lads and felt hungry, so I buttered the last piece of bread in the house. I didn't know it was the last piece then. But I do now.'

'And that's what this is about?'

He nodded, then winced, rubbing at the back of his neck. 'I also said I wouldn't be home for as long as I thought I was going to be. That went down like a ton of coal down the chute. She said I should spend all my leave with her. I s'pose I should have really, but I just needed to unwind . . .' He continued to rub at the nape of his neck.

John was fair and lightly built, though taller than Daw. Daw was well built, big busted and broad in the hips. Mary Anne asked the obvious. 'Did she hit you?'

He looked surprised by the question, as though he didn't quite understand.

'Your neck,' said Mary Anne. 'You keep rubbing it.'

'That's because I've been sent packing from the bedroom.' He pointed to the settee. 'I slept there last night.'

'Oh dear.'

He grimaced. 'The trouble is that when Daw gets on her high horse, there's no knowing when she's going to get off.'

Mary Anne sighed. 'I'll find you something to eat.'

Daw marched stiffly along, shopping basket containing ration book, identity card and purse banging against her side.

The queue outside the vegetable shop was long, but she joined it anyway. Vegetable soup with plenty of potatoes would fill a gap. There were a few things underneath the counter in the corner shop that she could add to make it more flavoursome. She was tall enough to look over some of the heads in the queue. Women wearing headscarves tied in all manner of ways chatted and smoked ahead of her. The smell of Woodbines brought on a craving she'd been trying to do without. She searched in her coat pocket for her cigarettes and brought out only an empty packet.

'Damn,' she muttered. Tipsy, he'd said! Drunk more like! He'd not only been hungry, he'd wanted a smoke, couldn't find his own and smoked the last of hers.

'Have one of mine.'

She turned round. For a brief moment a strange sense of déjà vu seemed to flash between them. Although the woman was slimmer and taller than she was, Daw was taken aback.

'Thank you,' she said, taking a cigarette from a case that looked to be made of gold. The woman offered her a light. Daw's gaze never dropped from her face.

'I'm sorry for staring,' said Daw, 'but we look so alike.'

'I thought that too when I saw you join the queue,' said the woman. 'Perhaps we're related. May I ask your name?'

May I! A relative who spoke like that? Highly unlikely.

'Doreen Smith, but I was born Doreen Randall.'

'Ah!' The woman nodded thoughtfully.

'Are you a Randall or a Hodgeson?' asked Daw. Hodgeson was her mother's family name. She lifted her chin and spoke down her nose as she said it.

The other woman laughed in a short, sharp manner, the kind of laugh that is dropped in like a kind of challenge or even an insult.

'Well, one can never be sure who one's people are, can one? History and families make such chaotic twists and turns, one can be a prince one day and a peasant the next.'

Daw blushed at the thought of where she fitted in and it angered her. Damn the woman and her cigarettes, the stuck-up cow!

She made a rueful face. 'Ugh. That tastes disgusting,' she said. Although only its tip had burned to ash, she threw it down, grinding it into the ground with the heel of her shoe.

Surprised by her action, the woman's lips parted slightly as though she were about to comment. Daw turned her back on her, a sure sign that she neither wanted to listen nor speak any longer.

When she next turned round the woman was gone. The fact that they'd looked so alike had unnerved Daw. She craned her neck, seeking a glimpse of the burgundy suit, the handsome black fedora with the green goose feather at the side.

Expensive clothes, she mused. Now how could any relative of hers afford such expensive clothes?

Her mother's family of course – not that she ever saw them nowadays. She wondered why. She was sure Harry knew, and Lizzie would of course. But neither of them imparted secrets to her. They were different from her. As her mother kept saying, she was more like her father than they were, and to be honest she was glad of that.

Mary Anne was sewing huge brown buttons on to the patch pockets of the winter coats when Gertrude came calling. She looked glum and stood with her hands folded in front of her. Mary Anne immediately thought the worse. Once again Gertrude had decided to ban her from the shop because she was 'living in sin' with a man much younger than her. Deciding attack was the best form of defence, she held up her hands in surrender.

'Some coats are finished. You can take them with you. In fact you can take the lot if the thought of having me on your premises continues to cause offence.'

Gertrude's expression remained glum. 'That's not why I'm here. Lady Macory died in her sleep last night.'

Mary Anne looked at her blankly. She'd never heard of the woman.

'Edith,' Gertrude explained on seeing her confusion. 'I came to tell you I could do with more help and also that the funeral is next Tuesday. If you haven't got any mourning clothes, I'm sure we can fix you up with something.'

Mary Anne's shoulders slumped. No more Edith. No more tales of her romantic Frenchman.

'No doubt I shall see you tomorrow,' said Gertrude and without another word turned away.

Mary Anne watched her go, noting that a dowager's hump was forming between Gertrude's meaty shoulders.

'I'm sorry,' Mary Anne whispered to herself. A tear ran from one eye. Edith had been alive at this time yesterday. She'd been licking her lips salaciously, about to tell more lurid tales about the love of her life, the handsome Frenchman who had swept her off her feet. Mary Anne was wracked with guilt. If only she'd stopped and listened. If only she'd asked her more about how one's past actions affect one's future.

Suddenly she wanted to tell someone about her past, about Elizabeth Ford. But who? She had no close friends who would understand as well as Edith. Daw wasn't approachable, and Harry and Michael were away. She and Biddy, her old neighbour, were not as friendly as they used to be. There was no alternative but to write to Lizzie and tell her everything. She'd have to send it via Patrick. Damn the war and the need for all this secrecy! Never mind. Down to the letter-writing.

She chose her words carefully, getting right to the point but without wanting to cause pain. She'd told Lizzie months ago that she'd had a child before marrying her father. She'd told her most of the circumstances, but not any hope that the child would one day turn up seeking her mother. Things were more simply outlined at the end of the letter.

> *I realize now that we never really escape our past. All that we have been and have done goes through life with us. I never expected Elizabeth to turn up, but she did. Now I regret not being more responsive to her. I could have done more, surely I could. I was told that giving Elizabeth away would be best for me and for the child. Now I know they were wrong. I should have fought like a tiger to keep her. No matter that we'd have been poor and ostracized, we would have been together. There would have been no gap between us.*

Thirty-Eight

The time at Margot's cottage passed quickly for Lizzie, though the feeling of loss and damaged expectations never went away. In December she packed her case and caught the bus to a home run by the Salvation Army for unmarried mothers, the one Bessie would have gone to had she not miscarried.

After reading the letter from Mary Anne, Margot had tried to persuade her to think again.

'Think how this half-sister must have felt when she found out she was adopted.'

'That's not supposed to happen.'

Margot had given her a 'things do happen' look.

'Your mother regretted doing it. So could you.'

Stubbornly she ignored Margot's advice. 'Everything's arranged.'

She purposely turned down Margot's offer of a lift to the nursing home. Her mind was made up, but Margot would have kept asking her to reconsider. She wasn't sure how long she could hold out. As it was, the question kept repeating inside her mind: could she really go through with this?

Yes, said a firm, nagging voice. *You must or your life will be ruined.*

The fat little bus snorted its way along the country road, the sound of its grating gears reverberating between high walls and hawthorn hedges. She stared out at the scenery but saw nothing.

They passed a factory making windows, obtrusive in the middle of fields, then storms of frosted leaves, remains of a beautiful autumn, raced before a cold north wind.

Lizzie's belly had grown and she had got used to it. *Strange how you get used to things*, she thought, like all these people wearing uniforms who seemed to be everywhere. Strange how she'd also become so used to being away from home.

When the scenery became boring and the nervous churning of her stomach too much to bear, Lizzie eyed the only other passenger on the bus. She was sitting at the front of the bus, smoke from a cigarette circling her head. The chignon at the nape of her neck shone a healthy pale gold. Pearl earrings glinted from her lobes each time she turned her head to look at the view or light another cigarette. She'd smoked a whole packet on the journey, Lizzie noticed.

Hidden by overhanging branches, the bus stop was not apparent until the bus slithered on wet leaves and eventually came to a halt. The other passenger got up from her seat first and came level with her. 'Need a hand?'

Lizzie's eyes travelled upward over a coat loosely belted over a stomach that was as big as her own. There was a confidence in her looks and manner that she instantly envied.

'It's not easy when there's a beach ball where your waistline used to be, but I'll manage.'

'Two beach balls together,' beamed the blonde.

She quickly judged the girl to be around her own age. She had wide-set blue eyes, high cheekbones and a straight nose above full, sensuous lips. The blonde with the pearl earrings had a handsome face, the sort seen on Greek statues at the British Museum. She also wore very nice clothes, not so much expensive as wisely chosen to appear that way. The blonde took the lead, moving sideways down the aisle. Lizzie struggled to her feet.

The conductor eyed them in a surly manner and didn't offer to help them off. Once their heels were digging into the soft grass verge, he sniffed and pointed to a sign and a gateway a few yards along the road. Like the bus stop it was half hidden by branches.

'That's the place for fallen women,' he said, his tone as contemptuous as the look he gave them. 'It's like a bloody great rowing boat in thur; oars on both sides!'

'Men!' shouted Lizzie and turned away, too angry, too humiliated to say anything else. All she wanted was to get this over with and then her life would be her own again.

The blonde set down her case, stuck her fists on her hips and jerked her head high. 'Whores! Is that what you mean, you dirty old sod? Now that's where you're wrong. Didn't you know? This place is being turned into a convent!' She jerked her thumb at Lizzie. 'She's got the job of Mother Superior, and I'm the bloody Virgin Mary 'cos I like being worshipped. Now sod off! Go on. Shove off and punch a few tickets, you bald-headed old coot!'

The bus conductor snorted. 'Tart!'

The blonde picked up a fallen stick and took a run at him. Despite her girth, she ran fast enough and looked strong enough to land a blow. She shouted all the way. 'And who makes us tarts, eh? Men! That's who! They're always Prince Bloody Charming until there's a bun in the oven!'

Firing puffs of black smoke from its noisy exhaust, the bus pulled away, its gears grating against the worn cogs as the dying pistons rapidly coated the engine with choking layers of carbon. Blown into the air by its passing, December leaves swirled like dancing dervishes, finally settling in crisp brown heaps at the roadside.

The blonde glowered after it, her cheeks pink from the morning chill. 'Men!'

Lizzie wasn't fooled by the jutting firmness of the girl's chin. Her own feelings of rejection and disappointment were reflected in the blonde's eyes, and yet she had to admire her guts.

Finally they stood alone. 'I'm Sally,' said the blonde, swiftly turning round and taking Lizzie unawares with a firm handshake.

'I'm Lizzie.'

Sally turned her classic features to the sign and the entrance to Pilemarsh Abbey. HOME FOR UNMARRIED MOTHERS was picked out beneath it in a more muted type than the original name. Her breasts, heavily expectant with baby milk, heaved her coat lapels apart when she sighed. 'Well. Let's get it over with.' Pouncing on her suitcase and gripping it with a firm hand, she began to walk.

Lizzie followed on, though more slowly than Sally, taking in the curling paint at the corners of the sign, the way the spindly twigs of the poplar trees rattled like tiny bits of metal, and the height of the walls – mostly the height of the walls. They were huge and meant to keep people in.

Sally got to the gate first, stopped and waited for Lizzie to catch up.

'Sorry,' said Lizzie, puffing and rubbing at the hollow of her back.

'What for?'

'I'm a bit slow and my back aches.'

The classic features softened. 'Nervous?'

Lizzie nodded. 'My stomach's doing somersaults.'

Sally laughed. 'Of course it is. There's a baby in there aching to get out.'

'I've never had a baby before.'

Sally's laughter died away. 'Neither have I. So it's a first time for both of us.' Turning, she scrutinized the gate as though she were looking for something in particular, perhaps for a way in that would be of advantage, unobserved by the authorities vested in the place. 'No,' she said at last. 'Can't find it anywhere.'

Lizzie eyed her with puzzlement. 'Can't find what?'

'The sign – the one that says "Abandon hope all ye that enter here".'

Lizzie laughed. 'I think we've already crossed that hurdle. What I had hoped for made a run back to his wife months ago.'

'Join the club,' said Sally resignedly.

'The pudding club?' said Lizzie raising her eyebrows.

They both laughed.

'Looks grim though, doesn't it?' said Sally, her bottom lip turning outwards in a half pout.

Lizzie eyed the entrance and gave a disdainful snort. 'Come on. Let's see what sort of place this is.'

'So what do your family think of your predicament?' Sally asked as they strolled up the gravel road towards the looming pile.

'I haven't told them. Have you?'

Sally shook her head. 'There's no one to tell. I'm an orphan. All my life I've been passed around the family like a parcel. No one wanted to keep me, so why should I tell them anything? What's your reason?'

Lizzie shrugged and narrowed her eyes as she thought about it. 'I'm not quite sure. I think I didn't want to see the pity in my mother's eyes. I'm not quite sure what she would say, probably something like, "Lizzie, you should have known better." But that's just it I suppose. I *should* have known better.'

'Don't tell me. Let me guess. He said he was going to divorce his wife for you.'

'And he told me he had no children. Turns out he has four.'

Sally smirked. 'Perhaps he forgot where he put them. Memory's the first to go when a bloke wants his own way. Now take my Cecil. Handsome as they come, pots of money and offered me the earth. But I held him off. No matter what he bought me, I said, "No; first put a ring on that finger right there."' Sally heaved her case high enough to point at the third finger on her left hand.

'And he said he would, so you finally gave in,' said Lizzie with a heartfelt sigh.

'No. I didn't,' said Sally, fixing her gaze straight ahead. 'I overdid the champagne one night and he wouldn't take no for an answer. I was black and blue in the morning, one eye closed and my bottom lip cut, my cheek swollen. I was also pregnant, though I didn't know it at the time. So! Here I am.'

'He didn't want to marry you.'

'Worse than that. He took back the keys of the flat. Lovely it was too. In South Kensington, in London. I had a bit of money and pawned some of the stuff he'd given me. Even then I had to eke it out, so I ended up living in a room above a pie and eel shop in Putney. Bit of a come down.' A sudden grin came to her lips. 'Except for the pies and eels, that is.'

Thirty-Nine

Henry Randall knocked back the dregs from the bottom of a pint mug. As he tipped back the glass, his eyes happened to land on Mary Anne unlocking the door of the Red Cross shop across the road. His unsteady gaze swept behind him to the clock behind the bar. Its face was fuzzy. Even when he squinted he couldn't tell what time it was. Bloody landlord! Why didn't he get it fixed?

He slammed his beer mug down on the bar. 'Time you got that bloody clock fixed, Jack Kitson.'

Jack Kitson's meaty fist swept a crumpled cloth over the brown pool that never really went away. He was wearing a look he reserved for good customers who were tolerated rather than liked. 'There's nothing wrong with my clock, Henry Randall. It's your eyes that's the problem.'

Henry's cheeks rippled with indignation. 'My eyes is as good as when I was pulling the trigger of a Royal Enfield.'

'But would the sergeant-major have let you handle a rifle after two hours in the snug of the local boozer? Think about that,' said Jack, raising a cautionary finger.

Henry shook his head. 'Poor old Sergeant-Major Ormrod. I wonder where he is now.'

'Not in 'ere,' said Jack. 'And neither should you be. It's two o'clock and I've got war work to do.'

Jack Kitson kept tight hours at lunchtime. The area above the bar was festooned with Union Jack flags and smaller ones from regiments and ships. Jack was a patriot of John Bull proportions, and few argued when he said he wanted to close – except for a fool, or the downright contrary.

'Two o'clock,' muttered Henry, peering into his beer mug as though expecting it suddenly to refill of its own accord.

'Are you 'aving another then, Randall?'

The question came from Alf Routledge. They'd been in the same outfit together in the Great War and like any old comrades they always had time for each other.

Henry slammed his glass against the man's chest. 'Only if yer buying.'

Routledge's bloated features crumpled with dismay. He didn't like forking out for anything. He'd only asked Henry in the hope of blagging a drink for himself.

Jack Kitson smirked to himself behind the bar. He knew Alf well. 'Didn't work that time then, Alf?'

Routledge scowled as he slammed the dimpled mug on to the bar. 'Bloody fool! His brain's turned to mush since his missus left 'im for a younger bloke.'

The landlord smiled broadly as he tweaked his curly moustache. 'Could be that 'is brain's turned to mush because of all the hops he's poured down his throat. They're mush too.'

Routledge wasn't listening. He too had seen Mary Anne enter the Red Cross shop. *Now here*, he thought, *is a chance to get even*. Michael Maurice had refused to pay him what he was owed for looking after the pawn shop when old Maurice had died. *Kill two birds with one stone*, he thought, sauntering back over to Henry, beer slopping from the pint pot he carried.

Through narrowed eyes, Henry stared unflinchingly at the shop across the road. Watching him, Alf saw his chance. He'd heard it was used as a place where mail could be forwarded to those who'd become homeless or just out of touch with loved ones or families. People who'd moved from elsewhere to work in munitions factories or down at the docks contacted the Red Cross when all else had failed. So did members of the armed forces.

Routledge nudged his arm. 'What d'you think they've been up to?' He nodded at three soldiers who'd just come out. One of them was waving a letter and looked mighty pleased with himself. Alf Routledge weighed up the situation. The soldiers were only collecting their mail, but good old Henry wouldn't see things that way – not with all the beer he'd drunk. All the same, a little push in the right direction wouldn't go amiss.

'What do you think then?' said Alf, indicating the boys in khaki on the other side of the road.

'What do you mean?' Henry's voice was slurred, his eyes bloodshot.

'Them,' said Alf. 'What do you think they've been up to in there?'

'It's a shop.'

Alf chuckled and nudged him in the ribs. 'Yeah! And you know what sort of shop, if you get my meaning. They may not call it a knocking shop, but I've heard some pretty spicy rumours, you know.' He paused as he waited for Henry to fully absorb what he'd said.

Henry's cheeks hollowed as he eyed the laughing young man. His jealousy was like a great big bonfire glowing inside, never going out. Sometimes it blazed, and this was one of those times. Mary Anne was his. She'd had no business leaving him, no business setting up house with that young German bloke.

Routledge saw the signs of jealousy, the burning in the eyes, the nervous tic quaking beneath Henry's skin. He twisted the knife deeper into the wound. 'I've seen a lot of blokes going in and out over there,' he lied. The truth was that few servicemen actually called there; Army Welfare kept them in touch with their families. But this was a means to an end.

A nerve twitched beneath Henry's right eye. The sound of grinding teeth accompanied his cold, hard stare. All around the shop was a blur of muted colour. Only the door to the shop concerned him – and more specifically whoever went in and out of it. He took another pint from Routledge but was oblivious to the man's wicked leer.

Routledge whispered into his ear. 'You ought to go and sort 'er out, chum. She's making you a bloody laughing stock, 'er and that Kraut bastard she's shacked up with.'

Henry's eyes flickered. His fist gripped the beer mug so

tightly that Routledge expected it to shatter. He took a step back.

Perhaps nothing more would have happened; perhaps Henry would have staggered home or slumped into an unconscious heap. But suddenly the shop door opened. Dressed in a dark red dress with a red and white checked belt, Mary Anne stepped out with a young fellow in a boiler suit. She appeared to be talking and smiling at him, and he was smiling back, both of them looking in at the window and then at each other.

Henry wasn't sure whether it was Michael Maurice or not; all he cared about was that his wife – and she still was his wife – was acting in a familiar manner with a very young man.

Seeing what Henry was seeing, Routledge stoked the flames. 'Blimey! That one do like a bit of variety!'

Henry slammed the beer mug against Routledge's chest as he'd done before, only this time Alf sidestepped and it smashed on the floor.

Jack Kitson watched in horror from behind the bar.

'Alf Routledge, you're banned,' he shouted as Henry charged out of the door.

Routledge smirked. 'Stick yer bloody pub. It's worth a ban just to watch old Henry go into action on that snooty cow!'

Tanked up with beer, Henry staggered across the road. 'Oi!' he shouted. 'You get away from my wife.'

He saw Mary Anne's cheerful expression change to one of total shock. Perhaps if he'd been sober he might have noticed that her glance at him was only brief. Her surprise was for someone beyond him, someone he did not know.

There was a man on the street cleaning windows, something he had resorted to after losing a leg at Dunkirk. He had dipped to fetch his cloth from his bucket when Mary Anne raised her head and saw Elizabeth Ford. Her first-born daughter was like a bird of paradise amongst a host of sparrows. The cut of her clothes, the quality of her hat and the beautifully made-up face set her apart from the midday crowds.

This was all too much. Henry and Elizabeth at the same time!

Taken off guard, her eyes flew from one to the other, unsure who to acknowledge and what to do. She hadn't expected to see Elizabeth again. Hadn't she said there was no room in her life for a mother who had abandoned her? Her heart would have leapt with joy, but just beyond Elizabeth and heading in the same direction, she saw Daw coming along the road with Mathilda in the pushchair.

Henry got to her first. 'Slut!'

A heavy hand slammed against her cheek, sending her sideways. Henry was a blur of staggering anger, lashing out at the innocent window cleaner and sending his bucket rattling along the ground.

'Keep away from my wife, you bastard!'

'Henry!'

Mary Anne grabbed the raised arm. 'He's only cleaning the windows . . .'

The fist meant for the window cleaner came back and smashed into her ribs.

'Dad!'

Daw shoved the pushchair between her parents. Her face was white with shock. Her father's eyes flickered. He saw her, recognized her, but his beer-fuelled anger was unabated. Routledge had done his job well. A red mist swirled before his eyes, obliterating any attempt to keep up the illusion he'd created for his children – that he was a good father and a good husband who never raised a hand to any of them.

To Daw's astonishment, he raised a fist in her direction, swearing at her and jabbing his knee into the side of the pushchair, sending it tilting on two wheels. Mathilda started to wail.

Mary Anne shouted, 'Henry! For pity's sake, this is your child and your grandchild!'

An elegantly gloved hand emerged from a mink sleeve, caught Daw's shoulder and pulled her away. The pushchair came too.

Henry's eyes narrowed. Mary Anne winced as his fingers dug into her neck. His other hand clawed over her face, digging into her cheeks and around her eyes. She heard Daw screaming at her father to stop; heard Mathilda wailing for her mother.

Another voice joined the melee. 'Stop that! Stop that, I say!'

Gertrude had come out of the shop and began beating Henry across the back with her umbrella.

'Leave me alone, would you,' Henry growled, hunching his shoulders against the blows raining on his back.

'I'm not surprised,' shouted Gertrude, suddenly changing tactics and prodding him in the ribs. 'No woman should have to put up with this. Emmeline Pankhurst certainly wouldn't!' Her swift jab knocked the breath out of him. His grip loosened.

Another body pushed in front of him. Something cold stabbed him between the eyes. 'Stop it or I shall be forced to shoot!'

The voice was female, but cold and clear cut. Henry froze. His eyeballs fixed on the muzzle of a small silver gun jammed between his eyes. Some small part of his brain that had remained sober took control. The woman was a toff, too well dressed to be from around these parts. She smelled of flowers and face powder. The words she uttered were like sharp glass cutting into his brain.

'Leave my mother alone or I shall shoot. Do you hear me?'

He tried to focus his gaze. This woman wasn't Daw and she wasn't Lizzie. He had only two daughters, didn't he? Yet she'd called Mary Anne her mother. He let Mary Anne go, his mind confused by what had been implied.

'Go home, Henry Randall. Go home now and sleep it off. If you don't it'll be the worse for you,' said the imperious voice.

'Or we'll beat you black and blue. Then shoot you!' The woman with the dangerous umbrella pointed it at him with as much intent as the woman with the gun. His arms fell to his sides. Wiping the drool from his mouth he turned away. He didn't understand. The world was a labyrinth and it was becoming more and more confusing. Suddenly he yearned for his bed. Perhaps he'd persuade Biddy to join him there. She was fat and filthy, but her body was warm. All thoughts of Routledge and his wife were wiped from his mind. Staggering from one side of the pavement to the other, he tottered off, his brain as mixed up as the world around him.

'Were you really going to shoot me dad?' No one had noticed Stanley arriving, but he had seen all that had happened. He sounded thrilled at the prospect. 'Is that really a gun?' he asked Elizabeth with round-eyed fascination.

'In a way.' She pulled the trigger. A small blue flame flared into existence. 'It fires flames at cigarettes.'

Gertrude Palmer chuckled as she sheathed her umbrella beneath her arm. 'A lighter! How very ingenious.'

Daw was crying great, slobbering sobs as she helped her mother to her feet. 'Ma! Oh, Ma!' Mathilda too was sobbing, though less vehemently than her mother.

Daw's face was a picture of contrition. 'I didn't know he was like that, Ma. Honestly I didn't.' She wiped at her eyes with the back of her hand. 'I've never seen me dad like that. He's a swine, just like our Lizzie said he was. A right swine.'

Elizabeth was dabbing at Mary Anne's bruises with a lace-edged handkerchief. 'I can think of worse things to call him. He should be horse-whipped.'

It came to Daw as though in a dream that this woman with the pretty handkerchief had said something truly surprising. She'd told Daw's father to leave *her* mother alone. *Her* mother?

'I think we'd better get some ice put on those marks,' said Gertrude, peering menacingly at the red welts on Mary Anne's cheeks.

Mary Anne allowed herself to be guided back inside the shop. Her ribs hurt, her face hurt and she was sorry the window cleaner had had to experience this.

'I haven't paid him,' she said through swollen lips.

'Never mind him,' said Gertrude. 'I'll see that he's paid once I've helped him get his false leg into some sort of order.'

The window cleaner wasn't the only person she was worried about. She kept looking over her shoulder, attempting to gauge Daw's reaction to her half-sister, and vice versa.

Looking apprehensive, even scared, Daw followed her mother into the shop, Mathilda in her arms.

Elizabeth was helping Gertrude and talking to the window cleaner, opening her purse and giving him money.

A practical sort, thought Mary Anne, and would have smiled if her lips hadn't been so swollen.

The crowds that had gathered around outside now began to disperse. One figure remained for a moment until, satisfied that everything was over, he shuffled off, a look of triumphant satisfaction on his face.

Mary Anne recognized Alf Routledge and remembered what he had done to Michael – or rather what he had got others to do.

'I know him,' she said, pointing to the shuffling figure

gradually disappearing among the afternoon crowds. 'His name's Alf Routledge. He's a trouble maker. He incites other people to do his dirty work. He got the local kids to daub a swastika on Michael's door.'

'Never mind that, Mum. It's in the past. You come and sit down.' Daw's voice trembled. Mary Anne could hardly believe how frightened she'd been.

'That man's a regular at the Lord Nelson,' she said to Daw. 'He's always been trouble. Michael ordered him off the premises when he first came to this country.'

Daw winced at the mention of Michael. 'Never mind, Mum. It's all over now.'

Mary Anne wondered if she'd ever accept him, but she didn't ask now. She did as she was told, sitting down on a bentwood chair usually kept for visitors. Where had her strength gone? And why did she feel so small?

She sighed and let the others take care of her. For the first time since turning forty, Mary Anne felt that her family was more mature than she was. *I'm slipping towards old age*, she told herself. It saddened her; not so much the thought of advancing years, but the ones wasted and long behind her now.

Her thoughts turned to Henry. She could guess what had happened. A few beers and Henry was easily swayed by male companions. Routledge would have goaded him on. *Wait till Michael comes home*, she promised him silently. *Just you wait*.

The shop was an oasis of silence after the scene in the street, the only sound being the clattering of Gertrude putting the kettle on.

She heard Elizabeth asking for a bowl and cotton wool with which to bathe her mother's injuries.

'Such a clod,' she heard her say. 'My mother deserves better.'

Daw sat, tears streaming silently down her face, her eyes bigger than usual, as though they'd just been opened to the way things really were.

'I'll be fine,' Mary Anne said to her, though the red marks hurt more than she'd ever let on.

'I . . .' Each time Daw attempted to say something, her voice failed. There were no words she could find to express how she felt. She'd been wrong. She'd believed her father could do no wrong because it had suited her to do so. She liked everything to be perfect, formed exclusively to suit her.

'We never really know anyone until we're married to them,' Mary Anne said suddenly. 'And we can't change what they are. It's impossible. Not everyone's as nice as John Smith, you know.'

It wasn't often easy to know what Daw was thinking, but Mary Anne thought she did now. Daw was thinking about the way she'd treated John when he wasn't on time for meals, or had been waylaid by family or friends. Daw had wanted him moulded to suit her vision of the ideal husband, doing everything together and never straying into doing something that suited him and him alone. But life wasn't like that, thought Mary Anne.

'Is John still sleeping on the settee when he comes home on leave?'

Daw didn't answer, but then she didn't need to. Mary Anne could tell by the look in her eyes that he was.

'You have to let John do things by himself at times,' she blurted. 'He'll be off again shortly and who knows when you'll see him again.'

Daw just stood silently, nodding her head in acknowledgement that her mother was right.

'This is going to sting,' Elizabeth said to Mary Anne, who smelled the unmistakable stink of witch hazel. She winced at the first dab. It wasn't so bad after that.

The kettle in the kitchen whistled for the second time. Gertrude popped her head around the door. 'Who's for tea?'

Everyone said yes.

Mary Anne looked into Elizabeth's eyes. Her daughter's touch was gentle, her fingers cool. Her daughter had fine hands. *Daughter*. It was hard to accept. Elizabeth looked as though she'd just stepped out of the pages of a fashion magazine. She was so elegant, so beautiful.

Elizabeth tended the last red mark and let the cotton wool fall into the bowl where it bobbed gently on the surface.

'Mother, what a brave woman you are,' she proclaimed, as though she'd just carried out a surgical operation.

Mary Anne caught the look on Daw's face. Perhaps she'd thought she'd misheard when Elizabeth had called her 'mother' earlier.

'I gave birth to Elizabeth before I married your father,' she said in answer to Daw's look of amazement. 'Her father was killed in France.'

Mary Anne Randall looked up into Elizabeth's face. One question above all others burned in her mind.

'I thought you wanted to forget me the other day. Why did you come back?'

The soft hands that now dabbed gently at her face with a dry towel barely paused when she answered. A slight smile hovered on her ruby-red lips.

'Aren't you glad I did?'

'Yes. Yes, I am.'

Daw sat silently, her eyes darting between the mature woman she'd known all her life, and this new sister, this woman who looked so much like herself.

'We could have been twins,' she said suddenly.

'Yes,' said Elizabeth. 'We look very much alike.'

Stanley hovered, fidgeting from one foot to the other. 'Can I play with your gun?'

She turned her calm eyes on to the little brother she'd never known. The cool, confident look persisted and for a moment it looked as though she would refuse.

'It's only a cigarette lighter,' she said. 'It's in my bag.'

'You shouldn't,' said Mary Anne. 'He'll dash off to play cowboys and Indians and that's the last you'll see of it.'

Elizabeth stopped what she was doing. 'Goodness! I hadn't thought of that. Stanley!' But Stanley was gone. 'Oh well,' said Elizabeth. 'There's obviously a lot I need to learn about my family.'

Daw's eyes stayed glued on her. 'I don't understand. This has all happened so quickly. We're your family? There's so much I don't know, yet everyone else seems to know about you. What happened to you? Why did we never know anything about you?'

Before Mary Anne could answer, Gertrude came in with the tea tray. 'We've got oatcakes today,' she announced. 'I made them with porridge oats and a few secret ingredients. Don't ask me what ingredients, they're a trade secret. And besides, I don't want you being sick even before you've tried them.'

For a change, Daw was totally uninterested in food. 'Tell

me,' she said, her velvety brown eyes flickering between Mary Anne, her mother, and Elizabeth, the sister she'd never known she'd had.

Mary Anne sighed. She'd told Lizzie and Harry all about her first love and the child she'd given away. Now she had to tell Daw, a prospect that worried her sorely. Daw was very traditional, very conservative and downright sanctimonious at times. *But it has to be done*, Mary Anne told herself. *You've told her the bit that was likely to shock her the most, and now she might as well hear the rest of it. It's only right.*

'Edward was my sweetheart. We were engaged to be married . . .' She went on to tell her about Edward being killed in the trenches, about discovering that she was expecting his child, about giving that child away, and about her parents paying Henry to marry her.

'We were happy at first, so happy that I thought I could trust him with the truth. I was wrong.' Hurt by the memory, she hung her head. 'I was terribly wrong. From that dreadful moment, everything changed. The man I thought I could trust turned to drink. I didn't know he'd made an effort not to drink when he married me. I didn't know then that he worshipped me. I was like a goddess to him, and then he found out that I was as human as he was.' She sighed, spreading her palms helplessly. 'My attempt to be honest didn't work because I'd been dishonest in the first place.' Her eyes misted over. 'At night I sometimes dream of Edward coming home and how different life would be if he hadn't been killed and we'd got married.' Her eyes drifted to Elizabeth. 'Different for all of us.'

Daw was like a broken doll, her features shattered and pale. She strained to keep her gaze fixed on her mother. She was like a rabbit caught in the headlights of a motor vehicle, afraid to turn away in case it was all an illusion.

Fixing her gaze on Mary Anne, Elizabeth leaned forward, her smooth fingers interlocked over her knees. 'I'm going back home tomorrow. George is in a hospital near Norwich. He needs me. I hope you'll understand. He's been so damaged by this war.'

Mary Anne's smile was wistful. 'I'm so sorry for you. Poor George.'

Elizabeth shook her head. 'No. Don't be sorry for me. A lot of husbands won't be coming back to their wives. I have to content myself with that fact. I've still got George, and in time he may well recover. I do hope you can find it in your heart to forgive what he did. He wasn't himself.'

Mary Anne felt her heart would break when she saw the pain in Elizabeth's eyes. She leaned across and covered her daughter's hands with her own. 'I understand, Elizabeth. I know what you must be going through.'

Elizabeth smiled through her tears, retrieved one of her hands and placed it on Daw's. 'I'm thrilled to have a family. I hope no one is offended by my intrusion into your lives. I only hope you can grow to love me as I already love all of you.'

Hot tears rolled down Mary Anne's cheeks. 'My dear girl. I'm so glad you came back. I've loved you all my life. I loved you before you were born and now I will never cease to love you.'

The two women embraced.

Gertrude, who had got the gist of what was going on during Elizabeth's first visit, now dabbed at the corners of her eyes, just as Edith had once done. 'Life is never what you think it's going to be,' she murmured as she blew into a mansize handkerchief.

Mary Anne filled up with emotion, her chest tightening with excitement, relief and happiness. She'd regained Elizabeth, but had she lost Daw? She looked at her daughter, sitting next to the pushchair, a blank expression on her face.

'Daw?'

Daw blinked and looked at her.

'Daw. There was a war on when all this happened, just as there is now. We seized the opportunity for happiness. Unfortunately, my sweetheart was killed. It happened so quickly. I'm sorry about not telling you . . .'

'It doesn't matter. I've got to see John before he goes back. I've got to . . .'

Make amends. Her mother sensed Daw's unspoken meaning.

Daw was suddenly all action, buttoning up her coat, adjusting her hat, fastening the apron on the pushchair so that Mathilda was protected against the chill December day.

'I'm going home,' she stated, firmly gripping the handle of

the pushchair and aiming it at the door. 'There's things I've got to sort out.'

'Of course you do. John's going back tomorrow, isn't he?'

Daw paused. Mary Anne saw the mix of regret and panic in her daughter's eyes. She guessed John would be sleeping in his own bed tonight. After what she'd learned today, Daw would never take John for granted again – at least, not while this war lasted.

'Will she accept me?' Elizabeth asked once the door had closed.

Mary Anne didn't take long to give her an answer. 'I think so.'

'I'm so glad,' said Elizabeth. 'I can't quite believe I've got a sister who looks so like me. I'd like to visit Lizzie and Harry too. Will you give me their addresses?'

'Yes, but let me write to them first,' Mary Anne cautioned.

Elizabeth gripped her hand. They hugged spontaneously; one moment they were looking at each other, the next they were hugging as though they'd never let go. Both knew that there would be many more such moments in the future.

Forty

Sally was polishing her nails and Lizzie was flicking through a woman's magazine that Sally had loaned her. Women in the most wonderful fashions imaginable looked out at her, their lips smiling broadly over perfect teeth.

Overawed by her roommate, she tried hard not to gush questions or comments about where the magazine had come from, how she managed to style her hair so professionally and whether they really made such wonderful underwear in Paris.

'Where else? You certainly wouldn't buy it in British Home Stores,' Sally said without pausing in the painting of her fingernails.

'And these models, they're so beautiful. I wish I could look like them.'

'You will, once you get rid of your little load.'

The words were harsh and brought the bile to Lizzie's mouth. Sally talked about parting with one's own child as though the living creature were a special offer bought in a sale and discarded because it didn't fit.

She took out the letter she'd received from her mother only days before arriving at the house. Again she read the news. Getting used to having a new sister wouldn't be easy, especially seeing as they'd never met.

First things first, she thought as she closed the magazine, placed it to one side and got herself ready for an examination by the doctor.

'I'll see you when I get back,' she said to Sally.

'I'll be here,' said Sally, still concentrating on her fingernails. 'Tell them to hurry things along if they can. I'm certainly going to tell them. I need to get on with my life.'

Lizzie thought about what Sally had said as she went downstairs. The heavy oak staircase led down to the brown pool of lino that was the reception hall. An arrow on a black and white sign pointed to the surgery, matron's office and doctor's office. To the right, fixed to a double doorway beside an oil painting of a woman wearing an old fashioned riding habit, was another sign saying Delivery Rooms.

Not yet!

The sign chilled her, but the letter from her mother chilled her more. Giving the baby away was no longer the easy option. Facing up to one's responsibilities was difficult and she was still young. There were fun times ahead despite the war. On the other hand, Patrick had made her a very good offer.

Suddenly the reality of her situation was right before her eyes. Needing to regain her self-control, she swept off to the left, found the appropriate door and entered.

The surgery's walls were painted in the most putrid shade of eau-de-nil; enamel-framed screens were folded loosely in one corner and a metal-framed trolley squeaked when a nurse wheeled it close to the examination couch.

A prune-faced nurse told her to take off her clothes behind a screen and to put on her dressing gown.

'Lie down, please.'

Lizzie heaved herself on to the examination couch.

The doctor had a baby face and pale hair. The merest hint of a moustache shadowed his top lip and she fancied he'd purposely deepened his voice in a bid to be taken more seriously. He was one of the few people here not dressed in a Salvation Army uniform. His hands trembled slightly as he approached her. Eyeing him sidelong, she tried to deduce what his problem was. *Drink*? *Stress*?

She couldn't believe that examining the bellies of young girls could lead to the latter, though there might be a case to answer for the former.

Her dressing gown was rolled up and a sheet placed across her stomach.

'Has she given Nurse a water sample?' He looked at the nurse as he said it and they continued to talk over her – *as though I'm not here*, she thought.

The nurse, her headgear as stiff and broad as a starched tablecloth, answered that she had and that the sugar test was negative.

The doctor made a humphing sound – something halfway between approval and curiosity.

The hands that pressed around the perimeter of the lump she carried were as cold as ice. She grimaced. He hadn't attempted to warm them beforehand, and neither had he apologized. His voice slid an octave higher as he looked into her face. 'A few days and it will all be over. A fortnight after that you can leave here and forget it ever happened.'

Forget it? How can I forget it?

But you will, she told herself. *You'll have to.*

Turning her face to the wall she squeezed her eyes shut and prayed it was all a dream. When she opened them again, nothing had changed. What had she expected? She forced herself once again to don the mask of indifference she'd worn for so many months. In a little while she could jettison the beach ball for ever – but would it be for ever? Her namesake, the first Elizabeth, had turned up. What about her child? Would it track her down too?

'You're very large,' said the doctor, and frowned thoughtfully. He straightened, sighed and made some notes. 'Be sure to see the receptionist on the way out,' he added, his pink cheeks glowing in his round, chubby face. 'I believe she has rules and information that may be of use to you.'

It was the first time a smile had lifted his baby-boy features but soon he resumed scribbling copious notes. The smile was tight and not really for her, merely the satisfaction of a man with too many patients and not enough time to deal with them all properly.

Sally and another girl named Hilary were sitting on metal-legged chairs outside the door. They both looked up as she came out.

'So what is it? A baby or just fresh baked bread making you a bit bloated?' said Sally.

'The proverbial bun in the oven,' said Lizzie.

'Hope he's warmed his hands up a bit. I can't stand cold hands.' She added a wink.

All that was happening made Lizzie more sensitive than usual. She couldn't help the sharp retort. 'All doctors have cold hands if they've washed properly. I suppose it depends what you're used to.'

The barb hit home, wiping Sally's smile from her face. Before she had a chance to react, her name was called.

Lizzie found her way to the reception desk. 'Sit here,' said the receptionist. She wore spectacles with round lenses and continually tugged at her tight collar. She was shuffling papers with the easy dexterity of someone used to collating information in strict alphabetical order. She drew a single sheet from of the bundle of manila folders and crisp paper. 'This is the Pilemarsh regime. Study it, memorize it if possible, and ask questions now if you wish. No one here has time for questions unless they're asked at the right time.' She passed the paper across the busy desk.

'And now is the right time?' Lizzie asked, her steady gaze resulting in the furtive haste of a woman who wishes to appear more efficient and important than she really is.

The woman's purple-thin lips tightened into grim accusation. 'Don't take that tone with me, young lady. It's your fault you are here, not ours. Rules are rules.'

The sheet of rules and a timetable were later discussed among the three girls.

Sally gripped the sheet as though wishing her hands would

turn into claws so she could more easily tear it apart. 'Looks as though everyone here is a chief. There's no Indians!' she said.

Lizzie got up and looked out of the window. She'd read the rules and regulations, but still her mother's letter was uppermost in her mind. *History repeats itself, so they say, and here I am doing the same thing she did back in the Great War.*

Sally was still going on about the rules and regulations. 'We've got to do all the cleaning, washing and ironing! I can't believe it.'

Hilary was strangely silent, a deep frown denting her dark brows. 'I've never done housework. We have servants back home.'

Sally stared at her.

Lizzie glanced over her shoulder and smiled. 'They obviously like to keep costs down here.'

Sally stared at her newly painted fingernails and sighed. 'And they were just getting nice as well.'

'I've got some cream,' said Hilary, reaching into a crocodile skin vanity case and passing Sally a pink jar with a gold-coloured top.

'Thanks all the same,' she said suddenly and handed it back. 'I think I've got something better than that. Vaseline,' she added. 'It cost only pennies and is just as good as anything.'

The morning bell summoned the girls to lay the table for breakfast at six thirty. Those who had managed to doze off lurched into instant wakefulness. Few lingered too long in their beds. If they didn't report to the dining room on time, most of the porridge and butter would be long gone and breakfast diminished to tea and dry toast.

Lizzie groaned and buried her head under her bedclothes. 'I feel as though I've been sold into slavery. Is it too much to ask them to take on staff?' She raised herself up and pushed back the covers. She winced as she dragged her legs over the side of the bed, tucking her nightdress below her belly so she could more easily inspect her ankles. She sighed at the sight of them. 'Looking over my belly is like trying to peer over the top of a mountain. I vow that I will never allow myself to get fat again – certainly not on a permanent basis.'

'Are you alright?' asked Sally.

Lizzie nodded. The sight of the hem of her nightdress skimming her slim ankles was incredibly reassuring. 'Just a twinge – and look, my ankles are still slim.'

'Is that good?'

'I think so.'

'Your belly's pretty big.'

'That's what the doctor said too.'

'Oh dear. You don't think it's twins?'

Lizzie adopted a look of sheer horror. 'I hope not!'

They were interrupted by a knock at the door. Captain Gregory, a middle-aged woman with sandy hair and a ruddy complexion, poked her head around the door.

'Randall? You're wanted in the visitors' room.'

Captain Gregory had been about to shut the door, but stopped when she saw the surprise on Lizzie's face.

'Are you alright?'

'I'm not expecting a visitor.'

'Not even a friend?'

Thinking that Margot had come to see her, Lizzie visibly relaxed. 'I won't be a moment.' She reached for her clothes. Seeing Margot again would lift her spirits. Over a cup of tea they'd discuss Owen, men and the world in general. Margot would be discreet; she wouldn't let her eyes drop to Lizzie's fat belly or mention the impending birth.

Despite her girth Lizzie flew down the stairs and into the small room to the right of the staircase. The room held a small bookcase, six chairs and a giant aspidistra in an olive-green pot.

A sincere smile plastered to her face, Lizzie breezed into the room. The woman got up as she entered. At first she wondered why Daw was here and reached the obvious conclusion that Patrick had spilled the beans. Perhaps her mind was playing tricks: this woman looked like Daw, but wasn't Daw. Her sister was handsome but never looked elegant, and neither did she have the money to wear mink, good-quality tweed skirts and handsome leather court shoes.

As realization dawned, Lizzie's smile turned to jaw-dropping surprise.

The woman got to her feet. 'Do forgive this intrusion, but I had to see you.' Her voice rang like a bell.

This was Daw and yet it wasn't Daw; it was her mother's face but not quite her mother's face. First and foremost, why was she here? Lizzie waited for her to explain.

Elizabeth Ford looked at her with imploring eyes. 'I expect you're wondering who I am and how I found you. Patrick didn't give your secret away, if that's what you think. On the contrary, he was very reticent until I told him why I wanted to see you. He understood then. We both knew that I had to come and that my coming here might help you reach the right decision.'

She was talking in riddles. The only part that made Lizzie react was her mention of Patrick. He'd sworn not to tell anyone.

'Your mother wrote to you about me, I believe.'

Lizzie sank into a chair. 'Yes. You're Elizabeth!'

Her gaze was steady. 'So are you.'

Lizzie nodded. Their mother had named them both Elizabeth. Everything had been in the letter. Reading about the other Elizabeth had been so impersonal. Face to face was not so much disconcerting as strange.

Elizabeth Ford waved a gloved hand at one of the chairs. 'Please. Sit down.'

Lizzie lowered herself into the chair as though in a dream, her eyes never leaving her half-sister's face. 'So you got hold of Patrick and he sent you here? Have you told my mother where I am and what's happening?'

Elizabeth shook her head. 'No. I had to promise Patrick that I wouldn't. It was agreed between your mother – our mother – and me that she would write to you first before I came visiting. She told me your address was secret but that Patrick would know. I visited him first and explained the situation. He begged me to tell you that his offer is still open.'

'And you know about his offer?'

'He told me.' Elizabeth paused and leaned forward. 'Think very carefully about what you are doing. Think of what your – our – mother went through.'

Lizzie eyed her quizzically. It was difficult to accept that this elegant woman had had such an unpromising start in life. Orphanages and Dickensian stories usually accompanied a baby being given away at birth.

'What sort of upbringing did you have? Were people cruel to you?' she asked.

Elizabeth shook her head. 'No. I was one of the lucky ones.'

Lizzie gave a little gasp as the child kicked inside her.

Elizabeth noticed. 'Is it coming?'

The sudden twinges she'd been feeling all morning intensified. She nodded. 'I think so.'

Elizabeth looked at her watch. It looked to be made of silver and studied with stones. 'I have to go. I have to visit my husband.'

'I hear he's under lock and key.'

'Until he's better,' Elizabeth sighed and looked sad. 'Whenever that may be.'

'He caused a lot of problems.'

'I'm sorry he did, but also thankful. I would never have found you if he hadn't applied his skills to the task.'

Lizzie nodded. 'I suppose so.'

'I always wondered,' Elizabeth said suddenly. 'Once I knew I was adopted, I always wondered who my mother was, why she'd abandoned me and who my natural family were. Wanting to know stays with you, but not as strongly as the feeling of abandonment.'

Lizzie stared at the floor. What now? This visit was totally unexpected. This woman had been a baby just like the one inside of her, and now she was a person with feelings and hopes and dreams for the future, but also with problems. It was obvious from the sadness in her eyes that she was worried about her husband.

'Will you be seeing Patrick again?'

'I don't know. He said he would call in on you.'

'Male visitors aren't allowed.'

'Not even those who want to marry the mother?'

Lizzie didn't answer. Of course he'd be let in, but was she ready for him? The baby moved again, as though urging her to act before it was too late. 'Tell him I won't object.'

'I will.'

'Have you seen Harry?'

Elizabeth smiled as she pulled on her gloves. 'I have. He hugged me and called me "sis". I love him for that.'

'I'd like him to visit if he can.'

Elizabeth headed for the door. 'I'm not sure whether he can, what with this business at Pearl Harbor.'

Lizzie looked at her blankly. 'Pearl Harbor? What's that?'

News was slow entering the walls of Pilemarsh Abbey. Like visitors, the outside world was held firmly at the door.

'Yesterday the Japanese bombed Pearl Harbor in Hawaii. The United States has now entered the war. Goodness knows what will happen from here on. But never mind,' she said and kissed Lizzie on both cheeks. 'I'm so pleased I have a family. So pleased I've found my roots.'

In the early hours of the morning of December 9th 1941, Lizzie gave birth to twin girls – Mary and Elizabeth – named after the two living queens, one the mother-in-law of the other.

The almoner came to talk about having them adopted.

'It's easier to place one than place two,' she said. 'Rest assured they'll be placed with two separate families who will take good care of them.'

Exhausted after her ordeal, Lizzie lay back against the pillows and collected her thoughts. The prospect of the twins growing up separately appalled her. Her children had suckled at her breasts, and even now her body was reacting to their presence, the sticky birth milk seeping into her nightdress. Nothing would ever be the same again. She knew that now. Her life was no longer just for her. She had seen her beautiful children and in a flash had turned from a pussycat into a tiger.

'I have a form for you to sign,' the almoner continued. 'Well, two forms actually. One for each child.'

Taking her inaction and silence for exhaustion, the almoner pushed the pieces of paper beneath Lizzie's fingers and pressed a pen into her right hand. 'There. A signature on each and it's all over.'

Lizzie stared at the screen surrounding her bed, but didn't see the dull green cloth. All she could see was a future alone when in fact it could be so different. The choice was hers and hers alone. The paper crumpled beneath her fingertips. The pen rolled on to the counterpane. 'No.'

The almoner raised her eyebrows. 'No?'

'No. I've decided to keep them.'

The almoner looked outraged. 'But you've no husband?'

Lizzie smiled weakly. 'Not at the moment. But I will shortly. I definitely will.'

Forty-One

Michael explained in his letters that all leave was cancelled due to the worsening situation in the Far East. Once she'd opened and read them, Mary Anne hugged them against her heart. There were long gaps between writing and his infrequent visits. She'd written to his parents in the hope of finding out more. They had written back, addressing her as though she were Michael's landlady and not the love of his life. They remarked on some photographs he'd sent them of a 'young English girl'. Whose photographs had he sent? She wouldn't tackle him about it, preferring to brood over what might be while hoping for something better.

'Mum, you're worrying unnecessarily,' said Lizzie. 'You've been down that route before.'

Having two new grandchildren helped her cope, although she didn't know the truth about their father and Lizzie hoped she would never find out. Christmas would have been a subdued affair if it hadn't been for Lizzie, Patrick and the twins. A special marriage licence had been granted so their wedding was celebrated alongside Christmas.

'Best time of the year,' Patrick had quipped. 'Christmas and wedding anniversaries all in one!'

Daw sobbed all the way through the ceremony because she was missing John. After seeing what her father was capable of and meeting Elizabeth Ford, Daw had forgiven her husband for whatever he'd done – or hadn't done.

'What did he do to upset her?' Lizzie asked.

Her mother shrugged. 'Knowing our Daw it wasn't that dreadful. She's such a stickler for having things done her way.'

'Never been any different,' said Lizzie dismissively.

The event was low key. Patrick, Lizzie and two of his army pals had gone to the Register Office. Mary Anne had been left to look after the twins and Daw had come over with

Mathilda. The wedding feast was held in the rooms above the Red Cross shop. By collecting coupons and receiving donations from Harry's black-market friends, a tea time spread of cake, jam and bread and butter, along with a little fruit jelly preserved by Gertrude Palmer, covered an oblong table.

The wedding was too short notice for Harry and Michael to come. John's aunt and uncle from the corner shop were there, and so was Gertrude although she didn't look her normal self. During the celebrations, she called Mary Anne over.

'I've something to tell you,' she said, looking very down in the mouth. Mary Anne wondered if she was ill and asked her outright.

'Right as rain,' said Gertrude. 'Right as rain.'

'Then what . . .?'

'I need someone to run the shop for a short time. There are some family matters I have to take care of. Well?'

Gertrude's manner was abrupt at the best of times, but more so today. There was something defensive about her voice, her eyes and her lack of expression. Mary Anne guessed that the family matters she had to attend to were serious. There was no point in asking why. Gertrude kept her family life very separate from her work for the Red Cross.

'Just a yes or no will do,' Gertrude continued in her usual brusque manner.

'I'll do it.'

For a moment Mary Anne got the impression that Gertrude had been expecting her to probe further. There was a look of relief when she didn't.

'Right,' said Gertrude, her stiff features brightened with a smile. 'Then let's toast the couple well.'

Glasses were raised to the happy couple. The day was perfect. Patrick looked like a dog with two tails and Lizzie looked good in a black and white checked costume trimmed with velvet on the collar and cuffs.

Henry Randall, Lizzie's father, had not been invited to the wedding feast, but Patrick's mother had. She sidled up to Mary Anne, a brown ale in one hand and a cigarette in the other.

'Lovely spread, Mary Anne. Lovely couple, aren't they?'

'I think so.' Mary Anne held her breath as a cloud of cheap perfume and face powder threatened to choke her. The baby girls were the twin apples of her eyes. Her only regret was that Lizzie hadn't told her sooner so she could have been there at the birth.

'I didn't want to shame you,' Lizzie had said. 'And I didn't want to force Patrick's hand. I wanted him to marry me for myself, not because I was pregnant.'

Rosie, Patrick's mother, was still gabbling on between sips of brown ale.

'Twins too! I suppose they are his,' she said glibly.

Mary Anne looked at her in amazement. Men had breezed in and out of Rosie Kelly's life as frequently as a trail of ants over the doorstep. 'I'll caution you to shut your trap. Not everyone's tarred with the same brush as you, Rosie Kelly!'

'What?' Rosie eyed her quizzically. The penny suddenly dropped. 'No, Mary Anne, you've got me all wrong. I wasn't casting doubt on your Lizzie. It was just the miracle of my Patrick becoming a dad. He had mumps when he was little, you see. That's why him becoming a father at all took me right off guard.'

Mumps! She knew the implications of small boys getting mumps. She told herself that Rosie could have got it all wrong. Patrick had been neglected from the moment he was born, but still looked in on his mother despite her defects. Patrick could have been suffering from anything. Rosie wouldn't have worried too much about him so could easily have been mistaken.

Don't let it worry you, she said to herself.

Patrick and Lizzie looked so happy together. They'd been friends since they were small. Something of her concern following Rosie's comments must have showed on her face, and Patrick came over.

'Now don't you worry, Mrs Randall. You've gained a son who'll always look after your Lizzie – and the little 'uns, of course.'

She smiled and couldn't stop her eyes watering. Patrick was such a kind young man. 'I know you will, Patrick. I know you two have always looked out for each other.'

There was something about the sudden look that came to his eyes that made her start, an unguarded moment when the truth had risen to the surface and then been instantly hidden.

'I know you will,' she said softly and kissed his cheek. 'I know you will.'

She told herself that all was well, that Patrick was definitely the twins' father. But a small doubt remained. Why hadn't Lizzie told her when she was expecting? And why had she stayed away until they were born? Memories of a private nursing home run by nuns came back to Mary Anne. She had given birth to her first born in secret, away from prying eyes – just as Lizzie had done. Adoption papers had been drawn up just before the birth. Her parents had signed them because she hadn't yet been twenty-one. Lizzie was old enough to sign her own. Again she pushed the doubt away, but it kept coming back. In time Lizzie might tell her the truth, but for now Mary Anne would keep her doubts to herself.

The beginning of January was cold and thick with frost. Mid January brought a rise in temperature, but the leaden sky was heavy with snow. Children snapped icicles off window ledges, sucking them like ice lollies.

Stanley and a few of the other boys had made a cart for collecting coal out of an orange box and some old pram wheels.

'We're charging threepence for delivery,' he explained to his mother, his red nose shining like a beacon in his icy white face.

'Threepence is it?' She handed him a threepenny bit. 'We're down to half a hundredweight until the coalman can get through. Another sack of Welsh steam wouldn't go amiss.'

Wrapping her cardigan around herself, she went back inside. The back part of the house that had survived the fire kept fairly warm, shut off from all that remained of the front part which had been totally gutted. The back half of the roof was still intact and so was the chimney. The door between the living accommodation and the shop remained tightly shut. The old counter and the glass-fronted display cases no longer existed, the lingering smell of charred wood a continuous reminder of what used to be. The door to the front bedroom was all that separated them from falling from the upper floor to the ground.

After giving the coals a good poke, Mary Anne filled the kettle and put it on the hob. A rich stew simmered on the other hob, its delicious aroma rising with white steam and a satisfying bubbling sound.

She heard the back door open and then close, followed by clumping footsteps going upstairs. She presumed Stanley had gone upstairs to fetch his balaclava. Then she heard the door open and close for a second time.

Funny, she thought, *I didn't hear him come back down. Maybe you're going deaf.*

She grinned. Most likely a wheel had come off his cart.

'That smells good. You always were a good cook.'

Immediately recognizing Henry's voice, Mary Anne straightened, still tightly gripping the poker.

'What are you doing here?'

His face was red. Cold or drink? She settled on the latter.

He was wearing a thick muffler around his neck. She caught a glimpse of a white shirt collar and dark tie.

His smile was hesitant. He rubbed his hands together. 'Just been to a funeral. Old Alf Routledge has passed over.'

'I hope he burns in hell.'

'Aye,' said Henry, his eyes flickering. 'There's a few that think he's gone in that direction.' He glanced towards the stew again. 'If you've a drop to spare, the church was freezing, and course, being Methodist there was no chance of a drink to warm the cockles.'

'There's no stew either. Get out.' The tip of the poker glowed red as she raised it above her head.

Henry eyed a curl of smoke as it spiralled upwards from the red-hot tip. 'Is our Stanley around?'

'No.'

'Where is he?'

'Gone for coal.'

He jerked his chin by way of a nod. 'I would have liked to see him.'

'So you can beat him again?' Mary Anne shouted. 'So you can leave red marks across his back, just like you used to across mine?'

She had never really forgiven herself for going back to him for that short period of time. She'd written to Michael about it, trying to explain. He'd been understanding – almost too understanding. In a strange kind of way he'd made her feel worse than ever.

'It was what you thought best at the time,' he'd said. 'But all the same, it makes me feel like killing him.'

'I was drunk,' Henry said now. 'I'm sorry.' He looked up suddenly, his eyes piercing. 'I could make it up to you. I could change.'

She stared at him in disbelief. How many times would he say that?

'No! I want you to leave.' She backed off, feeling behind her for the door to the stairs. 'Leave me alone. Go away.'

His face was like a stretched mask, his mouth forming an obscene oval as though he were uttering a silent scream. She saw the disbelief in his eyes.

'You're me lawfully wedded wife, Mary Anne. You're not his, not that Boche bastard that took you from me. You'll never be his, 'cause you're married to me.'

Gripping the poker with one hand, she felt behind her for the door knob. The door was charred and rough beneath her fingers. Backed into a corner, she had no choice but to face him. She saw his inner ugliness, the vindictiveness of the power he'd had over her. She'd promised to love, honour and obey him and for years she had done just that, purely for the sake of the family. By doing so she had forgotten herself. There was no chance of her ever going back.

'Michael's twice the man you are, Henry Randall. Being with him is as different as chalk is from cheese. There's no forgiveness in you, no understanding whatsoever.'

At first he seemed rebuffed by her words, but he recovered quickly. With a contemptuous scowl, he looked her up and down. 'Look at you! A middle-aged woman long past her best. What do you think he wants you for? Yes, yer definitely past yer best, Mary Anne. He's years younger than you. How long do you think he's going to stay with you? Until yer hair turns grey and yer teeth fall out?' He laughed. The sound of his laughter echoed in her head. He could be right, but somehow she didn't care. Michael was *her* choice, just as Edward had been.

'He'll stay with me. I know he will.'

Henry laughed again. 'You've got four kids. Does he know that?'

'Five,' said Mary Anne, her eyes shining. 'I've got five. Remember? Edward's daughter, the child I was forced to give away. She held a gun to your head, or at least you thought it was a gun.' Despite the situation, she began to laugh. 'You looked so scared. Henry Randall, terrified of a novelty cigarette lighter!'

Henry's jaw dropped and as his anger rose, his eyes turned bloodshot, his jaw clenching and unclenching. 'Make a fool of me, would you?' he growled, his hands clenched into tight fists.

If she could just get out into the passageway and up the stairs . . . She wasn't sure where she would go from there, but it might be her only chance of escape.

Hanging on to the poker with one hand, her fingers folded over the door handle with the other, she turned it, swinging it open.

She ran up the stairs, stumbling halfway and dropping the poker. She heard it clatter to the ground. There was no time to go back, no time to retrieve it. Unarmed and frightened, she ran along the landing. If she could barricade herself in . . .

The door was shut. She tried the handle. Swollen and misshapen after the fire, it jammed. There was no time to force it. Henry was right behind her. He reached the top of the stairs, barring her way to the bedroom.

Henry raised his fist. 'That beating I gave you the other week weren't enough, I reckon.'

Mary Anne swallowed hard. The bruises she'd received outside the Red Cross shop throbbed. She was trapped. Helpless. 'Henry. No. Please don't,' she implored.

He stopped as though a sudden thought had occurred to him. 'You're right,' he said, his tongue sliding along his bottom lip. 'We don't want it to show, do we? This is a matter between husband and wife, and best kept secret.'

For a moment she dared believe that he'd had second thoughts. But her moment of hope was short lived. Slowly, his eyes never leaving her face, he began to take off his belt. Her stomach churned with fear. She watched the leather slide out from his waistband and saw the wicked glint of the steel buckle.

Her breath caught in her chest. 'No,' she whispered as fear swelled her breasts and caused her blood to race to her face. 'No. I will not allow this to happen.'

He gave no sign that he'd heard her. His eyes narrowed as he wrapped the belt around his fist, leaving the buckle hanging. It was hard to drag her gaze away from its cruel glint. The years of submitting to such treatment fuelled her anger. No, she would not submit this time. Not this time and never again.

She sidestepped away from him, sliding along the wall until she was in front of the door that was never opened, the door that had once led to the front bedroom. Her heart thudded against her ribs. She knew what she had to do, but could she do it? Could she time it right?

The consequences of what she was about to do were as frightening as what would happen if she failed. It was the only way out for a desperate woman. But she knew she had to do it.

She braced herself across the doorway, fumbled behind her for the handle, found it and pushed the door open.

Daylight flooded in from what remained of the shop frontage. Above her was sky. Below her was rubble, blackened pieces of roof timber and shards of broken glass.

'If you touch me I'll jump.'

At first he looked surprised, but then slowly a cruel smile slithered across his face. 'Go on then. Jump.' He began slapping the belt buckle into his left palm. 'It's your choice. The belt or that. Please yourself.'

Like a woman hypnotized, she stared at the belt and its shiny steel buckle. From behind the cold wind tousled her hair and played with her skirt. She glanced over her shoulder. It was quite a height. Jumping might not kill her, but she could be seriously injured. Sharp glass and broken masonry would see to that.

'Choose,' he said cheerfully as though he were offering her a choice of fur coats or gold bracelets. 'Choose your punishment. And you do deserve punishment, Mary Anne, by Christ you do!'

'I don't . . . How can you say . . . Think about what you're doing, Henry!' As her breath caught between words, her eyes strayed to the slowly opening door of the front bedroom. A shaft of light coming through a gap in the bricks glinted off something shiny.

The footsteps charging up the stairs had been Stanley's after all!

Suddenly the door swung open, slamming against the wall. Stanley leapt out. He was clutching what looked like a gun.

No, she corrected herself. It was just Elizabeth's cigarette lighter.

'Leave my mother alone!'

Surprised at first, Henry swung round. He laughed when he saw who it was and what he was holding.

'Go on then. Shoot me!' He ripped open his shirt and spread his arms wide. 'Go on then! What are you waiting for? It's only a cigarette lighter.'

Mary Anne immediately regretted telling him that the gun wasn't real.

'No it isn't.' Stanley dropped to one knee and took aim, his eye aligned with the barrel of the small pistol. 'I will do it. I will shoot you if you don't leave my mum alone.'

While Henry's back was turned, Mary Anne moved away from the doorway. She did it quietly, easing herself along.

Henry's laughter turned to a determined snarl. 'Keep out of grown-up business, son. This matter's between me and your mother.'

'I'll shoot,' said Stanley, his voice trembling and tears streaming from the corners of his eyes. He'd seen this scenario too many times before; he knew what his father was capable of. He wouldn't have his mother hurt again. He wouldn't allow it to happen. 'I hate you. You deserve to die!'

His father stood squarely facing him. 'Then you'll have to shoot me in the back. First I'll deal with yer mother, and then I'll deal with you.' Henry turned swiftly, lunging to where Mary Anne had been standing.

Just as he did so, Stanley fired the gun. A shower of ceiling plaster fell on Henry's head. A soldier, trained to react quickly, Henry threw himself to the ground. If he'd been three feet further back he would have hit only the landing floor. As it was he'd been in the process of lunging at Mary Anne. But she'd moved aside. Henry fell out through the door and landed on the mound of rubble and shards of broken glass.

One hand covering her thudding heart, Mary Anne stared wide-eyed at her son.

'The man gave it to me,' Stanley said before she'd had a chance to ask him the obvious question.

'George Ford,' she murmured. It could only have been George Ford.

Forty-Two

Henry Randall was buried on a sunny day in Arnos Vale Cemetery. Harry was granted compassionate leave to attend.

'It's a lovely day,' he said to Lizzie and Patrick. Out of regard for appearance rather than respect for his father, he did his best not to smile. It wasn't easy. Only Daw looked sad.

It was Daw who threw the first handful of earth on to the coffin. 'Whatever he was, he was still our father.'

Her mother nodded and did the same. Harry and Lizzie followed suit.

They were passing a tomb shaped like the palanquin of a maharajah, an elephant supporting each corner. It was said to be the tomb of an Indian prince. That was when Daw voiced what she was thinking. 'However did he manage to fall through that door? He had his faults, I know, but I would have thought he was more careful than that.'

Mary Anne and Harry exchanged secretive looks that Daw did not see. If she had she might have questioned what was going on, but only Harry was party to that.

For what seemed like ages after the accident, Mary Anne had stared down at Henry's twisted body. She'd had no doubt that he was dead. It was how to explain his death that mattered now.

'Stanley. Give me the gun,' she'd said.

As if in slow motion, Stanley had handed over the gun. It was small, though not as small as Elizabeth's cigarette lighter, and light in the hand.

'Did George Ford give you this?'

He'd nodded. 'To protect myself.'

Mary Anne had looked at him in horror. 'Against who?'

He'd shrugged. A mix of anger and frustration had overwhelmed her. Still with the gun in her hand, she had shaken him by the shoulders, so hard it was a wonder his head didn't fall off.

'Against who, Stanley? Tell me. Tell me now!'

He'd struggled out of her grasp. 'Me dad, of course. He told me to shoot me dad if I had to.'

For a moment she'd been speechless, horrified that George Ford had told him to commit murder, and sad that war had made a monster out of Elizabeth's husband.

'How many more will be affected like him?' she'd said to Harry when he'd first arrived at the scene.

'Where's the gun now?'

She got down on her hands and knees, reached beneath the bed and brought out a willow-pattern chamber pot. 'Here it is.'

If the situation hadn't been so serious, Harry would have burst out laughing.

'In the jerry?'

'In the po. Why do you call it a jerry?'

He smirked. 'Looks like a German helmet – don't you think so?'

He didn't hold it up in front of her for long as there was work to be done. He'd changed into his favourite grey suit over which he wore a navy-blue overcoat. He slipped the gun into his inside pocket. 'I'll find a home for this.'

Mary Anne didn't ask him where that home was likely to be. That was his business. Harry was what he was and nothing was going to change him.

Henry Randall's death was treated as an accident. No one noticed the hole in the ceiling where the bullet had smashed through to the rafters. No one knew what had really happened except Mary Anne, Harry and young Stanley.

As they walked back from the cemetery after the funeral Harry took hold of his mother's arm. 'You alright, Ma?'

His eyes slid sidelong when she didn't answer straight away. His breath caught in his throat. No woman had ever stirred him like his mother did. There was serenity in her eyes, composure in her fine features. Silver strands ran like fine threads through her honey-coloured hair. Her beauty had been enhanced by age rather than diminished. To his mind, she was not just the perfect woman, but the perfect person, one he had loved and would love all his life. He knew her so well, and without her saying anything, he also knew what was troubling her.

'You're wondering about Michael.'

She sighed. 'Michael hasn't been on leave for a long time and the last letter I had was three months ago.' She hung her head. 'Perhaps it's funerals that bring it on, but I'm beginning to wonder . . . After all, your father was right. I *am* a lot older than him . . .'

'Don't say that.' He tugged her arm closer. 'Michael will be back. There's been a lot going on . . .'

There was something about the tone of Harry's voice that jolted her out of her mood. 'What is it, Harry? Where is he? Is he in danger?'

Harry smiled in that lazy way of his that only slowly reached his eyes, almost as though he was holding something back, withholding the final truth that would make everything alright.

'There's a lot going on in the Mediterranean and North Africa.'

'He's there?'

'You know I can't tell you where he is – not that I'm saying I know where he is, only that I couldn't tell you even if I did.'

Mary Anne fixed her eyes on the road ahead of them. The winter sun glowed that little bit brighter. Green shoots were erupting from grey branches and bare stems. Birds were singing. She told herself she should be feeling happy. Harry had hinted at where Michael might be. All she wondered now was whether he was alive or dead.

'I had a letter from his parents,' she said, purposely eradicating the worry from her voice, adopting not exactly a smile, but at least a casual fortitude. 'They believed I was his landlady and asked that I forward their letter on to their son. They said something about him being engaged to a pretty English girl. He had sent them a photograph.'

'How do you know it wasn't your photograph he sent to them?'

'I'm not a pretty young English girl.'

'You're pretty, you're English and you're female. Besides, you take a very good photograph. Any young chap would fall in love with you. I certainly would.' He gave her a peck on the cheek.

'You're biased,' said his mother, laughing and warmed by his concern.

'Not at all.'

Harry's secretiveness about Michael and his comments about the Mediterranean helped restore her spirits, but at the back of her mind the suspicion remained. Who was the lovely young girl in the photograph he'd sent to his parents? And why hadn't he written? She wanted to know that above anything else.

Forty-Three

Gertrude Palmer's face was ashen. They were sitting in the kitchen at the back of the shop, the door between the two rooms tightly closed so the other voluntary staff couldn't overhear.

Gertrude still had her hat on. It was grey and emblazoned with the insignia of the WRVS. She looked at her tea before pursing her lips over the brim of the teacup, her sips small and considered.

'I do not want a word of our conversation going beyond this room,' Gertrude began. 'Do you promise not to breathe a word to a living soul?'

This was certainly something different to discussing how best to market ancient underwear or jars of home-made polish.

'I won't tell a soul,' promised Mary Anne.

'I do not make a habit of discussing personal problems with professional colleagues. However, I think we know each other a little better than that so I can tell you why I have reached the decision I've come to.'

Mary Anne sipped thoughtfully at the tea she was drinking from a rose-patterned cup. Both cup and saucer were gilt edged, from a set Gertrude had brought from home.

'This may come as a bit of a shock, but I'm going to have to give up the shop.'

Gertrude always got straight to the point, her words firing

out of her mouth like bullets from a machine gun. Today the words came just as quickly, yet Mary Anne sensed a slight trembling of her voice.

'That's a great shame,' she said, putting her cup down in the saucer, and both back on the table. 'Does this mean the shop will have to close?'

Gertrude looked at her askance. 'Don't be a dunce! You'll take over, of course.'

'Oh!'

She could have said 'Why me?' or expressed her gratitude at being chosen, but Gertrude's reasons for leaving the shop had not yet been disclosed. What dreadful thing could have happened to bring her to this decision?

Prying into Gertrude's reasons was not an option. The woman had never responded well to personal questions.

Gertrude's shoulders suddenly seemed less broad, her stance less stiff, and her features no longer resembled the hard lines of a smoothing iron.

'The fact is that my nephew, Christian, has been incarcerated by the Japanese. His wife is beside herself and alone with three children. I have to go to her. I'm sure you can see that. Family comes before duty to one's country.'

'Family is as much about one's country as duty,' blurted Mary Anne. 'We have a duty to both, and both, in their own way, are about family. The country is a family. I suppose so too is humanity – don't you think?'

For the first time ever, she saw the softer side of Gertrude Palmer. There was pain in her eyes and fear for her captured nephew.

'Yes,' she said, having regained her composure. 'I suppose that's what duty and patriotism are all about. We are all one big family – all over the world – except for the Germans, the Italians and the Japanese.'

Mary Anne hid her smile by taking another sip of tea.

Gertrude's next comment was just as surprising. 'I see no reason why you shouldn't move back in to the rooms up above.'

But what about when Michael comes back? She corrected herself. *If he comes back.*

'That's very kind of you,' she said aloud.

'Not at all. You're a widow now. I presume you'll marry

your Michael when he does come back. I would. There's no point in letting the grass grow under your feet at your age. You can both move back in – once you're married, that is.'

Mary Anne surprised herself by stating what was on her mind. 'He may not come back . . .'

Gertrude raised her iron-grey eyebrows. 'Really? Well, yes, I suppose you could be right.'

'I hope your nephew gets through things and comes home.'

Gertrude merely nodded. 'I hope so too.'

'We'll help you move in,' said Lizzie a few days later, once Mary Anne had told her and Daw what Gertrude had said. 'Fancy the old bat relenting like that.'

'Her nephew was captured at the fall of Singapore. She doesn't know when or if he'll come home. Families are important at a time like this. Her family needs her.'

Lizzie pretended to tend one of the twins. Both were actually asleep, but if she wasn't careful her mother would see the look in her eyes and guess.

Each time she looked into the tiny faces lying side by side on the settee, she saw Guy Hunter. He was there in their eyes, in the shape of their tiny noses, the rose-red pinkness of their mouths. She wondered how he was. Had he too been captured at the fall of Singapore? And what about his wife and children? Despite his deceit, she hoped that both Guy and his family were safe. These were not times to hold grudges against past wrongs. Life goes on.

John, Harry and Patrick had all returned to where they were needed. It was left to the women to move the few bits of furniture out of the ruined pawn shop and back into the flat above the Red Cross shop. The bed and other heavier things would have to be moved later, with help from Jack Kitson from the Lord Nelson and the one-legged window-cleaner who'd been at Dunkirk.

'It's the least I could do after what happened to Henry,' Jack had said.

Mary Anne looked back at the tree still growing in the back yard despite the black soot staining its bark.

She welled up at the thought of leaving. Even though it was broken and burned, it was hard to close the door on the old place. It was too special, almost sacred, the place where she and Michael had found love.

Tonight would be her first night back in the flat. Stanley's single bed had already been taken over there. That's where she would sleep tonight, and yet when she finally lay in it, sleep wouldn't come.

Drawing back the curtains revealed a clear sky heavy with stars. Gunfire sounded from faraway Purdown, courtesy of a gun nicknamed Purdown Percy by the local population. Searchlights pierced the night of stars, their arcs of light tracing small, black silhouettes moving like bugs across a counterpane.

The promise of spring mixed with the cloying stench of cordite. There would be other raids, other nights of stars, but tonight somehow felt special. She had moved on. The future was hers, the past consigned to the prospect of nightmares she hoped would never come.

Pulling a skirt on over her nightdress and a coat on top of that, she found her shoes and crept down the stairs and through the shop.

The clothes hanging on rails loomed in dark battalions, like soldiers standing to attention, saluting at her passing.

Her footsteps led her across the road, down the alley and into the back yard of the ruined pawn shop. The first buds of spring nodded at her as she made for the door. It was unlocked, the hinges having shifted and making locking it difficult.

She entered the building accompanied by a feeling of nostalgia for everything it represented. It was her symbol of freedom, a torch in her darkest hours.

Memories of that first time came flooding back. She'd been beaten and injured, the child she'd been bearing aborted and bleeding. Michael had rescued her. Michael had made her whole again.

The curtains drawn back, she sat in the old leather chair in the bedroom where she'd first lain with Michael. The heavens outside the window were a riot of rippling lights, enemy bombers and RAF fighters. She sat watching and praying for everyone serving in the armed forces. Eventually the bombers and fighters disappeared. She was alone in the room with her thoughts and her memories. Eventually, she slept.

* * *

What was that?

Mary Anne opened her eyes. Daylight flooded into the room showing up the shabby furniture, the stub of candle and the old bed. Not remembering the moment of falling asleep, she looked in surprise at the arms of the old chair she was sitting in.

Aware that something had woken her, she sat upright. Her eyes went straight to the gap at the bottom of the door. The strip of daylight altered as a pair of feet moved on the landing outside.

Holding her breath, she hugged her cardigan around her. The door knob turned and the door opened. A man stood silhouetted against the light behind him. Suddenly she let her breath go.

'Michael?'

'Marianna.'

He was leaner, had more lines in his face, but the look in his eyes and the smile on his lips was unaltered.

'I've been fighting a war,' he said simply, and fell on to the bed.

His eyes closed. He looked pale and drawn, and she was totally surprised that he could topple and fall asleep so quickly. It worried her. Then she heard him breathing.

While he slept, she put his things away and sorted his washing. A photograph fell out of a book of poetry. It was of her long ago, just after the Great War, a pretty English girl with the future in front of her. She'd saved a few from the fire.

She smiled. At least for now, all her doubts had flown away. He wouldn't be home for long and not until this war was over would she cease to worry about whether he'd come back.

That was the way things would be. She smoothed his hair back from his forehead. A line from a poem came to her. *Gather ye rosebuds while ye may* . . . For now that was all anyone could do: live for today, for tomorrow might never come. Michael was home and that was all that mattered for now.